THE LITTLE
TEASHOP OF
LOST AND FOUND

Trisha Ashley

BANTAM PRESS

LONDON · NEW YORK · TORONTO · SYDNEY · AUCKLAND

TRANSWORLD PUBLISHERS
61–63 Uxbridge Road, London W5 5SA
www.penguin.co.uk

Transworld is part of the Penguin Random House group of companies
whose addresses can be found at global.penguinrandomhouse.com

Penguin
Random House
UK

First published in Great Britain in 2017 by Bantam Press
an imprint of Transworld Publishers

A CIP catalogue record for this book
is available from the British Library.

ISBN 9780593075586 (hb)
9780593075593 (tpb)

Typeset in 12/15 pt Adobe Garamond by Jouve (UK), Milton Keynes
Printed and bound in Great Britain by Clays Ltd, Bungay, Suffolk

Penguin Random House is committed to a sustainable
future for our business, our readers and our planet. This book
is made from Forest Stewardship Council® certified paper.

3 5 7 9 10 8 6 4 2

For
Louise Marley
with love

TEASHOP OF
LOST AND FOUND

www.penguin.co.uk

For more information on Trisha Ashley and her books, please visit her Facebook page (Trisha Ashley books) or follow her on Twitter @trishaashley.

While Haworth and the beautiful moorland surroundings exist, Doorknocker's Row, Blackdog Moor, Upvale and all the characters portrayed within the novel are purely the product of my own imagination.

– Trisha Ashley

Prologue

West Yorkshire

Liz
2 March 1978

There had been no signs to warn me of the imminent catastrophe about to overtake me, or if there had been, I was oblivious to them. When everything kicked off that night, I felt as if I'd been catapulted straight into a horror movie, and a gross one at that – or the nightmare from hell.

Fear and confusion were quickly followed by realization, panic, shock and revulsion, for who'd have thought a birth involved so much goriness? Certainly not me, even though, ironically enough, my sights had refocused on gaining an Oxford place to read medicine the very moment my brief first love affair the previous summer had come to an end.

But then, that wasn't because I felt any kind of vocation to heal the sick, the halt and the lame, it was simply part of my plan to mould myself so much in Father's image that he forgot I wasn't actually his biological child at all.

As these thoughts jostled chaotically together in my normally clear, cool and analytical mind, my eyes met Mum's over the small, misshapen, skinned-rabbit of a thing that lay weakly mewling on the bed between us and I expect the expression on her ashen, stunned face mirrored my own.

Her mouth moved silently once or twice, as if it had forgotten how to shape words. Then finally she whispered, 'Liz, your father must never find out!'

She always was entirely mistress of the bleeding obvious.

1

Once Upon a Fairy Tale

Alice
Autumn 1995

I grew up knowing I was adopted, so it was never a shocking revelation, merely one of the things that defined me, like having curly copper-bright hair, distinctive dark eyebrows, a fine silvery scar above my upper lip and pale green eyes (like boiled gooseberries, according to Mum, though Dad said they were mermaid's eyes, the colour of sea-washed green glass).

As a little girl I'd sit for hours painting with Dad in his garden studio, while his deep, gentle voice wrapped me in a soft-spun fairy tale, in which my desperate young birth mother had been forced to abandon her poorly, premature little baby, hoping that someone like Mum and Dad would come along and adopt her.

Or like *Dad*, at any rate, since eventually I came to see that Nessa (she'd insisted I call her that rather than Mummy, practically the moment I could string a sentence together) had had no maternal yearnings; she'd just been paying lip-service to his longing for a family, smug in the knowledge that she couldn't physically carry a child even if she had wanted to.

'A bad fairy had put a spell on baby Alice, but when the nice doctors had made her lip all better, everyone agreed she was the prettiest princess in the whole of Yorkshire,' he'd finish his story, smiling at me over his canvas.

'And they put the wicked fairy in a metal cage and everyone threw rotten tomatoes at her,' I'd suggest – or even worse punishments, for some old fairy-tale books given to me by my paternal grandmother, including one strangely but wonderfully illustrated by Arthur Rackham, had had a great influence on my imagination. We lived near Granny Rose in Knaresborough until moving to a village just outside Shrewsbury when I was eight, and I can still remember her reading to me the long, long poem by Edith Sitwell about Sleeping Beauty, once she'd tucked me up in bed. I'd slowly drift off on a sea of musical, beautiful words about malevolent fairies and enchantments.

Other favourites of Granny's included *The Water-Babies* and *Alice's Adventures in Wonderland* – the latter a favourite of mine, too, since the heroine had the same name. I begged for her lovely old copies after she died and Dad made sure I got them, even though Nessa was hellbent on having a clearance firm empty the whole house. She was a minimalist sort of person . . . except when it came to her own clothes, jewellery and shoes.

Our house was a tale of two parts, with most of the creatively chaotic clutter in Dad's studio, which might have been stables once upon a time – until he married a wicked witch disguised as a flamboyantly beautiful ex-opera singer and she banished him there.

Anyway, you can see why I have a tendency to turn everything that happens in my life into a dark-edged fairy tale – I can't help it!

'They threw stinky rotten eggs at the wicked fairy, too,' I'd once added firmly to the familiar story.

'Well, perhaps, but only until she said she was sorry and then they let her out,' Dad had amended, kind-hearted as always.

Over the years we embroidered the story with increasingly ridiculous flourishes at every retelling, but it had served its purpose, for I grew up knowing that I'd been abandoned in the village of Haworth in Yorkshire and adopted, and the filament-fine silvery scar was all that remained to show I'd been born with a harelip.

Of course, later I realized Dad had had no way of knowing whether my birth mother was young or not and also, once I became quite obsessed with the Brontë family and Haworth, I knew that it was extremely unlikely that she'd tiptoed up to the steps of the Parsonage in the middle of the night and laid me there, in the expectation that he and Nessa would shortly swing by and scoop me up. I mean, it was a museum by then, so it would have been closed, and also, adoption didn't quite work like that. (I'm still surprised they let Nessa on to the register. I can only think that her opera training kicked in and she hadn't been able to resist throwing herself into the role of eager prospective mother.)

But while Nessa might make extravagant expressions of affection towards me only when her London friends were visiting (one of whom once cattily let fall the information that she hadn't had *that* brilliant a voice even before the operation on her vocal cords that ended her career), I'd known *real* love from Granny and Dad.

And I also had Lola, my best friend, and her lovely parents, who owned a nearby smallholding, growing herbs commercially. There we helped look after the hens and goats, ran wild in the fields and learned to bake in the long, cool, quarry-tiled kitchen. All my life, baking – even the scent of cinnamon and dried fruit – would have the power to transport me back immediately to those happy days and transfuse me with warmth and comfort.

So it was an idyllic childhood on the whole, though once the rebellious teenage hormones kicked in I began to clash more and more with Nessa.

Still, the finer details of my distant past didn't seem to matter . . . until Dad suddenly died from a massive heart attack when I was nearly eighteen and my safe, secure world collapsed around me like a house of cards.

In any ordinary family, his loss might have pulled Nessa and me together, but she was not so much grief-stricken as filled with a volcanic rage, mainly directed at me. And she became so obsessed with money that immediately after the funeral she sold the entire contents of Dad's studio (he was quite a well-known artist) to an American collector without a word to me beforehand, locking the door so I couldn't even go in there to find solace among the comforting, familiar smells of oil paint and turpentine.

That was bad enough. But then, with even more indecent haste, she moved a new man into the house – and a horrible one, at that, who was scarily over-friendly in an old-lech kind of way whenever she was out of earshot – and I came to realize that now I was just an encumbrance and she couldn't wait for me to go off to university the following year.

The pain of Dad's loss was still raw and I couldn't bear to see another man in his place, so I had the row to end all rows with Nessa, culminating in my saying that I hated her and I was going to go and find my *real* mother.

'She has to be an improvement on you!' I finished.

'You're a foundling, darling, so there's no way you can find her,' she snapped cuttingly. 'And bearing in mind that she dumped you out on the moors on a freezing cold night, she'd be unlikely to welcome you with open arms, even if you did.'

Stunned into silence, I stared at her while I took in the implications of what she'd just told me. 'She . . . didn't leave me in Haworth village, but up on the moors, where she didn't think I'd be found?' I asked eventually.

Nessa looked at me, the fury dying down slightly into a sort of malicious, slightly shame-faced pleasure that shook me: I knew she'd never *really* loved me, but until recently I'd thought her as fond of me as her self-absorbed nature would allow.

'Your father never wanted me to tell you the truth, but I think that was a mistake. And maybe she was batty and thought someone *would* come across you,' she suggested, possibly divining from my expression that she'd gone too far.

'No, if she left me at night out on the moors, then clearly she hoped I'd die and never be found,' I said numbly, for the spell of Dad's fairy tale was now well and truly shattered and there was no way it could be glued together again. I felt empty, alone and lost . . . and unwanted – totally unwanted – by anyone.

'I hate you!' I cried with sudden violence as hot tears rushed to my eyes. 'I wish *you'd* died instead of Dad – though you couldn't have had a heart attack, because you haven't got a heart. You've never loved me like Lola's mum loves her.'

She shrugged. 'I expect Dolly actually *wanted* children, which I never did, even if I could have had them. Your father finally wore me down into agreeing to adoption and he was over the moon when we were offered a baby. But you'd only just had the surgery on your face and what with that and the carroty hair, you weren't exactly prepossessing, darling.'

Now the floodgates of frankness were open, there seemed to be no stopping the hurtful revelations, so I added one of my own: I told her that the day before, when she was out, her creepy new lover had tried to kiss me and made suggestive remarks.

'You lying snake in the bosom!' she hissed furiously, clutching those generous appendages as though she'd just been bitten there by an asp.

And though of course she didn't believe me (which was why I hadn't already told her), there was no going back after that.

Dawn found me on a coach heading to Cornwall, with the loan of Lola's birthday money in my bag, to tide me over. I took only one case with me, leaving with her for safekeeping my most precious possessions, including Granny's books and a small portrait of me in oils, painted by Dad.

Of course Lola had wanted to tell her mum what had happened, but I'd sworn her to secrecy until I'd found a job and somewhere to live.

'I'll stay in a bed and breakfast at first, and there are lots of hotels and cafés there where I can get some casual work until I find my feet,' I assured her.

Inspired by some of Dad's old stories of the Newlyn artists, and our holidays in Cornwall, I had romantic ideas about joining an artists' colony, where my aspirations to become a writer and painter could be nurtured, though later I realized this was not only unrealistic, but several decades too late.

The stark reality was that my arrival, late in the evening and off-season, when many places were shut up for the winter and no one was hiring, left me without any option other than spending the first night huddled in a shelter on the seafront . . . and all too soon my over-active imagination was peopling the darkest corners with evilly muttering goblins and foully hellish Hieronymus Bosch creatures.

When the cold breeze blew a discarded cardboard cup across the prom I thought it was the clatter of running footsteps and even the soft, constant susurration of the sea sounded like an unkind conversation about me.

I'd begun to write my own contemporary mash-ups of fairy tales, fables and folklore, spiced with an edge of horror, but when it came to the crunch, *this* princess was no kick-ass kind of girl able to rescue herself, but a frightened waif in urgent need of a handsome prince . . . or even a kind, ugly one.

Hell, I'd have settled for a reasonably friendly frog.

Tears trickled down my face and I shivered as the cold wind picked up and wound its way around my legs.

Then, all at once, I heard the staccato tap of high heels and the excited yapping of a small dog. Before I could attempt to shrink even further into my dark corner, it dashed in and discovered me.

A torch snapped on and I screwed up my eyes against the dazzling beam, though not before I'd glimpsed the small and unthreatening shape behind it, so that my heart rate steadied.

'Well, what have we here, Ginny?' said a surprised female voice with the hint of a highland lilt. 'A wee lassie?'

After completely putting the events of that dreadful night out of my head for so many years, it's odd that now I've moved back to live with Father in Upvale, I should suddenly find them creeping back in again.

I have decided to write a full account of what happened, and outline the perfectly logical reasoning that led me to act in that way, in the hope that it will exorcise them. My conscience is, and always has been, entirely clear about the matter.

2

The Bonny Banks

My knight in shining Burberry was Edie, the owner of a small local hotel, who'd been giving her Pomeranian a bedtime stroll. She was a brisk, acute, businesslike woman somewhere in her late fifties, five foot two of pugnacious Scottish determination, though with a soft centre for waifs and strays.

'Not such a wee lassie after all,' she said as I stood up and towered over her and then, once she'd grasped the essence of my situation, whisked me back to her hotel.

There, she thawed me out with hot soup and consigned me to bed in an empty room in the staff quarters on the top floor, with the admonition that I was not to worry, things would seem better in the morning.

When I finally got a chance to phone Lola next day to assure her I was fine, she confessed that she'd got cold feet and told her mum everything, even where I'd been heading.

'But of course, I didn't know *exactly* where you were going,' she explained. 'Only that it was Cornwall.'

'It took a lot longer to get down here than I expected, so when it started to get dark, I thought I'd better get off at the next seaside town we stopped at,' I said.

'Mum said she wished you'd told her right away and she wants you to come back and live with us, until we go off to university, Alice.'

'That's really sweet of her, but I don't want to go to university any more,' I said. 'I only agreed to apply for teacher training courses because I couldn't think of any other option after I was turned down for fine art.'

Whatever art departments were looking for these days, it appeared it wasn't a girl who strongly resembled the Pre-Raphaelite muse Lizzie Siddal, but drew a contemporary world with fairy-tale echoes and a hint of horror in ink and wash, like a nightmarish Arthur Rackham. I could possibly have tried for a degree in literature and creative writing, but I didn't see the point – I read everything I could get my hands on and you certainly couldn't say my modern takes on traditional fairy tales weren't *creative*.

Then I told Lola that I was living in a small hotel on the seafront called The Bonny Banks, and the owner, Edie, was going to try me out in various jobs to see what I was best at.

I'd already discovered that it wasn't making beds.

We quickly found that my *métier* wasn't cleaning, either (too prone to fall into a dreamy trance), or waiting at table, since I was not only very reserved, with a full-lipped mouth that made me look permanently sulky, but when I *did* utter, tact didn't seem to be my middle name. I expect I was too used to giving back as good as I got, having grown up with Nessa, the expert in barbed and belittling remarks.

I think Edie was starting to worry that her lame duck would never turn into a decent swan, until finally I came into my own – in the kitchens. For thanks to Lola's mum's cookery lessons, I could make cakes and pastries to die for and if my mind was wandering in a warped fairyland while I was dreamily rubbing the fat into the flour, then that must have been a good thing, for there was always a touch of magic in my baking.

Predictably it was Dolly, Lola's mum, who drove down to see me a couple of weeks later. Though I knew she would have told Nessa where I was, there had still been no word from her, so I assumed she'd washed her hands of me.

I hadn't really expected the Wicked Witch to get on her broomstick and fly down there to check that I was all right, but still, it was another total abandonment. First my birth mother, then Dad (even though he couldn't help dying, I was still angry with him for doing it), and now Nessa had finally cast me adrift. Or maybe I cast myself adrift and she simply decided not to toss me a lifejacket.

It seemed I was right about that. Dolly, once she'd had a chat with Edie, took me out for tea and told me that she'd been round to talk to Nessa as soon as I'd told Lola where I was.

'I thought she'd be desperately worried about your safety and relieved to know you were all right,' she said. 'But she told me you'd accused her fiancé of such dreadful things that she wouldn't have you back under her roof again.'

'I did, but it was all true.'

'Yes, I told her that you'd always been such a truthful girl that if you said he'd made a pass at you, then he had.'

'Did you say fiancé?' I asked. 'She's *marrying* that creep?'

'Apparently, and they're moving to London once the house is sold. There's already an estate agent's board up in the garden.'

I felt a pang of sadness – not so much for the house as the studio in the garden, which held so many happy memories of Dad. But in any case, by now the entire contents had probably been loaded into a container and shipped off to America.

'I really don't understand how any mother can behave that way,' Dolly said, shaking her head sadly so that fine, silky strands of white-blond hair came loose from a mother-of-pearl butterfly clip and fell around her face. 'She'd already packed up all your belongings and was about to give them to a charity shop until I said I'd store them. They're in my attic now, though Lola's sent you a few things she thought you might need.'

'You're so kind,' I said gratefully, wishing not for the first time that she was my mother, rather than the Wicked Witch.

'Well, we all love you, darling. You know you could come back with me right now and go off to college in the autumn with Lola, don't you? And, of course, you'd make your home with us during the holidays.'

I was so touched I felt choked. She meant it from the heart, I was sure of that. But still, I didn't want to be the bit of jigsaw that didn't really fit into their happy family picture, but had to be squeezed in somehow.

'I'll be OK,' I assured her. 'I'm going to stay in Cornwall and work, and get a place of my own eventually. And there are evening art classes and writing groups I can join . . . I like it here.'

Which was true, because it was a lovely place. Of course, it wasn't really *my* place, any more than our village near Shrewsbury had been. Nowhere was.

Not even Haworth, once the Avalon I'd both longed and feared to visit – a fear arising from a suspicion that it wouldn't live up to Dad's comforting stories about my abandonment. For now I knew that I'd been left out on the moors, probably miles away, I could have come from *anywhere*.

But I settled in Cornwall for the next few years, even if my roots were never more than shallowly put down.

Edie became a good friend, despite the difference in our ages, and Lola's family provided support and a bolthole I could always return to, sure of a warm welcome.

Of the Wicked Witch I heard nothing more, once the house was sold and she decamped to London. It felt as if all those years she'd only been *pretending* to be my mother . . . which actually, I suppose, was the truth. She was thrust into the role but the run was lengthier than she'd hoped for.

Lola went off to university the following autumn to study history but then, instead of carrying on and doing a postgraduate teaching course as she'd intended, fell in love with a visiting historian older than her father and settled in Hampstead to raise three children. She said Harry, her husband, had a young soul and the same sense of humour, which, when I met him, I discovered was true. They were genuine soul mates and, if the stars were not quite in alignment regarding their ages, then they were prepared to take what happiness they could together.

Meanwhile, I drifted from job to job, baking in a café, working as a pastry chef in a big hotel, torturing icing into edible fantasies for a celebration cake maker . . . all kinds of things. In between, I'd return to Edie, where my room was kept ready for me and I was always welcome. In my spare time I took painting classes and accepted that my talents lay more in illustration than fine art, tried on several writing groups for size and socialized in one of the artier pubs with a group of bohemian and often transient friends.

And that's where I eventually met and fell for Robbie . . . though by then I'd become so used to having my own space that I never actually moved in with him. I'd climbed up the housing ladder slowly, from rented room, to bedsit, to minute flat. It wasn't easy to find anything affordable in a tourist resort on my wages.

Robbie was a bit like my father, I suppose, in that he was a big, easy-going and comforting bear of a man, given to warm, wonderfully consoling hugs. He was a dentist, of all things, though his real love was surfing, kayaking, hang-gliding or any sport that had a dangerous edge to it. I was always afraid I was going to lose him, though not in the way I finally did, when he emigrated to Australia.

He wasn't big on permanent commitment and though he suggested I follow him out there once he'd found his feet, I didn't believe for one minute that he really meant it. In any case, I didn't *want* to go. I mean, I have ghost-white skin, red hair and wilt even in mild sunshine, so I'd have to live the life of a vampire to survive in a hot country.

The day he flew off, leaving me with his old and sea breeze-blasted Beetle car, with the hippie-style daisies painted up the side, as a keepsake, it felt like yet another abandonment.

Still, as Lola pointed out to me when I was staying in London with her and Harry soon after Robbie left, my life was also a series of lucky breaks: against all the odds I'd been discovered alive after my abandonment, I'd had a wonderful father, and Edie had rescued me on my very first night in Cornwall from who knows what danger.

'And you and your family have always been there for me,' I said gratefully. 'I'm OK about Robbie really, because I can see now that we were just drifting along together and he was never going to commit to marriage or a family, but we did have some good times.'

I looked back at over a decade spent in Cornwall and added, surprised, 'You know, when I moved down there I didn't think I'd be spending my life working in café kitchens! Somehow, I imagined I'd magically be able to earn my living from writing and painting.'

'You have sold some of your paintings and you've had short stories published,' she said encouragingly.

'I've given up trying to sell my pictures, because in my heart I know now I'm not that good, and *all* my novels have been rejected.'

'I think your pictures are great, but probably a bit of a niche market,' she suggested tactfully. 'And I expect readers just aren't ready for dark, adult fairy tales yet. Perhaps you should try a change of direction?'

And I did, though not quite in the way she meant. In the spring of 2007 I loaded my entire worldly possessions into the old Beetle car and upped and moved to Scotland, to work in Dan Carmichael's Climber's Café.

Looking back now at my teenage self, I'm amazed that I managed to drive up on to Blackdog Moor while still weak and shivery with shock, and negotiate the maze of narrow, rutted lanes in the pre-dawn darkness.

Father had given me the Mini only a few weeks before, after I'd passed the test first time, and it was my pride and joy . . . or it was until it became for ever tainted with the happenings of that night.

The vile Thing – I couldn't think of it as a baby – was bundled into a once-white sheepskin rug and lay still and silent in the passenger foot-well. Indeed, I presumed it to be dead, since it had shown no sign of life after those first mewling weak cries, for which I was profoundly thankful. I felt like Frankenstein, repulsed by the monstrous creation that had resulted from my first – and, I was determined, only – love affair the previous summer.

It held the power to destroy my safe, comfortable future, should Father ever find out about its existence, but I was totally determined he would not.

3

Sad Café

That move from Cornwall to Scotland was a culmination of several things, not least turning twenty-nine and suddenly spotting thirty looming on the horizon like a slightly forbidding cloud.

And, once he'd emigrated, Robbie had communicated with me only during the short, drunken, self-pitying intervals between a series of leggy and beautiful Australian girlfriends. (When later we became Facebook friends, I actually got to *see* the girlfriends, since he pasted his whole personal life on the page.)

My local friends were moving away, getting married or settling down – sometimes all three – while I didn't even have a Significant Possibility, let alone a Significant Other. So when Edie decided to semi-retire, selling her hotel and purchasing a guesthouse in her native highlands, I felt increasingly lonely and stuck in a rut. And *that's* when Dan's advert for kitchen help in his Climber's Café, in a village not too far from Edie, caught my eye.

Dan was ten years older than me and an inch shorter, but a wiry, charismatic character and a rock-climbing legend even *I'd* heard of. With his spiky fair hair and bright blue eyes, I'd found him immediately attractive, but it had still taken him nearly a year – not to mention an engagement ring – to persuade me that happy-ever-after wasn't just the stuff of fairy tales and to get me to agree to move into his square stone Victorian house next door to the café.

I should have known better. A handful of years passed, yet we were still no nearer setting a date for the wedding or starting the family of my own I desperately wanted – and then he went and got himself killed while scaling for a stupid TV programme some coastal stack of rock he'd climbed a dozen times before.

He was tackling the very difficult route up Gannet's Rock on Lundy Island for the first programme. You're only allowed to climb there before April, or late in the year, and he'd chosen early March. I'd been cross with him because he'd forgotten my birthday was on the 2nd and seemed to think it didn't matter if we celebrated it later . . . Afterwards, I kept thinking that my last words to him had been angry . . . and now, no matter how illogical it was, I was *still* angry with him, but this time for leaving me permanently.

He was so vibrant, alive and charismatic – I simply couldn't believe he wasn't going to walk through that door at any moment.

He'd always jokingly called me Rapunzel, but there was no way I could have helped him to the top of that particular tower . . . and anyway, it wasn't lack of climbing skill that killed him, but a great chunk of rock that fractured off and fell from above, sweeping him away as casually as if he'd been a worrisome fly. One of his friends explained it to me – how the rain and ice must have been secretly weakening a tiny fissure deep down into the rock and it was just sheer bad luck that Dan had chosen that moment to make the ascent.

Eventually the anger wore off and my old friends Grief and Despair moved in instead, not to mention an all-too-familiar feeling of abandonment. I wanted to give in to my emotions and lie down and howl like a dog, but instead I battened them down and focused on making all the arrangements to lay both Dan and my dreams to rest, getting through one minute, one hour, one day, at a time.

The day before the funeral we reopened the café while I baked up a storm in the kitchen, for I expected all Dan's climbing friends to come back there after the ceremony and some would have travelled a long way – he was very popular.

I was still moving through a miasma of despair and grief, but was a little assuaged and comforted by the familiar smells of allspice and dried citrus peel, the sound of the springy metal whisk beating eggs into a yellow froth and the feel of the butter and flour between my fingers as I rubbed it into tiny, light golden crumbs.

I'd just taken the last of the baking out of the oven when Jen, the café manageress, said there was someone who wanted to speak to me. I thought it might be Edie. She'd rung when she'd seen the news on the TV, but it would be like her to just turn up when she had a moment. Or possibly it was a friend of Dan's, returned from a climbing expedition and hotfooting it over to offer condolences.

But the woman sitting at one of the café tables was none of these things. She was at least a decade older than me, about Dan's age, and with a hard, salon-tanned face, eyebrows plucked to thin threads and blond hair that showed an inch of dark roots along the parting. I'm never quite sure these days if that's a Look or not.

But whatever it was, I was certain she wasn't one of Dan's climbing buddies and if she was a rep trying to interest me in her firm's latest line of meat pies, she'd chosen the wrong day (and anyway, *I* made them all).

She didn't get up when I approached, so I slipped into the chair opposite. I hadn't really meant to sit down, but I'd been on my feet for hours and I couldn't remember the last time I wanted to eat anything, so my knees suddenly went wobbly and the room spun round.

'I'm Alice Rose. You wanted to see me?' I asked her. 'Only if you're selling something, this isn't a good time and—'

'Oh, I'm not *selling* anything,' she said, eyeing me with curiosity. 'I'm Tanya, Dan's wife, though I went back to calling myself Tanya Carter after we split.'

Something clicked in my brain. I knew Dan had been married long ago but they'd both been very young and it hadn't worked out. There had been no children and they'd separated by mutual consent.

'Of course, you're his ex-wife, aren't you?' I said. 'I—'

'*Wife*,' she broke in firmly, 'and now widow!'

I stared at her blankly as this pierced the fog of grey misery that hung around me, my own permanent wet blanket. 'But . . . you can't be, because we were engaged! We were getting married.'

Or eventually we were . . . for now I remembered all the times he'd put off setting the date.

'He'd need to divorce me first, and although it's been more than ten years since I even *saw* him he knew where I was and he never got round to asking me for one. So when it said on the telly that famous rock climber Dan Carmichael had died in an accident – bit of a shock, to hear the news that way, actually – I thought he'd probably not bothered making a new will either. In which case,' she added triumphantly, 'everything he had would come to me. And when I rang our old solicitor, he confirmed I was right.'

'That can't be true!' I cried, but even as I said the words I remembered that Dan's solicitor, Mr Blackwell, had called only yesterday asking me to search Dan's papers to see if I could find a newer will than the one he held. I'd been too dazed by grief to get round to it – or even wonder what the old one might say.

'When we got engaged, Dan told me he'd always look after me, no matter what happened,' I heard myself saying. I think I was having an out-of-body experience. Or possibly an out-of-my-mind one.

She shrugged. 'He'd never get round to doing anything unless you made him. I mean, I'd heard on the grapevine that he was living with someone, but any normal man would have asked his wife for a divorce before he got engaged again, wouldn't he?'

I didn't reply. I couldn't, because this final blow felt like the *ultimate* abandonment of my life, shrivelling my heart and hopes like an arctic blast. Recently we'd discussed finally setting a date for the wedding, talked of starting a family . . . and all the time he'd known he was still married to someone else.

And now, after all the work I'd put into his café and creating a lovely home, I had no claim on any of it. It would all go to the woman sitting opposite, tapping acquisitive turquoise talons on the table as she looked round the room.

'We used to live in a hideous old rented cottage about forty miles from here, but he seems to have done well with this business – and I understand the house next door was his, too?'

She didn't wait for an answer, or even any response, which was just as well because I was frozen right to the heart. It wasn't just a house she was talking about, but my home and somewhere I'd finally begun to put down tentative roots.

'The café can stay open, so when I get probate I can sell it as a going concern. I expect my turning up has been a bit of a shock to you,' she added, flicking an impatient look at me as I continued to remain silent and stunned.

'I'd better take an inventory of everything now, though, and then I'll know what's what.'

You'll know what's missing after I've gone, you mean, I thought.

She took a notebook out of her large and expensive handbag. 'You can show me round and tell me what's your personal stuff,' she suggested.

'Over my dead body!' I exclaimed, fury finally waking my tongue into action. 'I've no proof you're even who you say you are, let alone have any claim on anything. Dan *told* me he'd make sure if anything ever happened to him I'd be all right, so—'

'Oh, you'll find it's all true. I just thought I'd save myself another long trip up here to do an inventory and note down anything of any value,' she said, and then, glancing at one of my paintings, which hung on the wall nearby, she added disparagingly, 'I don't think much of Dan's taste in art these days.'

The picture had been a particular favourite of his. He'd loved the strange goblin-like kitemen who whirled in the sky on paper wings, unaware that below them a white she-wolf had gathered up the kite strings in her mouth and was running away with them.

That pretty well summed up my present situation, I thought, and then, as if the she-wolf had jerked *my* string tight, I stood up so suddenly that the heavy pine table overturned, pinning Dan's wife to the floor.

Pausing only to unhook my painting from the wall and tuck it under my arm, I walked out into the cold dusk, still wearing my chef's whites.

The slam of the door behind me shut off the steady stream of screaming invective from Tanya who had, as Dan would have been the first to acknowledge, a mouth on her.

I finally turned off the narrow, rutted lane on to the track that led towards the Oldstone, a stark finger of rock on a hill, its weathered sides carved with ancient symbols.

It was a natural outcrop on a small plateau, though a small circle of standing stones had once been erected around it, their purpose long forgotten and their fallen remains now serving only as seats for tired ramblers.

Since a popular hiking trail passed nearby, it had its share of visitors from late spring to early autumn. But so early in the year, with the stiff frost still scrunching up the grass under my wheels as I came to a stop, it was left to the sheep and the occasional bird.

4

Packing Up

When the big oak front door was safely closed and locked behind me, I leaned against it for a moment with my eyes shut, trying to remember how to breathe normally.

And when I finally opened them, I saw the place with new eyes: no longer as my home, just one more temporary resting place on the root-less journey that was my life.

The house was furnished in an eclectic mix of Victorian mahogany furniture Dan had inherited from his parents and a few quirky modern pieces and junk shop finds we'd bought together. Most of my personal possessions were either in the kitchen, or the small boxroom I used for my writing and illustrating, but a few treasures were dotted about the rest of the house: the portrait of me painted by my father, a box made of shells, a small Venetian mirror, a good rug in colours muted by age that I'd once impulse-bought in an auction in Cornwall . . .

I fetched down a stack of cardboard cartons from the attic that were still marked in my own hand from the move up to Scotland: kitchen equipment, books, clothes, bedding, art materials . . .

The doorbell rang later, but I didn't answer it in case it was Tanya Carter. But whoever it was persisted, so I put my head into the hall to listen. It fell suddenly silent, then the letter box clattered and the familiar voice of the café manageress called, 'Alice, are you there? It's me, Jen.'

She looked relieved when I opened the door.

'Thank goodness – I could see all the lights on, so when you didn't answer I was starting to get worried.'

'I thought you might be that woman,' I said, not able to bring myself to call her Dan's wife. 'What happened to her?'

'Well, I think she was bruised by the table, but she was screaming blue murder when she got up, so we knew she was OK, really,' she said, following me into the kitchen and looking at a half-packed box into which I was stashing my favourite utensils. 'There's nothing wrong with her lungs, that's for sure.'

'Do you know who she is?' I asked, wrapping up a glass lemon squeezer and then putting it inside the blue-glazed interior of a Mason Cash mixing bowl, along with a kitchen timer shaped like a hen and a few other small items.

'Yes, I overheard what she was saying – in fact, half the people in the café did, because she's a bit shrill, isn't she? She threatened to report you for assault, but we told her she'd only got what was coming to her . . . and then Col said she'd need witnesses and he was sure no one there had seen a thing. Most of the customers were locals or Dan's friends.'

'That must have cheered her up,' I said, my hands automatically continuing with the wrapping and packing.

'She quietened down when she realized she wasn't getting any sympathy and went away, but she said she'd be back as soon as she'd sorted things out with the solicitor.'

'So . . . she's not intending to go to the funeral tomorrow?' I asked, wrapping newspaper round my set of good kitchen knives and putting them in the box, one at a time.

'No, I don't think even she had the brass for that. She said she was off back down south, she'd forgotten how freezing cold it was up here and how much she'd hated living in Scotland. And . . .'

She paused, clearly uncertain how to put what she wanted to say. 'Alice, we're all really sorry about what's happened. We know Dan loved you and how good you were for him, grounding him and making the café so popular.'

'He wasn't grounded enough to get a divorce,' I said, slightly bitterly.

'You know Dan – he would have *meant* to, he was just so laid-back he never got round to it.'

'Well, it's too late now,' I said. 'I'll be packed and gone, right after the funeral.'

'But shouldn't you speak to the solicitor first? Surely you're entitled to something, after all the work you've put in on the house and the café?'

'The solicitor just rang *me*, to warn me that Tanya Carter might appear – and she *will* get everything. He suggested I check Dan's papers again, in case there's another will, but what's the point when I know very well he won't even have given it a thought.'

'I'd double-check anyway,' she said, 'and surely you don't have to pack up and go straight away?'

'Perhaps not, but I can't bear to be here any more, and the sooner I find a new job and somewhere to live, the better. You can carry on managing the café, meanwhile, can't you? It's a good business, so when she gets probate and puts it up for sale, someone will snap it up and, if they've got any sense, you and the other staff with it.'

'I can keep it going, but it won't be the same. No one can bake the way you can, for a start. One climber said the thought of your syrup sponge pudding and custard had kept him going through a snowstorm on Everest.'

'Dan said much the same,' I said, tears suddenly smarting in my eyes. 'And that my chocolate fudge cake was to die for . . .'

I looked down and realized I was now trying to cram a milk jug into an overflowing box. Only part of my brain was doing rational things, while the rest was desperate to retreat somewhere dark, and howl.

'Look, why don't you come and stay with me and Mum for a bit?' Jen suggested, just as she had after we'd heard the terrible news about Dan.

'You're very kind, but I feel I'd like to get right away. I'll phone my friend Edie in a bit – you know, the one with the guesthouse? She called me after she saw the news and invited me over there for a change of scene after the funeral was over. She can probably put me up until I find another job.'

Back where I started, skivvying for others in a kitchen somewhere – up the ladder and down the snake. The chimera of marrying and having children and a forever home of my own shivered and vanished into the air.

Whatever I wrote in my stories, in real life Princess Alice was destined never to have her happy-ever-after ending.

I said so to Lola when she called me, as she'd done every day since I'd had the news about Dan.

'I shouldn't say that, when *you* haven't either,' I said contritely, for Lola had been suddenly widowed two years ago and had moved back to her parents' smallholding, with her three children.

She'd been absolutely devastated by the suddenness of her loss and I'd spent as much time as I could in London, supporting her through the funeral and helping her to pack up afterwards.

'But your situation is entirely different: I found and married my soul mate and we had our happy-ever-after, even if the after didn't last as long as we'd hoped,' she assured me.

Then she urged me again to go and stay with them, even though the cottage was now bursting at the seams with people, until the annexe they were building was finished. But going back to Shrewsbury, even though the Wicked Witch had long decamped to London, would have been even more of a return full circle.

You know those metal bangles made out of a snake eating its own tail? Well, I felt just like one of those.

I left phoning Edie until early next morning and by then I'd searched Dan's papers again for a will I knew didn't exist. His idea of filing had been to shove everything into the big roll-top desk in the corner of the sitting room and his long-suffering accountant would come over once a year and stuff it all into a box and take it away to sort, so that narrowed down the search area.

I had trouble getting out the words, because my throat felt as if something had been tied tightly round it – my heartstrings, possibly – but once Edie had grasped the situation she offered me one of her three guest chalets for as long as I needed it.

'There's one in need of a bit of renovation that I will nae get round to till next year, so I'll not be losing money by it,' she said, businesslike as ever.

'But I could rent it – I've got savings,' I suggested, for Lola had been wrong about the market for adult fairy tales. A year earlier I'd put a novel and a couple of my novella-length stories out as e-books, with my own artwork for the covers, and the sales had been quite good. I'd bought a nice new laptop on the proceeds.

'You'll do no such thing!' Edie declared. Then she added, 'You know, you were lucky that woman didn't press charges for assault; she sounds the type.'

'She might have done, if Jen and the other staff hadn't told her they would swear they never saw any assault if she tried it,' I said. 'I can't imagine how Dan came to marry her in the first place . . . or why he never told me he wasn't divorced.'

'He was a nice man, but a feckless creature when it came to anything other than climbing mountains,' she observed. 'Like that Robbie you used to know down in Cornwall – sweet nature, but never quite made the leap into adulthood.'

'I suppose you're right,' I said. 'Though it turns out that Dan wasn't totally feckless, because I've just found a life insurance policy . . . and it named me as the beneficiary. I think when he signed up for this documentary he must have had to have it.'

'Oh? That's something then, at least. How much was it for?' she asked, very brisk and practical.

'I don't know. I don't suppose it's a lot,' I said disinterestedly. 'I'll read the documents later when I can think straight. I've packed them with my stuff.'

He'd probably had the insurance forced on him, but at least he'd cared what happened to me enough to name me. He really had loved me and this must have been what he meant when he said he'd see me right if anything happened to him.

I could feel grief poised to spring out of me like an unloosed jack-in-the-box, but crammed the lid firmly back down.

'Shall I come over and pick you up?' Edie offered.

'No, I know you're busy and I think the old car has one journey left in her before she needs some urgent mega repairs. I've got everything packed so I can load it up and drive over early this evening, after the funeral tea at the café. I – I'd just finished doing the baking for that when his wife turned up. I was going to cut the sandwiches and leave them in the fridge under a damp tea towel, but Jen said she'd make them this morning, instead.'

My mind seemed to run automatically along catering lines, even at a time like this.

'That old car of yours should have been scrapped long since,' Edie said.

'I can't bear to, I'm attached to it after all these years. I'm sure it can be fixed and it's so old, it's probably collectable.'

'Only to someone really keen on rust, and hand-painted flower-power bodywork,' she observed drily. Then she offered to come and support me through the funeral, but I knew she was busy in the guesthouse, so I assured her I'd be among friends.

And I was. So many of Dan's climbing companions and local friends had turned out that the little church was packed, and so too was Climber's Café when we all adjourned there afterwards.

Mr Blackwell, Dan's solicitor, had put in an appearance, which was kind of him, and he apologized for the way things had been left, even though it was hardly his fault. For some reason, I'd expected him to be tall, desiccated and remote, but in fact he was the exact opposite: small, plump and friendly in an avuncular kind of way. I found myself talking to him as if I'd known him for ever.

'There was no sign of another will, but I did find an insurance policy,' I told him. 'I think it must have been something to do with that documentary he was making and it names me as sole beneficiary.'

'If it actually *names* you then Tanya Carter has no claim on it,' Mr Blackwell observed.

'It did, though I can't say I really took in much beyond that, and I've packed it up with my papers now,' I said. 'Edie – the old friend I'm going to be staying with – said she would go over it with me later.'

'Let me know if you need my assistance with that, or anything else. I'll be happy to help,' he said kindly, before shaking my hand and driving off in a sporty little red car. I'd had him down as a sedate dark saloon kind of guy.

When the other mourners began to depart – or decamp to the pub to make a night of it, in the case of some of Dan's climbing friends – I left Jen and the others clearing up while I went to pack my worldly belongings into the Beetle. I must have had more than when I arrived, because everything only just fitted in, even utilizing the passenger seat and footwell. Then I popped back to the café, as I'd promised, to say goodbye.

The staff were all waiting for me and I think they knew I'd never go back there again, because they'd clubbed together to buy me an antique Cairngorm brooch.

I'd been holding it together fairly well until then, but their kindness nearly cracked the shell over the heaving sea of emotions beneath. I stood, swallowing hard and blinking back tears as Jen pinned the brooch to my moss-green hand-knitted jumper, one of Edie's creations, and kissed my cheek.

A fine, pervasive rain was falling as I waved once out of the car window and then drove away, my vision blurred and a thumping in my head that beat in time to the windscreen wipers.

I felt pulled tight, almost at breaking point. I wanted to close a door on everything, including thought, to be alone and silently scream like that Munch painting.

The car valiantly hauled and wheezed and clanked itself over the hills to where Edie's Victorian guesthouse stood on its plateau overlooking a small loch. But that last pull up the drive to the sweep of gravel at the front proved too much and as I came to a halt, the Beetle made a most horrible noise and died on the spot.

I wasn't just having that sort of day – I was having that sort of life.

The cook, William, came out to help me carry my things to the chalet from the defunct car. The three wooden lodges were set back among a stand of pine trees and mine was the furthest from the house, shabby but cosy, with a bedroom, fake log fire (Edie prudently didn't trust her guests with logs and firelighters) and a small kitchen area for any cooking, though most guests took their meals in the main house.

He didn't linger, since he had dinner for the guests to prepare, but said Edie would be down shortly, when she got back from the cash and carry.

Left alone, I just sat down and listened to the wooden building ticking gently, the thumping of my heart and the ringing in my ears, some of which was possibly due to a lack of eating and drinking.

After a while I stirred myself to get out my overnight things and put the kettle on. There was one of Edie's welcome packs in the kitchen area, with the basic necessities for drinks and breakfast in it.

I made coffee as soon as she arrived and she switched on the log-effect fire, causing the room to suddenly look a lot cosier, even though I'd started to feel as if I'd never be warm again.

I apologized about the heap of junk in the car park.

'It's all right, I've already rung the local garage to come and take it away tomorrow,' she said. 'Don't worry your wee head about it.'

'Can you give them my mobile number, so they can tell me what's wrong with it?'

'I think it might be past fixing,' she suggested.

I must have looked upset, because she amended quickly, 'but I'll ask them to do their best and they'll let you know when they've had a look at it.'

She'd brought a wide, squat Thermos of stew and some fresh bread rolls. 'I thought you wouldn't feel like coming up to the house for dinner after the day you've had.'

'No – you're very kind,' I told her. 'I just want to be alone for a bit, because I feel so overwhelmed by everything that's happened. I can't seem to take it all in.'

'Well, we'll talk in the morning,' she said, getting up. 'Now, mind you eat some of that good stew that William sent down for you, or his feelings will be hurt. Are you sure you wouldn't like me to pop back later, after dinner – or you come and spend the first night in the house?'

I shook my head. 'I'll eat and then go straight to bed,' I assured her.

And I did try to eat but my throat closed up, so I abandoned the attempt and crawled into bed. I'd thought I'd never fall asleep again, but the moment I lay down I sank fathoms deep into welcoming darkness, too far for dreams or nightmares to catch me.

The moor was supposedly haunted by a giant black dog with blood-red eyes, so it was just as well I wasn't the imaginative kind. The full moon cast strangely shaped shadows around me as I followed a sheep track round the base of the rocky outcrop and shoved the bundle deep into one of the many crevices, to join the debris of last summer's picnickers. It struck me that that was bizarrely apt under the circumstances . . .

I looked back only once and thought I could make out a glimpse of white, though it was probably just a bit of old fleece caught on the gorse, nothing out of the ordinary in that terrain.

5

Catatonia

Next day I didn't so much wake up as float about just below the surface of full consciousness. My senses felt muffled, as if I was buried in an avalanche.

I couldn't think – but that was all right, because I didn't *want* to think. In fact, I didn't want to do anything except lie there like a leaden log. Inertia weighed so heavily that I could hardly move my arms and legs. It was all very odd . . .

In the other room my phone began to buzz spasmodically, like a dying fly. Then later there was an urgent tapping noise that might have been a woodpecker . . . or someone rapping at the door. I curled into the smallest possible ball and pulled the covers right over my head.

Edie, discovering my near-catatonic state, called the doctor out, who diagnosed delayed shock and prescribed some pills, which she duly forced down me by sheer strength of will.

I'd always hated popping pills and though they eventually set my feet on the path back from Catatonia, I seemed to have almost entirely mislaid April. There were fuzzy memories of the two kind sisters who were Edie's live-in staff, taking turns to spend the nights on the sofa in the living room, and of William popping in with little delicacies with which he hoped to tempt my non-existent appetite, but that was about it.

Even after I started to come out of the fog, my mind still tended to make sudden sideways darts down the nearest dark burrow, like some other Alice. I resisted, because there wasn't much prospect of finding any kind of Wonderland down there, and anyway, I was afraid I wouldn't be able to climb back into the light again.

When I mentioned the rabbit holes to the doctor, he changed my prescription to an antidepressant, instead of whatever he'd been dosing me with before.

They seemed to do the trick . . . or at any rate, turned me into a fully functioning zombie, going through the motions of living and communicating in quite a lifelike manner, though with all the sharp emotional edges rubbed off.

It certainly fooled Edie into thinking I was well on the road to recovery, but I knew Lola suspected there were still rats gnawing at my sanity, because in early May she made a flying visit north to see me, despite being so busy helping in the family herb-growing business, not to mention the burgeoning one she'd set up with her mum, under the trade name Dolly and Lola's Perfectly Pickled and Preserved Company.

They'd started off with their Jam Session line of traditional jams, curds and marmalade and had recently added a Get Pickled range of chutneys and relishes. Lola had commissioned small wooden display stands and several local shops were now stocking their products.

Lola is quietly determined and makes you do things by stealth, so before she went home she'd prised me out of the cabin for a drive and several walks, since she said that although I was naturally pale, I'd started to look like a mushroom. Then she made me promise to answer my phone when she rang every day, since I couldn't access the internet from my cabin.

I suppose getting out did do me good, because after this I started to help out with the cakes and pastries in the hotel kitchen. William was a wonderful chef, but his puff pastry might as well have been shortcrust and his sponge cakes never looked as if they were about to float off the plate. Edie was still refusing to take any rent for my chalet, so I felt I was doing something in recompense.

And it was thanks to Edie that I was to have a little nest egg in the bank, for she remembered what I'd said about finding Dan's insurance policy and insisted on coming up to the cabin and unearthing the paperwork from the depths of a mixed box of my belongings.

Reading through it, she made a discovery. 'There are *two* policies here, Alice,' she said. 'There's the one you mentioned, which appears to be part of Dan's contract with the TV company, and a second policy, an annual one. Perhaps he needed life insurance to run his business leading groups of climbers?'

'Yes, I expect he did,' I agreed.

'And whoever the beneficiary of the annual one was originally, it's in your name now,' she said bracingly. 'I'm surprised the insurers for the TV programme haven't contacted you already.'

'They might have tried, but I still haven't opened most of the post,' I confessed. I'd left Jen the keys to the house and she'd been sending on any letters for me, which I'd simply dumped in a cardboard box. 'And I haven't checked my emails since I moved in, either.'

'You'd better let me go through the mail and throw out the junk for you before you tackle the rest,' she suggested.

A thought suddenly struck me, which made a change, because I hadn't been having a lot of those lately. 'Edie, if there are two policies, does it mean I'm rich?' I asked, though without an awful lot of inter-est. The riches I'd been seeking all my life hadn't been that kind: you can only warm your hands on money if you set it on fire.

'I think you'll find you'll be more than comfortably off,' she said, scanning the end of the second document and then laying it down. 'In fact, I think there should be plenty to buy a nice wee home of your own and more to spare. Perhaps even enough to purchase Climber's Café, if you wanted to?'

I shuddered. 'No, there's no going back. In fact, I seem destined never to belong anywhere, really. I'm the human equivalent of tumbleweed.'

'Oh, no,' she said. 'You were found in Yorkshire, so you must have been born there, which makes you as much a Yorkshirewoman as I'm a Scot. *That's* where your real roots are.'

'I suppose you're right, and I've always been fascinated by Haworth and the Brontës, because of all the fairy stories Dad used to spin me about my being found there, on the Parsonage steps. Even after I'd real-ized he'd made most of it up, I still assumed I'd been left somewhere in the village, but I had a feeling that going there would somehow break the spell. But then, of course, my mother shattered it anyway, when she told me I was actually abandoned up on the moors.'

'That was wrong of her; she behaved very badly to you,' Edie said disapprovingly.

'It certainly made me resist the pull of the place, so I've never been there,' I agreed. 'Of course, by then I'd already read everything about the Brontës and Haworth that I could find. I like Emily best – she was so awful in company and preferred to be with her dogs on the moor, or baking in the kitchen. She was her own woman and a bit of an enigma . . . and I do love her poetry.'

'You have a lot in common with her, then,' Edie said drily. 'I went to Haworth many years ago and it was very interesting. You can see the moors spreading out beyond it, where you must have been found – savage and wild, just like that Heathcliff in *Wuthering Heights.*'

'It's lucky I don't identify with him rather than Emily, isn't it?' I said. 'I wouldn't want to wreak vengeance on my birth mother and any family she might have, even if I found her, and I just want to forget all about my adoptive one.'

'No, you're not the vengeful type, Alice. And though your adoptive mother behaved very badly, I don't expect your birth one was thinking in a rational way when she abandoned you, so you shouldn't take it too much to heart.'

'Dad thought she was probably very young and frightened, and that when she came to her senses later and realized what she'd done, she must have been relieved to know I'd been found in time.'

'Your dad sounds a lovely, warm man,' Edie said, which brought the first tears to my eyes I'd shed since arriving at the chalet. Maybe Sleeping Beauty was starting to wake up?

With her usual brisk efficiency, Edie insisted we contact the insurance companies right away, then downloaded, printed out and filled in all the endless forms, right up to the point where she put a pen in my hand and pointed to the boxes for me to sign.

When she'd gone back to the hotel, I searched out a framed photograph of Dan from one of the boxes: he was standing quite casually on what looked like a stone springboard over a chasm, his blond hair sticking up in spikes and his blue eyes sparkling. And then, finally, I allowed myself to weep a river of tears for what we'd had and what might have been.

It was lucky Edie had sorted out the insurance for me, because Mr Blackwell called shortly afterwards to tell me that Dan's wife had finally asked about it.

'I thought I'd better just check that the policy mentioned you by name,' he said, in his warm, friendly voice, and I remembered how kind he'd been at the funeral.

'Actually, there are two policies, *both* in my name. The friend I'm staying with helped me notify the insurance companies and put in the claims.' I explained what we'd found.

'Edie did most of it, because it was all beyond me. I still can't seem to think straight,' I found myself confessing, probably because he'd been so nice to me at the funeral that he'd felt like my favourite uncle . . . if I'd ever had any uncles. 'But perhaps it's the pills the doctor has put me on and I could stop them now. I hate taking pills anyway.'

'Do trust his judgement and only stop taking them when he says you can,' he advised me. 'These things take time.' Then he kindly said he'd always be happy to hear from me if I needed his assistance in future on any matter, and rang off.

And as if by serendipity, only ten minutes later two texts from the insurance companies popped up, one after the other, saying my claims were being expedited. That sounded painful – they mustn't have wanted to part with the money.

Now I was emerging into the land of the living, I finally began working through the backlog of texts on my phone and then my overflowing email inbox.

Among the junk in the latter I discovered several messages from Robbie, who, entirely oblivious to what had happened to me, was angsting about losing his latest leggy blonde beach babe in his usual self-obsessed fashion.

I found it strangely refreshing. I'd only seen him once in the six or seven years since he moved out to Australia, when he was over to visit his parents, but I was still fond enough of him to hope a Great White Shark didn't gobble him up on one of his surfing trips.

I sent him a brief message back, saying I was staying with Edie for a bit, so he'd probably just assume I'd broken up with Dan.

I deleted most of the rest of the emails unread: they were from so long ago no one would still be expecting a reply.

It felt fairly cathartic and my brain was clearer. I thought I might even be able to return to my writing at some point soon – I'd left a novella half-finished on my laptop, but when I looked for it, I stumbled across a whole story I'd no recollection of writing at all. I *vaguely* remembered a nightmare I'd had while catatonic, but it seemed from the April date on the document that I'd actually got up and written it all down!

It was a take on the story about a mermaid who falls in love with a mortal, then takes on human form by day so they can be together. At night, she goes back into the sea. But he jealously suspects she's returning to a merman lover, so imprisons her in a lighthouse. He cuts off her long hair, too, so she can't do a Rapunzel, but an albatross brings her a long strand of seaweed and she slides down that and escapes. The prince hears the pebbles on the beach murmuring her name as she hurries towards the sea, the damp salt air turning her skin scaly . . . and then, just as she's about to dive under the waves, he grabs her. The tale ends with her pulling him under the water with her and, since he won't release his grip, he drowns.

It was dark, but not bad at all, and definitely my style. How odd to have written something and not remember doing it! All it needed was a polish and it was good to go.

Feeling encouraged, I went up to the hotel again and checked the Amazon reviews for my e-books, and there was a really horrible one that made me feel quite sick. But it also made me so furious that I immediately wrote a story about an author who'd had such a vicious book review that she'd tracked down the perpetrator and unleashed on her a series of revenging goblins, boggarts, wicked fairies and other dark creatures, who all inflicted punishment on her in different and inventive ways.

I felt *so* much better after that and it seemed to light a little spark of me-ness in my heart again . . . whoever I actually *was*.

In my imagination I'd cast my infant self in many roles, so much more comforting than searching out the truth: I'd been Moses in the bulrushes, the baby princess abandoned in the forest to die, the child left as a sacrifice to the gods on a blasted heath . . . a Heathcliff heath.

But I was none of those: I was *me*, Alice Rose, and for the first time I felt a real need to stop running away from the past and discover who I really was and where I came from. But to do that, I'd finally have to go to Haworth . . .

The blackberry-dark sky had begun to lighten towards the east as I drove away. I thought I'd be safely home before anyone else was stirring, which made it all the more of a shock when I came round a sharp bend in the narrow, twisty lane and caught the briefest glimpse of a tall figure dragging a large dog on to the narrow verge, her pale face with eyes screwed shut against the sudden glare of my headlights.

Even in that split second, I recognized who it was . . .

6

Agent of Change

I woke up one morning in early June with the decision to stop taking the antidepressants already fixed in my mind.

I hoped that I wasn't also cutting the invisible umbilical cord to my sanity, but actually, once the drug had worked its way through my system, I felt instead that the world had shifted fully back into focus, that was all. Everything was brighter, louder, clearer.

The breakdown seemed to have been cathartic, for though I still grieved for Dan and what might have been, I now felt strangely distanced, as if losing him had happened so long ago that I'd come to terms with it.

Perhaps, too, it was partly because I now had a new obsession. What Edie had said about my belonging in Yorkshire had sparked off the idea of moving to Haworth and now I was consumed by it. I had a *right* to live there. I'd buy a cottage and, if there was enough insurance money left, I'd be able to eke out a living from my e-book sales. I loved baking, but I really didn't want to work in someone else's kitchen all my life.

Once I was there, I'd try to trace my real mother. I even took the first step in that direction by ordering a copy of my birth registration document, though I had no idea what kind of information I'd find on it. I'd never bothered before, because since I'd been abandoned there wasn't going to be any major clue as to who I actually was on it, was there? My parents must have had one, because I'd had a passport for school trips to France and Switzerland, but I'd never seen it.

When I had a rough idea of how much money the insurance would be I spent hours in Edie's small back office, surfing the internet to see what kind of property I could afford in the Haworth area.

Lola looked too, when she had time, and sent me links to cottages she thought nice and also suggested we meet in Haworth for a couple of days to view anything suitable together.

But actually, you can virtually tour most properties on the internet and . . . well, something was *still* holding me back from going there. It was a sort of spell, an evil enchantment that I knew would be broken the moment I bought my stake in the village. No frog required.

The birth registration certificate was a brief and not very illuminating document, giving the parish where I was born, which wasn't a surprise, and my birthday as 2 March, the day I'd been found. I discovered I'd been registered as Alice Oldstone, but although I'd always been Alice, I had no idea where the Oldstone came from, unless it was the name of the person who found me, or something like that. It wasn't my social worker, because she signed the certificate as Janine Parker. I suppose *someone* had to.

Alice Oldstone . . . It sounded quite *Cold Comfort Farm*, unlike Alice Rose, which I'd always felt was a bit Victorian miss.

They say good things come in threes and following hard on the heels of the insurance money came number two: an offer from a large and well-established publisher for my next full-length novel, and they also wanted to do a deal for my self-published e-book novel and the two novellas.

After all those years of submitting adult horror fairy tales and being rejected, now they were actually asking *me*! I thought about it and felt it might work to my advantage. Also, I rather liked the idea of print books that I could hold in my hands.

But I really needed the guidance of an agent and I'd been firmly rejected by a few of those in the past, too. Then I remembered that I'd once actually *met* one.

I didn't just read horror, supernatural and fairy stories; I liked a bit of historical romance, too, especially by my favourite author, Eleri Groves.

Just before I moved up to Scotland I'd been lucky enough to win the prize of an afternoon tea with her at Framling's Famous Tearoom in London, along with two other fans. I'd travelled up from Cornwall by train, feeling very nervous, but Eleri was a lovely, friendly and interesting person, and it had all been great fun.

I'd also looked forward to seeing the swish Framling's Tearoom, and it had certainly been quite an experience. Everything had seemed to sparkle: the light bounced off the pristine white tablecloths, the rose-pink china and the silvery teapots. And the food was wonderful, especially the cakes, although I was a *little* critical of the Battenburg. It should have been soft squares of vanilla yellow and pale pink, wrapped in a good layer of marzipan, not a garish chequerboard of primrose and cerise, the squares stuck together with thick red jam and then the whole wrapped in marzipan so thin you couldn't taste it. Mine was definitely better.

Also at the tea had been Eleri's agent, Senga McWhirter – a name so odd that it had stuck in my head – so I thought I'd try her first, reminding her that we'd once met. The slight connection *seemed* like a good omen and I was always keen on signs and portents. She'd had a liltingly familiar Scottish accent that had made me feel relaxed in her company, but she struck me as a tough cookie under her soft baby-blue cashmere twinset, which I suspected was exactly what you needed in a literary agent.

I contacted her via her website and within hours she rang me and talked at length in that persuasive voice. She wanted me to go down and see her until I explained the circumstances . . . and then somehow it appeared that I'd agreed terms with her and she was to send me a contract to sign in the post.

In return, I was to email her all my published backlist e-books and my new novel as soon as I'd finished it.

'What's it about?' she asked, obviously assuming I was in the middle of writing it.

'About?' I repeated blankly. 'I . . . well, it's about Sleeping Beauty – when she wakes up, her bower's been transported to the middle of a run-down housing estate and she mistakes one of the locals for her prince,' I gabbled.

Now, where the hell did *that* idea come from?

'Wonderful,' she enthused. 'I'll look forward to reading that very soon.'

I realized I'd sold my agent a fairy tale, so now I'd have to put my money where my mouth was and write it!

Once business matters had been settled to her satisfaction, we chatted a little about the time we met, and Eleri Groves' amazing Brontë find: the previous year she'd discovered a formerly unknown mention of Charlotte Brontë in the diary of a school friend, revealing she'd frequently walked out on to the moors in the hope of seeing a certain farmer, who inspired her to create Mr Rochester. Eleri, when researching the novel she'd based on this, met and married a descendant of that farmer and settled there, near Haworth. It had been in all the papers around the time of the book launch, which was held at the farm's teashop.

'It's quite a coincidence, because I'm hoping to move to Haworth myself soon,' I told Senga.

'Great idea! I sometimes travel up to see Eleri and I'll be able to kill two birds with one stone,' she enthused. 'She's holding the second *Tea with Mr Rochester* book launch at her husband's farm in September and I'll be there for that – perhaps you could get a ticket?'

'I'm sure they sold out long ago – probably the moment they were released,' I said.

'Perhaps, but I'll tell Eleri to squeeze you in.'

'No – please don't,' I said quickly. 'It's only a couple of months away and I may not have moved by then. Perhaps next year, though.'

'We'll see,' she said, then broke off to hum a little of 'We'll Keep a Welcome in the Hillside', before saying she'd be in touch soon and ringing off.

Edie, when I told her about Senga, said I'd done a sensible thing and was predisposed to think that a Scot would naturally be the best kind of agent to have.

'I hadn't realized your books were doing so well, dear,' she added.

'I was surprised when they took off too, really,' I admitted. 'Lola always said they were a bit of a niche market, so I'm going to ring her and tell her the niche is about to get a lot bigger.'

*

I soon discovered that Fear of Agent overcomes creative inertia. Idea sparks flew around my mind until they coalesced and the glimmering of a story formed around the dark heart of the Sleeping Beauty.

'I could remove the evil spell that makes you so spiteful and vile-tongued,' suggested the fairy. 'Just give me a little sweet cake to eat and a drop of honey wine first.'

'Bugger off,' said Princess Beauty. 'I've hated you and all your kind ever since I was cursed in my cradle, and there's no cake or wine here for you.'

'Your stupidity would appear to be a natural curse, but perhaps I should add a little something to remember me by?' the fairy mused, then spun herself into a ball of bright sparks, before vanishing through the window.

The cursed princess congratulated herself on getting rid of her unwelcome visitor until, on looking in the mirror, she saw that where once her forehead had been as smooth as silk, now something was pushing up in the centre . . . and even as she watched, a fine spiral horn emerged and grew, until the tip touched the surface of the mirror and she fell back with a dreadful scream.

Luckily, it turned out to be a twenty-four-hour spell, but it reminded her that it never paid to be rude to a fairy.

I didn't immediately tell Edie or Lola about the *third* lucky thing that happened soon after, but instead hugged it to myself.

For by another seemingly fortuitous stroke of good fortune, I'd stumbled across Mrs Muswell's online advertisement for the Branwell Café, just off the main street in Haworth, and fallen in love with the place.

We chatted via email and exchanged Facebook messages, and then she sent me photographs of the café, which also had a flat over it . . . And I don't know what came over me, because I bought it, sight unseen, despite the warnings of Mr Blackwell, when I asked him to act for me, and the disapproval of Edie, once the cat was out of the bag.

It seemed a great bargain, even though I hadn't been looking for a business – but there was living accommodation too and, after all, I did know about cafés.

I can't have been totally rational, even though at the time I *thought* I was, because I ignored everyone's warnings and carried on with the purchase regardless, taking everything Mrs Muswell said at face value.

From her Facebook photo I could see she was a fat, jolly-looking woman with a glinting smile and even more glinting huge hooped gold earrings. She informed me that the café opened seasonally and, since she was based in Spain, was run when she was absent by a manageress. It had just closed early for the winter for updating and redecorating, after which she'd intended increasing the price, so I was getting a bargain by buying it now. Anyway, from the pictures I could see it looked fine, if a little old-fashioned.

The bare minimum of searches and surveys that my solicitor insisted I needed were soon done, showing nothing of any great moment. The café fronted a small dead-end alleyway, a little cobbled backwater off the main street, but there was parking behind the premises and the sale included all fixtures, fittings and catering equipment.

Mrs Muswell even promised to come across and meet me there once the sale was completed, to show me the books (though she said there was lots of potential to increase the profits), tell me about local suppliers and introduce me to her seasonal staff.

It all sounded almost too good to be true, much like my own fairy stories . . . and so it was.

All I can say is, never surf property for sale when you have a huge insurance cheque in your bank account.

The first cloud on the horizon was an email from Mrs Muswell as soon as the purchase had been completed, saying she couldn't come over after all, due to family circumstances. However, the deeds, keys, accounts and any other useful paperwork would be at her solicitors in Keighley, waiting for me.

But then she suddenly vanished into the ether. I could no longer see her Facebook profile and all my emails bounced. I contacted her solicitor's office, but they wouldn't divulge any information or contact details for her, though they did confirm they had the keys and a folder of paperwork for me.

'I did say perhaps you weren't wise to buy a property sight unseen,' Mr Blackwell said mildly, when I told him. 'However, the café is now in your possession and you must let me know how you get on.'

Edie was more forthright. 'I smell a rat and there must be something wrong with the place,' she declared. 'Buying a property that way was a silly idea, as I'd have told you if you hadn't turned all secretive on me till the deed was done!'

'I know – I wasn't thinking straight and I expect I knew you'd stop me,' I agreed.

I *was* worried, though I consoled myself that however odd Mrs Muswell's behaviour was, the property did actually exist and was now mine – and I'd seen the photos so I knew there couldn't be anything *too* awful to find out.

'If it's dreadful, mind – infested with vermin, or falling into one of those sink holes, say – then put it straight back on the market, cut your losses and return here,' Edie said, still fretting. 'There's always a place for you at Lochside House.'

'I know – and you've been so kind to me always,' I said gratefully, and kissed her wrinkled cheek.

'Och, away with you, you great daftie,' she said, but affectionately, even though I was pretty sure that that was her exact opinion of me, now I'd bought a place I'd never seen.

There was no going back: I'd broken the spell and was now as eager to see my new home as I'd been reluctant to visit Haworth in the past.

Yet still, I'd recognized something that resonated with me in Emily Brontë and I'd reread *Wuthering Heights* so often that I knew passages of it by heart. This simply had to be the place where I could put down roots at last.

When I'd left my hysterical mother she'd been dosing herself with tranquillizers and sleeping tablets, so I knew she'd be out for the count for hours. Probably just as well.

Luckily our house was right at the edge of the village, the last on the road up to Blackdog Moor, so I didn't have to pass through it, risking being seen. I remember I was shaking when I finally turned the car into the gravelled drive, but from cold, exhaustion and relief, nothing more. I closed the metal gates behind me with finality.

7

Alice in Brontëland

The first Wednesday in September found me travelling down to Yorkshire by train, which was *not* the way I'd envisaged embarking on my new life.

My car had been in the local garage since dying on the drive the day I arrived. The owner's son, Rory, happened to be a vintage Beetle enthusiast, so had been carefully and slowly restoring it in his spare time. It had become such a labour of love that it seemed as if he'd never stop tinkering and get it back on the road. Now, apparently, he wanted to put the finishing touches to it before driving it down to Haworth himself, to see how it ran.

I strongly suspected he'd been put up to this by Edie, who didn't think I was yet ready for the long drive, but since she'd insisted on paying the garage bill as a leaving present, I didn't feel I could really argue.

I took one wheeled suitcase and an overnight bag with me and Edie assured me that she and Rory would pack my worldly goods back into the Beetle and he'd follow me down on Sunday. I couldn't even wait and travel with him, since there simply wouldn't be room. I'd only managed to get all my possessions into it when I'd arrived at Edie's by utilizing every inch of space except the driver's seat.

Anyway, the second I'd exchanged contracts on the café, it was as if every restraint that had held me back from going to Haworth before had suddenly snapped, so that now I couldn't wait another single moment to get there.

It was a long journey and I arrived late and had to spend the night in

56

a small hotel in Keighley near the station, waking to a rain-washed morning with a faint rainbow in the sky. I hoped that was a good sign.

The solicitor's office was only a short walk away and I got there as soon as they opened, eager to collect the keys. They handed over a bundle of papers relating to the property too, but though I asked if I could have Mrs Muswell's contact details in case I had any queries regarding the café, they wouldn't divulge them. I didn't even see an actual solicitor, just a secretary, and she was so close-lipped she strongly resembled a bearded clam.

I collected my suitcase, which had the small overnight bag strapped to the top of it, and set off for Haworth in a taxi. At the very moment that I closed the taxi door the weather reneged on its earlier half-hearted promise. The sky glowered blackly and cascades of water fell on to the roof of the car, a frantic drumming that echoed my thoughts.

Reality had finally and belatedly set in and I wondered what on earth I'd done. Was this sudden Stygian gloom an omen? Was the churning in my stomach panic, fear, excitement, anticipation or an indigestible mixture of all four?

The heavenly carwash was still in action when the taxi driver halted with a sudden jerk that set the eye-watering pine air freshener attached to the rear-view mirror swinging. I knew exactly where I was, because Haworth was so familiar from books and documentaries: we were near the bottom of the cobbled road that led up towards the church and Brontë Parsonage.

'Why have you stopped here?' I asked the driver. 'I want Doorknocker's Row, not the main street.'

'Aye, I know,' he said, then pointed to the entrance of an alleyway so narrow that I hadn't noticed it until that moment.

'It's a few steps up t' ginnel,' he said, laconically.

'But I thought you could drive right up to it? I know it's got parking.'

'Not at the front, it hasn't,' he said. 'See for yourself – nowt but a motorbike would fit down there.'

He didn't offer to get out and help me with my luggage, but stayed snug and dry while I struggled to extricate my suitcase and overnight bag, which was now weighed down with the bundle of documents as well as my laptop. I paid him, but without a tip, and he gave me a look that was even blacker than the sky and drove off in a cloud of spray.

There didn't seem to be anyone else about, which was hardly surprising. I scuttled into the shelter of the passageway, a sliver of slippery cobbles between the steep sides of two substantial buildings.

I'd have been certain the taxi driver had brought me to the wrong address, had it not been for the street sign on the wall above my head, so I dragged my suitcase along and discovered that beyond the narrow entrance, Doorknocker's Row opened up into a bottle shape.

Through the curtain of rain I could just make out a forlornly flapping café sign to my left, but if this was the Branwell Café, then the photos I'd seen must have been taken using trick photography! Either that, or they'd been of an entirely different place, for there was no wide expanse of cobbles fronting it and the tubs of bright flowers had turned into two rotting half-barrels bursting their metal hoops and containing no hint of life.

It appeared that some bad fairy had cast a blight over the place – and my dreams. Story of my life in a nutshell, really.

Still, there was no going back, so I fished out my keys, one of which was helpfully labelled 'Café door', before trundling my baggage across at a run. I fumbled the key into the lock, huddled under the inadequate shelter of a trellis-sided wooden porch. The gutters, unable to cope with the sheer volume of water, overflowed in cascades on either side.

Maybe I should have bought an ark, instead of a café?

The key turned easily once my wet fingers managed to insert it and the door swung inwards so suddenly that I stumbled forward down an unexpected step into the gloomy interior. Recovering my balance with an effort, I pulled my case inside and shut the door. The deafening waterfall noise abruptly quietened to a murmur. That was a mercy.

I fished out the torch I kept in the bottom of my handbag and took a good look around me. There was a light switch, which didn't work, but by then I wasn't altogether surprised to find the power had been cut off.

I shone the torch beam around the long, narrow room, which had a counter at the furthest end, backed by a mirror in which my pale face floated like an apparition. There was a door to the left, which presumably led to the kitchen premises, and steps to the customer conveniences vanishing down into the darkness on the other side.

Apart from having a wooden floor, the room bore little resemblance to the old-fashioned pine, chintz and polished brass cosiness of the pictures sent to me by Mrs Muswell, for it was instead furnished with speckled Formica tabletops and tubular chairs with pale blue plastic seats, some ripped and leaking grey stuffing.

There was the gleam of a glass cake display cabinet on the counter and the outline of a hatch through to the kitchen behind it . . . unless the rear premises had magically vanished into one of the sink holes that Edie had been so worried about.

I'd have said the café had been abandoned years ago, except that even by torchlight I could see that it was as clean as a whistle, for every surface, however cheap and shoddy, shone.

I supposed that was something . . . and when I went through the swinging door into the kitchen, *that* was spick and span, too. It was outdated, the work surfaces and flooring worn, and I spotted immediately that there were spaces where equipment had been taken out. Now I was getting Mrs Muswell's full measure, I was fairly positive they would be items she'd included in the sale, though I'd have to unpack the list of what she said she'd leave to be sure.

I hung my wet raincoat on the back of a chair, dumped my bag on the wooden table and went to explore further.

There was a cubbyhole of a windowless office, with built-in desk and wooden shelves, and a utility room through an arch where, to my relief, I found that the big fridge, freezer and chiller cabinet were still there, turned off and with the doors slightly open to air. Like the one in the kitchen, the Belfast sink was scrubbed a spotless white, too. It was as though someone had done their best to turn a sow's ear into a silk purse, and I was certain it wasn't Mrs Muswell. On one wall was fitted the obligatory staff hand-washing basin, and next to it a floor-to-ceiling cupboard was full of cleaning materials.

The back door was in a little hallway, but whatever was outside could wait until the end of the apocalypse, if it ever came. There was another flight of steps vanishing down into darkness in there, too, but I'd seen too many horror films to go exploring the basement with a torch. I didn't remember any mention of a cellar in the details.

Anyway, it was the flat, where I hoped to make my home, that I was most eager – and afraid – to see now. There was a door at the bottom of the stairs that led up to it. Mrs Muswell had told me that in the days when it had been a holiday let, the café and flat shared the rear entrance.

She'd also said she'd rarely used the flat herself, preferring to board with friends who had a nearby guesthouse when she was over here, so I unlocked the door with some trepidation. Who knew now what was true and what wasn't? Because it was plain that I'd been sold, if not a pup, then an elderly and slightly flea-bitten mutt.

Those pictures I'd pinned my dreams on must have been from some long-ago incarnation and hadn't included the flat.

Still, I'd sort of assumed that whatever I found, it would at least be as clean as the café, but I was immediately disabused of this idea by the furry festoons of cobwebs that clutched at my face as I went upstairs. I opened another door at the top with a metal latch and shone my torch round a kitchen-cum-living room that stretched from front to back of the building. Old lino had worn into holes and dust lay like thick felt along every surface . . . except the bare places where furniture had once stood and the marks of footsteps going to and fro. It clearly hadn't been occupied for years, except by about a million huge black spiders.

There was a sliver of a bathroom, containing the smallest bath I'd ever seen, and two bedrooms, one of them partly over the passageway between the café and the next building.

It all looked dismal, dank, chilly and unwelcoming, though the ghastly weather wasn't helping it any. I'd need to spend time and money refurbishing it before I moved in, which I hadn't banked on, and I wouldn't even let myself *think* about what I'd have to do to get the café up to scratch!

I went back downstairs, ducking below the cobwebs this time and feeling glad I'd booked myself in for the first night at a guesthouse . . .

the one recommended by Mrs Muswell, now I came to think about it. If they were her friends, I wasn't too sure how good an idea that was.

I felt damp and cold, and there was no point in lingering there. I'd get a better look next day in good light and perhaps things wouldn't seem quite so dismal.

So I unstrapped my overnight bag and tucked the suitcase under the desk in the office, then put on my wet anorak and went out, locking up carefully behind me even though there wasn't a single thing in there worth stealing.

The cascades of rain had finally stopped, but it was still Waterworld out there and I was now so stiff from the damp and cold that I felt as if I'd been hung to petrify in the Dropping Well at Knaresborough for a century or two.

Next day, although physically I felt as if I'd been fed through a mangle, mentally I'd entirely returned to my usual calm and logical self. This was more than could be said for Mum, once she finally awoke from her pill-induced oblivion.

'What did you do with—' she began fearfully, when I took her some early lunch in on a tray. With her bleach-blond hair and pale, pond-water eyes, she always looked like Marilyn Monroe's less attractive sister, especially now her generous curves were running to fat. Luckily, I take after my long-absent father in appearance . . . and presumably in intelligence. I must have got it from somewhere.

Then Mum added quickly, in a trembling voice, 'No – don't tell me! I don't want to know.'

8

Away with the Fairies

Luckily the Gondal Guesthouse was only a short walk away, but it was not the welcoming haven I'd hoped for. Instead, it wore a slightly depressed, shabby, end-of-season air and I was checked in by a morose and pimpled youth, who seemed to take positive pleasure in informing me that they didn't do evening meals.

But at least my room was clean and warm, with a kettle, tea and coffee. I changed into dry clothes and then, over a hot drink, looked through a menu I'd picked up from a box on the café counter on the way out, then read through the paperwork the solicitor had given me when I'd collected the keys.

Facing the reality of what I'd actually bought had had the effect of shocking the last lingering miasma of mingled grief and antidepressants right out of my system and I'd snapped straight back into my old self – the one who operated on a practical level to earn a living, but was away with the fairies whenever she could escape into her writing . . . though actually I really *must* have been away with the fairies when I bought the café sight unseen.

Why hadn't I so much as looked at Google Street View? Or checked for reviews on travel sites, to see if customers had mentioned the place?

But no, I'd blindly trusted Mrs Muswell and rushed straight into the biggest purchase of my life with less care and thought than I'd have given to the buying of a pair of shoes.

The papers the solicitor had given me contained no promised file of catering suppliers, addresses for the staff, useful contacts – nothing.

There wasn't even any indication of the café turnover. And when I came to look more closely, most of the documents were those passed on by the previous owners of the property, which had operated under the not very upmarket name of The Butty Box.

I made another hot but disgusting cup of instant coffee, sat on the bed and phoned Lola.

'You told me you visited the Branwell Café when you came to Haworth with the WI, and it was a thriving business in the middle of the village,' I told her accusingly, though that was rather unfair, seeing that I'd already bought the place before I'd mentioned the name to her.

'The *Branwell* Café?' Lola exclaimed. 'Oh, I misheard you – I thought it was that wonderful teashop in the heart of the village that's been there for ever.'

'No – how could I have afforded that, even if it was for sale?' I demanded. 'And though I was expecting the Branwell Café to need a lot of updating, it's a far cry from how Mrs Muswell described it to me. She sounded so nice and genuine, too,' I added bitterly. 'I should have smelled a rat when I couldn't see her Facebook profile once the sale went through and my emails started to bounce.'

'Is it *very* dreadful?' Lola asked tentatively.

'It's run down and grim, and it looks as if she's sold off all the kitchen equipment of any value, even though everything was included in the price. Not only that, but the flat obviously hasn't been used for years and it's totally bare – not even a cooker up there, just a space where one has been.'

'How sneaky, removing things she said she'd leave! Isn't that illegal?'

'Possibly, but I expect it would be difficult to take her to court over it since she's in Spain and no one will give me her contact details.' I sighed. 'Still, it might look better in the light of day, if it ever stops raining.'

'I hope it does, but I suppose you could always cut your losses and sell it again, if not,' she suggested.

'No,' I declared with sudden determination, 'I've sunk all my money into the place, so I'll just have to make a go of it – though *not* as the Branwell Café, because I found one of the menus and it seems to have been a cheap burger and sandwich joint.'

'Have you considered shutting the café down and turning the whole premises into a house?' she said. 'I mean, that's what you were looking for originally, wasn't it?'

'I suppose I could, but either way, renovating the place will take most of what's left of the insurance pay-out, and I don't think I'm going to make enough to live on from my books, even with a proper publisher and an agent.'

'You'd have to get another job?'

'Yes, and since baking is all I know how to do – well, I might as well do it in my own café as someone else's.'

'You're right,' Lola said. 'I hadn't thought of that. Oh, I do wish I could come and help you sort things out!'

'So do I, but I know it's impossible: you're already doing too many things.'

'It'll be easier when the extension is finished and I can move in with the girls,' she said. 'At the moment, running the jam and pickle company with Mum, the school run and juggling all the children's activities means I never seem to have a second free. Just as well I like being busy.'

'Yes, and I need to just get on with it, like you did after you lost Harry.'

'But I was lucky because I could move back in with Mum and Dad and then, once I'd sold our house, there was enough to fund the extension *and* a new building for the jamming and pickling. Things have really taken off with the business, and it's *fun*,' she said.

'I think you've just infused a bit of backbone into me,' I told her. 'The Branwell Café will be reborn as something new – onwards and upwards!'

'That's the spirit!' she said, then made me promise to ring her again next day when I'd been back and seen it in daylight.

'I think the electricity might be back on, too. When it wouldn't work, I assumed Mrs Muswell had had it disconnected, but they said here there'd been a power cut earlier.'

'If it's light enough to take pictures, send me some.'

'With or without the giant spiders?' I asked.

'Without!' she said firmly.

*

I borrowed an umbrella from the moronic youth and had a quick meal in the bar of an almost empty nearby pub.

I was tiring now after all the ups and downs of the day, but as I made my way back to the guesthouse, it suddenly struck me that I was actually here at last, right in the heart of Haworth!

Perhaps I hadn't been born in the village, as in Dad's stories, but I must have come from the immediate area and I felt ready to embrace the part of me that belonged here . . . if I could find it.

There was a thin, brisk woman with cropped iron-grey hair behind the reception desk when I returned the umbrella. When pressed, she admitted that she was Hattie Voss, the owner of the guesthouse, and asked me if everything in my room was OK, though not in a tone to indicate that she cared one way or the other.

'OK' was about the most you could say about it, but I took the opportunity to ask her about Mrs Muswell, since she'd told me she always stayed there and was friends with the owners.

'Well, yes . . . she does stay here sometimes,' she said reluctantly, then suddenly called out, 'Jim!'

A short, balding man with a military haircut and moustache, who had been visible through a door laying the tables in the dining room for breakfast, stopped clattering plates and joined us.

'Our guest was just asking about Mrs Muswell and I told her she occasionally used to stay here.'

'Ah . . . yes,' he agreed. 'Handy for the café. She had a good manageress, but she liked to pop over from time to time and personally check on things.'

They were oddly cagey and insisted they didn't have any contact details for Mrs Muswell in Spain. I didn't believe them: they smiled and smiled but were probably still villains, just like Mrs M.

I wasn't getting anywhere, so finally I gave up and retired back to my room, where I fell into that state of exhaustion where you become febrile and wide awake, but in a slightly nightmare, spaced-out kind of way.

Since the guesthouse had broadband and I had my laptop with me, I sat at the rickety dressing table and began some of the internet searches I should have done before I signed the contract – and quickly discovered there was a surprising amount about the Branwell Café out there. None of it was good.

Visitors appeared to have stumbled on the café by accident and then wished they hadn't. The food was poor-quality burgers and sandwiches, as the menu I'd found had suggested, the premises shabby, the facilities basic and the ambience non-existent. *And* they had the rudest staff ever.

I could sympathize with the latter, for my sharp tongue had got me into trouble once or twice when I'd been pressed into serving customers rather than working in the kitchen.

Then I struck gold with two video clips of the café interior that had been uploaded to YouTube. The quality wasn't brilliant, but I was riveted.

In the first, the camera panned round the café and then settled on a tall, gaunt and elderly waitress as she pushed a large mobcap out of her eyes and then slapped a plate of food in front of a beady-eyed and noisy small boy.

He looked down at his plate and asked suspiciously, 'Are these Brontëburgers made out of *real* brontosauruses?'

'Aye, they breed them up on t' moors,' she said.

'I never knew that before,' said his mother indistinctly, having already taken a large bite of what was probably, having seen the menu, a Charlotte Chicken wrap.

She seemed to be serious. They were both now looking at the waitress with wide eyes and bulging hamster cheeks.

'Like *Jurassic Park*?' the child asked. Then he added through a second larger mouthful, 'This tastes kinda weird.'

'Shut tha moaning and get it et,' the waitress advised him, then stumped off.

The other clip was of a customer complaining to a different member of staff – perhaps the manageress Mrs Muswell had left in charge, whenever she'd gone back to Spain. She was younger, possibly late forties, but as tall and gaunt as the first one and clearly related. Mother and daughter?

'Can you take this toastie away and remove the onion? I can't eat onion,' said the man.

'You ordered a cheese and onion toastie, you great daft lump – what were you expecting to find in it?' she said, looking scathingly at him from under a pair of heavy, straight, Frida Kahlo eyebrows.

'I didn't come here to be insulted!' the man said indignantly.

'Well, if tha don't like it, take thisen off,' she advised him. Then her eye fell on those customers near enough to hear the exchange, who were sitting, stunned, with their mouths hanging open.

It was like a halibut convention.

'What are thee all staring at?' she demanded. 'Tha dinner'll be as cold as a stone if tha don't get a shift on and et it!'

Well, Edie'd always said I was so brusque with customers that I should never be allowed out of the kitchen, but clearly I had *nothing* on the staff at the Branwell Café.

They were women after my own heart, sisters in sarcasm . . . and as I finally fell asleep in my lumpy bed with the hard, flat pillows, I was visited by the firefly glimmer of a Good Idea . . .

'There's nothing to know, you just had a bad dream,' I told her, putting the tray down on her lap. 'Now, eat this and forget all about it.'

'Oh, I couldn't eat a mouthful – and how can you look and sound so normal after what happened last night?' she demanded.

'The natural resilience of youth,' I said, which was a bit of a low blow, considering the way she struggled against the signs of ageing, a female Canute battling to hold at bay a sea of wrinkles. 'And we're never having this conversation again, right?'

'So cold and hard . . .' she murmured, wincing and shutting her eyes.

But when I went back to collect the tray and tell her I had to go out for a short while, it was cleared to the last crumb and she was watching some mindless soap series on the bedroom TV.

9

Up the Creek

I finally fell asleep from sheer exhaustion, but was awake again at the crack of dawn with a complete scene in my head from *When Beauty Goes Bad* (as I'd called my new novel), which I got down on the laptop before I forgot it.

'It is your birthday,' said the stepmother, who wasn't so much wicked as at the end of her tether. 'I know how you love a game of hide-and-seek, so I have concealed a beautiful necklace of sparkling diamonds in the bower deep in the woods and if you find it, you may keep it as my gift.'

Of course, when the stepmother adds that if Beauty doesn't find the necklace she'll give it to one of her own daughters, Beauty is off in a flash.

And after this, *I* was off like a flash too – down to a large, chilly dining room to eat a fortifyingly huge breakfast with the only other occupant, who might as well have had 'sales rep' stamped all over him.

The food was served by the military-moustache man, who seemed even less talkative than the previous night and, while the place wasn't quite in the Fawlty Towers league, it wasn't far off. I had the uncomfortable feeling that the owners were surreptitiously observing me and reporting back to Mrs Muswell, too.

I packed and settled my bill right afterwards. I wasn't sure where I would be staying that night, because it would take some time to make the flat over the café habitable, but there had to be a better option than the Gondal Guesthouse.

I decided to worry about it later, when I'd seen the café in daylight and, I hoped, electric light, too.

When I emerged from the guesthouse, the sun was attempting to come out from behind a lot of billowing dove-grey clouds and, though the cobbles of the main street were still slick and damp, I felt my spirits rise slightly.

I longed to explore the village and visit the Parsonage and church, not to mention walk beyond them on to the moors, as Emily Brontë used to do. But there would be time for that later, when I'd got to grips with the realities of my impulse buy.

I turned into the narrow entrance-way to Doorknocker's Row, which was easier to spot in the full light of day, and noticed for the first time that a shop faced the café across the courtyard.

'Small and Perfect' boasted the sign over it. Curious, I veered over and had a look. It seemed to be some kind of curio shop. I could dimly make out various bijou objects by peering through the bow window, which was made from small squares of thick greenish glass, just like that of the café. The door was locked, with a sign on it that more or less said, 'Tough luck if I'm not open, but call this number to make an appointment', only it put it marginally more politely. It was signed 'Nile Giddings'. There weren't any opening times.

I wondered if the proprietor of Small and Perfect was small and perfectly . . . I veered away from finishing that thought. He was probably elderly and retired, keeping the business on as an interest and opening when he felt like it.

And what sort of name was *Nile*? Did he have parents with a river fetish? Siblings called Zambezi, Seine and Mersey?

I pulled my mind back to my present task and turned to scrutinize the café. Set in the good Yorkshire stone walls, the shallow bullion-glass bow window resembled a painted harlot smile on the face of an honest, plain woman, but the sacrilege had clearly taken place a good century or more ago.

The way the light fell into the courtyard revealed that the Branwell Café sign had been roughly painted over the previous one, so the raised outline of 'The Butty Box' could still be seen.

Then I narrowed my eyes and peered again and was certain I could pick out an even earlier stratum that might have said the Copper Kettle.

The damned thing had more layers than an archaeological dig!

The wooden, lattice-sided porch was another Victorian addition, as incongruous as the window, but sort of charming in its way – or it would be when the broken and rotten bits were mended.

Apart from the café and Small and Perfect, the walls around the little courtyard were the blank stone backs of other properties, only broken by the entrance to the narrow passage next to the café, which ran under part of the flat above.

When I let myself into the café (remembering the step down, this time), rays of weak sunshine were fingering a pile of junk mail on the window ledge like a dubious shopper. The long room looked marginally lighter and less dismal, though no more upmarket than before. I suspected Mrs Muswell had merely changed the name to something fancier when she bought the place, but kept the greasy spoon ambience and menu.

Crossing my fingers, I pressed down the light switch . . . and lo, there was light! I switched it off again (I was going to need all the money I had left from the insurance to turn the café and flat around, so I might as well start being thrifty), and went through into the kitchen, dumping my overnight bag next to my suitcase in the office.

Down to business: I took the contents inventory, a pen and notebook out of my tote and started to check off what was supposed to be there against what actually was.

All the tables and chairs were certainly present, but I'd naturally assumed they'd be the pine farmhouse-style ones in the photos she'd sent me. Those tubular Formica and plastic monstrosities looked as if Mrs Muswell (or perhaps the proprietors of The Butty Box) had bought them as a job lot from a failed low-end diner. They didn't really go with the rustic charm of the wooden floor, either, which was a bit battered at the moment but would probably strip and seal well.

There was a rustic, Spanish-style wooden light fitting in the middle of the room and matching wall lights, all fitted with dim bulbs that left the corners of the room swathed in darkness. This was possibly why Mrs M had missed a couple of plates that hung on the wall next to the steps, which I discovered led down to two spartan and basic toilet cubicles. She hadn't taken the chipped sinks, the loos or the rusty hand driers with her, so I supposed I should be grateful for small mercies.

There was a door marked 'Private' beyond them, which, when I peeped through, led to a storeroom full of empty metal racking and stairs leading up – presumably the ones I'd noticed near the back door, on my first visit.

I went back up into the café to explore behind the counter, my ghost image in the mirror coming to meet me. There was an antiquated till and an even more antiquated but gleaming metal water geyser, racks full of thick white pottery mugs, saucers and fat, round teapots. A glass-fronted cake display unit sat on the counter.

I supposed Mrs Muswell had kept within the legal limits of our bargain in that the café was furnished with chairs, tables and crockery, even if not the ones I'd expected, but the kitchen, with its work surfaces denuded of equipment and the spaces where larger items had once stood, was another story. There was no catering-sized mixer, hob . . . or even an oven.

But then, after going through Mrs Muswell's menu last night, it didn't sound as if they'd done much in-house cooking at all, apart from some fancifully named burgers, wraps and cheese toasties. But there had been cake – what had they baked that in? Or hadn't they? Maybe they bought *everything* in and microwaved whatever needed to be served hot?

And come to that, the microwave from the list was missing, too.

I felt grateful that the chiller cabinet, large fridge and freezer had been left behind, for, though so ancient they looked fashionably retro, those still worked when I flicked the switches.

I sorted through the keys and unlocked the back door, stepping out into a paved courtyard surrounded by beds of overgrown, neglected roses, old inhabitants fallen on bad times.

There was a side gate that gave access to the passage under the flat if you turned right, but I went the other way along a path running between my garden and the high stone wall of the next building. I was looking for the parking space and found it was a large patch of rough ground next to a row of bins. There was plenty of room for my Beetle when it arrived – you could get two or possibly even three cars on it. I'd have to figure out where the alley led, so I could give Rory directions when he brought the car down, but that could wait for now.

I went back in and braced myself for another look at the flat. Downstairs had at least been *clean*. In fact, whoever was in charge of that aspect of the café evidently had a thing about it, for there were notices all over the place exhorting the staff to use good hygiene and food safety practice, along with a whiteboard with boxes to tick for daily and weekly cleaning tasks.

But whoever was responsible clearly hadn't extended their activities upstairs. I wondered if Sleeping Beauty had shared her bower with festoons of cobwebs and giant spiders . . . and, one thought leading to another, had to dash back into the office where my laptop lay on the table and type quickly:

Princess Beauty, suddenly drowsy, kicked off her high, gold-heeled shoes and lay down on the velvet couch, closing her eyes. A rattling noise, as many hard arachnid legs clattered towards her, made her open them again.

A gigantic spider stopped dead, as if they were playing a game of Mr Wolf.

'Are you a friendly spider, come to look after me while I sleep?' asked Beauty, who had never been the brightest bunny in the box, even when not fuddled by drowsiness.

'That's right,' he agreed, and proceeded to wrap her up as tightly as a parcel in a cocoon of strong spun silk.

When I dragged myself back to reality and went upstairs, the flat was, if anything, worse than I remembered and smelled musty from disuse, though not actually damp.

As to furnishings, there were a lot of useful things in the boxes Rory would be bringing with him, including some nice curtains from my last Cornish flat that hadn't been unpacked while I was living with Dan. I was sure they'd fit some of the windows here and I had everything else I'd need . . . apart from any furniture whatsoever.

I rang Mrs Muswell's solicitor and told him she hadn't left the items she'd agreed to, and also complained that she'd misled me by sending me photos of how the café *used* to look years before, not how it actually was now.

But it was just as I thought: in slippery, weasel words he gave me to understand that there wasn't a lot I could do about it, since she was domiciled in Spain. He still wouldn't give me any kind of contact information for her, either, but assured me he would pass on my comments. A fat lot of good that would do me!

I knew my own solicitor would say much the same, though. I'd made my bed and would now have to lie on it. Or I would, when I had one.

I thought I'd better try to put a more positive spin on things when I described the place to Edie, or she'd be down here strong-arming me into selling it again. And Lola would want an update, though I didn't need to pretend it was better than it was with her.

I let the tap water in the kitchen run until it stopped being a peaty brown and then filled the old and battered kettle, which had obviously not been worth taking. I'd purloined teabags, coffee and little pots of milk from the guesthouse, but now I discovered a whole box of Yorkshire Gold teabags, like a treasure trove, in one of the cupboards.

The kettle was just coming to a boil, along with a few more ideas that had germinated and begun to sprout from the original one of the night before, when I heard the brass bell on a spring attached to the café door jangle. I was sure I'd locked up when I came in – and anyway, even if I hadn't, the 'Closed for Renovation' sign that had been stuck to the glass and the lack of lights should have put any potential customers off.

I got up to investigate and as I came through the swing door a tall, raw-boned woman turned from switching on the lights and stared at me. She had grey-streaked dark hair cut in the sort of sixties Mod bob that was very short at the back, but came down in two wings on to her cheeks.

She looked familiar, too, but the feeling clearly wasn't mutual because she was eyeing me with deep suspicion.

'Well, I'll go to the foot of ower stairs! Who the hell are you, flower?' she demanded.

The last thing I felt like doing was going out, but I urgently needed to buy a few things at a chemist and I also thought I'd better get a replacement for the sheepskin bedside rug while I was at it – both as far away from home as possible, just in case . . .

Luckily, our weekly cleaner wouldn't be here until Thursday next week, by which time I'd have removed every last trace of what had happened and restored the house to the condition of pristine order and cleanliness that Father insisted on.

10

Burger Queen

'I might say the same,' I replied, but then the penny dropped and I realized who she was. 'Oh – you work here, don't you?'

'In season I do,' she admitted. 'I'm Tilda Capstick and I manage the place and do what cooking there is. But out of season I come in Fridays to clean and air it, that's why I'm here today. Have you come about the renovations? I suppose Mrs Muswell gave you a key, but she didn't tell me what was happening.'

'No, actually, I'm Alice Rose, the new owner,' I said, and then, seeing she now looked both blank and suspicious, added, 'Surely Mrs Muswell told you she'd put the place on the market and I'd bought it?'

'Eh, I'd no idea she was even *thinking* of doing that, the sneaky bugger!' she said, looking gobsmacked. 'She was over here the end of August to close the café up early for renovations – and about time, too, we thought.'

'She told me she'd intended doing that if the café didn't sell as it was – but for a higher price than I paid.'

She ruminated over this, glowering. 'You know, if I'd been thinking straight I'd have realized she wouldn't part with her brass that easily. Oh, I can see it all, now! That's why the flat was emptied and most of the appliances in the kitchen vanished. Nell and me just thought it was about time the place went a bit more upmarket, and maybe then it would open all year round, so we wouldn't have to go out working for a cleaning agency from late September to Easter.'

'Nell?' I queried.

'My aunt. I'm mostly in t' kitchen, but I managed the place too, when Mrs Muswell wasn't here. She only came over every three or four weeks and someone had to be in charge of ordering, stock control, cashing up and the like. My aunt Nell just waits on and makes the coffee and tea.'

'Of course – I saw you and your aunt in some video clips on YouTube.'

'Aye, my cousin's girl, our Daisy, showed me on her iPad thing. Mrs Muswell saw it too and she said we'd better shape up to be more polite to the customers, or she'd fire us,' Tilda said darkly. 'But it was all hot air. Where else would she get two trustworthy and reliable workers for so little money?'

'She wasn't a great payer?'

'Both of us were on minimum wage and seasonal contracts, so we'd never know from one year to t' next if we still had jobs or not. Looks like we're out of them now, though . . .'

She looked at me assessingly. The first shock had passed and she'd clearly begun to wonder what I intended. 'So . . . you've bought the place. Do you have any café experience, blossom?'

'*Years* of it,' I assured her. 'Ever since my late teens I've worked in hotel kitchens, cafés, restaurants and even a specialist cake shop. Baking's my thing, especially pastries and cakes. I . . . recently came into some money and when I saw the Branwell Café for sale online, it seemed too good to be true.'

I smiled ruefully. 'It was! The pictures Mrs Muswell showed me must have been taken years ago when it was a different café entirely.'

'It was probably the Copper Kettle. Two sisters had it and you've never seen the like for starched gingham tablecloths, spider plants in macramé pot holders and vases of plastic flowers,' she said. 'But it's all been downhill since then and I told her, if she didn't replace the kitchen flooring and put in new worktops, we'd be losing our hygiene rating, however hard I worked to keep the place clean. You've bought a right pig in a poke.'

'I realize that now and, of course, all my friends and my solicitor warned me not to rush into buying it without looking at it first. But I wasn't thinking straight, because of a recent bereavement,' I explained.

79

'I'm not usually so trusting, but I exchanged emails with Mrs Muswell and talked to her on Facebook too, and . . . well, she seemed really nice.'

'It's all put on. She fools lots of people that way. And now you *have* seen it, I suppose you're going to sell up again?'

'I could, of course, but I've got one or two ideas,' I said. 'Look, I was just about to make some tea in the kitchen, so why not have a cup with me and talk things over?'

'All right. I usually make a brew first before I start cleaning,' she agreed, following me through the swinging door. 'And come to think of it, Mrs M still owes me for cleaning the café and kitchens right through before we shut up for the season. Who's going to pay me now?'

'I was struck by how everything looks spick and span, except the flat – that's filthy,' I said.

'She didn't ask me to go up there. It was never used for anything that I recall.'

'Do you have her address in Spain and phone number?' I asked hopefully. 'She vanished off the internet and her solicitor won't give me her contact details.'

'No, when she was in Spain I had to tell a friend of hers at a local guesthouse if there were any problems and they'd ring her.'

'The Gondal Guesthouse? I stayed there last night and they denied knowing where she was.'

'Well, they would, wouldn't they, if she's taken you in over buying the café? Thick as thieves, they are, and they'll be closing up come October and going out to stay with her, like they do every year.'

'The solicitor will forward mail for me, but that's a fat lot of good, isn't it? I had a whole list of things she was supposed to be leaving behind as part of the sale, all the kitchen equipment and the furniture in the flat, and most of it is missing.'

'Kettle's still here, though,' she said, switching it back on. 'And I've got a little flask of milk in my basket so we won't be needing those pots of weird stuff you've got there.'

'I stole them from the guesthouse,' I confessed. 'It says on the sides that they taste like milk.'

'Nothing tastes like milk, except milk,' she said. 'Why not just have milk?'

There seemed no answer to that. I let her 'wet the tea', as she put it, in a white china teapot and fetch thick white mugs from the café.

'So, you hadn't seen the place till this morning?' she asked.

'I got the keys and came here yesterday afternoon, though it was such a dark, rainy day that I couldn't see clearly and the electricity was off – there was a power cut, I found out later – so I didn't stay long.'

I sighed. 'I'd meant to move into the flat, but it's been stripped bare, it's dirty and it needs repainting.'

'Just as well you'd booked the guesthouse then,' she said.

'I only booked one night, because I expected to find the flat habitable. Someone's driving my car down from Scotland with all my stuff on Sunday.'

'Scotland's all right,' Tilda commented grudgingly. 'I had a holiday in The Trossachs once, and except that it rained the whole week and they gave us fried haggis for breakfast, it was fine. Probably a sight better than the Gondal Guesthouse.'

'I'm not going back there, because apart from the owners lying to me about Mrs Muswell, it wasn't very nice. They seemed so pleasant on the surface too, just like she did.'

'You don't seem the type to be taken in so easily,' she said. 'What made you do a daft thing like buy a property without seeing what you were getting first?'

I explained about my fiancé being killed and the insurance money. 'I was looking for a cottage when I stumbled across the café. I thought it would give me some income and I could live in the flat – it seemed quite a sensible thing to do at the time.'

'But why Haworth? You're not from Yorkshire, are you?'

'I was born not far away,' I said vaguely. 'We lived in Knaresborough for a few years and then moved to a village near Shrewsbury.'

'That would account for it, then,' she said, though she didn't define what 'it' was. Maybe the lack of accent. I'd noticed hers was considerably less broad while talking to me than in the YouTube clips – perhaps she and her aunt put it on, along with those strange mobcaps and stripy dresses?

'In those old photos, the café and flat looked really nice, just in need of a bit of updating.'

I fetched the printouts to show her and she studied them with interest.

'That's the Copper Kettle, all right! Nell was the waitress for the Misses Spencer, but I had a decent job at Betty's of Harrogate at the time – I was easier-going then, though some customers would turn the best nature sour over the years, with their complaints.'

'The Misses Spencer's café would be quite some time ago?' I ventured.

'Years. Then it became more of a coffee bar and they called it The Butty Box. Mrs Muswell gave it a posher name when she bought it and took me on as well as Nell, but it still wasn't much better than a sandwich bar.'

'I read the menu, such as it was. There didn't seem to be a lot of cooking involved.'

'There wasn't, it was all microwaved. And she insisted on doing everything on the cheap, even buying tubs of ready-made fillings for the sandwiches. I told her it was a false economy, because I could have made much nicer ones myself for very little more money, but she wouldn't listen. She bulk-bought economy burgers, too. I reckon they make them from the bits of meat they scrape off the factory floor.'

She gloomed into her tea, which was the colour of overdone fake suntan.

'You can't have got a lot of passing trade, tucked away down here?'

'No, and it wasn't like anyone who found us would tell other people about our great food, was it? Though, of course, Haworth's standing room only with tourists in season and people have to eat somewhere.'

'How would they even find the Branwell Café – did you advertise?' I asked.

'There used to be a sign fixed on the side of the shop by the entrance to the main street, but it dropped off at the end of last season and hasn't been put back. She probably stopped paying them to let her have it there, thinking on it. The antiques shop opposite puts a board out when he's open, but he doesn't keep regular hours. He's away a lot.'

'It's a funny way to make a living . . . if he does?'

'I asked him once and he said he finds things for special clients, so he doesn't rely on selling to the public.'

'Oh, right.' I wasn't that much interested, to be honest, I was more concerned with what I was going to do with the Branwell Café. And now, especially after talking to Tilda, all the vague ideas that had been swirling through my head since last night suddenly coalesced into a cloud of enlightenment – or maybe unfounded optimism.

'So, what *are* you going to do with the place?' she asked, as if she'd read my mind.

'I have a plan to breathe new life into it – but I'll need you and Nell as permanent staff to do it.'

I didn't know how I'd pay their wages at first, but they were both *vital*.

'Seasonal?'

'No, I'll open all the year round, except perhaps for a couple of weeks after Christmas.'

A smile tweaked the ends of those straight, grim lips. 'That'll be champion,' she said, then qualified cautiously, 'or it will be, provided you're not as daft as you look.'

'I'm not,' I assured her, and then, clearly feeling that some kind of celebration was in order, she fetched a packet of gingernut biscuits from her basket and piled six up beside my mug like oversized gaming counters.

I certainly had a lot at stake.

In the unlikely event of the bundle up on the moors being discovered, I wondered whether the person I'd passed in the lane on the way back had been able to recognize the distinctive shape of a Mini and might put two and two together.

With this in mind, I decided to stop at the petrol pump in the heart of the village to fill up the car so that, if asked, people would recall that I'd behaved perfectly normally that day. Or normally for me, at any rate, since I don't see any point in making observations about the weather to someone who can see it perfectly well for themselves.

11

Small and Perfect

'So,' Tilda said, removing the lid of the teapot and giving the remaining contents a good stir with her teaspoon, before refilling our mugs with treacly liquid, 'what's this plan for the café, then?'

'I'm going upmarket and we'll reopen as a premier afternoon tearoom.'

Her hand, which had been in the process of dunking a gingernut into her tea, stilled as she stared doubtfully at me. 'You mean, like Betty's of Harrogate, where I used to work?'

Then she noticed that the soggy bottom of her biscuit had fallen off. 'Oh, bugger! I hate it when there's a gritty silt on the bottom of the cup.'

'Not really like Betty's, I'm thinking more Framling's Famous Tearoom,' I explained.

'What, that posh place in London? No one here will pay those prices!'

'I know, but it has the kind of ambience I'm aiming for – and the concept, too: we'd only serve full afternoon teas. We wouldn't be a regular café, which are two a penny round here.'

'They are, that's true enough,' she said, ruminating. Then she looked up and said, 'The Harry Ramsden's fish and chip restaurant had got chandeliers and posh tablecloths when I went over there once with our Daisy, and folks do seem keen to part with their brass when it comes to fancy eating.'

'Yes, they'll pay for something special and that's what we'd have to provide – starched white tablecloths and napkins, tiered cake stands and fine china. And the cakes and sandwiches would have to be excellent too, of course, with some proper Yorkshire treats.'

The ideas were simply pouring out of me now I'd opened the sluice gate. 'We'd have two sittings every afternoon – say at two and four – so that customers could take their time. Everything would be made or baked on the premises and we'd even provide little boxes for those who wanted to take home any leftover cakes and sandwiches.'

'Who'd be doing all the baking, then?'

'Mostly me – I'm great at cakes and pastries,' I said immodestly but truthfully. 'I'd buy the bread in for the sandwiches, though, so I'd need a good supplier.'

'The Copper Kettle was a genteel kind of place and pricier than the other cafés at the time,' Tilda said, 'and that did all right, according to our Nell. So your tearoom might just work . . . but would you get enough customers through the door to make it pay, that's the question?'

'I'm hoping people would soon start booking tables in advance for special occasions, but if there are tables free, anyone passing by could come in and have afternoon tea.'

A thought struck her. 'But if it's going to be that posh and upmarket, would you still *want* me and Nell to work here?'

'I certainly would!' I assured her. 'You'd still be manageress, too, because once it's up and running I'll want to spend more time on my other interests.'

She didn't ask me what those were, which was probably just as well, seeing they currently involved writing weird novels and trying to trace my birth mother.

'I suppose we'd have to mind our p's and q's?' she said doubtfully. 'Mrs Muswell said we were notorious for being the rudest waitresses in Yorkshire, though we were only speaking our minds, like.'

'No, I want you to carry on being your natural selves – plain-speaking Yorkshirewomen. In fact, I'll be positively *promoting* the idea that we have the rudest waitresses in Yorkshire and I think it will be such a draw that it'll provide the icing on the proverbial cake.'

She seemed pleased but puzzled by this idea. 'Really? Well, there's nowt so queer as folk.'

She stirred the silt at the bottom of her mug with a look of disgust.

'We'll need better nicer china than this thick white pottery stuff,' I said, adding it to one of the ever-extending lists, which I was going to put on the laptop as soon as I had time.

Tilda laid down the spoon and looked up. 'I wonder if all the good blue and white willow-pattern china from the Copper Kettle's still at the back of the cupboard under the stairs to the conveniences?'

'I wouldn't bank on it. I expect Mrs Muswell remembered it was there and sold it off with everything else she could lay her hands on,' I said, without much hope.

'I wish she'd sold those mobcaps and long striped dresses she made us wear to wait on,' she said darkly. 'A right pair of gawks we felt in those.'

I'd already noticed the limp garments hung behind the kitchen door and recognized them from the YouTube video. They hadn't exactly been becoming.

'You won't have to wear them, just tie big white aprons over your ordinary clothes, instead.' I added aprons to the list, the all-enveloping Victorian sort.

'That'd be better. And happen Mrs M might have missed the china, seeing as it's right at the back, behind the old vacuum cleaner I use in the basement, and she'd never think of using that,' she said, getting up.

I followed her down the short flight of steps to the basement and she opened a large panelled cupboard underneath them. It had been painted the same dark mushroom colour as all the walls and skirting boards, so it didn't stand out.

She pulled out an antique Hoover and then bent down, reaching far back into the depths, before dragging forth a large and tattered wicker hamper. 'Still here – thought as much.'

There were a couple more boxes behind it and we brushed the dust off, before carrying them up into the kitchen to unpack on the large pine table.

The stacks of willow-pattern china entirely covered it, there was so much, and I was surprised and delighted to see the words 'dishwasher safe' stamped underneath each piece. I expect that was still a new and trendy concept at the time the Copper Kettle was opened.

There were cups and saucers, small and large plates, sugar bowls, soup bowls and serving dishes. Some things we wouldn't need, but those could help fill the empty display shelves in the café, once I'd repainted them.

'This is brilliant!' I told Tilda gratefully. 'I can probably find extra bits and pieces on eBay, too, because any inexpensive blue willow-pattern china would blend in.'

'Well, I suppose it's a start, and one less expense,' she said.

'It is, and I'll start to put batches of it through the dishwasher today . . . that is, if it works? If it does, I'm surprised Mrs Muswell left it behind!'

'I expect it was too old to be worth selling, but it works OK,' Tilda said. Then she offered to go up and clean the flat, instead of the café, which was only in need of a light dust.

'But it's filthy,' I protested.

'That's all right, I like a challenge,' she said, her eyes gleaming keenly. 'Though for extra pay, naturally.'

'Of course,' I agreed, and she vanished up the stairs with the vacuum cleaner and a bucket of cleaning materials as eagerly as if I'd offered her a rare treat.

While the first lot of crockery was chugging its way through a dishwasher cycle, I counted up the tables and chairs in the café. I didn't think anyone would *buy* them, but if I listed them on one of the free recycling websites they might appeal to someone. Then I remembered the plates hanging in the dark corner by the stairs and went to see what they were like and, while I was doing that, spotted a big spider's web up there that Tilda had managed to miss. Or maybe it was a fast worker, like the one in my new novel?

Stopping only to shove my hair into one of the despised mobcaps in case the occupant fell on my head, I climbed up on one of the tubular chairs and had at it with a long-handled feather duster.

With all the surprise of finding a total stranger in the café, Tilda mustn't have locked the café door behind her, for the brass bell suddenly jangled on its spring and then the light was blocked by a tall, slender, but unmistakably masculine figure.

'Can I help you?' I said, climbing down from my perch. 'I'm afraid the café's shut.'

'I'm not a customer. I just saw the light was on and I wanted a word with Molly Muswell,' he explained. His voice held no trace of the local accent or, indeed, any other. It was slightly posh and smooth as dark, expensive chocolate.

'Wouldn't we all,' I rejoined tartly, wondering if he was a delivery man she hadn't paid, despite the upmarket accent. 'But she's not here, I'm afraid, so you might as well go away again.'

Instead of taking this strong hint, he shut the door behind him and came down the step into the light.

Two thoughts skipped across my mind faster than flat pebbles across still water. The first was that, with his curling blue-black hair, pale olive skin, aquiline nose and a full mouth that turned up enigmatically at the corners, he looked so much like a Greek god that if he'd handed me a bunch of grapes and an invitation to an orgy, I'd probably have gone.

In fact, he was the most handsome man I'd ever exchanged words with outside my imagination.

My second thought was that he wasn't any kind of delivery man, because he was wearing a silky, beautifully cut suit, worn over a soft, snow-white shirt with the neck open. I suddenly felt quite cheap and grubby in my jeans, sweatshirt and trainers.

My answer had clearly not been the one he wanted to hear, because he was scowling. 'When will she be back? I've just returned from a trip to America and I saw the sign on the door saying the café was closed for renovations, so I thought when I saw the lights on that she'd be here.'

He glanced around. 'Not that I can *see* any sign of renovations – unless that's why you're here?'

'Well, I'm certainly going to make some *changes*, because I've bought the place,' I told him. Seeing he looked as blank as Tilda had, I added helpfully, 'She's gone – I'm the new owner of the Branwell Café.'

'She's . . . gone? Permanently?' His dark eyebrows twitched together in an alarming frown. 'But she owes me money!'

That didn't surprise me. 'What for?' I asked curiously.

'Antiques, if it's any of your business,' he snapped. 'I run the curio shop opposite.'

'You mean *you're* Small and Perfect?' I exclaimed, and then felt myself glowing pinkly. With my auburn hair, that's *never* a good look.

'You could say that,' he agreed drily, and one corner of his rather beautifully moulded mouth twitched, though whether with amusement or anger, I couldn't tell. 'I certainly *sell* small and perfect antiques and curios. Mrs Muswell suggested at the start of the season that I display a few things in the café and give her a small commission on any sales. I tend to source special items for collectors, rather than sell directly to the public, but there are always extra odds and ends I pick up in job lots at auctions, so it seemed like a reasonable idea.'

He indicated the two plates that I'd just released from their coverlet of spider silk. 'Those are mine, but I can't see any of the rest, and Tilda – one of her staff – told me that instead of sending customers over to my shop if they're interested in buying something, she's been selling them herself and pocketing the cash.'

'That doesn't surprise me. She's stripped out everything of any value from the café and flat, even those things included in the sale.'

'Kind of her to leave the plates behind, then,' he said sarcastically.

'She probably overlooked them, because they were in this dark corner, covered in spider webs.'

'I'd still like to know where the rest of my stuff is.' He pulled out a piece of paper from his pocket and a slim and expensive-looking pen. 'This is a complete list of everything she had and their value – and there are five things missing.' He circled them and handed me the paper.

'But it's nothing to do with *me*,' I protested, looking in alarm at the prices of the missing items – a small watercolour, three Dresden plates and an eighteenth-century sampler. 'I bought the property, but I didn't buy her debts with it!'

'*Someone* owes me,' he said, his jaw jutting.

'Well, it isn't me,' I said indignantly. 'And *I'll* have to replace all the kitchen equipment she's taken and furnish the flat, so I'll need every penny I've got left.'

'Got left from what?'

'Mind *your* own business,' I told him.

'You're not going to make your fortune selling Brontëburgers at the Branwell Café,' he pointed out with, I thought, unnecessary sarcasm.

'Yes – thanks for that,' I said, then added bitterly, 'It was bad enough that Mrs Muswell conned me over the state of the flat and café, but now I expect I'll get a whole stream of people like you turning up and demanding to be paid.'

I tried to run a distracted hand through my hair and only then realized I was still wearing that ridiculous mobcap. Snatching it off, I threw it with some force across the room, while my hair, released from bondage, exploded out in a cascade of tight, coppery curls.

The man stared at me narrowly from a pair of surprisingly light grey eyes. Then a sudden and unexpected grin softened the angles of his face and he said, 'I might have known you were a redhead.'

'I can't imagine why!'

'And you remind me of someone . . .' he added, thoughtfully.

'Someone local?' I asked quickly. My colouring was so distinctive, with my dark eyebrows, red hair and light green eyes, that I'd wondered if I might come face to face in the street with a woman so similar that I would know immediately she was my mother.

'No, I've got it now. You look like that woman in all the Pre-Raphaelite paintings, Lizzie something.'

'Lizzie Siddal. I get that a lot,' I said resignedly. 'I can't see it myself, apart from the hair, and I can hardly help that.'

'It wasn't a criticism,' he said mildly. 'She was very beautiful, in a sulky sort of way.'

'I am *not* sulky!'

'Who said you were?' he asked, with an air of innocent surprise. Then he seemed to lose interest in winding me up and said, with a sigh, 'I suppose I can't really expect you to pay me back for the stuff she's stolen, so I can kiss my money goodbye.'

'You could try her solicitor. You might have more luck than I had in getting contact details for her.'

'I suspect that would be pointless, though I'll report what's happened to the police, so maybe they can nab her for theft if she should come back over here – her signature is on the list of items and Tilda was there when we came to the agreement, so I have a witness. I'll take the plates she's left away with me now, though.' He suited his actions to the words, unhooking them and laying them on the nearest table.

'You'd better brace yourself, because if she left owing money to any of her suppliers, you might have to pay them off before they'll agree to deliver to you,' he suggested helpfully.

'I'm not liable for any of her debts and I'm not going to pay them,' I insisted stubbornly. 'I'm as much a victim of Mrs Muswell as anyone else.'

'I doubt they'll see it that way, so you'll just have to make a speedy success of running the place, won't you? I'm Nile Giddings, by the way.'

'Alice,' I said. 'Alice Rose.'

'A rose by any other name,' he said flippantly. 'And shouldn't you be in Wonderland, not Brontëland?'

I ignored that sally. 'I've got plans for the café and I won't need any of the suppliers Mrs Muswell used, because I intend reopening as an upmarket afternoon tea emporium.'

'*Really?*' His face expressed mild disbelief. 'Good luck with that, then.'

'I'll do it, you'll see!' I insisted.

'I hope for your sake you do. And what are you going to call this little oasis of refreshment?' he asked sardonically as he turned to leave, clutching his reclaimed antiquities as if I might leap forward and snatch them back.

A vision of Molly Muswell's social networking avatar flashed across my mind, her plump face bunched up in a friendly smile, so that her small eyes looked like deeply set currants in a bun.

'The Fat Rascal,' I told him.

Luckily, my grammar school was closed on the Friday, since it was a staff training day. Although normally I resented the way these Baker days interrupted my lessons, this time it had worked to my advantage.

And of course none of my school friends noticed any difference in me, because, being a year younger than the rest of my class but twice as clever, I didn't have any.

12

The Blasted Heath

I felt strangely unsettled by this encounter, though I suppose unexpectedly coming face to face with so much male beauty was enough to throw anyone! And Nile Giddings appeared to have the mercurial temperament to go with the Greek god looks, too.

We didn't seem to have got off to a good start, though admittedly I'd been just as spiky and sarcastic as my visitor. But then, anyone would be who'd been brought up by Nessa: I tended to give at least as good as I got.

I went to check on how Tilda was doing and found she'd thrown herself into cleaning the flat with huge enthusiasm. Although I offered to help, she said firmly that she could do it quicker and better without me.

So I dusted the café and kitchens instead, though they barely needed it, and then settled in the office with my laptop to type up the first of several lists from my notes. If I was going to wave a magic wand over the café and undo Wicked Witch Muswell's evil spell, I'd need more elbow-grease than fairy dust to achieve it, so it was time to get practical.

But unfortunately, I strayed again.

The evil fairy lay on her deathbed, suffering from a fatal surfeit of spite. She contemplated her life of misdeeds and wickedness with satisfaction but then, with a deep sigh, waved her wand weakly.

'Unspell!' she cried. It was that easy.

All over Fairyland, frogs turned into princes and geese stopped laying golden eggs. And deep in a wood, where an impenetrable thicket grew around the bower where Beauty had fallen asleep, a portal shivered into existence and a small mouse took the opportunity to scurry through into another time and place . . .

A loud thump in the flat over my head brought me back to the present and I firmly closed the *Beauty Goes Bad* document and opened a new one called, simply, 'Tearoom Lists'.

The shortest was of those items I wanted to get rid of, like the café chairs and tables and all the thick white crockery, since Mrs Muswell hadn't left much else behind. I followed that one with the list of replacement equipment and furniture I'd need, which ran to two pages without my even having to give it much thought.

But the very first thing I'd have to buy was gallons of paint, step-ladders and brushes to transform the dingy café – and I'd do as much of the work as I could myself, because I'd have to be on a tight budget if I wasn't to find I'd run out of money before I reopened.

There'd be *some* major things I wouldn't be able to do myself, like renovating the café cloakroom and fitting new work surfaces into the kitchen. I'd have to ask about for a reasonably priced local handyman.

I was still giving myself a headache over some financial calculations when Tilda called me upstairs to see the fruit of her labours.

'Oh, wow!' I said when I did, because although it was still bare and dingy, it was now totally clean and smelled of pine disinfectant and lemon antibacterial cleanser – tangy. It practically made your eyes water. You could see through the windows now, too – the back one at the kitchen end overlooking the small garden and the front directly facing Small and Perfect. There was a light on behind the thick bull's-eye panes of the shop window, so Mr Small and Perfect was probably polishing his curios.

'It's absolutely amazing – thank you so much!' I said gratefully.

'Eh, I'm black as a sweep, but I've had a grand time,' she assured me, 'and you're paying me for it. There's nothing else up here needs doing now, bar a lick of paint and some curtains, carpets and furniture.'

That was a slight understatement, but at least if it came to it, I could camp up here from Sunday, once my car full of belongings had arrived.

'You're not completely on your own down here in Doorknocker's Row, because you've got a neighbour in t' shop across the ginnel,' Tilda said.

'Yes, I just met him.'

'Oh? He's a proper handsome lad, that one. When he first moved here and the local girls got a good look at him, it was like putting a cockerel in a hencoop, there was such a flutter.'

'I can imagine,' I replied, and immediately determined to make it clear in any future encounters with Nile Giddings that there was going to be no fluttering from *me*. 'He said you warned him Mrs Muswell had been selling the antiques she was displaying for him in the café, and pocketing the cash. When he saw the lights were on, he thought she was here.'

'I put a note through his door, but he's been away a while so I expect he only just got it,' Tilda said. 'Bit too late to do anything now.'

'Yes, though Mrs Muswell had missed a couple of things that were hanging in that dark corner near the stairs and he's taken those. And he's reporting the theft to the police.'

'I don't know that they can do anything about it and she's too wary a bird to show her face here again,' Tilda said, shaking her head. Then she looked round the room with the satisfaction of a job well done and added, 'I'd get someone out to service that old gas boiler in the kitchen before you light it. The name of the man who does the one in the basement is on a label stuck on the side; I'd ring him.'

'Good idea – I shouldn't think it's been used for donkey's years.'

'That's right, you don't want to start off by blowing the place up,' she agreed. 'Now, here's my phone number if you need me to help with anything else, otherwise I'll be back Friday as usual, to clean through again, shall I?'

'Yes, do, but I might ring you before that, because I'd like to meet Nell when my plans for the teashop are clearer in my mind.'

'Where are you staying till you can move into the flat, then?' she asked. 'Did you find somewhere else?'

'I haven't got round to looking yet, but I'd better do that now. At the worst I expect they'd have me back at the Gondal Guesthouse – I could survive one more night – then just camp in the flat after that.'

Tilda looked doubtful about this idea and said she'd have put me up herself, except she only had a two-bedroomed cottage and Nell lived with her, but I assured her I'd find somewhere.

But when she'd gone, I wondered how I'd set about it, because the telephone landline wasn't yet connected and I was waiting for a router as well, so I could get the internet . . . and now I came to look, there was no sign of a local phone book.

I really ought to upgrade my phone, too. The one I had was an old one of Dan's.

My laptop, with the latest list up on the screen, was still blinking at me in the office and on impulse I had a quick look at internet connectivity . . . and discovered I could piggyback someone else's open connection!

Quick as a flash I was in, and emailing short updates to Edie and Lola. Then, just as I was embarking on a search for a guesthouse, that damned doorbell did its loud jangle.

'Is that you, Tilda?' I called. 'Did you forget something?'

She'd certainly forgotten to lock the door behind her again, for Nile Giddings suddenly appeared in the doorway, then pounced before I could slam down the lid of my laptop.

'Aha! I had a feeling it would be you,' he said triumphantly, and I felt myself going guiltily pink.

'Oh, was that *your* internet connection I borrowed?' I said innocently. 'Sorry, I just wanted to check out local guesthouses . . . and anyway, how did you know?' I asked, as the thought occurred to me.

'Because it was taking me for ever to download new photographs on to the Small and Perfect website,' he said grimly.

'Well, I'm very sorry,' I repeated, 'but my router is supposed to arrive tomorrow and my landline will be connected early next week, so I won't need do it again.'

'You'd better not,' he said tersely. Then he looked around and clocked all the empty spaces in the kitchen.

97

'She really *did* clean you out, didn't she?'

'The only things she left were fixed in or screwed down, apart from a fridge and freezer so old they belong in a museum,' I agreed. 'You should have seen the flat: not only was it stripped bare, it was filthy, too.'

'So you won't be moving in any time soon, hence the guesthouse search?'

'Oh, Tilda has spent most of the day cleaning the flat so it just needs a lick of paint and some furniture now,' I said, hoping I sounded more upbeat about it than I felt. 'I'll move in when the rest of my belongings arrive along with my car on Sunday. I don't want to go back to the guesthouse I stayed at last night, if I can find a different one – preferably cheaper.'

'Even off-season, Haworth is still pricey,' he said, then paused, frowning. 'I've got a better idea. My family live just out of the village and my mother takes paying guests when she can get them. The house is a big old place, a bit ramshackle and run down, but it's cheap and she's a great cook.'

'I'm sure it's wonderful, but I need to be within walking distance of the café until I've got my car, so even for a couple of nights—' I began, but he interrupted me.

'I divide my time between home and the flat over my shop and I'm there most weekends, so I'll give you a lift in and out.'

I was very far from sure that I wanted to be stuck out on the moors with strangers and dependent for transport on Mr Tall, Dark and Stroppy. 'I don't want to put your mother out, when I need somewhere for only a night or two. She's probably shut for the winter like a lot of the local guesthouses, isn't she?'

'Sheila's doors are never shut,' he said enigmatically. 'I'll ring her.'

'Sheila?' I repeated and it suddenly occurred to me to wonder if he had a wife stashed away there, too. He might well have, for he was about my age – mid-thirties, or possibly a year or two older . . . Maybe one of those hens Tilda had told me about had fluttered a little more attractively than the others?

'My mother – I always call her Sheila. She'll be delighted to hear you're going to stay at Oldstone.'

'*Oldstone!*' I exclaimed, sharply.

'Yes, do you know it?' he asked, surprised.

'No . . . it's just an odd name,' I said weakly, and he gave me a considering look as if wondering whether taking me home with him was a good idea after all. Then he seemed to make up his mind.

'I've got a few things to do first, so I'll come and collect you around half five or six. Be ready.'

'But dinner—' I began, feeling railroaded and even surer I didn't want to go with him.

'Oh, she'll feed you, don't worry,' he assured me. 'She always cooks enough for an army anyway, though she's part Scandinavian, so you're never quite sure what's on the menu. Do you like Norwegian food?'

'I'm not sure I've ever had any.'

'It's good, except for the time she produced a whole sheep's head for dinner. It's a Norwegian delicacy, but all those teeth and the eyeballs are too off-putting.'

'Eyeballs?' I echoed faintly.

But he was gone, leaving me feeling totally unsettled. Not only was I about to be marooned on the moors with the unknown family of the strangely unnerving Nile Giddings, which might be all too *Wuthering Heights*, but the house was called Oldstone, the name I'd been registered under on my birth certificate!

Might I be connected to the place? I could have been given that surname because I'd been found near it (in which case I *hadn't* been found miles from habitation, like Nessa had said), or perhaps I had been found further away, but by a member of that family?

Now I was actually here and Sleeping Beauty had woken up, it was hard to understand why I'd never checked out all the available details of where and by whom I was found, though I had sort of pushed it all away to the back of my mind after Nessa's revelation, following on from losing Dad . . .

But, I thought, there must be lots more information out there than my birth certificate, and once I had an internet connection I'd be right in there looking for it.

Princess Beauty woke up after the best sleep of her life, to find herself bound tightly in a cocoon of silk and unable to wiggle even her smallest finger.

A mouse was sitting on the end of the couch, washing his whiskers.

'Hello,' said Beauty. 'Can you help me? A friendly spider wrapped me up warmly before I fell asleep, but now I don't seem able to move.'

'You're very stupid,' the mouse said witheringly. 'It's a silk shroud — you've been asleep for aeons and so has the huge spider in the other room. He's wrapped you up to eat later and he's stirring now, so he's probably ready for a snack.'

I closed the lid of the laptop with a snap.

There wasn't much more I could do at the café by then and, having already snipped through the first ring of briars and freed myself from my self-imposed imprisonment, I went for a walk around the village.

I passed several better and more established cafés than mine and, despite the time of year, there were still plenty of visitors about.

I found the church and the graveyard, which lay before the Brontë Parsonage, exactly as it looked in photos, but I didn't go inside that or the museum. They'd have to keep for another time, as would the moors that tantalizingly beckoned beyond.

I paused by the Parsonage steps, though, remembering Dad's fairy-tale description of how the young princess had crept up and left me there late one night.

I thought he'd have been happy I was there now . . .

After a while, the cold breeze wandering around my legs got me moving again back down the hill. No one at all stopped dead and exclaimed at my resemblance to someone local that they knew, as I'd thought, hoped, or even feared that they might. In fact, no one had given me a second glance, probably because in a place as popular with visitors as Haworth, tall strangers with long copper curls and pale green eyes were nothing out of the ordinary.

By the time Nile reappeared I was waiting by the café door with my baggage, the lights off and the key in my hand. I hadn't until that moment wondered where he'd left his car, but he wrested the case out of my grasp and set off down the passageway to the parking area at the back of the café. I should have guessed.

'This is *my* land,' I said indignantly, catching up with him.

'Well, that side certainly is,' he said, pointing. 'But this patch I bought from the people who had The Butty Box, before Mrs Muswell took over, so I'd have somewhere to park. I'm afraid you're going to have to share it.'

'I'm sure that didn't come up when my solicitor did the searches on the property,' I said suspiciously.

'Maybe not, but I had a deed of the sale signed in front of my own solicitor, and Mrs Muswell knew about it when she took over,' he said. 'I've no idea why it didn't come up in your searches.'

'Well, I *suppose* it's legal then, and I can't do anything about it,' I said grudgingly.

'Gee, thanks!'

His car was a dark Mercedes estate with an interior that smelled of leather combined with the faintest hint of an expensive and subtle after-shave. I half expected the boot lid to go tight-lipped at the sight of my inferior luggage, but no, it popped up and stayed open. He slid my case in as if it weighed nothing and then we were off into the gathering dusk.

At least it gave me an opportunity to see where the alleyway led to and how to get through the small streets to the main road. The car climbed and took a turn or two, then came out on the moors above the village and continued on until all the other houses had petered out.

'If you carry right on along this road it takes you over Blackdog Moor to a crossroads with a motel, just above Upvale village, which is in the next valley. But if you turn down any of the small side roads off it, you could be missing for a week.'

'Maybe I'll stick to the main road for a while, then, till I get my bearings,' I said, shivering, because now the light was almost gone and a fine, driving rain was moving in, we seemed to be surrounded by darkness and blasted heath.

Had I really been left somewhere out there, at the mercy of the elements and passing predators?

Then we were turning off the road sharply right by a large sign that said 'Oldstone' and, rather bafflingly underneath, 'Pondlife'.

The drive was more of a rutted farm track and led over a small bridge made of stone slabs to a stretch of gravel in front of a long, low stone building that looked as if it had been squatting there, glowering defensively at the nearby hills, for a *very* long time.

'Here we are,' Nile said unnecessarily, switching off the engine. 'Welcome to Oldstone, the Giddings family's ancestral pile.'

I was to be glad I'd taken all those precautions when, against all the odds, the discovery was made – and even before I'd read the newspaper reports, I'd guessed who by.

Predictably, Mum became hysterical and asked me if I'd known the baby was still alive when I'd left it . . . not that I'd thought of it as a baby at the time, since I was so filled with shock and revulsion.

'Of course I didn't, or I'd have put it somewhere I'd be certain it would be found quickly,' I assured her.

'Some doctor you'll make!' she scoffed, which I thought was pretty rich, considering she'd originally trained as a nurse, even though once she'd snared my father she'd given up work.

But I was still determined that medicine would be my career, even though I now intended to have as little to do with obstetrics and gynae-cology as possible . . .

13

Pondlife

'It looks ancient – or what I can see of it does,' I commented, for although the rain had stopped, a heavy wet mist obscured the full extent of the house and anything beyond it. It didn't look like my idea of a moorland farm, but at least the situation didn't seem as bleak and exposed as that of Top Withens, which was reputed to be the inspiration for Wuthering Heights.

There was a battered carving on the lintel, illuminated by a large glass and metal lantern that hung over it from a wrought-iron bracket. I was sure I could pick out a Pan-like creature and also a bunch of grapes, though they can't grow many of those up on the Yorkshire moors, can they?

The huge front door below it was open on to an inner hall, despite the dark and the autumnal chill. A large, elderly golden Labrador trudged out, stared at us, and then plodded dejectedly back in again with his tail down.

'Doesn't he like visitors?' I asked.

'Yes, but whenever a car pulls up he still hopes it's my father, even though he died a few years ago, just after the family moved up here permanently,' Nile explained. 'He's disappointed, but he'll come round when we go in.'

'Poor old thing,' I said, and then added, awkwardly, 'and I'm sorry you lost your father. I know how that feels, because mine died when I was still a teenager.'

'It was . . . devastatingly sudden,' Nile said, his profile in the light cast from the lantern looking severe and shuttered – and, it has to be said, still very handsome.

The car's engine ticked quietly as it cooled and he added, with a brisk return to his usual manner (or his usual manner to *me*), 'Well, there's no point in sitting out here half the night, when you can get a better look at the exterior of the house tomorrow in daylight.'

'It's certainly much bigger than I expected,' I said.

'The central hall is the original part of it and very old, but the rest of it's been added on over the years, so there's plenty of room for everyone to be sociable or not, as the fancy takes them.'

'Everyone?' I repeated. 'How many people live here?'

I hoped it wasn't some kind of weird hippie commune! Though, thinking about it, I decided Nile wasn't really hippie commune material.

He shrugged. 'All the family. Sheila's letting rooms are in the Victorian part and we live in the rest. My brother, Teddy, and his wife and their baby have a sort of apartment in the eighteenth-century wing, but it's not completely closed off. It's all a bit of a hotchpotch.'

'It sounds it.'

I got out of the car and followed Nile round to the boot to retrieve my luggage, shivering in the cold dankness.

It didn't seem to affect Nile, who gestured into the murky darkness and said, 'There's a stable block over there, partly turned into offices where Ted and Geeta run the family business. Did you see the sign on the way in?'

'Pondlife?' I asked. 'Aquarium supplies? Garden ponds?'

The wet grey misty curtains opportunely parted at that moment to allow a slightly sickly moon to briefly reveal a large pond in a hollow below the house, equipped with a hut and jetty. Everything glistened and it looked a little surreal.

'More that kind of thing,' Nile said.

'Right. Not your average plastic garden liner with a fake heron standing at the edge, then.'

'Not really. I'll explain at dinner,' he promised, hauling out my suitcase and refusing to let it go when I tried to take it from him. I'm five

105

feet nine inches and I can carry my own luggage, but I only just managed to grab my overnight bag before he got that, too.

'Come on,' he said, as a small, plump figure appeared in the open doorway. 'Here's Sheila, wondering where we've got to.'

Nile's mother drew us into the hall, closing the outer door behind us, and then shook my hand with a square, firm grip.

'There you are! Welcome to Oldstone,' she said warmly. She was blue-eyed and with pale golden hair, so totally unlike Nile that he must have got his darker colouring from his father's side of the family.

'Thank you for letting me stay at such short notice,' I said.

'Not at all: we're delighted to have you here and dinner's nearly ready. All my guests eat with the family, so I'll show you to your room and then you can follow your nose down to the kitchen when you're ready.'

Nile had already vanished through one of the doors with my case and it was waiting for me in my room when we got there. Since we hadn't passed him on the stairs, I don't know where he went after that. Perhaps he flew out of the window like a giant bat?

Or maybe I've watched too many old Dracula movies.

It was just as well that there was nothing of the Victorian Gothic about the room, for it had been remodelled in a modern and slightly incongruous Scandinavian style, with light wooden furniture and the walls and paintwork in shades of white, warm cream and a soft greyish-blue.

'I know it's all too modern for a Victorian room,' said Sheila, with whom I'd been on first-name terms before we were halfway up the stairs. 'But the roof had leaked and brought the ceiling down, so everything was spoiled and we had to start again. I already had this furniture from our previous house.'

'I like it,' I told her, and she beamed.

'I can *see* the dark antique furniture goes with the age of the house, but here and in my own bedroom I decided to have things the way I like them, instead.'

'I think Nile said you were Norwegian?' I ventured.

'Only a quarter – a grandmother,' she said. 'But I often spent my summer holidays there, as a child.'

She opened a door in one wall to reveal a bathroom. 'It's what they call a Jack and Jill bathroom, with a door to the bedroom on the other side too,' she explained. 'But there are no other guests, so you have it to yourself. Now, I'll leave you to unpack and settle in, but come down in about an hour for dinner, or earlier if you're ready.'

She bestowed another naturally warm smile on me, so that I felt my last reluctance at the prospect of being marooned out at Oldstone melt entirely away. Nile might be insufferably overbearing and bossy, but it had worked out all right this time.

Even the cheerful Scandi-style ambience was just right because, given my overactive imagination, anything antique would have conjured up not only vampires, but Cathy's hand tapping at the window to come in, just when I was falling asleep.

I hung up my clothes, which were getting perma-creased from never being unpacked, then washed and tidied up in the bathroom, which was an austere but pristine black and white tiled apartment. There was a shower attachment over the claw-legged bath, and though the radiator was barely lukewarm to the touch, the towels were huge and fluffy.

I changed into a clean pair of jeans, a long green shirt and my favourite pair of Minnetonka beaded moccasins, then went down the stairs I'd come up. This time I noticed a door on the landing that must lead into the rest of the house, so maybe Nile hadn't flown out of the window, after all.

As Sheila had suggested, I followed my nose through dimly lit passages booby-trapped with random steps up and down, until I reached the kitchen.

The door was ajar, and warmth, light and a cheerful babble of conversation spilled out, so that I paused for a moment feeling rather shy, before entering.

The large room was brightly lit after the dim passages and seemed very full of people. Nile was facing me, sitting at the head of a long table and holding a lively dark-eyed infant upright, while it flexed its knees and bounced up and down, as if revving for take-off. When he looked up and caught my eye, his expression was still amused and tender, which was quite a revelation . . .

A slender woman with a long plait of hair hanging like a black silk

107

tassel down the back of her deep pink salwar kameez was laying out soup plates.

'Here's Alice,' said Sheila, turning from the large Aga range with a dripping ladle in one hand. The Labrador, obviously used to these moments, caught the soupy drops before they touched the floor.

'Alice, this is my lovely daughter-in-law, Geeta,' she said, indicating the woman laying the table, 'that's my son Teddy, and Nile's holding their baby, Casper . . .'

A timer pinged, distracting her from her introductions, and she began to haul bread rolls out of the oven. 'Introduce yourselves, the rest of you.'

'Hi,' said Geeta with a friendly smile, sitting down near Nile and taking the baby away from him, to his obvious relief.

'I feel like a springboard,' he said, ruefully.

'I'm Bel, Nile's sister,' said a woman of about my own age, with curling fair hair and periwinkle-blue eyes. She patted the seat next to her.

'Come and sit here, between me and Teddy – we're twins, you might have noticed?'

I nodded, because now I was looking at them they were as alike as a pair of perfectly matched pearls. 'You both take after Sheila, too.'

'I know, except we're about two feet taller, like Dad,' she agreed. 'Casper very cleverly takes after both parents – he has Geeta's wonderful brown eyes and Ted's fair hair – that's a really unusual colour combination.'

I didn't like to ask where Nile got his looks from – these things can be very tricky and he could well be Sheila's son from a previous relationship – and no one volunteered any information on the subject. Anyway, I was feeling a bit glazed and disorientated by exhaustion and lack of a decent meal by then, so when the familial banter that had ceased when I entered the room began again, I let it wash over and enfold me like a soothing wave.

'Who's for mulligatawny soup?' asked Sheila, dumping a large porcelain casserole dish in the middle of the table and turning for the basket of warm bread rolls.

Until that moment, I hadn't realized how totally ravenous I was.

The finding of a baby up on the moors and the entirely futile search for the mother proved little more than a seven-day wonder, quickly superseded by sensational news of national importance.

Back at home, relations between Mum and I were soon no more strained than they had been before the events of that night, which neither of us ever referred to again. In fact, by the time Father finally got back, I'm sure she'd developed total amnesia on the subject, which was just as well, since he'd have pounced on any sign of a secret and bullied it out of her.

14

Pot Luck

By the time I'd got outside a big bowl of hot, spicy soup followed by a roast chicken with all the trimmings, I felt back in the land of the living, and began to tune in to the conversation around me. I'd never been in the heart of a big family before – Lola's was warm and friendly, but she had been an only child.

I found I felt strangely at home, rather than the outsider I really was.

'Nile's told us how you were taken in by Mrs Muswell when you bought your café,' Bel said to me, passing plates of apple pie and thick cream in a blue and white striped jug.

'She got what she deserved, because only an idiot buys a property without going to look at it first,' Nile said.

'It's not polite to call our guest an idiot,' pointed out Geeta, giving him a reproving look, before resuming the spooning of gloop into Casper's mouth. The baby was now in a highchair next to her, with the Labrador seated underneath it, looking up hopefully.

I gave Nile a level stare. 'I admit that it was a stupid thing to do, but Mrs Muswell fooled *you* into letting her sell your antiques and then pocketing the money, so it's a case of the pot calling the kettle black, isn't it?'

'That's true,' said Teddy, grinning.

'Yes, you tell him,' Bel encouraged me. 'He's got too much into the habit of being the bossy older brother and he needs taking down a peg or two.'

'I just give out good advice,' he said, looking surprised. 'It's your own fault if none of you ever takes it.'

'I suspect it's going to be pointless you even trying to boss Alice about,' Sheila said, with one of her warm smiles at me. She added, 'Nile told us you expected to find the café and flat only needing a little updating and that all the furnishings and fitments were to have been included in the price?'

'Yes, but Mrs Muswell must have come over from Spain and cleared out anything she could sell the very moment I agreed to buy it,' I told her, then described the state I'd found the place in. 'I thought about camping in the flat until the rest of my things arrive on Sunday, but there isn't a stick of furniture. It was totally filthy too, and the gas boiler doesn't look as if it has been used for half a century.'

'You need to be so careful with gas,' Teddy advised me.

'I know. I'll get it serviced by the people who've been doing the boiler in the basement,' I agreed. 'And at least the flat's now clean as a whistle, because one of the seasonal staff turned up this morning and volunteered to do it instead of the café – she seemed to enjoy the challenge.'

'Clean or not, you still can't move in until you have heating, furniture and something to cook on, can you?' said Geeta practically. 'Especially in September – it's so much colder here than where I was brought up.'

'Where was that?' I asked, though I thought I could guess from her accent.

'Bradford,' she said. 'My family all think I'm mad, living up here in the back of beyond.'

'Well, we're all glad you do,' Sheila said fondly.

'Nile said you'd got some plans for the café, but he didn't say what they were,' Bel told me.

'Airy-fairy ideas, rather than plans,' Nile put in.

'They're not at all airy-fairy, though perhaps it'll be a bit of a gamble,' I said evenly, giving him a cold look. 'I'm going to totally refurbish it and reopen as The Fat Rascal Afternoon Tea Emporium.'

'I rest my case,' Nile said.

'*I* can't see any problem with that, Nile,' Teddy said. 'Sounds fine to me.'

'Ah, but it won't be just any old tea emporium, but an *upmarket* one,' Nile revealed, as if it proved his point.

'It *will* be pretty swish, because I'm using Framling's Famous Tea-room in London as my inspiration,' I said. 'I'll only serve classic afternoon teas, with sandwiches, scones, cakes and savouries – with a Yorkshire twist, where I can find suitable recipes.'

'Like the fat rascals,' agreed Teddy. 'I've had those in Betty's café in Harrogate, split and buttered, and they're wonderful.'

I smiled at him. 'Yes, they're lovely and I can make a miniature version of them for the cake stands.'

'*I* can't see anything airy-fairy about your plans either,' Bel said with a teasing look at her elder brother. 'I mean, Haworth is awash with cafés and restaurants of all kinds, so something a little different is bound to catch on.'

'Not if she's so fancy she prices herself out of the market,' Nile objected.

'I only said "inspired by Framling's",' I told him. 'I'm not going to attempt to recreate it in Yorkshire, with the same prices! Of course I'll be charging more for afternoon tea than anywhere else locally – I'll have to sneakily check up on what's on offer – but then, they'll get a special experience *and* wonderful food for the money.'

'Do you know anything about running cafés?' asked Sheila with interest.

'Yes, I've worked in them all my life, though mostly in the kitchens, but my late fiancé had a café in Scotland, so even though there was a manageress, I still had a lot to do with the running of it . . .'

I stopped for a moment, thinking how long ago that seemed now, even though it was only five months, really – but my long journey down the rabbit warren of depression and grief had distanced it, so it seemed another world, another time, an entirely different Alice.

And Dan, so impulsive and living each moment to the full, would have been the first to urge me to embrace the future, not look back sadly at the past . . . I blinked back a sudden tear.

'I'm sorry for your loss,' Sheila said gently, and I didn't tell her that loss and abandonment punctuated my life at such regular intervals that I was becoming quite accustomed to it.

'So, you know all about running cafés,' Bel said, 'which means there's no reason why it shouldn't be a big success. And it's really lucky that you're going to stay with us for a while, because we can pick your brains about *our* café.'

'You have a café?' I said, surprised.

'Not yet, but Mum and I have got plans to open one in the old stables, between our two workshops and the Pondlife offices.'

I must have looked puzzled, because Sheila explained. 'Bel and I are both potters. I've always sold my work through the Crafts Council, exhibitions and galleries, because I do big sculptural pieces. But Bel works in porcelain and makes more accessible, smaller things that she could sell directly to the public, if we could entice them to turn off the main road.'

'I was teaching art in London and working at my ceramics in my spare time till my divorce, but now I've moved home again I'd like to see if I can earn my living from it,' Bel said.

'I suppose there's quite a lot of passing tourist trade in the summer?' I asked.

'Yes, so if we hung a "Pottery Open" sign at the end of the lane, people could come and watch us work, then perhaps buy some of Bel's pieces,' Sheila said. 'Mine aren't really impulse buys, though I might get one or two commissions that way, and I don't mind if people watch me,' she added. 'Once I'm working, I won't know they're there.'

'I don't mind either,' Bel said, 'but I thought if we could offer refreshments, too, then that might make more of them decide to turn off.'

'Yes, it's not going to be a *proper* café, just coffee, tea, cold drinks and cakes,' Sheila said. 'I'd make the cakes – maybe one or two Norwegian specialities like Bergen buns.'

'They're delicious,' said Geeta. 'Sort of sponge cakes filled with apple – not really a bun at all.'

'I think a sign advertising a pottery and refreshments would bring people in in droves,' I said. 'But you can't work and serve food at the same time, can you?'

'True, though I'm a lark and like to get up early and into my workshop in the mornings and we could open to the public just in the afternoons,' Sheila said.

'Once it's up and running, we could get someone in to help anyway,' Bel suggested. 'There's a local girl, Jan, who takes care of the baby while Teddy and Geeta are working in the office and I know her elder sister's looking for a part-time job.'

'I saw the sign for Pondlife on the way here,' I said to Teddy and Geeta. 'Nile told me you sell garden pools.'

'In a manner of speaking,' agreed Teddy. 'Geeta and I run the family business, creating swimming ponds.'

'Swimming ponds?' I echoed blankly.

'Ponds big enough to swim in,' Geeta explained. 'They're expensive to put in, but ecologically sound, because they keep clean naturally and are easy to maintain.'

'Dad started the firm up originally, when we lived near Bristol,' Teddy said. 'He dropped out of university after his first year and went to work for some family friends in Germany, who had a swimming pond business – it was popular there much earlier than it caught on here. Our business has slowly built up over the years.'

'I've never heard of the idea, but it seems a good one,' I said.

'It was – and you have to admit, Nile, that taking the plunge with what might seem an expensive and airy-fairy idea sometimes works out,' Sheila said to him pointedly.

'*Touché,*' he said with a grin that transformed his face to something much more human – and dangerously more attractive – than a Greek god. 'I'm sure there'll be a huge market in Yorkshire for potteries serving Bergen buns and expensive posh teashops.'

'There will,' Bel said firmly. 'And we can help each other too, can't we, Alice? Pool our resources. Sink or swim together.'

'Splash out and go for it?' I suggested.

Teddy groaned.

'You have the catering experience we lack, while I'm ace at painting and decorating,' Bel said.

'Sounds good to me,' I agreed.

'Perhaps you should have a Plan B, in case your teashop doesn't take off?' Nile suggested to me pessimistically.

'Oh, I'd cut my losses, sell the place, buy a small cottage and scrape a living,' I said, though I didn't say that it would probably come from writing horror fairy tales.

'Or just move in here permanently and help me renovate the house, because it's going to be an ongoing project for ever, like painting the Forth Bridge,' Sheila offered. 'But ignore Nile – his glass is permanently half empty. I'm sure your tea emporium will be a huge success.'

I was starting to feel as if I'd known the Giddings family for a long time and I took this opportunity to put the question I'd been dying to ask for hours.

'How did Oldstone Farm get its name?'

'Oh, from the natural stone outcrop on a hill nearby – didn't you see it as you arrived?' asked Teddy.

'No, it was starting to go dark and you couldn't see much because of the wet mist.'

'The Oldstone isn't actually that close, but it's a landmark. At some point a circle of stones was erected round it, but they've all fallen down now,' Nile said.

'It's a nice place for a picnic in summer,' Geeta commented. 'If you know the way through the small back roads you can park quite near it, though there's a hiking trail that goes right past it, too.'

'And there's a bit of a Brontë connection,' Bel added. 'It's said that it was a favourite spot of Emily's, though I don't think there's any proof, and it would have been a long hike from Haworth.'

'It's an odd sort of spot. The wind seems to whistle round the stones even on a summer's evening,' Sheila said.

'There are all kinds of stories about it. Apparently, a baby was once found abandoned there, though I don't know how any mother could do that to her child,' Geeta said, tenderly stroking Casper's downy head.

The room swirled around me.

'Is that an old legend?' I heard Bel ask, as if from a long distance away.

'Actually, I think it was fairly recent, now you come to mention it,' Sheila said. 'In fact, not many years before Paul brought me here after we got engaged, to meet his father and grandparents for the first time – Oldstone is the family home, you know, so Paul had always spent a lot of time here.'

Then, catching sight of my expression, she looked at me with concern and asked, 'Are you all right, Alice? Only you've gone very pale.'

'Yes . . . fine,' I said and then blurted out, without in the least meaning to, 'Only . . . I think that baby might have been me!'

Fortunately, at the critical moment Father had been on one of his lengthy tours of duty with the medical charity I-Cee. An ophthalmic surgeon, he'd taken early retirement when he came into a substantial inheritance, but kept his hand in by working in countries where a simple cataract operation could be a miraculous and life-changing event. People often said how kind and wonderful it was of him to devote his time unpaid to this work, but personally, I think he just enjoyed his god-like power to make the blind see.

15

On the Rocks

The whole family turned as one to stare at me – even Casper moment-arily stopped banging his plastic spoon on the tray of his highchair – and then Sheila asked gently, 'What makes you think it might have been you, Alice?'

'Because I was a foundling and my adoptive mother told me I was abandoned out on the moors near Haworth. On my birth registration document I was given the surname of Oldstone, so when Nile told me what this house was called, I thought perhaps I'd been left nearby . . . or even that someone from the family here had found me.'

'I don't think so, because I'm sure if that was the case it would have been mentioned when I was first told about it,' Sheila said.

'Then it would appear that you were literally called after the place where you were found,' said Teddy, interested. 'I must say, *I'd* never heard the story before.'

'The last cleaner told me, *and* about the headless ghost dog that Blackdog Moor is named after,' Geeta said, with a shudder. 'It has red eyes and brings bad luck.'

'I don't see how you'd know if the dog had red eyes if it was headless,' Nile objected.

'No, and if that cleaner had spent as much time working as she did gossiping, she'd still be the present one, not the last,' Sheila put in.

I'd been lost in thought, but now I looked up and found Nile's light, clear grey eyes fixed on my face. His expression was softer than it usually was when he looked at me, but then, we had managed to get off on the wrong foot right from the start.

'Didn't your birth mother ever come forward to claim you?' he asked.

I shook my head. 'Dad said it was extremely likely that she was very young and perhaps hadn't even realized she was having a baby until she gave birth, so she abandoned me in a panic.'

'I believe that often *is* the case,' Sheila said.

'I hope your adoptive parents were nice?' asked Bel.

'Well, Dad was great, but he died when I was in my late teens and I left home soon after. I never got on with Nessa – my mother – so we didn't stay in contact.'

'That's rather sad,' Sheila said.

'And now you're back where you came from,' Bel said, looking fascinated. 'Have you thought that if you take after either of your birth parents in appearance, perhaps someone local will recognize you?'

'It had crossed my mind,' I admitted.

'Light green eyes and long auburn hair,' Sheila mused. 'It doesn't ring any bells . . . but then, we've only lived here for a few years, though of course we used to visit for holidays and long weekends before that.'

'I think she looks sort of familiar,' Bel said. 'I did from the moment I saw her.'

'That's because she's a dead ringer for Lizzie Siddal, the Pre-Raphaelite muse,' Nile told her. 'You'll have seen her in loads of paintings.'

'I am not!' I snapped automatically, and he grinned, seeming happy to have got a rise out of me.

'Actually, I think he's right, though you're *much* prettier,' Bel told me. 'Did you come to live in Haworth in the hope of finding your birth mother, Alice? Are there any clues as to—'

'Bel, all this is none of our business,' Sheila chided her gently. 'Now, would anyone like a second helping of apple pie before I put the coffee on?'

'Me, but I shouldn't,' Bel groaned. 'My waistline is vanishing since I moved back home.'

'I don't think I've ever had one,' Teddy said. 'Maybe we're just built differently, Bel.'

'She will be, if she carries on eating so much,' said Nile.

'Just because you don't have a particularly sweet tooth and can resist temptation, it doesn't mean us lesser mortals can, too,' she told her brother indignantly. 'Anyway, it's better to be a little on the plump side than so skinny the wind rattles your bones.'

This was an exaggeration, for although Nile was on the willowy side, his shoulders were broad enough and I knew he had hidden strength because of the way he'd hefted my heavy suitcase about as if it weighed nothing.

'I put all this weight on when I was pregnant with Casper and all I wanted to eat was pistachio and rosewater kulfi and Mars bars,' Geeta said. 'I didn't have any problem before that.'

'It's not a problem: I like you cuddly,' Teddy told her, and they exchanged an affectionate glance.

I gratefully let the give and take of family conversation wash over my head again after that, thinking about what I'd learned: ever since Nile had told me the name of the house, I'd thought I *must* have been found nearby and that Nessa had exaggerated the loneliness of the spot where I'd been abandoned just to be cruel. Now I realized she'd told the truth, it somehow reinforced my determination to find out as much as I could about it.

Teddy and Geeta went to their apartment right after dinner to put the baby to bed and I refused coffee, pleading tiredness after the long day, then went up to my room.

My mind was whirling and I wanted to be alone to think, but the moment I saw the bed, with its crisp white sheets and the billowing expanse of an old-fashioned quilted blue satin eiderdown, huge waves of tiredness practically knocked me off my feet.

I got ready quickly and climbed in, feeling as if I'd like to sleep for a hundred years, though preferably without the giant spiders of my story for company.

'Gnaw faster!' Beauty ordered the little mouse. 'I can hear the spider stirring!'

'This web stuff is disgusting,' he said, spitting out a mouthful and then pulling a strand off his whiskers. 'You owe me big time, for this!'

'Anything,' she promised, fearfully looking over her shoulder. 'A life-time supply of cheese – whatever!'

'Cheese is so overrated,' the mouse said. 'I prefer a good single-estate dark chocolate.'

'What's chocolate?'

The mouse sighed. 'Of all the portals in all of Fairyland, I had to choose this one,' he said.

I woke much later than usual, probably because the previous day had lasted about half a lifetime . . . or that's what it felt like, anyway.

When I went downstairs, the kitchen was empty apart from Bel, who was eating toast and reading the newspaper.

She said she was on breakfast duty. 'Since Mum likes to get to her studio early, while I'm more of a laid-back, later kind of person, I always cook the breakfast when we have guests,' she said, pouring me coffee. 'I'll scramble you some of our free-range eggs.'

'Not if it's any trouble,' I told her. 'Toast is fine.'

'It's no bother. Some visitors expect a full English breakfast, but we're not geared up for it out of season.'

'Where's Nile?' I asked, hoping he'd remembered his offer to drive me into Haworth later.

'He took Honey out for a walk, but he says he'll run you into the village as soon as you're ready.'

'I don't want to put him out, if he doesn't need to go – I could ring for a taxi,' I suggested.

'Oh, he doesn't mind. He often comes home for the weekend – he can't resist Mum's Sunday lunch, for a start – but he has a client coming to the shop to see him today, so he has to get back.'

'That's OK then,' I said, relieved. 'When my car arrives tomorrow, it won't be a problem and I can camp out in the flat over the café as soon as I've got a bed.'

'Oh, but we're hoping you'll stay for at *least* a week!' Bel protested. 'Sheila's going to charge you half-price, because we intend milking you for lots of free advice about starting up our café.'

'I'd do that anyway,' I told her. But it really would be more comfortable to stay at Oldstone Farm until the flat had some heating as well as a bed. Once I had my own transport and independence back, that was.

The kitchen was at the rear of the house and while Bel was scrambling eggs I took my mug of coffee over to admire the view across the rolling moorland. The weather had changed entirely and the morning was bright, sunny and so clear that the finger of rock on a distant hill stood out like a bold black exclamation mark.

'I presume that's the Oldstone I can see?' I asked her, feeling both attracted and repelled by the monolith in equal measure.

'Yes, that's it. On the maps it's called the Devil's Finger, but I think the Ordnance Survey people must have made that one up.'

'It looks very near.'

'I know, but it's deceptive – it's miles away really,' she said. I suspected she was dying to talk about my having been found up there, but didn't want to bring it up herself.

I felt strangely comfortable with Bel already, as if she was someone I'd known for years, but I wasn't yet ready to confide everything in her, as I did with Lola.

After breakfast Nile came to see if I was ready to go. He was wearing jeans instead of his natty suit, and a soft blue-grey sweater, which just *had* to be cashmere: he reeked of elegance even dressed down.

In an old cream Aran jumper knitted by Edie and cheap chain-store jeans, I didn't feel so much dressed down as downmarket.

Before we left, Bel offered to drive in later and show me the nearest big stores. 'I love shopping, especially for home furnishings, and we could pick up some paint charts, too. Anyway, I'm just dying to see the café,' she added candidly.

'Don't you want to work?' I asked.

'No, I mostly take the weekends off, unlike Mum. But then, she has some commissions to spur her on, while I'm still trying to build a name for myself.'

'I'd like to see your studio and what you make.'

'You can do that later, or tomorrow, can't you?' Nile said, impatiently jangling his car keys, so I took the hint and went to fetch my coat.

Nile was silent at first on the drive in, though I thought that might be due to his being stunned by my emerald-green acrylic fur jacket, which he hadn't seen before; but then he said right out of the blue, 'You haven't seriously come to Haworth to try to find your birth mother, have you?'

'I certainly didn't move here with that intention *alone*,' I said, thrown off balance. 'It was just that I've never really felt I belonged anywhere until Edie – an old friend of mine – pointed out that I must have been born round here, so if I was going to feel at home anywhere, this would be it.'

'I suppose that's true enough, but I'd abandon any ideas of tracing your birth mother,' he said, to my surprise. 'After all, if she's never come forward to claim you, she might not welcome you back with open arms. Life doesn't always give you the happy endings you expect.'

So far, life didn't seem to have dealt me *any* happy endings!

'Thank you, but I'd already thought of that scenario,' I told him. 'I want to find her so she can tell me who I am and what the circumstances were that led her to leave me out on the moors. I don't feel angry or judgemental about it, I'd just like to *know*.'

'She may have a new family by now and have told them nothing about you.'

'I've thought of that one, too. If I find her, but she doesn't want to meet me, then I'll respect that.'

'I'd still leave well alone, if I were you, and concentrate on this far-fetched tea emporium of yours, instead. God knows, it's going to need all the help you can give it.'

'Gee, thanks for that vote of support, Mr Small and Perfect,' I snapped sarcastically, and after that we didn't speak again until he'd wound his way through the back streets and up the alleyway to the parking space.

I expect he wasn't used to women not drooling over him and lapping up his every word, but it would do him good.

When we got out, he said curtly that he'd see me later, but I knew where to find him if anything came up.

Then he strode off, a stiff breeze blasting back the blue-black curls from his forehead, like a heavenly hair dryer.

I'd kept my brief romance the previous summer a secret from Father, since I knew he would disapprove of anything that deflected my attention from studying, so there was nothing to cause the least suspicion to enter his head.

He'd been quite right, too, for I'd realized long before that catastrophic night that 'falling in love' was merely a midsummer night's dream of illusion and fantasy, in my case caused by a rush of teenage hormones. I had no intention of ever succumbing to anything of the kind again.

Having dealt with the consequences of my stupidity, I worked hard for my exams and duly went on to take up my place at Oxford to read medicine. Father was extremely pleased and made me a generous allowance.

16

Lost Lambs

I spent the morning washing and putting away the rest of the willow-pattern china and adding yet more things to the lists for both the café and flat, which were now longer than the novel I was currently supposed to be writing . . .

Though actually, I was feeling increasingly interested in Beauty and what was going to happen to her. Eventually, I knew I'd have to settle down and fuse all the little scenes I'd written together and hope it turned into a book.

The moment she was free, Beauty leaped for the door and, slamming it, turned the key, though not before catching a brief glimpse of the monstrous shape within. Clearly, the spider had grown even more enormous during its long sleep.

Beauty was glad that she *hadn't, since she'd already been a plump girl when she fell under the enchantment. On the other hand, she wouldn't have minded losing a few pounds . . . Still, her nursemaid had always said that princes liked girls with curvy figures – and as soon as she escaped this pesky enchantment, she'd go and find one to test that theory.*

Unless, of course, he found her first, for she could now dimly hear the sound of hacking.

The new internet router arrived in the mail, though of course it was entirely useless until the landline was reconnected. But I'd have to manage without it until then, because I'd learned my lesson about using Nile's without permission.

Along with the router came a bundle of ominous-looking envelopes for Mrs Muswell. At a guess, I'd say they contained a full set of final demands, so I readdressed them to her solicitor. I only hoped Nile hadn't been right when he forecast a steady stream of debtors turning up in person at the door . . . though just after the post, a man turned up and said he'd come to collect the old kitchen table and chairs, which he'd bought from Mrs Muswell. He hadn't been able to pick them up earlier because his van had been in an accident, and he was more than a trifle angry and belligerent when he realized he wasn't going to get them at all. I wasn't going to back down, though, and sent him off to Mrs M's solicitor, too.

When Bel arrived, I gave her a tour of the café and flat and then we went out to look at beds, the top item on my list.

First, though, we bonded further over a burger and fries during a drive-through lunch (glad that Nile wasn't around to criticize our food choices). The odd thing about Bel was that the moment I'd met her, I'd felt as if she was an old friend I hadn't seen for ages, and she said it had been just the same for her.

'Perhaps we knew each other in a previous existence?' she suggested, but I was having enough trouble coming to terms with the present one to want to explore that idea.

I told her a bit more about my past in Cornwall and how I'd moved to Scotland and thought I'd finally found the man I could settle down with – until he was killed in an accident.

In return, she explained that she was divorced – not amicably, since he'd had an affair with her best friend – and now just wanted to stay at Oldstone and throw herself into her career.

'I hated teaching and I don't think I was very good at it,' she confessed. 'I spent all my spare time in my studio shed in the garden and Chris – my ex – got very jealous of the time it took up.'

'Dan – my late fiancé – was the only man I ever lived with,' I said. 'He was away a lot, though, so I had time to myself to write in.'

'You write? What kind of thing?' she asked with interest.

'Sort of updated fairy stories with a horror twist. When I was a little girl, Dad told me a fairy-tale version of how I was abandoned as a baby, and as I grew up we added more and more over-the-top detail to it, so I've just carried on from there, really, only darker.'

'Fun!' she said. 'Mum's been a successful artist all her life, while Dad built up the swimming pond business. I suppose I take after her, but our work is very different. The whole family love Oldstone – we'd spent so many happy holidays here before we moved in permanently – so we're pulling together to renovate it in our spare time.'

'I can understand that, because the setting's beautiful in its way, even when it's so bleak.'

'I just love to watch the changing skies over the moors and the way the dark clouds close in suddenly, like curtains,' she agreed. 'But in summer, with the bees buzzing and the birds singing, it's a different place entirely.'

'And the tourists buzzing, too?'

'Well, we're certainly on the tourist trail, because they pass us on their way to landmarks like the Oldstone and the Hikers' Café and the restaurant over near the Standing Stones Motel. I just need to lure them down the track to our pottery.'

'Don't you already get lots of visitors interested in swimming ponds? I assume that's a demonstration model below the house?'

'No, that was just put in for us – we all prefer natural swimming, but then, that's what we grew up with. Most of the orders for ponds are generated through the website and word of mouth, so not many customers actually turn up here. Teddy or Geeta visit the potential clients and then do site visits till it's completed. They have a team of installers, but they're still based in Bristol where the warehouse is, so they travel up and down quite a bit.'

'That must be tricky, with the baby.'

'Teddy's been doing most of the travelling since Casper arrived, and Geeta has taken on more of the management side, so it's worked out, and as Geeta says, children aren't small for very long. She has a very nice local girl to help with Casper, called Jan. You'll probably see her about the place.'

'So, it looks like we're both making a fresh start – and we'll build successful businesses and stay here for ever!' I said.

'Sounds like a plan to me,' she replied cheerfully, and then drove me to a nearby retail park, where she encouraged me to buy a pretty white-painted metal bed with moulded swags of roses on the headboard, rather than the plain and economical divan I'd been looking for. Then we bounced our way down a long row of mattresses until we found the right one, like Goldilocks, but without the bears.

After that we picked up armfuls of paint charts and a few tester pots (I was feeling inspired by Sheila's Scandinavian décor), some cheap white paper globe lampshades and a few other minor bits and pieces for the flat. I didn't want to buy too much until I could see which of my curtains fitted the windows and whether I had enough bedlinen for a spare bed, when I finally got one.

It was late afternoon by the time we'd finished, so we headed straight back to Oldstone Farm and, once I'd dumped the carrier bags in my room, Bel gave me a tour of the grounds.

They weren't extensive, since it had long ceased to be a working farm and the land had been sold off, but it did extend to a drystone-walled vegetable garden, where the hens also lived, and a substantial U-shaped block of outbuildings.

The barn at one end was now used as a garage, but the hayloft over it had been converted to the Pondlife offices, with an original flight of stone steps leading up to it.

Some stables in the central part had been turned into two pottery studios, a kiln room and storage. Bel showed me round those first.

'The stable doors will be ideal, because we can open the top halves to the studios when there are visitors, so they can watch us working,' she said. 'Then, when that palls, they can go and stoke up on coffee and cake and buy some of my smaller pieces of work, like the jewellery.'

'You make porcelain jewellery?' I asked, surprised.

'Yes, when I was at art college I used to collect Victorian china brooches, usually flowers, and that inspired me. I'm starting to get a name for it, I suppose because it's wearable art.'

She showed me some pieces, which were lovely, though not at all Victorian or flowery.

I was allowed a glimpse of a huge heavy example of Sheila's work, too, which was waiting to be packed up.

'Everything she makes sells almost instantly. The galleries can't get enough of it,' Bel said proudly. 'Come on, I'll show you the carriage house, where the café is going to be.'

It proved to be a large, stone-flagged space sandwiched between the studios and the Pondlife office. I thought it would be ideal . . . with a lot of work. I wasn't sure that either Bel or her mother realized quite *how* much would be involved before they could serve even the light refreshments they were contemplating.

'We could have the tables in the middle and my ceramics displayed around the walls, to tempt them into impulse buys,' Bel was saying. 'Maybe later we might take other craftspeople's work, too, or even convert more stable for studio space.'

I looked round at the stone walls and the lovely beams in the roof. 'You'd need to glaze in the big entrance doorway; that would let more light in. Those high windows help – are they original?'

'No, I think there was some Victorian remodelling,' she said. 'We've already had electricity put into the studios and the Pondlife office, of course, which will be handy.'

'And presumably you've got water laid on? You'll need a staff hand-washing sink behind the counter if you're selling food to the public. There are all sorts of hygiene and safety rules to comply with.'

'I suppose there must be,' she said vaguely. 'You can see now that Mum and I really *need* your help with the café idea, because we simply don't know where to start, so it's a huge stroke of good fortune that you've come to stay!'

'Yours will be simple to plan and set up compared to my teashop,' I said, 'though you'll still have to comply with all the same planning and hygiene rules.'

'That sounds daunting.'

'Don't worry, I'll help. I need to update myself with the current regulations anyway.'

'I can see you're going to be worth your weight in cooked breakfasts,' Bel said, smiling.

The early wintry spell had mercurially reverted to golden September sunshine with a little warmth in it, and on the way back to the house we paused to look down on the swimming pond.

'It looks quite inviting with the blue sky reflected in it,' I said.

'We do sometimes swim in it in September if we have an Indian summer. Not this year, though; it's too chilly even on a day like this.'

I shivered. 'I still think I prefer heated indoor swimming pools.'

'We'll see if we can change your mind next summer, when it's hot.'

Bel finished her tour by taking me round the house, which was a total mishmash of styles that somehow melded into a homely whole. The oldest part had lots of small, dark, panelled rooms and one large formal dining room, which she said they never used, preferring to eat in the kitchen.

'Mending the roof took most of our money, so Mum's doing the rest of the house up one room at a time,' Bel explained. 'We all join in with the wallpaper stripping, sanding, painting – all the rest of it. Then we have a couple of weeks off and start on another. I think one of the letting bedrooms in your wing is next, so she can take more paying visitors next summer.'

Two letting bedrooms had been finished, including mine, but three more were dingy and in need of attention.

'There are former servants' bedrooms in the attic, too,' Bel said. 'But some are full of junk and they can all wait until we've done the rest of the house. Mum goes up there occasionally to take a lucky dip into the furniture and usually comes back with something interesting.'

I saw a little of Geeta and Teddy's rooms through the open door off the living room and glanced into the bedrooms occupied by the family, which had all been redone. Nile's had a vast four-poster bed and a large wardrobe eminently suitable for hanging vampire cloaks in.

The house had been quiet and deserted until we opened the kitchen door and found baby Casper in his highchair, banging a spoon on a tray quite happily while Sheila cooked.

'There you are!' she said over her shoulder. 'Stewed chicken and dumplings – and it's just us tonight, because Nile is having dinner with that client and Geeta and Teddy have gone to see friends for the evening.'

The chicken smelled lovely. I was *so* glad it wasn't a sheep's head. Perhaps Nile had only been joking about that.

Over dinner I told Sheila that the Scandinavian décor in my bedroom, all chalky grey-blues, warm cream and soft white, had inspired my entire colour scheme for the flat and café.

'It's very tranquil and soothing, but not cold, so I think it will be perfect, and also fit in with the blue and white patterned china.'

Sheila wrote down the contact details of her handyman, who was very good, for those jobs I couldn't do myself. 'And if you need plumbers and electricians, he can organize that for you, too,' she added. 'You can trust Jack.'

'That will be really useful – thank you,' I said gratefully. 'The bed we ordered should be delivered on Friday – if they can find me,' I added, 'but I'd like to paint the flat before I move in, if you don't mind my staying here till then?'

'Of course not – stay as long as you like,' she said hospitably. 'In fact, I was banking on you still being here over next weekend, at the very least.'

Honey the Labrador, who as usual had been lying under the high-chair waiting for any descending gobbets of food, thumped his tail approvingly.

After dinner Sheila went off to put Casper to bed and then watch TV in the apartment until Teddy and Geeta got home, while Bel and I stacked the dishwasher and cleared up.

Then Bel suggested we take our coffee into the library and do an online search for newspaper articles about my being found up on the moors.

'The connection's really slow, but we could give it a go, if you like?'

'I'm dying to,' I confessed. 'I should have tried to find out more long ago – I don't know why I didn't. I suppose part of it was this silly idea that the first time I walked down the main street of Haworth I'd come face to face with my mother, who I'd recognize because she looked just like me, but that kind of thing only happens in fairy stories.'

'And children don't always look like their parents, do they?' she pointed out. 'Teddy and I are tall like Dad, but he had wavy brown hair, while we're both fair and blue-eyed like Mum.'

I was longing to ask where the dark and mysterious Nile fitted in, but didn't want to appear nosy . . . or over-interested. It seemed increasingly likely he was Sheila's son by an earlier partner.

'Were there any clues found with you?' Bel asked.

'*Clues?*'

'Things that might help to trace your mother, like the clothes you were wearing? I read once that penniless mothers in Victorian times used to leave their babies at foundling hospitals with a token, so they could claim the baby back if their circumstances improved. They were so poor, it was often something like an acorn, or a button. Heartbreaking, isn't it?'

'Yes, and I imagine practically none of them ever did reclaim their children,' I agreed. 'Dad never mentioned anything like that being left with me, so I've no idea. Come on, let's have a look and see what we can find.'

'We'll start with the national newspapers,' she suggested. 'Some of the local papers might have more details, but we can get the overview first using the year you were born and your birthday.'

'*Official* birthday, the day I was found,' I said. 'I was only a few hours old at most, so it had to be that day or the one before.'

It took a bit of searching, using various combinations of wording, but finally we struck gold. It appeared I hadn't made the major news, since there was a lot going on at the time including a big murder trial, but all the dailies initially covered the story, though it petered out when it became clear the mother was neither coming forward, nor likely to be discovered.

'I was out before dawn looking for a lost sheep up near the standing stone on the hill – we call it the Oldstone, but it's down on the maps as the Devil's Finger – and I heard something,' said local farmer Joe Godet. 'I thought it might be an early lamb, but it was a baby crying. It was wrapped up in a white sheepskin rug, the kind you get in all the tourist shops round here, and pushed down into a hole in the rocks. I don't know how it survived the cold, except maybe it hadn't been there long and the sheepskin protected it.'

The reporter went on to say that the farmer seemed overcome by emotion as he added, 'It was a lass, a poor little thing with a harelip and scrawny as a featherless chicken.'

'How weird – a sheepskin rug,' I exclaimed.

'That farmer sounds a sweetie,' Bel commented. 'I didn't realize you'd had a harelip, Alice? You wouldn't know at all now!'

'I was lucky, because it wasn't a serious one and Dad said I had a really good surgeon. I do have a thin scar but it's gone silvery now and with a little makeup you can't see it at all.'

Most of the dailies carried variations on the same story, and then I seemed to have lost my charm for the readers, because there was only one further update, in the *Mail*:

The baby abandoned near a local landmark on Blackdog Moor in West Yorkshire has been named Alice, after the late wife of the farmer who found her. Although slightly premature, she is now doing well and will have an operation to correct a cleft lip as soon as she is strong enough. A medical source said that it was amazing what early surgery could do in such situations and there was a good chance of an excellent outcome with little, if any, scarring . . .

'Well, they were right about that,' Bel commented, looking up.

'Despite extensive police inquiries, the mother has not been found,' continued the article, 'so the baby will be fostered once her medical treatment is completed.'

'They say the Oldstone is near Haworth, but didn't you tell me it was actually much closer to another village?'

'Yes, Upvale is a lot nearer. I expect they only put Haworth because everyone's heard of it.'

She got a map and showed me and really, it was *miles* from Haworth, while Upvale was tucked right down next to it, in a small valley.

'I suppose I must have been born *somewhere* round here, but maybe not Haworth after all.'

'She must have been local enough to find her way through the back lanes to the Oldstone, though,' Bel pointed out. 'The only other route is the hiking trail that passes it and I can't imagine she went that way in the dark.'

'Assuming it was my birth mother who took me there,' I said. 'It could have been someone else.'

'I suppose it could, now I come to think about it, but they still had to know the way because, at the time, only a handful of tourists used to visit the Oldstone. It's more popular now because of the Charlotte Brontë connection to a nearby farm. They found a diary last year saying she was inspired to create Mr Rochester by the farmer living there. Did you read about that?'

I nodded. 'Yes, it was discovered by one of my favourite novelists, Eleri Groves, and she went on to marry the current owner of the farm,' I said, and then something struck me. 'Didn't it say in that article that the farmer who found me was called Godet? Only Eleri married a Henry Godet.'

'Oh, yes, so it did – but I think there are loads of Godets round there and they're all related.'

'Curiouser and curiouser,' I said. 'It's so odd how these coincidences keep happening. I mean, I've actually *met* Eleri Groves! Years ago I won afternoon tea with her at Framling's Famous Tearooms in London – that's what sparked my idea for the tea emporium!'

'It's serendipity, and truth being stranger than fiction,' Bel said.

'Yes, and it means that at least I should be able to track down the farmer who found me, with that name. When I feel brave enough, of course . . .'

'There might be more detail in some of the small local papers,' Bel suggested. 'The *Upvale and District Gazette* is the biggest and it covers Haworth, too.'

'I'll look another time,' I said. 'I want to take in what we've found first – and it's getting late.'

'OK, one step at a time,' Bel agreed.

As I drew my bedroom curtains against the dense, starless darkness of the night, I thought of the ancient stone topping the distant hill and shivered.

I'd have to make a pilgrimage up to the bleak spot where I was found one day soon, and I couldn't say I was looking forward to it.

I completed my medical training with flying colours, having no interest in the student drinking culture and general silliness that distracted so many of my peers.

At one time I considered becoming a pathologist, since the dead don't require their doctors to exhibit any kind of bedside manner and I was forever being told that I didn't have one.

But in the end I joined a general practice near a well-known Scottish golf course. Having initially taken up the game in my early teens to please Father, I had soon become the better player and found it a pleasant and healthy exercise. A relaxing non-alcoholic beverage or two in the members' clubhouse afterwards formed the main part of my social life and I was perfectly content.

17

Beetle Drive

Next day I was to meet Rory at noon in the main car park near the Brontë Parsonage Museum, which would be easier than his attempting to find the way to the back of the café alone. A friend who was studying at Leeds University would then pick him up and they'd spend a couple of days together before he returned to Scotland.

Bel had told me that Nile usually stayed at Oldstone until after Sunday lunch, before returning to his flat, and she volunteered to drive me into Haworth instead.

'We could set off early and get the paint for the flat on the way, if you like?' she offered. 'Unless you want to try the test pots first?'

'I think I know what I want for the flat now, so that would be great,' I told her. 'I'll need to get some brushes and rollers, too, I suppose.'

'Unless you're going to paint the walls with your fingers,' Nile commented, having wandered in in search of breakfast.

He hadn't yet shaved and his hair was unusually rumpled, which oddly I found rather more attractive than his normal vision of manly perfection . . . in fact, my heart seemed to stop for a moment and then resume with a heavy thud. I looked away quickly, though I could feel myself blushing.

'Would anyone like to cook my breakfast for me?' he asked, with a winning smile.

'No, but you've got plenty of time to cook your own, because *I'm* driving Alice in,' Bel told him.

'Is your car on the way?' he asked me.

I busied myself with clearing away my plate and mug, so I didn't have to look at him. 'Yes, Rory sent me a text very early when he set out, so you won't have to worry about having to give me lifts any more.'

'I wasn't actually worried,' he said enigmatically, then began getting out the ingredients for what looked like a breakfast banquet for six, so we left him to it.

'If I can paint the flat before the bed comes on Friday, I could actually move in at the end of the week,' I suggested to Bel later, as we headed back to Haworth with the paint.

'I think I'd make the official move next Sunday or Mum will be upset and think you don't like staying with us,' Bel said with a grin. 'You could go back after lunch, like Nile does.'

'Well . . . if you think so,' I agreed.

She dropped me off at the back of the café and I carried my purchases up to the back door in relays: paint is surprisingly heavy.

Then Rory sent me another text, this one saying he was running a little later than he'd expected, so it would be some time after one when he arrived. I decided to fill in the time by having a leisurely walk around the village, ending up at the Parsonage. The sky was gloomily overcast, and I thought how bleak it must have been for the Brontës looking out on the graveyard, especially once the siblings began to die, one by one. How short their lives had been, yet so full in many ways.

I remembered how I'd embellished with increasingly ridiculous flourishes Dad's story about my being left on the Parsonage steps, like the Wicked Witch arriving in a pumpkin carriage to curse me with the harelip and how one of the horses accidentally turned back into a rat and bit her . . .

The breeze was too chilly for me to stand around for long, so I had a bun and a cup of coffee in a nearby soon-to-be rival establishment, so that I was on hand when Rory finally arrived.

He said the car had driven beautifully, he'd just been held up in a queue because of an accident. Then, once I'd greased his palm with petrol money and a bit extra, his friend came to collect him.

Rory did kindly offer to go back with me to the café to help unload first, but I could see the boys had things planned for the rest of the day, so I assured him it would be no problem.

Really, I could have done with some help, because after carrying all those cans of paint earlier, I was convinced my arms had grown two inches longer. Still, I'd manage.

I found my way round the back streets and up the alley to my parking space without any problem and then I had a cup of coffee before starting the slow process of ferrying everything from the car to the house.

Next time I went shopping I vowed to get one of those little carts for trundling heavy objects about ... or at the very least, a sturdy wheelbarrow.

Edie and Rory had carefully packed into the Beetle all the boxes, bundles and bags I'd left ready in the chalet, together with my folding easel, some bubble-wrapped pictures and a selection of battered suit-cases. Edie was a great one for delegating, so I expect she just stood and directed where each item would fit, like doing a giant jigsaw by remote control.

But I discovered she'd somehow managed to insert a house-warming gift into the rear footwell, too: a Dundee cake in a tin and a bottle of Scotch whisky.

There was a kind note attached to the bottle that suddenly made the tears come to my eyes and I was standing there, resolutely blinking them back, when Nile's car appeared and parked next to mine.

'So, flower power is still going strong in the highlands?' he asked, getting out and surveying the freshly repainted and improbably col-oured blooms up the side of the green Beetle.

'Vintage Cornish old hippie style,' I told him. 'It's a surf dude special.'

'It's going to stand out like a sore thumb round here.'

'Shouldn't you still be at Oldstone, with your feet in the trough?' I asked coldly, and he looked at me in surprise.

'No, lunch was ages ago, and actually I'd have been here even sooner if Sheila hadn't insisted on making you a picnic lunch so you didn't starve to death. Not that you seem likely to,' he added, looking at the cake tin I was holding.

'House-warming gift from my friend Edie,' I explained. 'But woman can't live on cake and whisky alone.'

'I'm glad to hear it,' he said, handing over a large plastic sandwich box and a fat, short Thermos. 'You might want this hot soup and the chicken and stuffing rolls, after all.'

'I do,' I said, feeling ravenous. 'How thoughtful and kind Bel and Sheila are!'

'*I'm* kind, too,' he told me. 'I'll just drop my things off at the shop and then carry all this stuff up for you.'

'Oh, I can manage, don't bother,' I said airily. I mean, I'm not exactly a fragile little flower and on the whole men seem to expect me to get on and do things myself. But I was feeling tired, so when Nile returned and insisted, I gave in gracefully and watched as he ferried everything up to the flat, where we stacked it in the smallest bedroom. I could unpack it at my leisure when I'd painted and perhaps got a bit of carpet down – something else I'd need to buy.

'It's certainly clean as a whistle in here,' he said, after depositing the final box, which because it was full of cookbooks made a heavy thump as it hit the floor. 'But apart from the built-in kitchen units and the sink, there doesn't seem to be any furnishings at all.'

'No, Mrs M cleared the place, but now I've got all my things I'll soon have it looking like home. Once the bed arrives I can manage until I find some inexpensive furniture. It'll have to be cheap, because I've got the whole of the café to refit and paint, and I can't do *all* of the work myself.'

'I expect Bel will give you a hand with some of the painting, and so will I, when I'm around,' he offered, to my surprise. I didn't have him down as the handyman type. 'And tomorrow I'll take you to see a friend who has a big old barn full of furniture, where you can probably find a few bargains.'

'Well, that's kind of you, but if you give me directions I could go on my own, now I have my car,' I pointed out. 'It'll have to be in the afternoon anyway, because my telephone landline is supposed to be reconnected in the morning and I think I need to be here for that.'

'But you don't know your way around yet, so it would be easier to go with me the first time,' he said. 'Chill – take help when it's offered, because you still have plans to make, suppliers to find . . . more of those endless lists to write. Every time I see you, you're scribbling down something new.'

'They're not endless, it's just that as soon as I cross one thing off, I think of several more.'

'That's what I meant.'

'Well, at least I won't have to try to persuade Mrs Muswell's suppliers to deal with me, because everything except the bread will be prepared or baked on the premises, and the ingredients will be top quality, not bought in bulk on the cheap,' I told him.

'Very grand: I hope you know what you're doing.' One dark eyebrow went up quizzically, in a way I was starting to find familiar.

'I've spent most of my adult life working in cafés and teashops so I know *exactly* how I want my own to be, and I'm not going to be skimping on the food, that's for sure.'

'The opposite of Mrs Muswell, then,' he said, then added, 'Just a thought: have you got a handset to plug into the phone landline when it's reconnected? Only I haven't noticed one about.'

I stared at him. 'No – you're right, there isn't one. I'd forgotten about that.'

'I've got a spare somewhere. I'll dig it out and bring it over first thing in the morning,' he offered.

Then his mobile rang and when he looked down at the number he turned partly away while he answered it, so I assumed it was a girlfriend.

'No, I can't come at the moment, Zelda,' he said in reply to some query. 'But I'm hoping to pick up a very special piece at a local auction for one of my London clients and, if so, I'll be down next week to deliver it personally.'

Presumably, this was not what his caller wanted to hear.

'I'm sorry,' he added after a minute. 'I know I haven't seen you for a while, but I can't get away before that. You can always email me whatever the problem is if you don't want to discuss it on the phone. Look, I'll ring you back later. I'm a bit tied up at the moment.'

He grimaced as he put the phone back in his pocket, but didn't give me any explanation. 'Well, I'd better get off,' he said, back to being Mr Terse, which was just as annoying in its way as Mr Bossy. 'I'm away to Keswick, in pursuit of a bit of Ming. Or *alleged* Ming, which would mean a wasted journey.'

'Ming the Merciless,' I said absently, still wondering about his caller. A man so handsome, even if he *was* a bit on the bad-tempered side, must have hordes of women after him and it sounded as if this Zelda was one of them.

'I didn't have you down as a *Flash Gordon* fan,' he said, looking at me in amusement, and I amended that thought to 'sometimes bad-tempered but can suddenly turn on a stun-ray of a smile'.

'My late fiancé . . . it was his favourite film,' I explained.

'Oh, right,' he said, the smile vanishing as quickly as it had appeared.

Left to myself, I went up to the flat and unpacked my kitchen equipment into the cupboards, then flattened the empty cartons. This time I'd get rid of them because I was determined that I was here to stay.

It was chilly in the flat – having the boiler overhauled so I could switch the radiators on was right at the top of my priority list – so after I'd discovered that most of my curtains were long and narrow, while the flat windows were shallow and wide, then painted test patches on the walls and skirting boards, I gave up and drove myself back to Oldstone.

Nile still hadn't returned, so I hoped he'd found his Ming and it was all that he had hoped for.

Back in my comfortable room at the farm, I wrote another scene before dinner.

*'My prince is coming to free me and we'll live happily ever after,'
Beauty said.*

*'But it might not be the right happily-ever-after,' said the mouse.
'Something's wrong with this enchantment, or you'd have stayed
asleep till your prince had kissed you. This must be a prince from the*

Here-and-now, while you need one from the Once-upon-a-time.
You'd better wait.'

And indeed he was quite right. Where once a forest had flourished,
an estate of shabby, rundown houses, with gardens growing crops of
rusty cars and old prams, had encircled the bower without the occu-
pants realizing it was there.

Now, as the enchantment faded, it would beckon to them like a
jewel in a sea of mud.

Dinner was just me, Bel and Sheila again, which was cosy. I was starting to feel very at home at Oldstone, considering I'd barely been there
five minutes.

'Nile is taking me somewhere tomorrow afternoon to look at
second-hand furniture and antiques, but I thought I'd start painting
the flat in the morning while I'm waiting for the phone engineer,' I
told them. 'And maybe I can get hold of someone to come and
service the boiler in the flat, because it's freezing up there without the
heating on.'

'I'll come and help you paint in the morning for an hour or two,' Bel
offered. 'But then I'll come back and work: I'm exhibiting with two
other potters at a gallery in York before Christmas, so I'll have to start
stockpiling pieces.'

'Only if you've got time and feel like it,' I said.

'I'm putting you in my debt, so you have to help us plan out and convert our little café before spring,' she said. 'It's my cunning plan.'

'I'd do that anyway,' I told her.

After dinner, Sheila said she was going to the studio she'd created
out of what was once a small Victorian orangery at the back of
the house, a concept I would have thought as entirely alien to the
surrounding moorland as the carving of a bunch of grapes over the
front door.

When she'd gone, followed by her shadow, Honey, Bel told me she'd
checked out some local newspapers online that afternoon and had
printed out what she'd found.

'I hope you don't mind, but I couldn't resist it.'

'No, it will save time,' I assured her. 'Did you find anything interesting?'

'Yes, and there was a lot more detail in the *Upvale and District Gazette* than any newspapers on the Haworth side.'

'What kind of detail?' I asked.

'Well, for a start, there was a second person on the scene when you were found. I'll show you.' She spread the printouts on the table.

'Here we are – read this one,' she said, pointing.

It started with the now-familiar story of how the farmer found me, right up to the moment when Joe Godet picked me up and discovered I was a baby and not a lamb. But then he said sensationally, 'I looked up and saw one of the Upvale witches standing right next to the Oldstone, staring down at me,' and went on to add that at first he'd thought she'd put the child there, but it seemed she'd appeared at the same moment he did by pure coincidence.

'Witches?' I said, looking up. 'There are *witches* in Upvale?'

'He certainly seems to think so. But read this one – it's an interview with the "witch" from the same paper.'

'I don't know why Mr Godet has a bee in his bonnet about witches,' said Emily Rhymer, of Upvale. 'I simply decided to walk up there to watch the sun rise over the hills, something I'd done several times before.'

When asked if she wasn't nervous about walking the moors alone in the dark, Miss Rhymer replied, 'No, there was a full moon so it was quite bright, once I was out of the lane. And not only can I take care of myself, but I had my dog with me. A friend had said she might drive up to the Oldstone at dawn, too, but there was no sign of her. Then I heard noises and my dog started barking and when I looked down over the edge, I saw a farmer holding what I took to be a lamb . . .'

'The plot thickens,' I said, looking up.

'I know, it's quite a drama, but it seems as if the police cleared this

Emily Rhymer from suspicion: it says so in the next bit.' She frowned. 'The name Rhymer sounds very familiar, somehow . . .'

I read on, but there was only a little more.

'He'd found a baby and accused me of having put it there. But my friend turned up just then and she told him I'd been at her house till late the previous evening and she'd have noticed if I was heavily pregnant or had given birth: the idea was ridiculous. Then, since the priority was to get the baby somewhere warm, we all got into her car and went back to Mr Godet's farm, where we rang for the police and an ambulance, because the poor little thing was only just alive.'

The article concluded by saying that Miss Rhymer had been cleared of any involvement and it was still a complete mystery as to who the mother was and how she'd got the baby up to that remote spot.

'That's all very difficult to take in,' I said, sitting back at last. 'It's really weird that *two* people should have just happened to be there at that particular moment. It's hard to believe it was a coincidence.'

'But the police evidently decided it was, so your fairy godmother must have been looking out for you and sent not one, but two rescuers,' Bel said.

'Yes, and even though Emily Rhymer can't be my mother, I'd still like to talk to her,' I said, then added, 'Let's keep what we've found out to ourselves for a bit, OK?'

'Yes, fine,' Bel said. 'And you've got lots to think about before you try to find out any more.'

'When I'm ready, I'll want to visit the Oldstone and talk to the eye-witnesses, though I'm not really expecting them to add anything that might help me trace my birth mother. I think it will be a dead end, and that's probably going to be as far as I get.'

'Unless you go public at some point with a newspaper appeal, asking her to get in touch?' Bel suggested.

'I might consider that one as a last resort. Nile told me I should let sleeping dogs lie, because my birth mother might very well not want to be found.'

'Then she needn't come forward! And anyway, it's your life, Alice, so you do what you want,' she advised me. 'Nile's always come the bossy older brother with all my friends; just take no notice.'

I thought that might be easier said than done, given I was living two steps away from him in Doorknocker's Row and he tended to turn up as unexpectedly as a pantomime Demon Prince through a trapdoor.

*I didn't remain entirely celibate, but had a couple of short-lived affairs –
conducted on my own terms, of course. If you believed everything you'd
read you'd assume most men were looking for sex without commitment,
but in my experience this was not so. All too soon they demanded more
from me than our original bargain and perceived my emotional disen-
gagement as both an insult and a challenge.*

*This was tedious in the extreme, so eventually I decided the game was
not worth the candle and purchased a small dog to fulfil any need for
companionship, without the complications.*

*Bichon Frises have the advantage of not shedding hair all over the
furnishings.*

18

Mapped Out

It was a delight to be able to drive myself into Haworth next morning and the car had been so lovingly restored that it felt brand new. I wished I had a garage to leave it in, rather than it sitting forlornly on the rough patch of ground at the back of the café.

I'd just left a message for the man who serviced the café's gas boiler, asking him to come and do the same for the flat one, when Nile waltzed in through the unlocked back door, deposited the promised telephone handset on the table and left again with nothing more than a brief, muttered, 'See you later.' He seemed preoccupied: perhaps that was why he'd forgotten to knock.

To my amazement, and against all the laws of workmen, the boiler man appeared within the hour, right after my phone had been reconnected (so it was just as well Nile had remembered the handset).

He sneered at the antiquated boiler in the flat and said it probably came out of the Ark, like the one in the café, and if either of them broke down, he wouldn't be able to get the new parts, so they'd have to be scrapped. That I might have to buy two new gas boilers before very long was a cheering thought.

Still, it was a productive morning in that I had a working landline telephone, a functioning boiler and warm radiators upstairs, by the time Bel arrived. We applied the first coat of warm white emulsion on to the living-room walls, and if the entire interior of the café and flat hadn't been coated in shades of dark mushroom, one coat might even have been enough.

Bel could only stay for a couple of hours, but I painted round the edges of the walls and she rolled the middles, which made it speedy, and since we were chatting while doing it, it took my mind off what we'd discovered in the newspapers the previous day.

Images of the Oldstone and lost lambs had haunted my dreams last night. It was all starting to get way too *Wuthering Heights* for my liking. Why couldn't I have just been left in a cosy basket on the Brontë Parsonage steps, like Dad always told me I was?

Nile had been so preoccupied earlier that I thought he might forget his offer to take me furniture hunting, but he appeared after lunch. Or actually, he appeared *with* lunch, since he brought me a cheese and tomato sandwich in case I hadn't had anything.

I hadn't, and I was suitably grateful, though I fully intended stocking up the café fridge with a few basics like bread, cheese, eggs and milk at the very first opportunity.

Nile seemed in better humour than earlier, so I suspected he was one of those men who get grumpy when their blood sugar dips. It was very thoughtful of him, anyway, and I ate the sandwich while he drove me to his friend's barn showroom.

It was cosy and comfortable in the car, and once I'd demolished the sandwich and relaxed a bit, my mind strayed back to what Bel and I had discovered from the newspapers. In fact, I was miles away on a blasted heath when Nile's voice suddenly jarred me out of my reverie.

'What's the matter, Allie? You're not listening to a word I say and you don't even seem to have noticed that I've pulled over.'

'Don't call me Allie!' I snapped. '*Nobody* calls me Allie.'

He grinned. 'I thought that would get your attention! You've been lost to the world ever since we set out, so if any more devious Mrs Muswell dealings have come to light, you'd better tell me about them now, not keep them to yourself.'

'No, it isn't that,' I said, and then, without in the least intending to, found myself telling him about the newspaper articles.

'I'd only had my birth certificate to go on before, so all the extra

149

information about how and where I was found has really thrown me. It . . . made it suddenly real, rather than just a story.'

'I suppose it would, especially now you've seen what the moors are like. I expect you want to visit the actual spot soon, the Oldstone? We go on family picnics there in summer, but it's a bit bleak at this time of year.'

I shivered slightly, despite the efficient heater blasting out warm air. 'I can imagine, but you're right: going up there is something I'll have to do.'

'I could come with you, if you like,' he offered.

'That's kind, but I feel it's something I'm going to have to do alone the first time.'

'OK, I'll draw you a map of how to get close to it by road, instead, because it's impossible to find if you don't know the way.'

'That would be really useful, thank you,' I said gratefully.

'That's all right. Let me know if there's anything else I can help you with.'

'I think the next step after that will be to find the two eyewitnesses and talk to them. It's just to complete the picture – I'm not expecting it to lead to finding my birth mother.'

'Well, you know my opinion on that one,' he said. 'Better to leave it alone.'

'Now I know how remote a spot I was abandoned in, I have to admit you have a point, because she can't have expected me to be found . . . or not alive, at any rate, can she?'

'She may not have thought it through to that extent, Alice. We don't know the circumstances, but they must have been traumatic and desperate to make her do something like that.'

'That's what Dad said. He thought she was probably very young and when I arrived just wanted to get rid of me and pretend it never happened.'

'I think that's a fairly common scenario,' Nile agreed.

'But if you think about it, she can't have been *that* young, because how could she get me to a remote spot like the Oldstone in the early hours of a freezing cold March morning if she couldn't drive?'

'That's a point,' he said, frowning. 'There aren't many houses within easy walking distance, only a couple of farms, and I expect the police checked those out at the time.'

'It was miraculous the farmer found me at all, because I don't suppose I'd have lasted very long, even though I'd been wrapped in a sheepskin rug.'

'A *rug*?'

'Apparently, and it kept me warm, but even that wouldn't have saved me for very long, because I was slightly premature and had a harelip, too,' I confessed. It wasn't something I generally threw into the conversation with near-strangers . . . not that any of the Giddings family actually felt like strangers any more, even the irritating Nile.

'Oh? I hadn't noticed.' He turned his head and smiled at me, which I'd already discovered was way more disconcerting than the frown.

'I was lucky – there's only a very fine scar.'

'So, once you've talked to the two people who found you, will you give up on trying to discover who your birth mother is?'

'Probably not,' I admitted.

'Well, it's your call,' he said. 'But if the police couldn't trace her at the time, I don't suppose you will either, unless she finds out that you're searching for her and comes forward.'

'Bel suggested yesterday that I tell my story to a local newspaper in the hope that she sees it and does just that – and I might as a last resort.'

He started the engine again and gave me a half-smile that softened his distinctive face. 'In the end, it isn't who you started out as that really matters, it's who you become.'

'That's easy enough for you to say,' I snapped crossly.

'But *I* was adopted too – didn't Bel say?' he asked, sounding surprised.

'No!'

'Bel and Teddy are the real deal, Sheila and Paul's biological children, but I was adopted when I was eleven, so my circumstances are a bit different from yours.'

'I wondered why you didn't look like the rest of your family, but I thought you might take after your father.'

'I do – my biological one, who was Greek. Not that I ever met him, because he'd vanished from the scene by the time I was born. My mother had a drink problem and she couldn't cope, so I was in and out of care from the start.'

'That's terrible,' I said, and he shrugged.

'When she was sober – which was rare – she'd come looking for her darling child. Next bender, she'd abandon me and go off again. Eventually, she added drugs to the booze and moved to London and they stopped giving me back. I settled better after that, but I never saw her again and she's dead now.'

'That's so sad. I was adopted as a baby and although my mother wasn't great, at least my father was lovely.'

'It all worked out well for me in the end, because I was fostered by a friend of the Giddingses and when that broke down – I was a bit of a handful – they took me on instead and eventually adopted me,' Nile explained.

'And you became an instant big brother, with siblings to boss about,' I said, trying to lighten the tone a bit. 'Perfect!'

He'd pulled out again and was negotiating a road even narrower than the last, seeming to sense oncoming traffic long before it appeared, so that he could tuck into the small passing places.

'That's how Sheila and Paul got me to settle down, by telling me I needed to be a role model for Bel and Teddy, who are four years younger,' he said. 'They were wonderful parents and when they moved up here permanently, I missed them so much I finally upped sticks and moved too.'

'How long ago was that?'

'Oh – about six years ago, I suppose.'

'About the same time I went to Scotland, then,' I said, seeing our trajectories moving around the country until, finally, our orbits collided here in Haworth. 'How'd you get into antiques?' I asked curiously.

'Studied history of art at university, then worked for a large auction house in London. I've got a half-share in a stall in an antiques centre in Camden, too, but my partner, Zelda, runs it now that I've got my own place up here.'

He didn't specify if he meant business partner or another kind entirely – maybe even both?

'How do you manage to make a living from your shop when it's hardly ever open?' I asked curiously.

'Because I've built up a good client list of collectors and know what they're looking out for. I study the auction catalogues, go to country house sales, and scour antique's shops . . . and I have all kinds of contacts. That's where most of my income comes from. The shop is really more a base and somewhere to sell off the bits and pieces I buy in job lots.'

'Sounds fun,' I said, 'more fun than working in a café, anyway.'

'Oh, I get the feeling you're enjoying yourself, planning out your tea empire.'

'Emporium,' I corrected him, and he gave me that sideways glinting smile again, then swung the car through a pair of mossy stone pillars into a yard and stopped in front of a large barn that proclaimed over the double doors: 'World's End Antiques'.

It certainly *felt* like the world's end; I'd never have found it by myself, even with directions.

'Rick's got delusions of grandeur, as it's mostly junk, not antiques,' he said. 'Still, there are usually some solid pieces mixed in and I've found the occasional gem.'

The building was stacked floor to ceiling with furniture and bric-a-brac and, surprisingly, we weren't the only customers rummaging round in there. I spotted two huge willow-pattern serving dishes, both cheap because they were cracked and had been mended with old-fashioned metal rivets, but they would look lovely on display in the café. Then I moved on to the furniture and found a pair of white-painted bedside cabinets, a worn but still beautiful old rug for the living room, a Victorian wooden towel rail and a Lloyd Loom ottoman with a padded top. Nile haggled the prices down and then, with practised skill, he and Rick managed to insert all of them into the back of the estate car and we set off home.

'Thank you so much for taking me,' I said gratefully. 'I seem to have bought tons of stuff for amazingly little money, but I feel guilty because you didn't get anything.'

'I often don't find much there but, actually, I did today. I'll show you when we get back.'

And when he'd helped me carry my purchases into the café, where I put them in a corner until I'd finished painting upstairs, he produced from his pocket a small ivory parasol with a fist-shaped handle into which was set a little glass window.

'It's called a Stanhope. If you look through the glass, there's a magnified view inside. This has St Paul's Cathedral but there all kinds of different ones and they're very collectable. I have a client who'll snap it up straight away.'

'It's small and perfect in all ways,' I agreed, thinking how interesting it would be if you could peer through a bit of glass into the past, or into a parallel universe.

Or maybe not, depending on what you saw . . .

I got that thought down for a future book, before I forgot it.

My life continued pleasantly in this fashion, interspersed with golfing holidays in Portugal whenever I felt the need for a little change.

Mum died from cancer when she was only sixty, though Father, despite being many years her senior, continued with his voluntary medical work well into old age, until he began to manifest the first symptoms of Parkinson's disease. When this also eventually prevented him playing golf, a passion we'd shared, he rapidly deteriorated to such an extent that I arranged for live-in help until I could settle my affairs and move back to Upvale.

It wasn't what I wanted, but I knew my duty.

19

The First Cuckoo

With some faffing around, I managed to get my router working early next day and there was an email from Edie, asking me how I was getting on with my 'little Brontë café'. She'd be sorry for that 'little' when I started deluging her with requests for advice!

I emailed her back saying my afternoon tea emporium would probably merely be the start of a world-wide chain of Fat Rascals. Then I told her all about what I'd found out in the newspaper articles. I'd already given Lola a quick phone update last night after dinner and she'd been fascinated by all the details and supportive about my intention of trying to track down the two witnesses and, if possible, my birth mother.

'That's not what Nile says – he thinks I shouldn't attempt to find her,' I'd told her.

'Of course you must attempt to discover everything you can,' she'd said. 'I expect Nile is only afraid that if you find your mother and she doesn't want to meet you, you'll be terribly upset. He sounds such a nice, caring man.'

I don't know what I could have said to give her that idea!

'I suppose he has his moments,' I'd agreed reluctantly, and then it had occurred to me that for a man I'd only known for a matter of days, I must already have mentioned him so many times that his name was familiar to my oldest friend!

But he had been really helpful and I'd repaid him with spiky defensiveness . . . even more so since that moment in the Oldstone kitchen when

I'd suddenly realized that if I let myself, I could fall for him hard and be abandoned all over again: my own little Groundhog Day of the heart.

For the next couple of days I focused on getting the flat ready to move into.

Sheila, with experience gained from renovating Oldstone Farm, was an invaluable source of information on things like where to find the cheapest good-quality carpets and vinyl, and I got her handyman, Jack, to come round and give me an estimate for what work needed doing in the flat – mostly new worktops in the kitchen end of the living room, but there were also a couple of other odd jobs.

I liked him straight away: he was a man of few words, but those were all to the point and his on-the-spot estimate was very reasonable, so after we'd agreed terms I took him over the café, too.

Until he'd run his expert eyes over the premises, I don't think I'd quite grasped just how much needed doing and how little of it I'd actually be able to manage myself. Plumbing, flooring and electrics all needed to be done in the right order and by professionals, so when he suggested he site-manage the refurbishment between his other jobs, it seemed to me that it would be a practical move.

'And I'll repair that front porch first, before I start on the flat, or it's going to fall down,' he told me. 'Victorian, that is – it's a feature.'

Which I suppose it was, like the bull's-eye-glass windows – not original to the building, but having a certain strange charm.

I gave him a spare set of keys to the café – Sheila had said he was totally trustworthy and I could tell that for myself within a minute of meeting him.

Bel helped me with the painting again and though I didn't really expect Nile to make good his promise, he simply turned up later, carrying a folding stepladder and wearing a strange brown linen overall to protect his clothes.

'Leftover from my days at the London auction house,' he explained, but since he was painting the ceilings, it was a pity he didn't have a matching hat. He wouldn't even borrow one of the mobcaps, so it was his own fault if his mop of glossy blue-black curls got speckled with white paint.

Since I didn't want to keep popping down and letting them in, I gave both Bel and Nile keys to the café, too. Just as well I'd had a couple more spares made when I bought the paint.

In any case, if I was out and there was a delivery, I hoped Nile would let them in. I offered to do the same for him, but he pointed out that anything sent to him tended to be small, very valuable and couriered – and he didn't offer me a key to Small and Perfect in exchange.

The drive back to Oldstone Farm over the moorland in the late after-noons began to grow familiar, though the sky gave it an ever-changing beauty.

Over dinner in the evenings I'd discuss my plans for the café, and Bel and Sheila were finally starting to grasp just how much was involved.

'It's all the rules and regulations, the hygiene and food safety aspects, record keeping . . .' Bel said. 'I'd no idea.'

'Nor me,' said Sheila. 'It sounds a bit daunting, seeing we only intend selling coffee and a bit of cake.'

'You still have to register the premises and they'll be inspected and hygiene rated and all the rest of it,' I said. 'But don't worry, if we plan it out carefully right from the start, there won't be any problem with that.'

'Maybe we could go out to the coach house over the weekend and measure up to see what's feasible?' Bel suggested. 'If we're going to open next spring, we need to apply for planning permission soon, don't we?'

'Yes, organize that first step and then you can get to grips with the rest of it.'

'Teddy can draw up the actual plans, so that will save some money,' Sheila told me.

'The only bit *I'm* really looking forward to is the décor,' Bel said ruefully.

We'd entirely finished painting the flat by Wednesday afternoon, including two coats of gloss on the skirting boards. I thought one looked fine, but Mr Small and Perfect insisted it needed a second coat.

Still, it was dry by next morning, when the carpet fitters came and laid a nice hard-wearing oatmeal-coloured wool Berber throughout, except for the kitchen end of the living room, where I had a square of more practical vinyl.

It didn't take them long at all, for as well as being small, the flat was still empty, apart from the stack of my belongings in the spare bedroom and one of the rickety tables and a chair from the café that I'd set up in the living-room window for my laptop.

When they'd gone, I was dying to start getting my stuff out and turning the flat into a home, even if I couldn't stay there until my bed was delivered next day, but first I bit the bullet and ordered online the basic white goods I needed – a small fridge-freezer, oven, microwave and washing machine – with the promise of next day delivery.

All of that, plus the paint and carpet for the flat, had already bitten into the small reserves of cash intended for the teashop – which simply *had* to be a success!

I was about to begin hanging curtains – Sheila had kindly made my old ones fit by the simple expedient of turning them on their sides and sewing curtain tape along one long edge – when I decided to check my emails first. There was a maudlin one from Robbie, of the kind that had periodically punctuated the seven years of his absence, saying he missed me and perhaps moving to Australia hadn't been such a good idea, after all.

It had taken him a while to figure that one out, but I deduced from it that the current girlfriend had ditched him and he was drunk and feeling sorry for himself.

There was mail from Lola and Edie, too, but before I could read them one suddenly popped up from my agent, Senga McWhirter – almost as if she could magically divine that I was there looking at the screen. The whole table the laptop rested on seemed to quiver with tension, but then, all the café tables were so battered and flimsy that they trembled with every movement anyway.

Or perhaps it trembled from my guilty conscience? I'd become so engrossed with getting the flat ready that I'd barely written a thing in the last couple of days.

Still, I had to open it and she started off by telling me that the edits for the first of my backlist books to be reprinted by my new publisher would be arriving shortly. That was a bit of a surprise: I mean, it had already been out as an e-book, so why did I need to do anything else to it?

Then Senga really struck fear into my heart by adding that she hoped I was getting on with the first *new* book of the contract, because she was looking forward to seeing it *very soon*. And, of course, though I'd been writing down snatches of story and dialogue whenever they'd popped into my head, I'd just been drifting with the flow. Eventually I meant to pull it all together and finish it, but I had a feeling that 'eventually' wasn't a word in Senga McWhirter's vocabulary.

The postscript was probably the scariest of all: she was travelling up on 20 September – only ten days away – for the second Eleri Groves annual book launch party, which would be held at her husband's remote moorland restaurant, and Senga hoped to meet me there. I'd forgotten all about this.

I emailed quickly back, assuring her I was working hard (though I didn't say what on) and repeating that I was positive all the tickets for Eleri Groves' event would have sold out months ago. (And I might have to invent a pressing engagement elsewhere, when Senga was up here . . .)

She'd asked me for my new address and landline number, so I added those and then pressed Send, my heart thumping slightly.

On the only occasion we'd met, Senga had struck me as fierce, which I suppose is what you want in an agent, so long as it isn't directed at you. Or maybe it was what you wanted anyway, because the fear of her imminent arrival meant I'd really now have to throw myself into completing the new book the moment I moved into the flat.

And I'd need something more solid to put my printer and laptop on than the horrible café table, too, but which would still fit under the window: it was the perfect spot for a desk, where I could gaze absently across at Small and Perfect just as I was doing now . . . and then suddenly I remembered where I'd seen a lovely desk.

Hanging the curtains would have to wait until later.

*

When I bounced into Nile's shop five minutes later, he'd just started bubble-wrapping a tiny piece of netsuke. It was in the shape of a grotesque little skeleton and I'd seen it the day before, when I'd gone in and fingered all the curios, on the pretext of asking him where the nearest post office was, even though I already knew the answer.

'Nile, can you give me the directions to the antiques barn?' I asked now. 'Only I don't think I could find it otherwise.'

Actually, I wasn't sure I could find my way there even *with* a map – and I certainly couldn't get a desk in the back of my Beetle, so I was deviously hoping he'd offer to take me again.

'You want to go back there already?' he asked, surprised.

'I *urgently* need to buy a desk and I saw one there that would be just the right size.'

'Buying a desk is *urgent*?'

'It certainly is! My agent just rang and she's expecting me to have almost finished my new book, but I've barely started. I need something solid enough to put my printer and laptop on – and I could do with a decent chair, too. Those tubular ones from the café are hideously uncomfortable and they creak and sway.'

'Agent?' he said, raising a dark eyebrow. 'What sort of agent?'

'Didn't I say?' I said, distractedly. 'No – perhaps I just told Bel that I write sort of updated adult fairy stories. Darkish, with a twist. I self-published a couple and then a publisher offered me a contract.'

'There's no end to your talents, is there?' he said, taping the bubble wrap round the netsuke and laying the parcel down on a tray.

I gave him a look. 'My agent is dead scary, so I'll have to get on with my writing in the evenings, despite the café renovation. So – do you think you could draw me a map of how to get to Rick's?'

'I could, but I think you'd get lost and we'd never see you again. Delightful thought though that might be, I feel Sheila would hold me to blame.' He sighed. 'I've got to phone a client, but then I could run you out there, I suppose.'

'Not if you're really busy – I expect I'll find it. I really want something nicer and preferably cheaper than flatpack MDF.'

'Then I'll *have* to come so I can do the bargaining.'

I was pretty sure I could beat his friend Rick down on the prices myself, but I just smiled sweetly and suggested I buy him lunch on the way.

We returned with a sturdy and rather Arts and Crafts-style oak desk and matching cupboard, just the right height to put my printer on – and, as a bonus, a small gate-leg dining table and two wheel-back chairs. It was lucky it was a dry day, because some of it ended up tied to the roof rack.

We managed to unload them and carry them up to the flat between us, because I'm an Amazon, and Nile, as I'd already discovered, is surprisingly strong despite all that willowy elegance.

While we were at it, I got him to help me take up the ottoman that I'd stored in the café and the other bits and pieces before he made his escape to finish packing his netsuke.

Once he was gone, I finally began the pleasurable task of moving things about until I was happy they were in the right place, unpacking and turning the flat into a home, though my lovely new desk in the window, with one of the wheel-back chairs in front of it, kept beckoning enticingly . . .

Back in Once-upon-a-time, Beauty's not-terribly-evil stepmother was congratulating herself on having regained family peace. Luckily, her husband was both forgetful and unable to count to more than three, so that he seemed unaware of his eldest daughter's disappearance, until one day a prince came riding up in search of her.

'My mother told me I'd been betrothed to Princess Beauty when we were in our cradles, but I'd like to see her first – from a distance,' said Prince S'Hallow. 'If she's not pretty, the deal's off.'

'Beauty? We appear to have . . . mislaid her,' confessed her father, looking around him vaguely, as if she might be hiding behind the imperial purple curtains.

'I know where she is – leave it all to me, dearest husband,' said his queen soothingly, and he looked relieved and wandered off towards his library.

*

Since it was a weekday, I was surprised to find Nile at dinner that evening, though I don't know why I should be, since it was his home after all.

In fact, everyone was there, but until Nile commented on it, I hadn't realized quite how well I'd settled in and how much Oldstone Farm had already come to feel like home to me.

Sheila smiled at me across the table and said, 'Oh, yes, Alice is an honorary Giddings now. We've unofficially adopted her and even though her flat's almost ready, we hope she's going to spend this weekend and any more she can spare with us.'

'You know I'd love to – as long as you let me pay for my bed and board!' I said.

'Oh, no, because you'll be paying us with all your help in planning our little café,' she insisted.

'Not to mention roping you in to help with the house renovations,' Bel put in with a grin.

'I'd be more than happy to do that,' I said.

'I'm outnumbered by women anyway, so one more sister around the place doesn't make any difference,' Teddy said gloomily and then he yelped, so I think Geeta had kicked him under the table.

'You're all very kind and I'd love to stay this weekend, though I think I'll have to spend tomorrow night at the flat. I had a text saying my fridge and cooker were being delivered in an evening slot, so it might be a bit late to come out after that.'

'Well, you've got your key and can let yourself in on Saturday if we're not around,' Sheila said, and Nile raised his eyebrows.

'You really have got your feet under the table remarkably quickly,' he drawled.

'He wouldn't be so rude if he didn't like you,' Bel explained. 'And anyway, it's open house here, we're always having visitors and some of Mum's arty friends stay for *months*.'

'Yes, and it's a pity they're not the paying kind,' Nile said.

'I get lots of those in season,' Sheila said mildly. 'But it's lovely to have other artists around to bounce ideas off sometimes.'

'Dad was a painter and quite well known,' I told her. 'Alexander Rose – I don't know if you've heard of him?'

'Of course,' said Sheila, interested. 'I adore his work and I remember meeting him once, years ago, at one of the Royal Academy Summer Exhibitions. Such a nice man.'

'Yes, he was,' I agreed, thinking how much he would have loved the Giddings family and wishing he could have been there, too, though of course, if he hadn't died then I probably would never have ended up there myself. 'I have a portrait he painted of me and I'll show it to you when I've unpacked it. I paint a bit, but it's only for fun: the writing is more important to me.'

Nile gave an unsettling smile. 'Ah, yes, the writing . . . I assumed you'd be spending next weekend chained to that desk you just bought, knocking out a bestseller.' Then he told everyone about my novels and that he'd downloaded one on to his e-book reader and read the first couple of chapters. He didn't say what he thought of it.

'Oh, you told me you wrote, but I assumed it was a hobby!' Bel exclaimed. 'I didn't know you were a real, genuine novelist.'

Geeta, who had been quietly and efficiently spooning food into Casper's mouth, which opened and shut like that of a hungry baby bird, said she enjoyed a good love story.

'They're not really *love* stories as such,' I said. 'Well, not in the traditional sense, like Eleri Groves, for instance.'

'Oh, I adore her books,' Geeta agreed. 'She lives nearby, you know – over towards Upvale.'

'I did know and actually, her agent has taken me on,' I said. 'She emailed me today about my new book, which I've barely started, so Nile took me to the antiques barn to buy a proper desk I can work at. I got a couple of other pieces of furniture too, so when my bed arrives tomorrow morning I'll have everything I need to move in.'

'And then you can start work on your teashop,' Nile said. 'That and writing a book should keep you quiet for a while.'

'Not until she's had a nice rest over this weekend and recharged her batteries,' Sheila told him.

Bel, who had been abstractedly frowning and staring into space for the last few minutes, suddenly looked up and exclaimed: 'Eureka! All this talk about writing has made me remember why the name of that woman who was on the scene when you were found, Emily Rhymer, sounds so familiar!'

'What are you talking about, darling?' asked Sheila, puzzled, so then we had to explain about the newspaper searches we'd done and what we'd found out, though of course Nile already knew.

'Anyway,' finished Bel, 'I've just realized that Emily Rhymer is one of the daughters of Ranulf Rhymer, the biographer. There was a feature in a Sunday magazine about him ages ago – he called his children after the Brontës, so there's an Emily, Anne, Charlotte and Branwell.'

'I've heard of Ranulf Rhymer – but that's pretty odd,' I said. 'I don't think I'd want to call my children after such a doomed family, however brilliant they were.'

'I've read a few of his biographies and he's an odd kind of man,' Sheila said. 'His driving force seems to be to prove that all the great works of literature written by women were actually penned by their male relatives.'

'If the Rhymers are still living in Upvale, that should make finding Emily easy,' I said. 'As soon as I've got a little bit of free time, I'd like to talk to her and that farmer who rescued me.'

'Didn't you say he was one of the Godets?' asked Teddy. 'He should be easy to track down.'

'Are you sure about it?' Nile asked me. 'I don't suppose they can add anything to the newspaper reports.'

'I don't expect them to, but they were actually *there* – at the moment, they're the only links to my past I have.'

'That seems perfectly reasonable to me, Nile,' Sheila commented, then added, 'Did I hear you say you're off to London tomorrow?'

'Yes, early.'

'Then do give my love to Zelda.'

'That's Nile's partner,' explained Bel. 'She lives on a boat in Camden.'

'*Business* partner,' Nile amended, frowning down at his plate as if it had a disquieting message written across it in chocolate sauce.

I remembered the phone conversation I'd overheard and wondered if there was, or perhaps had been, more to it than that . . .

Not, of course, that it was any of my business.

*

Later, when Nile had gone and Bel and I were alone in the kitchen clearing up, she explained a bit more, some of which Nile had already told me.

'Nile and Zelda were at university together. She occasionally comes up to stay and we love having her, because she's fun, in a mad kind of way,' she added, and I felt a pang of jealousy, though if anyone was the cuckoo in the Giddings nest, it was me.

With suitable (as I thought) temporary live-in care arranged for Father, I returned to my home and informed my practice that in due course I would be leaving them. Of course, they were devastated to lose me, but I was fully aware that this was because of the increasing difficulty in finding doctors interested in becoming general practitioners, rather than on any personal level.

I began to wind up my affairs and put my house in the hands of the local estate agents. I was pleased to discover that it had increased in value to such an extent that I thought once it was sold, I might invest the proceeds in a property adjacent to one of the golf courses in Portugal I favoured. I could let it, until such time as I was able to retire there.

20

The Road Less Travelled

I think Nile must have left for London before dawn, for there was no sign of his car when I arrived at the café very early next morning.

Mind you, I was not quite as early as I'd intended to be, because I'd been scared witless by the huge, spectrally pale shape of a barn owl swooping low past my windscreen, returning late from a night's hunting. I hadn't realized before how *big* they were. I thought it was a ghost and had to pull in and wait for my heart rhythm to stabilize.

The bed and mattress were delivered soon after nine and when Bel came a little later to help with the last of the unpacking and curtain-hanging, I'd almost finished screwing the frame together. It was more complicated than it looked: I think there should be some sort of award for doing that kind of thing.

I hung Dad's small portrait of me in pride of place on the living-room wall and Bel admired it. 'It's a speaking likeness, though you must have been quite young when he painted it?'

'I was about fourteen. He painted a lot of pictures of me, but this is the only work of his I've got, apart from a few sketches. My adoptive mother sold the entire contents of his studio to an American collector soon after he died.'

'Harsh!' she said with sympathy.

'Nessa was like that, and she showed her true colours the moment Dad was gone.'

Seeing the memory still upset me, Bel quickly changed the subject, handing over the house-warming gifts she'd brought from the family to celebrate the first night I would spend in my flat. Sheila's was a ceramic cookie jar shaped like a sheep, full of iced biscuits; Geeta had sent a plastic box of spicy vegetable samosas; and Bel gave me a pair of her porcelain earrings shaped like pale fragments of fan coral, complete with minute sea creatures.

Since the post had already brought me a home-made wreath of dried leaves and flowers from Lola and her family, and a tea cosy from Edie, I was feeling very touched by everyone's kindness.

The wreath looked very *Country Living* when I'd hung it on the inside of the flat door, but I thought the light blue hand-knitted tea cosy with a pompom on top from Edie was a hat, until I put it on and realized that unless I'd grown a unicorn horn in the middle of my forehead, like Princess Beauty, I wouldn't need a hole there.

And then another scene dropped straight into my head and I got it down before it vanished like fairy dust.

'I'm afraid, dear Prince S'Hallow, that there's a teeny-tiny problem,' confessed the stepmother, when they were alone. 'Beauty was cursed in her cradle, which made her so spiteful to my own children that I had her imprisoned in an enchanted bower, where she must sleep for ever.'

'These things do happen,' he said, admiring his reflection in the mirror behind her and smoothing his butter-yellow hair. 'There's usually a solution.'

'Yes, the traditional kiss from a prince such as yourself should wake her up, though first you must follow her to another time and place. Of course, when you have set her free, you will be magically transported back here to the Once-upon-a-time and live happily ever after.'

My tapping at the keyboard slowed and then finally petered out altogether, like a slightly weary woodpecker.

I found I was staring directly across at the front windows of Small and Perfect, which were shuttered, dark and slightly mysterious . . . much as Nile's face often was when he looked at me . . . until he unleashed the ultimate weapon of that sudden and devastating smile.

He had to know the effect it had and was probably puzzled about why his charms weren't working on me the way they had on every other woman who'd ever crossed his path. Not that I was mad enough to think he was seriously interested in me: I was sure it was just an automatic reflex.

Slowly I became conscious of the sound of the Hoover zooming about downstairs and realized that it had been going on for some time: it was Friday and Tilda Capstick's day to clean.

I went down to say hello and Tilda said she'd called up the stairs and there had been no reply, so she'd just got on with it.

'But I packed all the white china into boxes and put it in the cupboard where the willow pattern was, first.'

'Oh, thank you,' I said. 'I meant to put it on one of the free recycling websites, because it isn't really worth selling, but I haven't got round to it yet.'

'It was cluttering up the place, but now it'll be out of the way till you do,' she said, then added slightly accusingly, 'Nothing much seems to have changed in the café yet?'

'No, but it soon will,' I assured her. 'I had to get the flat ready first. Come up and see it.'

'You've moved in, then?' she asked, following me upstairs.

'Not yet. I've been staying at a guesthouse on the moors – Nile Giddings' family home. I'll move in officially on Monday, though I will be here tonight because I've got to wait in for the cooker, washing machine and fridge to be delivered. I've got a four-till-ten time slot.'

'Eh, the world's gone mad, delivering orders in the middle of the night!' she exclaimed, then took a look round the flat and said approvingly, 'Well, this all looks grand now, doesn't it? So . . . are you still going ahead with the teashop, flower?'

'I certainly am,' I assured her and then asked if she and her aunt Nell would come for tea on Monday, when we could discuss it all.

As she turned to go she spotted Lola's gift hanging on the back of the door. 'Yon Christmas wreath's gone up a bit early.'

'It's not a Christmas one, just an all-year-round kind of decoration,' I explained.

'I wondered why there was no holly,' she said, then remarked

170

disparagingly that dried flowers were bad for collecting the dust and she herself wouldn't give them houseroom. I suspect she's not a reader of *Country Living* magazine.

My white goods arrived just after six, but the delivery man refused to take them up to the flat, instead leaving them in a forlorn row at the bottom of the stairs.

It would still have been early enough to go out to Oldstone Farm for the night, but I had something planned for next morning: Nile had drawn me a map showing the route over Blackdog Moor to the parking area near the Oldstone, and I intended setting out on my first visit there at a very unsociable hour, when I would be sure of having the place to myself.

In fact, dawn had only just begun to rim the blackberry sky with silvered steel as I took the by-now-familiar road up on to the moors, though this time I carried on past the turn to the house, where the Giddingses would probably all be fast asleep . . . unless baby Casper, who was teething, had woken his parents up early, or Sheila had been struck by inspiration and wandered down to her studio.

Thoughts of Casper, so wanted and beloved by the whole family, contrasted sharply with the baby that had been me, though somehow I didn't feel connected to that abandoned, sickly and malformed little thing. Perhaps I would, once I was up by the Oldstone.

I'd written Nile's instructions on a series of Post-it notes and stuck them along the dashboard. They started off clearly enough: 'Carry on along the main (!) road until you pass a sign on the right for Mr Rochester's Restaurant and the Hikers' Café'.

That was where Eleri Groves lived, having married her Mr Rochester. I hoped for her sake there were no madwomen in his attic, and also that he was not quite as irascible as the original.

The road dipped up and down, and the Oldstone on its rocky outcrop seemed to advance and retreat in a tantalizing dance. Then there was a level, straight bit of road and I spotted the sign on the right for the restaurant and paused briefly to peer up the track. Unfortunately, it took a bend and you couldn't see any sign of the house, apart from a hazy plume of wood smoke rising in the air.

On the sign it said the restaurant was open only in the evenings but the Hikers' Café proclaimed itself 'Now open all year!' though I wouldn't have thought many walkers would want to take advantage of that in autumn and winter.

I started off again, keeping my eyes peeled for a very narrow lane immediately before a crossroads, but I somehow missed it and had to turn in the car park of the Standing Stones Motel and go back.

I wasn't surprised I hadn't spotted it first time: stone walls bordered a thin ribbon of tarmac that meandered off in a series of twists and turns until eventually, just as it seemed to be deteriorating into a track with a grassy ridge growing up the middle and a hedge of blasted hawthorn guarding it like barbed wire, there was a gap and a weathered sign to the Oldstone.

When I turned in, it wasn't even a track, just twin grooves worn by the passage of many wheels through the turf. I bumped my way along this to where it ended in a half-circle of short turf and a couple of battered, lichen-spotted picnic tables, on one of which a large black crow was sitting, like the last diner reluctant to leave long after closing time.

It eyed me without hope, made a harsh and mocking noise and then flapped slowly and heavily off.

The wind was keen when I got out and the moors bleakly beautiful now that weak sunshine was gilding the picture. It didn't have any warmth in it, though: if anywhere else in the country was enjoying an Indian summer, it wasn't Blackdog Moor. The words 'blasted heath' were never more apt.

And if it was chilly *now*, what would it have been like right at the start of March, when I was found? You'd think only a Heathcliffian baby, an indestructible force of nature, would have survived such exposure, not the mewling little weak puny thing I'd been.

The finger of rock was now very near and stuck up like a rudely defiant gesture as I followed a well-trodden path that slowly ascended the ridge. It ended at a flattish plateau littered with the fallen remains of what had once been a small circle of stones around the natural monolith. One, flat and grooved, looked distinctly sacrificial . . .

My twisted-fairy-tale imagination stirred, but I shoved it firmly back into its box, for today it was time for a reality check.

The Oldstone had been carved with ancient cup-and-ball markings and, standing next to it, you could see for miles. The Giddingses' house was so far away it looked like a toy, but there was a farmhouse a lot nearer – perhaps even the one Joe Godet had come from.

It was the only other habitation I could spot, at any rate, and my all-too-fertile imagination offered me the image of a young woman in clogs and shawl trudging through the snow clutching her baby. Of course, that scenario was at least a century out of the right timescale – but which direction *would* my mother have come from? Was it along a path from some hidden, isolated cottage, along the road from Haworth, or from Upvale, the village in the valley below the motel? Or even, losing the clogs and shawl and transposing the image to the right century, from much further afield, if she'd driven, or been driven, here?

That last must surely have been how it was? It couldn't have been ideal weather for a night walk under any circumstances, let alone for someone who'd given birth within the last few hours . . .

Then I suddenly remembered that the newspaper had said that Emily Rhymer had actually walked to the Oldstone from Upvale in the dark pre-dawn morning, so perhaps they just bred a hardier race up here and it was quite possible my mother had walked here too.

I'd been numbing my bottom on a fallen monolith while turning all this over in my mind, recalling then that I hadn't been found at the top near the stones, but in one of the crevices beneath. I got up and made my way down sheep tracks to the tumbled rocks at the base of the stone outcrop. I had no idea into which hole I'd been pushed, but there were several likely candidates and I realized even more strongly how much of a miracle it was that I'd been found – and alive. Left there for long, I'd have been easy meat for any passing scavenger.

I shivered. Now I was on the spot, it really didn't help to speculate that my mother had been acting in a blind state of shock and panic. I mean, even thirty-six years ago having a baby out of wedlock wasn't such a cataclysmic event.

I suppose Dad could have been right about her being very young and perhaps in denial about the symptoms of pregnancy until the shock of my arrival – but then, if she was *that* young, mustn't she have had someone to drive her here? Or, if old enough to drive, not have been in a fit state to do so, for I can't have been more than a few hours old when they found me.

It was a puzzle and my thoughts were going round in unhelpful circles, so I began picking my way over fallen rocks towards the car.

I hadn't seen a living thing other than the crow, so when a sheep suddenly jumped up from under my feet and bounded away, bleating indignantly, I almost had a heart attack – and this was broad daylight!

So what must Joe Godet have felt when he spotted that white fleece and reached into the rocky crevice expecting to find a lamb, pulling out a barely alive baby, instead?

I hoped it hadn't been disappointment.

While I was still leisurely winding up my affairs in Scotland, convinced that Father would be well looked after until I could move back to the family home in Yorkshire, I received an anonymous letter. It informed me that Father's live-in carer was a designing hussy, who had him twisted round her little finger, and if I didn't watch out she'd marry him, or get him to leave her all his money, or both.

The anonymity of the sender was somewhat compromised by the address sticker on the back: it was Kim, our weekly cleaner.

21

Waffling

I hadn't got very far along the maze of narrow lanes that would eventually lead me back to the main road, when I met a small hatchback coming the other way. It was driven by a grey-haired woman of perhaps fifty, who simply stared coldly and impassively at me through the windscreen for what seemed like an hour, until I gave in and backed up to the nearest passing place, though I was certain she was a lot closer to one than I was.

A dog sat on the seat next to her, visible only as a small white head and a pair of bright dark eyes, so I thought she might be an early dog walker, though it seemed an oddly remote place to head for.

Unless, of course, she lived nearby? When I'd checked a map it had surprised me just how many buildings there were, dotted about the seemingly barren and empty countryside.

She swept by me without even a nod of thanks and I carried on my way. This time I didn't stop by the sign for the Hikers' Café and I wouldn't have been tempted to call for coffee and cake even if it had been open, in case Eleri Groves should just happen to be about. I mean, if she remembered me, it might seem a bit stalkerish, turning up on her doorstep. Or, if she knew about Senga taking me on, *pushy*, because I was just starting to make my way, while she was an established bestseller.

Instead, I headed like a homing pigeon to Oldstone Farm, where I thawed out over hot chocolate in the kitchen with Bel. It was quiet – Sheila was working in her pottery, while Geeta, Teddy and the baby had gone out.

'They do open the office at weekends if people book an appointment, but autumn is a slow time for ordering pools,' she explained. 'Anyway, it's Geeta's mother's birthday and there's a big family party, so they've gone to Bradford. Geeta was wearing her best sari and some of her gold wedding jewellery and she looked *stunning*.' She sighed. 'I wish that sort of thing suited me.'

'How did she and Teddy meet?' I asked.

'Teddy's best friend at university is her brother, and when Ted went to the house it was love at first sight. Her parents took a bit of winning round, but they adore Teddy now – and the baby.'

'I think I'm way too tall to carry off a sari,' I said, 'though I could probably get away with salwar kameez.'

'I'm only about an inch shorter than you,' Bel said. 'I take after Dad's side, the Giddingses were all tall.'

'You know, one of the nicest things about moving to Haworth is how many tall women there are – even Tilda, one of the Branwell Café staff, is almost my height.'

I'd told Bel yesterday that I meant to go and visit the Oldstone on my way here and now she said, 'So – what did you think of the Oldstone?'

I shivered, despite the warm kitchen and the mug of hot chocolate. 'It's bleak and deserted up there,' I said. 'And the question of where my birth mother came from is wide open, because I can see that while she might have been from a nearby cottage or farm, she could just as well have driven – or been driven – from almost anywhere else.'

'The police will have checked out all the houses within walking distance, so I think you can rule that one out,' Bel said. 'I mean, this Emily Rhymer may have walked up there from Upvale in the dark, but it's not something most women would contemplate.'

'No, and I'm looking forward to talking to her, in an odd kind of way, because she sounds eccentric, to say the least.'

Sheila came in just then, her moss-green corduroy trousers liberally besmirched with clay, followed by her shadow, Honey, and asked us what we were going to do today.

'Really, you should have a rest, Alice, before tackling the café renovations next week. Jack told me he was managing the whole thing for you between jobs for his regular clients and I think that's a really sensible idea.'

'I'd originally meant to do as much of it as I could myself to save money, but once I'd met Jack I realized that would be a false economy,' I agreed.

'We're having a busman's holiday today, Mum,' Bel said. 'We're going to measure up the coach house and work out the plans for our café so Teddy can draw them up. And I was just about to tell Alice that we've decided to go all Norwegian with the food!'

'Do you mean Norwegian cakes, like those delicious-sounding Bergen buns you mentioned?' I asked.

'No, we've scrapped the cake idea for something more unusual: we're going to serve Norwegian waffles with sour cream and black cherry jam.'

'Or *any* good home-made jam,' Sheila said. 'I like them with strawberry.'

'Are Norwegian waffles different?' I asked.

'They're floppy and you spread the cream and jam on one side, then fold it over to eat.'

'They sound delicious.'

'I must make you some,' Sheila promised. 'And I've come to the conclusion that it will be better to employ someone in the café than try to run it ourselves.'

'I think that's very sensible, and the catering facilities will be simple if you're going to need only a large waffle iron and tea- and coffee-making equipment.'

'It's going to cost a bit to turn the coach house into a café, but it's an investment to draw in the visitors,' Sheila said. 'A sprat to catch a mackerel.'

'I know. I keep going through *my* figures and trying to find ways of keeping the costs down that won't affect the quality of the teashop,' I said. 'But some things you just *can't* scrimp on.'

'So, you think a little Norwegian waffle house would be a draw?' asked Bel.

'A sign saying "Waffle House" would certainly make *me* turn off the road,' I assured her. 'It's your unique selling point, just as offering grown-up afternoon teas is mine.'

'Now I want waffles,' Bel sighed, 'and I've only just had a late breakfast.'

'I'll make some at lunchtime – I only came back for a cup of coffee really,' Sheila said, but when she'd made it she sat down again at the table. 'It will just be us three for dinner today, though I'm sure Nile will be back for his Sunday lunch tomorrow, come hell or high water!'

'He never misses one if he can help it,' Bel agreed, 'and he calls *me* greedy!'

'Nile said he'd told you about how he came to be part of our family,' Sheila said to me. 'I'm so glad, because normally he's very reserved about it.'

'He's normally reserved, full stop,' Bel said. 'Except with the family, of course.'

'I hadn't noticed that,' I told her. 'But then, I seem to rub him up the wrong way.'

'Oh, I think he likes you really,' Sheila assured me, though I expect that was more the result of her sunny optimistic nature than anything.

'I was very surprised when he told me he was adopted too. I suppose it gives us some common ground, though his experience was entirely different from mine, of course, because he knew his mother.'

'Yes, his early years were very traumatic, poor boy, and he saw some terrible things, though I'm sure that in her way his mother must have loved him.'

From what he'd said, it sounded to me as if she'd loved drink much more . . . which was just as tragic, in its way, as my being left in the middle of nowhere like a bit of discarded rubbish.

'My adoptive mother was cold towards me, but I had a wonderful, loving father. My best friend Lola's parents were great, too – really laid-back – and we had the run of their smallholding, with goats and hens and a donkey, so I suppose it was all a bit Enid Blyton.'

'And now you and Nile are forging your own careers and have turned into fine young people,' Sheila said.

'Not so very young,' I said wryly. 'I'm thirty-six!'

'Teddy and I are a couple of years younger than you, but Nile's thirty-eight, the poor old thing,' Bel said.

'Not so much of the old,' protested Sheila.

'Isn't Zelda about to hit the big four-oh, Mum?' asked Bel, then explained to me, 'Nile's partner spent a couple of gap years working her way round the world before she went to university.'

'You know, I think you're right,' Sheila said, looking struck. 'Time flies – and she's such a lovely girl that I'm surprised she hasn't settled down and had a family by now.'

'Oh?' I said, trying not to sound as curious as I felt, for Zelda was an unusual name so she had to be the one who had phoned him that time, and from my end, it hadn't sounded like just business. 'She and Nile aren't a couple?'

'I don't think they've ever really been anything other than friends,' Bel said. 'She's had a couple of long-term relationships, but they fizzled out.'

'Bel used to see a lot of her, because her ex-husband is a doctor at one of the London hospitals,' Sheila explained.

'I hated living in London,' Bel said. 'And in the end, I hated my husband, too! Once he became a consultant he seemed to expect everyone, including me, to obey his every word. And when I didn't, he would look at me as if I was a bad case of some nasty disease. And then having a fling with someone I thought was a friend was the finishing touch.'

'You were a bit of a mismatch from the start,' Sheila said. 'He was very handsome, though.'

'I think we both thought we were marrying different kinds of people,' she said. 'It didn't work out – and now I don't want to be married to anyone ever again. I'm going to live at Oldstone for ever and do my own thing.'

'I used to go out with a dentist years ago, when I lived in Cornwall,' I said.

'Really? Did he fix your teeth for free?' Bel asked interestedly.

'No, I was lucky and didn't need anything doing to them, because he was a rotten dentist. He was a lot more interested in his hobbies –surfing, white-water rafting, and hang-gliding – anything a bit dangerous.'

'At least he sounds *fun*.'

'He was, and I was very fond of him, but he emigrated to Australia eventually and I didn't want to go with him.'

'Do you still hear from him?' asked Sheila.

'Oh, yes, but usually when his latest girlfriend has dumped him and he's feeling lonely and sorry for himself. Then the next one comes along and he goes silent again. He's quite attractive in a big, boyish kind of way, though almost totally self-centred,' I added. 'I think he only gave me his old Beetle car because he forgot to sell it before he left.'

'Aren't they all,' Bel said gloomily.

'Then I moved to Scotland and got engaged to a climber – Dan Carmichael. You may have heard of him.'

'Of course – but wasn't he killed—' began Sheila and then stopped. 'I'm so sorry, Alice. You did say you'd had a recent bereavement.'

'It's about six months ago. Dan died in a freak climbing accident at the start of March,' I told them, and felt a sudden pang of guilt that I should have been attracted by Nile so soon. But then, the dark chasm of depression I'd fallen into after Dan died made it feel as if it had happened a lot longer ago. Now I only felt a poignant sadness when I thought of him.

'It was a shock,' I said, 'almost as much as finding out he was still married to his first wife just before the funeral.'

'Really?' Bel said, wide-eyed, so I told them all about Dan's dreadful wife, Tanya, coming out of the woodwork and grabbing everything with her pointed turquoise talons.

'But she couldn't grab Dan's insurance policies, because he'd named me as the beneficiary in them, and when they paid out I had enough to buy the café and flat. I *hoped* there'd be enough to live on if I was frugal, only now I can see it will all vanish into the renovations.'

'But it's an investment and I think it's going to be *great*!' enthused Sheila. 'We'll book a table for the very first sitting and all come!'

'That's kind of you and I hope you're right,' I said, and then she got up and headed back to her studio.

Bel and I collected clipboards and tape measures and soon followed her, to plan out the Norwegian waffle house. By the time we returned we'd got to the stage where we were bouncing silly promotional slogans off one another, like 'Jam yourself into our café for the waffle of the century!' and, my favourite, 'Waffle on in – Norwegians would!'

Next morning Teddy, Geeta and Bel went over to the Pondlife office to work on the waffle house plans, while I retired to the house's library with my laptop to contemplate the novel I was supposed to have almost finished by now.

I wasn't entirely sure where it was going and feared this horror fairy tale with a twist might well end up more twisted than most.

'There's something else you ought to know, too,' added the stepmother, and the prince looked pensive: it was all sounding very tiresome and he was by nature exceedingly lazy.

'The original curse, cast over Beauty's cradle, bestowed on her a beautiful face, but an evil nature,' her stepmother explained.

'A curse can be undone,' said Prince S'Hallow.

'Yes, but what if when you kiss her awake, breaking the enchantment, she has an evil face but a beautiful nature?' she asked.

The prince, who expected his bride to be the slenderest and fairest in the land, shuddered slightly.

'Then the deal would be off,' he said firmly.

True to Bel's prediction, Nile had set off from London so early next morning that his dark Mercedes estate came bumping down the track well before the palatial Sunday lunch of roast beef and Yorkshire pudding went on to the table.

He appeared to be in morose mood, but when I asked if the collector hadn't liked the pair of early Meissen shepherd and shepherdess figurines that had been the reason for the trip, he said that on the contrary, he'd been delighted.

Then he seemed to haul himself back from some deep thoughts with an effort and added, 'While I was down there, I asked around and one of my friends knows someone wanting to sell a job lot of café tables and chairs – all simple, good-quality white wood. I went and had a look and I've got some pictures and the dimensions on my phone.'

'That was very thoughtful of you, Nile.'

'Well, you needn't sound so amazed,' he said, then got out his phone, flicked to where they were and handed it across. 'They're solid, but they might want a fresh lick of paint.'

'That doesn't matter if they're the right size,' I said, scrutinizing the pictures. 'I wanted a mix of round tables and smaller rectangular ones, so if the measurements are OK, these look perfect!'

'I think I've found a home for your current Formica monstrosities, too,' he told me. 'Zelda knows a dealer who buys retro furniture, so if you like I can contact him and see if he'll make you an offer? It'll probably be peanuts, though.'

'Really?' I said, amazed. 'They're so vile I thought I'd have to pay someone to take them away!'

'Your tearoom is going to look very elegant,' Bel said, leaning over to look at the photographs. 'But our Norwegian waffle house will have a more homespun, country kitchen feel to it.'

'*Waffle house?*' repeated Nile.

Kim, the cleaner at Upvale, was a serious, silent and efficient woman with whom I had always been on perfectly good terms, so I was certain her warning was kindly meant.

And, once my eyes were opened to the possibility of Father's carer having designs on him, I recalled certain signs that she was right.

Father had recently ceased to press me to move home more quickly and, in fact, had only a day previously assured me that the current arrangements were very satisfactory and there was no rush.

Clearly, this was not so, and decisive and quick action was necessary. In the autumn of 2004, less than a fortnight after the warning letter, I was installed in Upvale, along with my rather elderly Bichon Frise, Drogo.

At my sudden advent, the chagrin of Father's carer, Patsy Dodds, was barely concealed, though she greeted me on the doorstep with the graciousness of a chatelaine welcoming an unexpected guest into her home.

I informed her in no uncertain terms that I required no assistance in finding my way about my own home and that she should return to the duties for which she was being handsomely paid.

Clearly, her pretensions were in sore need of a good squashing.

22

Slightly Listing

I'd meant to go back to the flat right after lunch, but time flew by while we were talking, so it was late by the time I set off home.

Home – that was a strangely permanent-sounding concept! And no one could take it away from me . . . or not unless the teashop bombed and I lost all my money. But I consoled myself with the idea that even if that happened, the premises would still be worth so much more than I'd paid for them, with a renovated and habitable flat and an updated café.

Oldstone Farm now felt like a second home too, one where I always seemed to be welcome.

Nile wasn't returning to Haworth until next morning, so when I parked behind the café everything was still, dark and deserted. And after I'd fallen over the recycling bins and then had to feel my way to the kitchen door, I vowed to get an outside light put in.

Inside the rear entrance hall, my fridge-freezer, oven and washing machine were still lined up at the bottom of the stairs – I'd entirely forgotten about them over the weekend. I'd have to try to hijack a strong man or two next day.

With Nile away and no other neighbours facing into Doorknocker's Row, the flat felt isolated, and yet, when I opened the front window a crack I could hear people talking on the main street beyond the end of the passageway.

It made me remember the many times in the past when, at the end of a long, hard day's work, I'd sat listening to distant voices in the street

185

below and the random yelps of seagulls, feeling content in my own little world.

I opened the laptop I'd laid down on my new desk and began spinning dreams, just as I always had: the baby princess left for the wolves in the forest, Heathcliff, the infant abandoned on the moor, Moses in the bulrushes and the child cursed at her christening by the evil fairy godmother . . .

Or, in the case of the current story, did the curse just work on what was already in Beauty? Thoughts swirled and sparks flew, until the shape of the next chapter began to form around Sleeping Beauty's dark heart.

Kev had walked along that street every day of his life – to school, to skive off school, to buy fags, to go to the pub with his mates and on his way to perform a spot of petty theft. He had no idea why he'd never noticed the overgrown plot full of trees, brambles and quickthorn before . . . or the domed roof of a small building rising above them.

It gleamed like dull gold in the orange streetlight, but it couldn't be gold. Maybe it was bronze, something like that. It would make his fortune in scrap value, that would . . .

There was no one about at this time of night; he was only on his own because he'd had a row with Shaz and left her in the pub. His house was two doors down and so he fetched a replica Samurai sword he'd nicked from a basement flat in a flash part of town, and began hacking his way in through the brambles.

Nile must have driven in early, because his car was already there when I set out next morning to buy paint for the café and kitchens. It was the same colour scheme as the flat, of course, just gallons more of it: that horrible mushroom paint everywhere would take some covering.

I wasn't out long, but Nile's car had vanished when I returned, though whether off on a trip, or hotfooting back to his London partner or . . . well, who knows what other interests he might have?

Or maybe he'd already gone to the café to speak to me about something, spotted the white goods at the bottom of the stairs and escaped before I could ask him to help me get them upstairs.

But no matter, because Jack the handyman, aided by a bashfully silent teenage assistant called Ross, did it later. Then he spread out a collection of new kitchen worktop samples, so I could choose what I wanted. Everything would be fresh, hard-wearing and easy to clean, and the kitchen table would be relegated to the back room so I could have a central island with cupboards instead.

After that, I went upstairs and left them to it. Jack had his keys and we'd agreed what needed doing, and in which order it should be done, so in theory my input from now on would be confined to a bit of painting and choosing fitments and fittings.

Just as well, because I still had to source equipment and find catering suppliers. I had a whole list of other things to do, too, including going through some of the official guidelines on taking over a catering business, which I'd downloaded from the internet.

Until Dan's death I'd been getting a salary from my work in the café but since then, my only income had been a small amount of royalties from the e-books and a modest advance from my publisher. Now I'd be the sole owner of a tearoom, with staff to pay, and I'd need to put a bit of the insurance money aside as a contingency fund for unexpected expenses and to tide us over until the business got going.

I started yet another list: 'accounts book, record books, whiteboards and pens, envelopes, files'. Thank goodness Mrs Muswell hadn't considered taking the heavy filing cabinet! 'Hanging files', I added. 'Filing trays' . . .

By then the day was slipping away and there was no point in starting painting anything before Nell and Tilda came for tea, so I spread my cookbooks across the gate-leg table and began thinking about what to have on the menu: the fun, easy part of setting up a tearoom.

I was lost in pastry heaven when Jack called up the stairs to say my visitors had arrived and Nell and Tilda clumped their way up.

'You were right, our Tilda: there *is* a wreath of dead flowers on t' door,' I heard Nell say as I got up to greet them.

I knew from the YouTube video that Nell was a skinnier, flatter-chested version of her tall, raw-boned niece. She was elderly, but it was hard to tell *how* old, for there was no question of a stoop and though her hair was grey it was thick, shiny and cut off at chin length. Parted in the middle, it was held back with butterfly-shaped slides at each temple.

Her eyes were a sharp periwinkle blue and her rather splendid nose was attempting to meet her chin and would probably one day succeed.

'Hello, come in – I'm glad you could make it,' I greeted them.

'Eh, you're a grand, strapping lass,' Nell said, eyeing me approvingly. 'Our Tilda said you were born round here too, though you talked a bit plummy, so there's good blood in you.'

'That's right,' I said, 'though we lived in Knaresborough till I was eight.'

'Well, there's nowt much wrong with Knaresborough, I suppose,' she conceded magnanimously.

'Sit down and I'll make the tea,' I said, pushing the books and notes aside. 'Or coffee?'

'Tea – and I'll wet it, I'll make a better job of it,' Tilda said, suiting the action to the words.

I took the lid off the sheep biscuit barrel, which Nell admired greatly, and offered her an iced biscuit.

'So,' she said, scrutinizing one closely before taking a bite, 'our Tilda said you were going to reopen t' place as a fancy teashop and you'd want us both to work here all t' year round.'

'Yes, you'd both have permanent jobs if you wanted them, though not full time.'

'Our Daisy could help out too, when she's not at college,' Tilda said, putting the pot with its knitted blue bobbled cosy on to the table and sitting down opposite. I'd brought up one of the two rickety kitchen chairs for me to sit on (the other was in the office) leaving the two decent wheel-backs for my guests.

'I hope to open by the start of November at the latest,' I said. 'I think that's realistic, because there's a lot to do and I want everything just right. And as much publicity as possible, too.'

'That gives you well over a month, plenty of time,' Tilda said, so I don't think she'd really grasped all that had to be done.

'My idea is that we open five afternoons a week, Tuesday to Saturday. What do you think?'

'Sounds good to me, if we get Sunday and Monday off . . . and you said we'd just open in the afternoons?' asked Nell.

'Yes, the first afternoon tea sitting would be at two, then the second at four, so people could have a leisurely experience. If any of the tables weren't reserved, then they could be given to casual customers coming in – we could have something on the sign outside like "Table reservations not always necessary."'

'You're not going to have a high turnover of customers doing that,' Nell said.

'No, our Nell, but they'll be paying a lot more for the privilege of sitting there stuffing their faces for as long as they like,' pointed out Tilda.

'Yes, it will be quite pricey, but the food, tea and coffee will be unlimited – we'll just keep it coming till they've had enough. And we'll only stock good-quality, traditional cold drinks, with natural ingredients. I might make lemonade myself in the summer.'

'I'm not faffing around with one of them fancy coffee machines what take an hour to make a cup of froth with a pattern on it,' Nell declared pugnaciously.

'You won't need to, because we're going the more traditional route. Coffee shops are two a penny now,' I agreed. 'We'll offer pots of proper Yorkshire tea and a range of speciality teas and herbal teabags. The coffee will be in individual cafetieres – I hate coffee that's been made and left sitting to stew on a hotplate.'

'As well as milk, you'll need lemons: some of them take their tea weak as cat's pee, with a slice of fruit in it,' Nell said.

'Yes, we'll have lemons sliced ready and jugs of extra hot water.' I made a note about that. 'I'll bake early every morning, but I'll need someone to cut sandwiches, set the tables and generally get ready to open.'

'I can do that and Nell can come in later,' said Tilda. 'And if I don't have to cook, then I'll be manning the tea and coffee counter after that and taking the money, as well as helping Nell wait on, I suppose?'

'That's right, though you might have to cut more sandwiches if we start to run out. You can give the customers their bills at the tables and they can pay at the counter.'

'I like waiting on best,' Nell said. 'I like to get them fed and watered, especially them poor devils of tourists what get off the coach more dead than alive, with only a couple of hours to see everything in.'

'I think most of our customers will be staying a bit longer than that,' I suggested. 'I'll leave leaflets at all the guesthouses and hotels.'

'Aye, and locals with more money than sense will come in, too. There are enough of those,' Tilda said. 'You won't have to hurry the customers out, though, our Nell. They'll be paying to sit there as long as they like, stuffing their faces and demanding more.'

'And complaining, most like,' Nell said dourly.

'I've been getting ideas about what to offer on the cake stands,' I said. 'I'm thinking of tiny dainty versions of classic cakes and pastries – but we'll be advertising it as a proper Yorkshire high tea, so I need some particularly local specialities. There'll be miniature fat rascals, of course, but if you think of anything else, let me know.'

'My mother always had a good big seed cake on t' table of a Sunday,' Nell said.

'Caraway seeds?' I asked, and she nodded.

'I'm going to have two large cakes on the counter every day, as well as the little ones on the stands, so the customers can choose a slice of those if they want to. Seed cake would be perfect.'

'There's going to be a generous lot of food,' Tilda said, not altogether approvingly.

'I'm still working out the options, but I think the classic tea will be finger sandwiches, scones or fat rascals, and cakes. There'll be a savoury option, too, with things like tiny cheese tartlets.'

'Our Graham has a couple of pigs, if there's going to be lots of crusts and such left over,' Nell said.

'Unofficially, you can take any leftovers you like,' I said. 'But food waste must be disposed of properly each day.'

'I'll just take the bread and he'll pay you back with a bit of bacon or such later,' she offered.

'What'll you have on the sandwiches?' asked Tilda practically, stirring the inky brew remaining inside the teapot and then putting the lid back.

If there was a dormouse at this Mad Hatter's party, it was probably tanned darkest brown by now, and there were certainly two mad queens, neither of them me.

'Roast beef and a hint of horseradish sauce, egg mayonnaise with cress, cream cheese and smoked salmon . . .' I listed.

'What about them vegetarians?' asked Nell, as if they were an entirely different species.

'Home-made vegetable pâté, cucumber, cheese and tomato, avocado . . . I'll look up a few recipes for interesting fillings,' I said. 'I might add a gluten free version later, but I thought we'd start out simple at first. I mean, we're a small teashop and if we had only one customer for a gluten free tea in a day, we'd be wasting a lot of food.'

'Gluten free!' Nell said scathingly. 'They'll all be thinking their systems can't take a bit of fresh air soon, and buying it in cans from the supermarket.'

She was probably right, but some people really *couldn't* digest gluten, so I'd have to work on that one later.

'So, it's all going to be cold food?' Tilda said.

'Unless anyone wants their cheese scone warming,' I agreed.

'What about kiddies? Mrs Muswell wouldn't have highchairs, because she didn't want to encourage people to bring small children in. Said they were more trouble than they were worth,' Tilda said.

'I shouldn't think many people would want to bring small children for a lush and expensive afternoon tea, but we'd better have a couple of highchairs just in case. But baby buggies will have to be left outside, because there simply isn't going to be enough room and it would block the exits in an emergency.'

'No, you can't have them in the way,' Tilda agreed.

'Disabled access will be difficult too, because of the nature of the old building. I thought I'd have a ramp over the one step down into the café, but I can't do anything about the steps down to the toilet other than put in good handrails.'

'You can only do your best with what you have,' Tilda said. 'I can see you're putting a lot of thought as well as good brass into making this work.'

'There's just one thing . . .' I said slowly, wondering quite how to phrase what I wanted tactfully. 'From a customer service point of view . . .'

'You want us to be nicer t' customers, however daft they are?' Nell asked, then looked accusingly at Tilda. '*You* said she didn't mind a bit of plain speaking.'

'No, I don't,' I said quickly. 'That's just it: I don't want you to change how you deal with the customers at all. In fact, you have such a reputation on YouTube for *plain speaking* that I'd like to advertise the teashop as having the rudest waitresses in Yorkshire – if you don't mind,' I finished in a rush.

'Well, I'll go t' foot of ower stairs!' Nell said, staring at me, though luckily she seemed amused rather than insulted.

And after that, we had more cups of treacle and got down to discussing the mundane behind-the-scenes nitty-gritty of running a café, most of which Tilda already had at her fingertips: I could see she was going to be a major asset.

When they'd gone and I'd shut the café door behind them, I began stacking the horrible tubular metal tables and chairs out of the way and putting down dustsheets.

I hated painting ceilings, so I decided I might as well get it over with right there and then, using the long-handled roller. I put on one of the mobcaps first, though, tucking my hair up into it. They might be hideously unbecoming, but they're surprisingly useful.

'"*O Sole Mio*"!' Jack sang in a pleasant light tenor from the basement, his Italian tinged with Yorkshire.

It had proved to be a surprisingly productive day.

Of course, it was as I thought and Father had simply been feeling lonely. Once he had someone of equal intellect to talk to, his carer found her nose put right out of joint.

I was considering how best to dispense with her services, when fortunately I discovered that several small but quite valuable items had gone missing from my mother's room. Patsy Dodds left precipitately and under a cloud.

I gave our weekly cleaning lady a bonus and a healthy pay rise.

23

Dragooned

I'd barely finished rolling the first coat of paint on to the ceiling when the phone in the office rang so loudly that I nearly fell over. I must have accidentally turned the volume up to maximum.

When I dashed through and picked the receiver up, all I could hear at first was someone softly singing, 'Will ye no come back again?' to the accompaniment of impatiently drumming fingertips. I guessed who it was – the energy was crackling down the line.

'Senga?'

'There you are!' my agent said, as if she'd found me by divination with rods. 'I knew you were around, though your mobile kept going to answer.'

'It's in my bag . . . up in the flat,' I explained. 'I'm in the café.'

'Café?'

'Yes, my flat's over a café and—'

'Handy,' she said, without letting me explain that I'd bought it with the flat. 'Now, as I said, I'll be heading up north for Eleri's book launch and annual Mr Rochester's afternoon tea this Saturday, the 20th.'

'Yes . . .' I agreed.

'So if you arrive there early, we can have a little chat. And your edits have apparently been delayed, but they'll be emailed to you within the next couple of days, so we can discuss any little points that might have come up.'

'But I'm not going to the book launch,' I said quickly. 'I mean, I did tell you I hadn't got a ticket and I'm sure it's been booked up for months – probably since right after the last one!'

'Oh, don't worry your wee head about that. I told Eleri I was sure she could squeeze one more in, especially since this year they're using the restaurant rather than the tearoom. Or *two* more, if you know a dishy man. There simply weren't enough of them last time and all the Heathcliffs except Eleri's husband were dismal. Do you know one?'

'I-I suppose I do,' I stammered, thrown off balance. 'My neighbour . . . though I'm not sure he'd want to come to a—'

'Great, I'll tell Eleri. And don't worry too much about the costume – anything vaguely Victorian will do.'

'*Costume?*'

'Everyone dresses up as a Brontë or a character from one of their novels.'

That put paid to the idea of my even mentioning to Nile the possibility of his going with me, though actually, I don't think I'd have dared anyway.

'But I haven't got time to get a costume by Saturday,' I began. 'I mean, it's Monday now and I'm terribly busy, so I really don't think—'

'I'll see you there, then – and I look forward to meeting your new bloke,' she said. 'Quick work!'

Before I could refute the idea that I'd pounced on the nearest unattached male the moment I arrived in Haworth, she'd gone. The line crackled for a moment, probably from Senga's excess energy, and then went dead.

'Gawd!' said Prince Kev, staring at her in amazement. 'How did you get in here, then? Is there an easier way round the back?'

'I'm Beauty and I was brought here from the Once-upon-a-time. I've been waiting for you to come and set me free, silly,' she told him, and he frowned as if she'd said something difficult to understand.

He was quite handsome in a darkly glowering kind of way, though dressed very strangely for a prince . . .

'If you kiss me, we'll be back home in a trice,' she said impatiently. 'What are you waiting for?'

I didn't see how I could get out of going to the book launch event, but I was quite determined I wasn't going to ask Nile to go with me!

I decided I'd be Emily, the tallest of the Brontës, though height was about the only physical characteristic we had in common. Apparently she was about half the width of a taper, an interestingly gruesome bit of information I learned from a book about the Brontës, because the coffin maker said it was far and away the narrowest adult one he'd had to supply.

I was very tall but not thin, which made finding a Victorian dress to fit me at a couple of days' notice almost impossible. My queries via the internet drew a blank that evening, so next morning, after slapping a second coat of paint on to the café ceiling, I began ringing round local fancy-dress shops.

This didn't meet with any success either (though I could have had any amount of naughty nurse outfits), but help was to come from the most unexpected direction. Tilda called in with Nell's seed cake recipe and when I told her my problem, she said she had the perfect thing.

'We all had to dress up one year for the Women's Institute Victorian Extravaganza – load of nonsense it was, really. Anyway, being tall like you, there was no way anything to hire would be long enough, so Nell ran me up a dress in sprigged muslin.'

I looked at her doubtfully: it sounded a whole unlikely Kate Greenaway step too far. 'Sprigged muslin?'

'Cream background and dusky pink and green pattern,' she said. 'I got her to make it loose fitting, so it was easy on and off, and the white petticoat's sewn in. Leg-o'-mutton sleeves.'

'It sounds . . . perfect,' I said weakly. 'And Nell made it?'

'Yes, she was a dressmaker back in the day, so she can alter it, too, if you like,' she said. 'I'll send her round with it shortly.'

'But surely you don't want to lend out your lovely dress,' I began. I mean, I was getting desperate but I didn't think I was a sprigged muslin kind of person.

'Why not? It's only hanging in the wardrobe, neither use nor ornament. In fact, you can keep it. Perhaps you'll be going to this grand do every year and get some use out of it.'

I gave in. Where else was I going to get anything else in time? And when, only half an hour later, Nell brought it round and unzipped the plastic cover, I was glad I had, because it was beautiful. It was plain and unfussy, and she'd made it all in one piece, with a long, long row of hooks and eyes up the back of the bodice.

Bel was there by then, intending to help me paint for an hour or two, so I told her about the invitation and we all went up to the flat so I could try the dress on without an interested audience – Jack and Ross were taking down the plate rack and china display shelves that ran right round the walls of the café, so the orange varnish could be sanded down and painted over.

I got in the dress and Nell hooked me up, then nipped in the waist, her mouth bristling with dressmaking pins.

'There,' she said finally. 'I'll bring it back tomorrow all finished and there's another inch or two to be got out of the hem – you're a bit taller than our Tilda.'

'It's very kind of you,' I said gratefully.

'It's nowt. I like to keep my hand in.'

'You'll be the belle of the ball,' Bel said when she'd gone and we'd resumed the café painting. The walls were going to be buttermilk below the plate racks (when they were back in place) and white above, like the ceiling.

'It's not a ball, just a book launch,' I pointed out.

'It'll be fun, though. I wish I was going with you!'

'You could, if you dressed up as Heathcliff, because Senga told me to bring one with me,' I joked. 'Any man, in fact, though she'd prefer it to be a handsome one.'

Bel looked at me. 'I think I'd rather wait and go next year, in full crinoline, but you could ask Nile. I mean, you can't say he isn't handsome.'

'There's *no way* I'm asking Nile to go with me. He might think I was inviting him out on a date,' I said firmly.

Bel's big blue eyes slanted a sideways look at me. 'Would that be such a bad thing? It wouldn't be the first time a girl had asked him out.'

'Exactly! I'm not going to do anything to make him think I've added myself to the drooling throng of his admirers. Even the postwoman knocks at his door, so she can hand him his letters personally, instead of shoving them through the letter box,' I said, and she giggled.

'Oh, well, as they say, treat him mean and keep him keen.'

'He's just as mean back and neither of us is keen,' I told her firmly.

Bel must have told Sheila all about the book launch as soon as she got home, because she rang later.

'The dress sounds lovely, darling – what fun! And I've been up in the attic and found you a warm paisley shawl to go over it, because you don't want to freeze between the car and the restaurant.'

'That's very kind of you,' I said gratefully.

'What about shoes?'

'I've got some silver ballerina flats that will do.'

'They sound perfect – and of course you must spend Friday night with us, so I can put your hair in rags to make proper ringlets for the party.'

'It mostly *is* in ringlets already,' I protested, but she insisted.

Then she totally distracted me by adding, 'Bel said your agent wants you to take Nile with you.'

'Not Nile particularly, she just suggested I take a man, because there weren't very many last time, but I'm sure dressing up and going to a book launch isn't his idea of a good time.'

'Well, it is now. I've just rung him and told him so. He needs to widen his horizons and get out more.'

'He seems to be always out!'

'Yes, but the wrong kind of out,' she said obscurely. 'He can wear a pair of Paul's old riding breeches and black leather boots, so a loose white shirt open at the neck and perhaps a dark cloak and he'll make a very dashing Heathcliff, don't you think?'

I thought he'd be more than a tad too elegant and handsome for Heathcliff. But he'd certainly meet the bill where Senga and the others were concerned, especially if, as I suspected, he'd been dragooned into it and would be in a deep and glowering sulk throughout the proceedings.

I had no idea where Sheila was going to lay her hands on a cloak . . .

When I checked my emails next morning, there were the edits Senga had told me to expect, with a covering letter from my editor, ten pages of notes and the manuscript itself attached, covered in coloured highlighting.

It proved quite a challenge because although they were mostly little queries, there were a couple of suggested changes right near the start of the book that I could see would be like the chaos theory in action: a butterfly would flap its wings and then the whole damned plot would unravel faster than knitting.

I emailed Senga urgently and got a terse reply telling me to do my best and she'd discuss the rest with me on Saturday. Which was all very well, but after waiting weeks for the edits to appear, the editor wanted them back by Monday.

I suspected this was how it was always going to be now.

Nile had returned from wherever he'd been, because later when I'd popped out to buy fish and chips, he accepted a parcel delivery for me and brought it over as soon as I got back. Maybe he could smell the chips from Small and Perfect?

'It's sample linen-look easy-care napkins, I think. Come up to the flat and I'll share my fish and chips and make some coffee,' I suggested, hoping to soften him up in case he was intending to complain about the book launch. 'They give you huge portions.'

'An offer I can't resist,' he said, following me up the stairs. 'And I deserve it, seeing Sheila's ordered me to take you to a fancy-dress party on Saturday,' he added, but he seemed gloomily resigned to the event, rather than cross, which was a relief.

I only hope he didn't think I'd angled for him to take me.

Father had already had a suite of rooms converted for himself on the ground floor, so once I had arranged for an efficient team of carers to come in from a good agency, he was entirely comfortable.

I subscribed to Sky Sports, so he could watch golf to his heart's content, and made sure those of his old cronies he was still on speaking terms with knew they were always welcome to visit for tea.

Father also quickly became attached to my dog, Drogo, who provided an interest and diversion. He had never before shown any interest in pets, so this was a surprise to me.

24

Edited Out

By Friday the café looked completely chaotic, with not only Jack and his assistant ripping things out, but an electrician gouging holes and channels in the plaster and a plumber consigning the cracked and chipped tiles, toilets and hand basins into the skip we'd managed to squeeze on to the parking area at the back, next to the cars. It was as if the place had been besieged by an army of large and destructive termites.

There was a constant cloud of dust, and grit underfoot, and when Tilda came round, she threw up her hands at the state of it and cleaned my flat instead. But she said she was looking forward to the day when she could give downstairs a good going over again. I didn't think I'd ever met anyone before who actually *enjoyed* cleaning.

Even outside the café, things had begun to change, for the sign had been taken away for repainting, the remains of the plant tubs removed and the rotten bits of the Victorian trellis-sided porch replaced.

Aided off and on by Bel and Nile, I'd finished painting the café walls and woodwork, too – and all the horrible tables and chairs had been sold to Nile's contact and removed in a box van. I only got twenty pounds for the lot, but it looked *so* much better without them.

Apart from painting the tiny office, there wasn't much more I could do until the professionals had finished their bit (although I was constantly called down for an opinion, information, or simply to admire some piece of work), so I retired to the flat to list all the things I wanted to ask Senga about next day . . . and then after that, by way of light relief, I wrote another scene of the new book.

'What's all this, then?' said a commanding voice, and a man in dark blue livery stepped into the room. 'Breaking and entering again, Kev?'

'I never broke nothing, Officer,' said Kev virtuously. 'This lady invited me in – didn't you, love?'

'In a way,' Beauty agreed, thrilled that already Prince Kev had called her his love.

Then the man in blue said, sounding puzzled, 'What beats me is why I didn't ever notice this place before? It doesn't seem right to me.'

'It's because it was enchanted, but something must have gone wrong with the spell, because I woke up before Kev kissed me,' Beauty told him.

'Am I dreaming this?' The man frowned.

'Not unless we're both having the same dream,' said Kev.

'Right . . .' said the man. Then his attention was caught by a sudden rattling noise from the next room and he added, suspiciously, 'What's through there, then?'

He flung open the door even as Beauty and the mouse both yelled together: 'Don't go in there!'

I got to Oldstone in time for dinner as Sheila had suggested, wishing I didn't have to go to the book launch party next day. I could have done with a restful weekend.

I certainly didn't get a lot of rest that night, once Sheila and Geeta had tightly bound up my hair in long strips of cotton ripped from an old pillowcase, because the only way to describe how my head felt was knobbly.

I was forbidden to remove the rags until after breakfast next day, too, so I was glad Nile wasn't coming over until later in the morning.

It was a huge relief when Bel and Sheila finally unwound them and then coaxed my hair into side ringlets, with more cascading at the back from a high topknot. Then they helped me into my dress, which was now a perfect fit.

Sheila had found me a green velvet reticule to go with the outfit, as well as the shawl she'd mentioned, which was a huge and fringed affair made from fine paisley-patterned cashmere.

'I feel a complete prat,' I said ungratefully, when they'd finished and we'd adjourned to the kitchen.

'But you look lovely,' Teddy said, coming in in search of tea and cake. 'Doesn't she, Nile?' he asked, and it was only then that I saw Nile had followed him in.

I think my jaw probably dropped a mile: imagine Johnny Depp in pirate mode, channelling Heathcliff, add a bit of dark and brooding edge, and you'd get a fair idea of how he looked.

'She certainly looks exactly like a Pre-Raphaelite muse,' he said, one eyebrow going up even more piratically.

'You're very swashbuckling, darling,' said Sheila admiringly.

'Actually, I think these tight breeches have buckled my swash permanently,' he said gloomily.

'There's lots of give in the fabric and they're supposed to be snug,' she assured him. 'Now, don't forget to put your cloak on, because the wind's cold out there and that shirt is very thin.'

'Where did she get the cloak from?' I asked, as we went out to Nile's car and the billowing folds of it threatened to envelop me like a heavy cloud.

'A friend who runs an amateur theatrical group.'

He was silent after that until we arrived at the venue. There were already two or three cars there, but they must have belonged to the family or staff, for there were no guests in the restaurant, which was a former barn in a courtyard, set at right angles to the closed Hikers' Café.

Inside, the dining area was a long space with a modern décor that still subtly fitted in with its rustic heritage. A middle-aged woman in an overall came through a swinging door with a stack of teaplates, put them down on the nearest table, and went out without a word or even glance at us. There was certainly no sign of Eleri or her Mr Rochester, though there was some interesting crashing and swearing coming from what I presumed to be the kitchen.

'Are you sure you got the right time?' asked Nile, just as I was starting to ask myself the same question. But then I spotted Senga, half-hidden by an antique wooden butter churn.

'There's my agent over there,' I whispered, as she waved what looked suspiciously like a gin and tonic at me, though at that time of day it was probably just lemonade. I'd have recognized her instantly anywhere, even though the afternoon tea had been years ago.

The recognition wasn't entirely mutual, for she got up and looked me over with piercing, light blue eyes. 'Alice?' she queried doubtfully, then answered herself: 'Yes – it has to be, because I remember your hair – we must get some publicity shots of you like that, you look *maaarvellous*!' She kissed me on both cheeks.

'But I don't usually wear my hair in ringlets . . .' I began, then noticed that I'd lost her attention: her eyes were on Nile and had widened appreciatively. She smiled, revealing a lot of teeth like a crocodile about to snap him up.

'And who is this hunk?' she said. 'Heathcliff, I presume?'

'Nile Giddings, a *friend*,' I said, with some emphasis. 'We both had to find costumes at short notice, so I'm not sure who we're meant to be.'

'Whoever it is, you look wonderful,' she said, and then you could see her business mind flip over. 'Do sit down, Alice. We need to talk before everyone else arrives.'

'I'll go for a walk and leave you to it,' suggested Nile.

'No – stay if you want to, because I don't mind you being here,' I said. 'It's too cold to go walking in that thin shirt.'

He'd discarded the cloak the moment we got in, presumably because it kept getting wrapped around things, like flypaper.

'There we are then, sit down,' said Senga, and then, shifting her focus, grilled me at length about the next novel, so it was just as well I'd finally got my ideas together.

'That sounds fine,' she said eventually. 'It needs to be *exactly* like the first backlist book they're republishing, only *totally* different. Crack on and get it finished.'

'I've been a bit distracted, because I'm opening a teashop soon and it's being renovated.'

'You haven't got time to be distracted. Delegate, dear, delegate!'

'I am, as much as I can,' I assured her.

'Yes, I've done more painting than she has,' Nile broke his silence to remark, and I shot him a quelling look.

'Can I ask you about those edits?' I said to her. 'I've done my best with them, but there are just a couple of things . . .'

I'd jotted down the two awkward ones, including the chaos theory one, which she told me to tweak slightly and then leave.

'And ignore the other one entirely, because you can't possibly change the sex of one of the main characters. It would totally throw out the motivation in the whole book,' she said, demonstrating that she'd actually read it. I was writing such different material from Eleri and her other authors that I'd been surprised when she took me on.

'Won't my editor mind?' I asked.

'Not if she's got any sense: I'll back you if they query it again.'

'Oh, thank you,' I said gratefully. 'They want it back on Monday and there was no way I could rewrite the whole novel by then, even if I'd wanted to, which I didn't. I mean, it's already been published as an e-book and no one had any problem with that aspect of it.'

'Quite,' she said, and then, business obviously completed, turned her attention back to Nile. She flirted with him outrageously until Eleri came out of the kitchens looking flushed, pretty and extremely pregnant, in a long, flowing, high-waisted dress.

'Alice, how wonderful to see you again!' she said, coming over and kissing me, as Senga had. I remembered all this kissing from London – they're all at it down there.

'I'm so pleased you've got a publishing contract and are with Senga,' she said, which was generous of her. I mean, last time we'd met I'd merely attended the tea as her adoring fan, so my suddenly popping back up in author mode had probably been quite a surprise.

'I can hardly believe it myself,' I said. 'But congratulations on your new book . . . and I see I should congratulate you on your future new arrival, too.'

'Yes, I've a first edition on its way,' she said, and Senga, predictably, remarked that she hoped she'd finish her new book before its arrival. She was clearly a slave driver.

Eleri called Henry, her husband, out to meet us – and he cut a dark and romantic figure in riding clothes similar to Nile's outfit and with much the same gloomy expression. He was thicker-set than Nile and rugged rather than handsome.

'Good to meet you,' he said, shaking hands and allowing a brief and very attractive smile to make an appearance.

He shook hands with Nile, too, and the two of them seemed to recognize in each other kindred spirits. 'See they've got you to wear fancy dress, as well,' Henry said.

'I can't wait to get out of it,' Nile agreed, and Senga looked as if she'd like to help him . . . or even both of them.

There was the faint sound of car doors slamming, footsteps scrunching on the gravel and excited voices.

'Here come the guests,' Eleri said.

'You go and sit down, darling, ready to sign books,' her husband suggested. 'I'll welcome them in and then give Martha a hand to bring out the refreshments.'

Eleri obeyed orders, heading for a table laden with copies of her new book – I think she was glad to sit down. But before she went, she invited me to come and have tea with her one day before the baby arrived.

'We'll have time for a proper talk then,' she said, and I told her I'd love to.

The room quickly filled up and began to buzz like a shaken hive of hornets, and the book launch went with a swing. There was a brief speech from Senga, the reading of the first chapter of the new novel by Eleri, and then a scrummy buffet tea of sandwiches, cakes and savouries that were along the lines of the food I intended serving in the teashop, only mine would be daintier. There was a toast in champagne, too, one of my many weaknesses, so I was glad Nile was driving.

Goody bags were distributed to everyone, containing fans, heart-shaped chocolates and a postcard bearing the facsimile of the Brontë sisters' portrait painted by Branwell.

Everyone mingled over tea and I talked to people from all over the world: Eleri had millions of fans, and the Brontës, of course, even more. In fact, I'd just met someone involved with the Brontë Parsonage Museum and was telling them about my plan to open a premier tearoom in Haworth, when Henry happened to overhear and said he hoped I wasn't stealing his ideas, so I could set myself up to be competition!

But then I decided he must be joking, in a straight-faced way, and Nile, who was standing next to me, said a teashop in Haworth was too far away to be competition anyway. Then he added that he'd heard how wonderful Henry's restaurant was and he must bring me to try it one evening.

'We're open all year in the evenings – and so is the café now, every afternoon between two and five,' Henry said. 'Since Eleri found that diary mentioning Charlotte Brontë and we put it on display, we get a lot more visitors out of season.' He indicated an illuminated glass display box on the back wall. 'There's a facsimile in the tearoom, but this one's the real thing.'

I left him talking to Nile and went to look at the journal, where I met two American sisters bent on the same errand. They'd both come as Cathy and had been at the initial tea party the year before.

'It was a smaller party in the café, and things got very exciting when it was breaking up, because there was a tractor accident right outside and Henry was a real, genuine hero,' said one of them. 'He was so brave, wasn't he, Eleri?' she said, appealing to her as she finally abandoned her book-depleted station and began to circulate among the guests. 'And you were too.'

'Oh, I didn't do anything much,' Eleri said modestly. 'My husband's cousin George managed to roll his tractor into the ditch while trying to turn it,' Eleri explained to me. 'Henry got right under it to help him until the emergency services arrived.'

'Yes, I'm a genuine hero,' Henry said sardonically, putting his arm round his wife.

'Not that George is at all grateful – or he was, but it wore off quickly,' Eleri said ruefully. 'He's such a grumpy, mean kind of man.'

'Not a bit like his father,' agreed Henry. 'You couldn't find a kinder man than Joe Godet.'

My ears pricked up: could it be *that* easy to find one of the two people I wanted to talk to?

'Does he live nearby?' I asked.

'Unfortunately, yes – Withen Bottom Farm, just over the hill,' he said, his face going all shuttered, so despite the rescue there was clearly no love lost between them.

I didn't like to ask any more, but my head was buzzing as Nile drove us back home, what with all the fascinating conversations, Senga's pep talk and instructions, and meeting Eleri again – not to mention knowing where to find one of the two people I desperately wanted to talk to.

I said as much to Nile and then thanked him for going with me. 'I know you didn't want to, really.'

'Actually, I quite enjoyed myself, and I liked Henry Godet,' he said. 'I'm going to keep my eyes peeled for more antique farm tools for him to display in the restaurant.'

'I'm glad you had a good time,' I said, surprised. 'I expect you'll be glad to get out of those clothes, though.'

'I've certainly had enough of the boots, and they're not the easiest footwear to drive in,' he agreed, and removed them at the first opportunity when we got back, utilizing a cast-iron boot jack by the front porch and going in in his stockinged feet.

The house seemed strangely deserted, though it was warm and there was the smell of something spicy baking in the oven.

'It's like the *Mary Celeste*,' he commented.

'Yes . . . but I need to find someone to unhook this dress,' I said, because there was no way I could undo the million tiny hooks and eyes down the back of it on my own.

'I think you're out of luck, unless you'd like *me* to unhook you?' he offered, with a slightly wicked glint in his grey eyes.

I dithered for a moment, but I was desperate to get back into my jeans and a sloppy sweatshirt. 'Oh, all right,' I agreed.

I turned round and he began at the top and worked his way slowly down. At one point his fingers accidentally brushed my skin and when I shivered he paused for a moment, then resumed, more quickly.

'There you are,' he said finally, and then I swear I felt his warm lips briefly brush the nape of my neck.

But perhaps I only imagined that. Because when I whirled round and stared at him, he was over by the stove, putting the kettle on.

He looked up, frowning, as if surprised to find me still there. 'What are you waiting for? First one back downstairs looking as if they belong in the present century gets to make the coffee.'

I took a part-time GP position in a Haworth practice and spent my off-duty hours playing golf, taking Father for small outings in the car and walking the dog on the moors. I came to an arrangement with the cleaner, Kim, who took on the weekday afternoon role of housekeeper. Life settled down quite pleasantly and I even got away occasionally to my villa in Portugal, though it was let for most of the year.

In due course, Drogo went to meet his Maker and was replaced by a new Bichon Frise, Hugo. He proved to be of a mischievous and stubborn character and I would have returned him to the breeder for a more amenable replacement, except that Father wouldn't hear of it, even after Hugo ate his slippers.

Kim promised to take him in hand and after a couple of unfortunate episodes, he began to behave with more circumspection, especially when he was out with me.

One day – I suppose this would be about six or seven years ago – I happened to hear that my former lover had moved back to the area, having inherited the family home, which lay up on the moors between Upvale and Haworth. However, this news meant nothing to me – and nor did I feel a pang when I learned of his sudden death the following year, for he'd long been dead and buried to me.

25

Flounced and Frilled

When I went back downstairs Nile had beaten me to it and, since he was his usual self in all ways, I told myself I must have imagined that moment in the kitchen . . . though I've no idea why I should, since I wasn't sure if I even *liked* him most of the time, however attracted to him I was. And he was *so* not my type.

But it was as if I could still feel the brief pressure of his warm lips against my skin and the delicious shiver that had run down my spine, so when my eyes caught his cool grey gaze I looked away quickly, blushing.

All the family were there for dinner and later, after Casper had been put to bed, Nile, Bel and I went to Teddy and Geeta's apartment and watched *Bride and Prejudice*, popped corn and, under Geeta's direction, attempted some Bollywood dance moves. Teddy flatly refused, but Nile proved better at it than either Bel or I, though his expression of grave concentration reduced us to near-hysterical giggles.

He had many hidden depths and goodness knew what was swimming round in them.

After breakfast on Sunday morning most of the family trooped off to inspect the bedroom that was next on Sheila's list of renovation projects and begin removing the furniture, but I was excused so I could finish off my edits in the peace of the library, and Teddy, because he had work to do in the Pondlife office.

When I got back to my flat after lunch – or, to be more accurate, after I'd snoozed off the sleepiness caused by eating a huge amount of roast chicken with all the trimmings followed by sticky toffee pudding and custard – I rang Lola and described the book launch party, my scary agent, and rather more than I meant to about how Nile looked in his shirt and breeches.

'When I'm up for my flying visit on Thursday, I hope I get to meet this paragon of manly beauty,' she said, with a laugh in her voice.

'He's not *beautiful*, but he's certainly classically handsome,' I said. 'I don't know if he'll be here or not, because he goes off on buying trips all the time or . . . just *off*. And he has a partner in London called Zelda – he seems to stay there a lot.'

'Partner as in personal or business?'

'He says just business. Sheila, his adoptive mum, told me they've been friends since they were at university together, but I overheard a phone conversation between them and I have a suspicion there might be a bit more to it.'

'Pity if so, because I'd like to see you settled with a nice man at last,' she said regretfully.

'I don't think Nile is the settling kind, even if he was seriously attracted to me, which I'm certain he isn't. And *I'm* not looking for Mr Right – I've got enough on my plate at the moment. If I get lonely, I'll get a dog.'

'That's not quite the same thing,' she said mildly. 'But I realize how big a project the teashop is, especially now you have to juggle it with writing books for your scary-sounding agent.'

'I'm enjoying it all – well, except for the dust, drilling and hammering – but I lie awake sometimes worrying that the tearoom won't be a success and I'll have to sell up again.'

'I'm sure it will be and I'm looking forward to seeing it – and you. It's been ages.'

'I've organized you a bed,' I told her. 'Sheila's loaned me a small brass one that was in the attic and Nile's offered to dismantle it and drop it off here when he comes back this afternoon. I'll order a mattress express delivery.'

'That's very kind of him, but I hope you aren't going to too much trouble when I'm only coming up for one night.'

'Only one night this time, but I hope you'll come again and I meant to get the guest room sorted out ready anyway, so it's just spurred me on a bit.'

'Well, actually you might see me more often than you expect, if you decide to use our jams and relishes in your café. I'm bringing you some samples. But there's no pressure to take them, because even if you don't I can still claim this trip as a business expense to the accountant.'

'That's a great idea! I don't know why I didn't think of it myself,' I enthused. 'And *I* must find an accountant too, before things get in a tangle. I'm keeping my accounts and filing all the receipts for the teashop, of course, but it's going to be quite complicated.'

'Yes, it's worth it,' she agreed. 'Perhaps Nile has one he can recommend?'

'He might. I'll ask him later,' I said. 'By the way, Sheila's invited us out to Oldstone Farm for dinner on Thursday night – is that OK? I said I'd run it past you first.'

'Of course and it's very kind of her. I do adore old houses and they sound a lovely family.'

'I'll tell her yes, then, and we can have a wander round Haworth before we go out there. I'll take the day off.' Then I heard a noise from below and told her, 'Either I have a very noisy burglar in the kitchen, or Nile's carrying bits of bed in.'

'He has a key?'

'Yes, I gave him one ages ago, because he's always in and out, though he hasn't given me a key to his place in return. Perhaps he thinks I'll sneak in and fondle his curios.'

'Or he's got a Bluebeard's chamber in his flat?'

'That's a nice thought,' I said, grinning, and then told her I'd better go and help Nile get the bits of bed upstairs.

I hoped he'd put it back together again for me too, but he seemed abstracted and left once he'd stacked it all in the small bedroom, saying he had calls to make, so I thought I'd get Jack to do it instead. Or perhaps it was time to augment my selection of screwdrivers and have a go myself.

*

213

I emailed the edits off early next morning, hoping the editor could make sense of them, because *I* certainly couldn't. All those changes in different colours were terribly confusing.

Still, they were gone and after that there was nothing to stop me finishing my new book . . . apart from the teashop, as I discovered all too soon.

For although Jack was site-managing the project between his other jobs elsewhere, I was constantly being summoned to make decisions, give an opinion, or simply admire the glossy white paintwork on the kitchen cupboard doors, or the installation of a gleaming new toilet in one of the two customer cloakroom cubicles. I could see every day would be like that until it was finished!

The almost silent youth, Ross, had sanded and painted all the plate racks and shelves now and they were reattached to the café walls. I don't think he enjoyed doing it, but he told me he was looking forward to sanding the café floor, once he'd worked his way all over it, hammering down any nails that were protruding.

What with the noise, the interruptions and organizing all the other things that needed to be filled in, ordered, sourced, registered or applied for before the teashop could be opened, it was dawning on me that most of my writing time would be at night, when I was tired. But since Senga was scarier than anything I'd ever thought up in my stories, I'd get on with it.

And once I was really into a novel, of course, I lost myself. The working title might be *When Beauty Goes Bad*, but in my head it was *Bad-Ass Beauty* – because she was.

Nile seemed to keep late nights too, because I didn't draw my curtains until I went to bed and whenever I looked up from my desk the lights were on behind the blind of his flat and occasionally a tall, dark shape moved across it. I found this strangely comforting.

'This is a good weapon,' Beauty said, picking it up from the floor. 'Did you see? He just pointed it at the spider and it dropped right down dead!'

'It's not dead – but he might be,' Prince Kev said, bending over the man, who had lost his balance and fallen, hitting his head. 'No – I

think he's just stunned, but I'm getting out of here before he comes round!'

'We'll both go,' Beauty said, taking his hand firmly in hers and drawing him out of the door.

Outside, a pleasant small glade had opened up and a circle of green-clad nymphs were dancing, diaphanous draperies floating.

'I think I must be having a nightmare,' Kev said faintly.

'If you kiss me, the enchantment will probably come right again and we'll be transported to our very own happy-ever-after. Do you think I'm pretty?' she added.

'I suppose,' he said, eyeing her generous curves, big blue eyes and corn-gold hair. 'I like a girl with a bit of meat on her bones.'

'Why?' asked Beauty, puzzled. 'Do you want to eat me?'

The previous day I'd remembered the white crockery that Tilda had stashed away in the cupboard, and quickly posted details of it on a free recycling website, hoping someone would take it off my hands.

I only had one taker, whose user name was the unpromising 'MrMajestic', but at least he wanted the lot and, when I gave my address, said he'd be right round to collect it and he didn't need directions, so I assumed he was local.

With hindsight I should have asked his real name, because had I known it was Jim Voss, proprietor of the ghastly Gondal Guesthouse, I'd have said the china had already gone..

He arrived the back way, which showed a familiarity with the former owner he'd previously denied, and I think he might have shown a certain familiarity with me, too, except that when he walked right past me into the kitchen uninvited, he came face to face with Nell.

She'd dropped by with a piece of her own lardy cake for me to try, which she was just releasing from its greaseproof wrappings, and she regarded him with acute disfavour.

'It's you then, Jimmy Voss, is it?' she said. 'I might have known you'd be after something for nothing, for a little snirp you were as a boy and you haven't changed that much since.'

'Ha, ha!' he laughed unconvincingly. 'You will have your little joke, Nell.'

'Miss Capstick to you, flower,' she corrected him firmly.

'The china's all in those boxes in the back room you just walked past,' I said pointedly.

'Right,' he said, glancing round at the chaos in the kitchen with beady-eyed inquisitiveness. 'You're certainly spending a lot of money on renovating the place. I suppose you're buying new crockery too?'

'There's no need, when all the Misses Spencer's lovely willow-pattern china, from when they had the Copper Kettle, was still sitting there in the cupboard,' Nell said.

'Oh? There was a lot of good china hidden in a cupboard?' he asked quickly.

'It wasn't hidden, it was just under the basement stairs – and it's about the only thing Mrs M didn't clear out of t' place, cheating poor Alice here out of what she'd paid for,' Nell said.

'Oh, well – I know nothing about all that,' he said hastily.

'I don't suppose you've heard anything from Mrs Muswell?' I asked. 'I'd still like to talk to her – and so would Nile Giddings, seeing as she sold some antiques of his that she was displaying on the café walls, but didn't give him the money.'

'I'm sure he must be mistaken about that,' Jim Voss said quickly.

'No he isn't, because either Tilda or me was there when she sold the things. It was when she was over here getting the place ready to close up early and Nile was away. She knocked them down at bargain prices and pocketed the cash.'

Jim Voss gave her a very unloving look. 'But I'm certain she would have kept the money separately, so she could pass it on to Mr Giddings. And I'm afraid I still don't have her current contact details, but then, now she's sold the café, she has no need to stay with us, does she?' He gave me an insincere smile, then looked at his watch, gave a stage start, and said he must be getting on and he'd fetch the boy, who he'd left in his car at the back, to give him a hand with the boxes.

'Like I said,' Nell remarked, once they'd finally gone, 'a little snirp!'

*

216

When Nile texted late in the afternoon to say he'd come round later and put the spare bed together, I didn't protest in the least.

To be honest, I'd had so much else to do that it had gone right out of my head and anyway, there's independence . . . and then there's sitting back and letting someone else do the tricky stuff.

It took him about fifteen minutes to put the brass bed together – I expect he was ace with Lego as a boy. Then he unwrapped the mattress, which had arrived earlier, and laid it down on top.

'You look as if you'd like to fall on it and sleep for a year,' he said, looking at me in amusement.

'So would you, if you'd been running up and down a flight of stairs all day, while trying to work, answer the phone and chase up deliveries,' I snapped.

'I spent a quiet day going through sales catalogues and ringing contacts and clients, but that is my work,' he said mildly. 'I thought Jack was doing everything and the boy – what's his name?'

'Ross. Jack is organizing everything, but he seems to want me to go downstairs about every fifteen minutes – and then I had an unwelcome visitor earlier.' I told him about Jim Voss and the way Nell had seen him off.

Then I yawned. 'I'm too tired to do any writing tonight, that's for sure.'

My legs suddenly felt a bit wobbly and I sat down on the edge of the pristine white mattress.

'I think you've been overdoing it – and what did you have for lunch?' he asked.

'I don't think I had any – though I ate a bit of Nell's lardy cake this morning and I think that might be still clinging to my ribs.'

'A piece of cake isn't enough. Come on, get your coat and we'll go round to a good pub I know and have a bit of dinner.'

I was too tired to resist and the pub was quiet, dark and warm, with good, plain food. I felt better once I'd got some steak and kidney pie and chips inside me.

'You've got some colour back,' Nile said approvingly, when I'd cleared my plate and, declining dessert, asked for coffee. 'You're doing so much already that you mustn't let Sheila rope you in to helping out at Old-stone at the weekends too,' he added. 'She seems to think we're all going to spend a jolly Saturday scraping off wallpaper in the bedroom opposite yours, and I, for one, will be out most of that day at an auction.'

'She did ask me for the weekend again and I don't mind pitching in with whatever wants doing. It's fun planning out the pottery café with Bel, too.'

'I hadn't realized, until Bel told me, just how many health, safety and food hygiene rules even a small café has to comply with,' he said. 'I only hope they can recoup the cost.'

'It's quite a large initial outlay, when you're creating something from scratch,' I agreed, 'but I'm sure it will bring more visitors to the pottery.'

'I'm not sure about the waffle house aspect – I thought it was just going to be coffee and cake.'

'Oh, I think that's a stroke of genius!' I enthused. 'When tourists spot the sign they'll be turning off in droves – and once they see Bel's lovely work, especially the jewellery, they'll buy that, too.'

'I hope you're right.'

'I wonder if Henry Godet will be cross when he finds out there's a rival for his Hikers' Café only a few miles away?' I said.

'I shouldn't think it would affect his business, because the Hikers' Café has been there a long time catering for walkers, and now tourists are heading for it, because of the Brontë connection.'

'Any tourists heading there from the Haworth direction will have to pass the Norwegian waffle house sign first,' I pointed out.

'Better not mention that when we go there for dinner, then,' he said, to my surprise.

'*Are* we going there for dinner?' I asked, staring at him.

'I told Henry we would and it's already got a reputation for good food so I'd like to try it. Wouldn't you like to go?'

'Well . . . yes, I suppose it would be nice,' I agreed, wondering exactly what kind of date this was – a friendly date, a bossy older brother date . . . or a *date* date?

'Is this a date?' I blurted, then felt myself going pink.

'I suppose it's a getting-to-know-each-other-better date – if you've no objection,' he said, raising one dark eyebrow.

This didn't really answer my question, but when he added casually, 'I'll book it for next week then and let you know when they can fit us in,' I decided there was nothing romantic about the invitation.

This was just as well, given how the pretty barmaid had flirted with him while he was ordering our food and the way he'd smiled at the two leggy blonde backpackers in the corner, who'd been eyeing him more hungrily than their scampi and chips.

I relaxed a bit. In fact, I was by now feeling so relaxed and sleepy from warmth and food that even the surprisingly good coffee couldn't wake me up.

'It's another strange coincidence that Henry should be related to the farmer who found me on the moors, isn't it? My whole life is a series of strange coincidences,' I said.

'It's not so strange when you think *where* you were found, because it's all Godet sheep-farming land round there.'

'I'll go and talk to Joe Godet soon. He must be getting on a bit by now. His son doesn't sound very pleasant, does he?'

'I could always come and protect you, if you're nervous,' Nile offered.

'I'm big enough to protect myself,' I said with dignity. 'I just need a little time to think things through first and then I'll track him down . . . and Emily Rhymer.'

'I can understand why you'd like to talk to them and hear the story of how they found you first-hand,' he said, 'but if you're hoping they'll reveal some clue to your identity, then I think you'll be in for a disappointment.'

'No . . . no, of course I don't really think that,' I said. 'But they must have been on the scene soon after I was left, or I wouldn't have survived, so they may have seen something.'

'I wouldn't get your hopes up. And the offer still stands: if I'm not away somewhere, then I'll come with you,' he said, which was very kind of him, though actually I thought it was something I'd prefer to do alone.

I sighed. 'I do accept I'm unlikely to find my birth mother, it's just an outside chance – though I could try Bel's suggestion and contact the local paper to see if they'd like to do an article about me. How I was found on the moors and now have come back to open my own teashop in Haworth – that kind of thing. It would be good publicity even if she didn't see it and come forward, but she might.'

'I'd advise against it, but that's only my opinion. I'd hate you to find her and then . . . be hurt because she doesn't want anything to do with you.'

'One final rejection,' I agreed. 'But perhaps then I'd feel I'd done everything I could and I'd be ready to move on with my life.'

'I suppose there is that.' His face had that brooding, dark, inward-looking expression again.

'Did you never want to try to trace your real father, or any other relatives?' I asked him curiously.

'Dad – Paul – asked me that once. He was keen on family history research and he'd just taken a DNA test through one of the genealogy websites to see if he could link up with any other relatives on the database. He suggested I try it, too.'

'I didn't even know you could do that! Did you have a go?'

'No, because I already knew my father was a Greek waiter. My mum told me once that he'd gone back to Greece soon after I was born, saying he'd send for her when he'd told his parents, but that was the last she'd heard of him.'

'That's so sad,' I said.

'I suppose it is, but I'm sure family pressure was brought to bear, once he got home.'

'You tried to find him, didn't you?' I guessed, and saw by his expression that I was right.

'Yes. I managed to trace the village he came from and went there . . . but he'd died a few years before in an accident. I've seen a photograph, so I know I look very much like him and I could see his family knew about me, but they denied it because they seemed to have the idea I'd come to claim my inheritance, such as it was.'

'I'm so sorry, it must have been horrible for you,' I said gently.

'I was more curious than anything and it did show me the background my father had come from,' he said, shrugging. 'I didn't tell

Sheila and Paul what I'd done because they were my *real* parents and I didn't want to hurt their feelings in any way.'

'I won't mention it then,' I assured him. 'And I can see now why you don't think searching for my birth mother is a good idea – though not all experiences will be the same. If I go public with the story and she *doesn't* come forward, then that's it, I really will let it drop.'

'Then I suppose you'd better go for it,' he said.

'Did your dad's research throw up anything interesting about the Giddingses?' I asked. 'I didn't even know you *could* trace your family history through DNA.'

'You can if there are any matches on the database, and he found several. It's a very old family, with lots of branches and several eccentric characters . . . like Teddy.'

'Teddy's lovely and not eccentric at all!' I protested.

'Wait till you've seen the scale of the model train layout he's got in one of the attics, or caught him wandering round the house in his replica Victorian stationmaster's uniform,' he said with a grin.

I myself like to chill out in a long, voluminous, Victorian-style, flounced and frilled white cotton dressing gown, which I call Miss Havisham . . .

I decided *not* to mention it.

Now that Nile had opened up to me a bit about his childhood, I could see that in many ways we'd been shaped by the same forces: abandonment, redeeming love and the search for who we really were. I felt I understood him better and that despite the way we seemed constantly to strike sparks off one another, deep down, we had a real connection.

It was odd that after giving practically no thought to the events of that dreadful night in the intervening years, once I was living in Upvale again I not only had the impulse to write down the details of what happened, but also found myself strangely drawn to the area around the Oldstone.

But then, the dog needed daily exercise, and since there was a convenient parking area nearby, it might as well be there as anywhere else.

Early in the morning I was unlikely to see anyone else up there, even during the summer months when one could barely move on the moors for Brontë-driven tourists, so there was no danger of my liking for the spot being noticed and commented on.

26

Perfectly Preserved

Lola drove herself up on Thursday and since the skip had departed again, we managed to squeeze her small hatchback into the parking place next to my old Beetle, while still leaving room for Nile, who appeared to have gone off somewhere early.

He was certainly home last night, though, because the flat lights were on. I think I'm becoming a curtain twitcher . . .

There were no workmen around, though Jack would be in later after another job, bringing the tiles we'd chosen for the kitchen and customer cloakrooms, and I knew Ross would begin sanding the café floorboards next morning, which sounded like another noisy kind of day.

We took Lola's overnight bag up to the flat and I gave her a guided tour, which, given the size of the place, took all of five minutes.

Then I made coffee and sampled some of the contents of the whole basket of tiny jars of jams, preserves, pickles and chutneys she'd brought for me to try. They were all so delicious that I decided that, as well as using them for the teas, I'd sell them from the counter in the café, too.

Lola showed me a picture on her iPad of the display stands she'd had made for stockists who were taking a range of Dolly and Lola's products.

'I haven't got room for a stand in the tearoom, but I wonder if Bel and Sheila would be interested in having one in their waffle house next spring?' I suggested. 'Remember I told you about that?'

She nodded. 'Oh, do you think they might?'

'They'd certainly have room, because their café will be in a former carriage house, so you can show them the photos when we go up to dinner later.'

'We've had some small carrier bags printed with our logo so I can bring you a supply of those for behind the counter, if you like?'

'It's OK, I'm having some upmarket doggy bags printed with our logo, for anyone who wants to take any leftover sandwiches and cake home from their tea, so we can use those,' I said. 'They're white card, with our logo up the side in a dark teal colour.'

'That sounds quite swish,' she said. 'What do you think of the lemon curd?'

'That and the orange version are so yummy, they'd make great tart fillings, garnished with just a twist of candied peel.'

I looked down at the pot I was holding, realized I'd eaten almost the entire contents of the orange one, and put my spoon down quickly. 'I'm glad you're making horseradish sauce too, because I'll need it for the roast beef sandwiches.'

'Dad started growing it a few years ago, along with the herbs, and Mum tried out lots of recipes till she came up with this one: it's not too explosive, but still strong enough to add a bit of zest.'

'It does that all right,' I agreed, and then we screwed all the lids back on the jars and went downstairs. I'd already sent her lots of photos of how the café looked before we started on the renovations and then some of the ensuing chaos, but now I'd painted the teashop itself, at least she could get some idea of what the final result would be.

'I love the colour scheme – it's just like the flat!' she enthused. 'All these chalky blues and whites and creams – light but somehow not cold.'

'Yes, that's what I thought. I nicked the idea from my bedroom at Oldstone Farm. Sheila Giddings is part Norwegian and she's decorated it in what Bel – that's her daughter – calls Scandi-style. It goes with the blue and white patterned china, too, in an odd kind of way.'

'I like the way the big mirror behind the counter at the back of the room reflects the light from the bow window.'

'I think it must have been there since the place was the Copper Kettle, and so had the signboard, because you could still make out the letters of the last two names before the Branwell Café. It's gone to be properly sanded down and repainted.'

I led the way out of the front door into the little cobbled courtyard, which was dappled by weak sunshine.

'I think The Fat Rascal is an inspired name choice,' Lola said. 'Are you going to have them on the menu?'

'Yes, miniature versions. In fact, I'll have a Fat Rascal Tea as an option to the Classic Tea with scones.'

'Good idea!'

'You can see where Jack has mended and undercoated the Victorian trellis porch,' I pointed out. 'I'm having all the outside paintwork dark teal picked out in white, to match the new sign.'

She caught sight of Small and Perfect opposite and said with interest, 'That must be Nile's shop? But it looks shut.'

'It isn't often open, because he makes his living finding expensive bits and pieces for wealthy collectors. His car wasn't there earlier so he must be off somewhere, which is a shame because you could have had a look round.'

'And I'd like to catch a glimpse of this mythical beast, too,' she said with a grin.

We went across and peered in the window anyway, though the distorting bull's-eye-glass panes gave everything a slightly rippled effect, not to mention a faintly bilious tinge of green.

'He has some lovely things, especially that small paperweight with the millefiori flowers,' Lola said, pressing her nose to the glass.

'It *is* pretty, isn't it?' I agreed. 'I love that tall, narrow blue and white jug with the pastoral scene on it. If I have any money left when I've finished the renovations, I might ask him how much it is, but the way things are going I expect to be totally skint.'

'You'll need to try to keep some in reserve to cover the running costs and staff wages till the tearoom takes off, won't you?'

'Yes, I've already set aside enough to keep us afloat for three months and if it isn't paying its way by then, I don't think it ever will, but I may have to use some of that money if anything major happens, like the boiler goes bust or something.'

'Well, then, fingers crossed it doesn't,' Lola said optimistically.

'I'll get some money from my publishers once I've sent them the new book – an advance on delivery – but it won't be a lot. *If* I ever finish it,' I added darkly.

'Of course you will! And won't it be wonderful to see it on sale in bookshops, not just on the internet?' she said encouragingly. 'What's it called?'

'*When Beauty Goes Bad.* They might change the title, though, I suppose.'

We went back into the café and Lola stood in the middle of the empty room, half-closing her eyes. 'I can visualize what the tearoom will look like when it's finished – very restful and swish and grown-up. The tables covered with white linen cloths . . .'

'Easy-care linen-look, with matching napkins,' I amended. 'I've seen samples and they're just what I want, so I'm about to place an order. And I've found a local laundry that'll collect and deliver daily.'

She closed her eyes again, like a medium summoning up the spirit of a tearoom: 'The quiet clink of cutlery . . .'

'Good-quality stainless steel that will go in the dishwasher.'

'The tables set for tea with tiered china stands . . .'

'I haven't sourced the right ones yet, but I'm working on it. They might have to be plain white, rather than willow pattern, though.'

'The soft gleam of crystal water glasses . . .' she murmured.

'Water glasses? Oh God, I knew I'd forgotten something!' I exclaimed. '*And* water jugs. Carry on,' I urged her. 'Let's see if I've missed anything else.'

'Preserve dishes and little pots for clotted cream and butter for the scones.'

'Hang on,' I said, and fetched the printout of my latest list, which was now more like an endless Dead Sea Scroll, and made some additions.

'Right, carry on,' I urged her. 'This is really useful.'

'Tea- and coffeepots . . . cups and saucers, sugar bowls, milk jugs.'

'Teapots I've got, large and small, though I could do with more, and I'm ordering glass cafetieres for the coffee,' I said. 'There's already a water boiler behind the counter, so Tilda or Nell can fill them there.'

'Larger glasses for soft drinks?'

'Yes, those are on the list, and I must find a supplier of old-fashioned bottles of traditional ones made from natural ingredients, like dandelion and burdock, ginger beer and lemonade, plus I'll make jugs of my own lemonade in the summer,' I added.

'People will probably ask for cola.'

'They might, but they're not going to get it *here*,' I said firmly. 'I'll set Nell or Tilda on to them if they get stroppy.'

'Your staff do sound a bit scary!' She looked around the room again. 'What is going in the glass display case on the counter?'

'Well, pots of your jams and preserves, for a start, but two large cakes of the day, too. One will always be some kind of fruitcake, but I'll vary the other with old favourites like Battenburg, seed cake, Victoria sponge, coffee and walnut . . .'

'Yum,' she said appreciatively, then suggested, 'Cake knives?'

'I think I'll buy some new stainless-steel dishwasher-proof ones.'

'Then I've run out of ideas,' she said. 'You've thought it through very well and you'll have time to fine-tune everything before you open, won't you? I mean, exactly when *are* you going to open?'

'November the 4th. That will give us the whole run-up to Christmas to establish ourselves and then perhaps I'll close and reopen in the New Year. Mind you, the speed Jack works at, I could probably have opened a couple of weeks earlier.'

'Then you can use the time to finish that new book, can't you?' she suggested.

'Good point – *and* track down and talk to the two people who rescued me when I was abandoned.'

'I'm sure that talking to the eyewitnesses will make it seem more real than just reading articles about it,' she suggested.

'It seemed pretty real when I was standing up on the hill by the Oldstone – so bleak and deserted,' I said, shivering at the recollection. 'I'd really like to know what made my mother leave me somewhere like that, where she must have been sure I wouldn't be found, so I think I'm going to put an appeal in the local paper, too, saying how much I'd love to hear from her.'

'I suppose that might be the only way to find her – if she comes forward,' Lola said.

'I was undecided about it, but Bel pointed out what great publicity the whole story would make for the teashop, even if nothing else comes of it, and she's right.'

'What does Nile think?' Lola asked innocently, and I looked at her suspiciously.

'Oh, that trying to trace her is a bad idea and even if I find her she might not be keen to meet me, so I'll get hurt. Because he had a bad experience of that kind himself, when he tried to trace his father, he's sure I will, too. Not that I actually *care* what he thinks,' I added pointedly.

'But if your birth mother comes forward voluntarily after the newspaper article, it'll mean that she *does* want to meet you,' she said. 'And if she doesn't then . . .'

'Then either Nile is right, or she's dead, or she's moved away and hasn't seen it,' I finished.

'So you might as well contact the newspaper,' Lola concluded.

We had lunch in the pub where Nile had taken me, before walking around the village and then visiting the Brontë Parsonage Museum, which we both found so fascinating we were there for hours and more than ready for tea and scones at a café on the way back.

'These scones are good, but mine will be better,' I whispered.

'So will your jam be if you stock mine, because this raspberry one is high sugar and low on fruit,' Lola said critically, after liberally spreading some on half a scone and taking a bite.

'Well, you're the expert on that,' I said, then asked her how the annexe to her parents' house was coming along.

'Almost finished, thank goodness. Dad's done as much of the work himself as he could, to save money, which is why it's taken so long. It'll almost double the floor space of the original house, so we were very lucky to get planning permission.'

'It's easier if there used to be a building there anyway, isn't it?'

'Yes, I think that swung it.' She sighed happily. 'What bliss it will be to have my own space again.'

'I'm already loving the fact my flat is my own and no one can take it away from me,' I said.

'Once I've moved into the annexe with the girls, Mum and Dad will be able to have a bit of peace occasionally and I can stop feeling guilty about all our clutter and toys spreading everywhere,' she said, though I was sure her parents loved having them there, however sad the reason for her return.

'Once we've moved in, you can come and stay, if you can get away. Though actually, I suppose you'll be working flat out till you're certain the teashop is a success – which I'm sure it will be.'

'I'm only opening five days a week, Tuesday to Saturday, so once things have settled down I could have a very quick visit. Tilda acted as manager for the last owner, so I'm sure she could cope alone later on. I'd love to see your parents again, and my godchildren – they're probably now at least as big as I am!'

'Oh, not quite!' she said, laughing.

It was lovely to be able to spend some time with Lola – my constant friend. We'd led such different lives, yet whenever we met again we just took up where we left off, as though we'd been parted for barely a heartbeat.

We set out for the Giddingses' early that evening, because Lola wanted a glimpse of the Oldstone first.

Miraculously, I remembered the twists and turns that led to the parking place, but then, I was always good at those puzzles where you have to guide a little silver ball bearing through a maze. I'd have escaped the Minotaur even without a ball of string.

We got out of the car but didn't walk up to the top of the rocky outcrop, just viewed it from below, while a surprisingly Siberian wind whistled round our ears.

'It's a godforsaken spot to abandon a baby in, isn't it?' I said. 'I was wrapped in a sheepskin mat and shoved into a hole in that rocky outcrop.'

'It must have been an act of desperation and panic,' Lola said charitably. 'And I expect your mother was terribly sorry for what she'd done later – and *so* happy and relieved when you were found alive.'

'I suppose I'd better make it clear in the newspaper article that I don't harbour any anger towards her for what she did – which I don't,' I said. 'I just want to understand why.'

'I'm still surprised that Nessa's never been in contact with you, even though she must have known she could have found you through us,' she said.

'*I'm* not, because after Dad died, suddenly it was as if she'd only been acting the part of my mother and she'd had enough of it – and of me.'

I seemed to make a habit of mislaying mothers.

By now, dusk was stealing over the landscape and the wind was revving up to a howl. 'Come on,' I said with a sudden shiver. 'Get back in the car and we'll go and introduce you to the Giddingses!'

Lola, with her sweet, serious expression and warm heart, was an instant success with the whole family, as I knew she would be. Even Nile, who'd turned up unannounced for dinner, thawed quickly and stopped glooming about some bijou bit of antiquity on which he'd been out-bid.

I told them all about Dolly and Lola's Perfectly Pickled and Preserved Company and my sampling session earlier that day.

'Everything was so delicious that I'm going to use them exclusively in my tearoom – *and* sell them from the counter, too. I'd have one of Lola's display stands if I had more room, but I wondered if you might like to have one when you open the waffle house?'

Lola, who'd been showing Geeta and Sheila a random collection of snaps on her phone, ranging from the three little girls, the hens and the goats, to the newly painted wooden building housing the preserve company, scrolled to a picture of the stands.

'Lovely,' said Bel, leaning over the table to see. 'I'm sure we'd have room for one of those.'

'And perhaps you could supply the black cherry jam for my waffles?' Sheila suggested.

'I prefer blackcurrant,' Nile said, coming out of his dark reverie at the mention of waffles.

'Or strawberry,' said Teddy, 'that's my favourite.'

'I'll bring samples for you next time I come up,' Lola said. 'The ones I brought have mostly gone.'

'You'd better keep the next lot away from Alice, then,' Nile said.

'They were very small jars, just for tasting,' I said indignantly. 'It's not like I was pigging out on gallons of the stuff.'

'I think Alice said you were opening your waffle house next year?' Lola said to Bel, quickly.

Bel nodded. 'Easter, if we get planning permission in time.'

'That's the time of year when things hot up on the swimming pond front, too,' Geeta said. 'People start to think about installing one ready for summer.'

'Oh, yes, Alice told me about those. I think natural outdoor swimming sounds a lovely idea.'

'If you come in warmer weather, you can try ours,' Sheila told her.

'What with Alice's teashop, Lola's preserve company and our soon-to-be waffle house, we're certainly sisters doing it for ourselves,' Bel said, then sang a snatch of the Annie Lennox song.

'Brothers are doing pretty well for themselves, too,' Teddy pointed out.

'True, you and Geeta have expanded the Pondlife business wonderfully, darlings,' agreed Sheila. 'And Nile's little shop is a success too.'

'Damned with faint praise,' Nile said.

'Now, Nile, you know I didn't mean it like that, you big grump,' Sheila told him affectionately.

'We looked in the window of Small and Perfect earlier, and there are some lovely things,' Lola said to him, soft-hearted as always, and then, since she adores babies, she went off with Geeta to help put Casper to bed.

When she returned, she said the smell of baby talc was enough to make her feel broody all over again, but for some reason this perfectly innocent remark seemed to cast Nile right back into his dark mood and he left before the coffee.

I noticed later when we got back to my flat that Nile's curtains were drawn and the lights were on, but who knew if anyone was home? Was the bear in his cave, or had he wandered off somewhere?

'Nile's even more stunning than you said,' Lola told me. 'And I think he really likes you, because at dinner I kept catching him looking at you as if he was absolutely fascinated.'

I gazed at her, astonished. 'I'm sure you're wrong – or if he is fascinated, then it's only because he can't understand why I haven't rolled over on my back every time he smiles, like practically every other woman.'

'*I* probably would, if he smiled at me,' she said. 'And I think you're in denial and really fancy him.'

'Well, OK, I admit I do find him attractive – but even if it was reciprocal, I'm not looking for yet another relationship with a short shelf life.'

Lola dropped the subject, but I kept thinking about what she'd said about Nile staring at me, when I wasn't looking . . .

The circle of dancing, diaphanously clad dryads pressed closer and closer around Kev, their soulless, beautiful eyes fixed on him and their grasping hands reaching out . . .

But Beauty hadn't been asleep all those hundreds of years just to let a bunch of airy-fairy nymphs get her man, even if he did now seem both mesmerized and acquiescent.

She pointed the weapon she still held and the magic force caused the nearest dryad to fall over in a heap with a loud and satisfying scream.

Beauty snatched Kevin's scimitar and would have followed on with a little letting of green blood, had the fallen nymph's sisters not scooped her up and run for the trees, where their fluttering draperies soon vanished into the foliage.

Given the situation of the GP surgery I'd joined, it was inevitable that my former lover's family would register there after they'd moved into the ancestral home on the moors just outside Haworth. Oldstone Farm was an extensive, sprawling affair, with the central part rumoured to be of great antiquity, though I have little interest in such things.

Nor do I have any idea why it should be called by that name, for it was miles from the rocky outcrop, and if the place had ever been a working farm, it had ceased to be one within living memory.

My practice was a large one and the family were registered with another of the doctors there, so I had little contact with them, though of course, whether I did or not was a matter of complete indifference to me.

27

Distant Views

Lola had to set out for Shrewsbury early next morning and once Ross arrived and started sanding the floorboards in the café, I began to wish I'd gone with her.

Bel had suggested that I went over to stay with them that day, though, so we could walk up to the Oldstone together very early the next morning, so in the end I put my overnight bag in the car and left Ross to it.

I had an appointment to meet a local artisan baker I'd heard about, who was young and enthusiastic about the idea of providing the bread for my teashop, then afterwards I went on to check out the stock of a cash and carry, before ending up at Oldstone Farm.

When I was there the previous night with Lola it was clear that Sheila assumed that I'd be spending my weekend with them, probably helping to paint the room she was revamping. It was a bit of a busman's holiday, but I didn't mind. It would get me away from the reek of the floor seal-ant too, which I hoped would have abated a bit by the time I returned to my flat on Sunday.

Just after dawn on Saturday morning, Bel and I set off across the moors in my car with an eager Honey in the back.

In fact, it was so early that we were surprised to find a glossy new Renault hatchback already parked on the turf below the Oldstone.

'I hoped we'd have the place to ourselves,' I said, disappointed. 'There was no one about last time.'

'It could be a twitcher, out watching birds,' Bel suggested.

'Is there anything much to watch at this time of year?'

'I have absolutely no idea,' she confessed.

But it appeared that it wasn't a twitcher, for as we headed up the path a woman appeared from the other direction, with a white Bichon Frise at her side.

'Early dogwalker,' Bel said.

'I thought that was a lamb, at first,' I said. 'They're very woolly little things.'

When we got nearer, I could see that she was perhaps in her fifties, of medium height and well built, without being stocky. She had steel-grey hair pulled back into an uncompromising plait, pale lipstick, chilly blue eyes and an expression to match.

But there *was* something familiar about her . . . and then I suddenly realized she was the woman I'd met driving towards me in the narrowest part of the lane the day of my first visit, when she'd simply sat there waiting for me to reverse miles to a passing place. You don't forget someone you've had that kind of stand-off with – especially when you came off the worst! So, either she lived nearby, or this was a favourite haunt of hers . . . or perhaps both.

The cold, uninterested gaze swept over us, though I thought her eyes lingered on me for just a moment, so the recognition might have been mutual.

'Good morning,' she said briefly.

I'm sure she would have continued on past, if Bel hadn't exclaimed, 'Oh, it's Dr Collins, isn't it? Perhaps you don't remember me – I'm Bel Giddings and we met when you were called out to Oldstone Farm one night. My baby nephew was running a high fever.'

'Oh – of course,' she said, stopping and shaking hands in a professional manner, but without any enthusiasm. Her ice-floe eyes rested on me again and Bel introduced us.

'This is my friend Alice Rose. She's opening a tearoom in Haworth.'

'Rather a crowded field, I would have thought,' she said in clipped tones, and the little dog, who had been exchanging friendly sniffs with Honey, looked up at her, its head on one side.

'I'm sure there's room for one more,' I replied pleasantly. 'We've actually come face to face once before, Dr Collins.'

'We have?'

'The Saturday before last. I was here a little earlier than this and our cars met in the lane as I was leaving.'

I didn't mention the reversing for miles bit, though it hadn't endeared her to me. 'This must be a favourite spot of yours?'

She shrugged. 'The dog needs to be walked and I like to be solitary at the start of the day – which can usually be counted on here,' she said rather pointedly. 'Excuse me, I must be getting back now. Come along, Hugo.'

The dog obediently trotted after her, though he turned his head with one of those lolling-tongued canine grins, his eyes bright, as if to say: 'Just you wait – I'll get up to some mischief as soon as we get home!'

'Well, I think that was meant to be a bit of a slap in the face,' I commented as we carried on.

'Yes, but she's very brusque like that. We all prefer to see one of the others at the practice,' Bel said. 'She's super-efficient, but I think she views people as cases to be dealt with, rather than as individuals, so she's not very popular. But they were desperate for another GP to share the workload, even if she's only part time.'

'Was she OK with the baby?'

'Fine. Geeta was convinced he had meningitis, though it turned out to be just a slight fever, but Dr Collins told her it was always better to get a professional opinion if a baby showed any symptoms, so she'd done the right thing calling her out.'

'Well, that seems . . . kind.'

'I'm not sure it was *intentionally* kind, just a statement of fact. I heard she was working in Scotland before, and then moved back here about ten years ago, because her elderly father was getting very frail. He has a large house this side of Upvale.'

'I suppose registering with a doctor is one of the things I should do soon,' I said.

'You'd better register with the same practice, then,' suggested Bel.

'It's the nearest. Just remember to ask for another doctor if you make an appointment!'

It took us most of Saturday to strip the wallpaper off the bedroom opposite mine. I think the Victorians must have invented some kind of Superglue-type paste.

Teddy joined us for the first couple of hours, before he and Geeta went out, and by the time Nile arrived to take his place with the water spray and scraper, we'd almost finished.

Bel accused him of getting there late on purpose and they had a bit of a battle with the water sprays. My hair went extra curly in the damp mist.

It was just the four of us for dinner and afterwards Sheila took her coffee out to her conservatory studio at the back of the house and Bel went to answer some urgent emails about the forthcoming exhibition of her work in York.

'Well, it's just you and me, kid,' Nile said in a fake American drawl. 'Film? Or shall I beat you at Scrabble?'

And he did win the first game, but only because some evil fairy had bestowed letters on me that naturally formed themselves into a series of such terribly rude words that I couldn't bring myself to put them down.

Then later, when I'd gone to bed and was in that delicious limbo state between awake and asleep, the characters in my novel suddenly decided to have a conversation in my head and I had to get grumpily out of bed and put it all down before it vanished like a popped bubble.

Annoying.

'Where did they go?' said Kev, looking after the dryads in a dazed kind of way.

'Never mind them – you're mine, so now stop messing about and kiss me,' she ordered impatiently.

'This is the weirdest dream ever,' Kev muttered.

'Kev? Where are you hiding?' yelled a voice like a corncrake from somewhere beyond the circling thicket, and his face cleared. In fact, he looked relieved. 'I'm in here, princess,' he called back.

'Princess?' Beauty scowled: she had competition?

A skinny woman with short, spiky pink hair, a cropped top that showed a washboard stomach and a navel-piercing set with a gold ring, stepped through a gap in the hedge – and at the same time, with a kind of popping noise, a tall, handsome, princely figure walked out of thin air and came face to face with her.

They stared deep into each other's eyes, and then the prince stepped forward and kissed her.

In fairy tales, especially mine, things were never quite as they seemed . . .

I could have done with a bit more sleep, because I set off with Bel and Nile before eight to a car boot sale on the outskirts of Keighley, the last local big one of the year.

Nile had insisted on the early start: he said you got all the bargains at the beginning of the day. I'd have thought car boot sales were beneath his notice, but no, he absolutely loved it, swooping down like a magpie on small sparkling objects and making several finds. He had a way of methodically but rapidly turning over the stuff on every stall and in every box and moving on, while Bel and I were more leisurely.

We quickly parted company with him, but met up later at the refreshment van, where a few plastic picnic tables and chairs had been set out for customers, where we compared our purchases.

I'd bought a battered but still lovely blue and white Minton teapot to display in the café – I wanted some variety, because you can have too much willow pattern.

'It reminds me of that beautiful jug you've got at the back of your window,' I said to Nile.

'Do you mean the Spode?' He looked at me as if I was mad. 'It's nothing like it!'

'It might not be to an antique dealer, but the pattern's the exact same shade of blue,' I said firmly.

'Show him what else you got,' Bel said quickly, scenting an argument brewing, so I opened the wooden box containing six mother-of-pearl-handled cake forks.

'I got them for a fiver, but they're for the flat,' I said. 'I don't want any cutlery in the teashop that I can't put through the big dishwasher.'

Bel had bought a strange and slab-like pot as a present for her mum. 'I can't find a mark on it, but it looks like Troika,' she said, passing it over the wobbly plastic table to Nile.

'Is that good?' I asked. I thought it looked more like the product of an evening class, but what do I know?

'I think you're right,' Nile told her, and then explained to me, 'Troika pottery is very collectable and you don't find much of it cheap any more. Sheila loves it and I buy it at auctions for her, if it doesn't go too high.'

Nile himself had purchased an old breadboard with a cute mouse carved on it, which he said was a genuine Mouseman, so it was my day for learning about obscure collectable stuff. His pockets were full of all kinds of other things too, including a domed greenish glass paperweight in which bubbles seemed to be rising in a cloud . . . which reminded me of something I'd been meaning to ask him.

'Is that small millefiori paperweight in your window as hideously expensive as I suspect it is, Nile? Only Lola spotted it and absolutely loved it, so I thought if I could afford it I'd buy it her for Christmas.'

'It is, but I'm sure we could work out some kind of discount – for services to be rendered,' he said, eyeing me speculatively, much as the three young women at the next table were regarding his handsome, austere profile and the tumbled blue-black hair.

'What kind of services?' I asked suspiciously.

'Free afternoon tea delivered to my door every day?'

'In your dreams, buster!' I said.

'You must be joking, Nile,' Bel said, grinning. 'If you ate a full tea every day you'd soon be like Winnie-the-Pooh after he guzzled all the honey and was too fat to get out of his hole again.'

'I might manage a small bag of sandwiches and savouries every afternoon, if you came over to pick them up,' I suggested. 'You did say you weren't a big fan of sweet things.'

'Oh, I like *some* sweet things,' he said, giving me that sudden and knee-quivering smile, so that I was quite glad I was sitting down. 'But in moderation. It's a deal – we'll arrange full terms later and sign it in icing sugar.'

When we got back, we found the rest of the family gathered in the kitchen, helping or hindering Sheila's preparations for the usual lavish Sunday lunch.

Casper was in his highchair, splashing a plastic spoon about in a bowl of something gloopy, while Honey sat in his usual position underneath, looking hopefully up.

'Here's the prospective bridegroom,' Teddy said with a grin at Nile as we walked into the kitchen. 'Do you want me to be best man, bro?'

Nile seemed totally taken aback. 'What on earth do you mean?'

'Don't tease, Teddy,' chided Sheila, turning round from the stove. 'Zelda rang while you were out, Nile, and she told me you were going to get married, which was a bit of a surprise, after all these years of thinking you were only friends.'

My heart did that weird thing again, where it seemed to stop dead and then restart with a thump, and I turned to look at Nile.

'It's a surprise to me, too,' he said drily. 'She was only joking.'

'She didn't *sound* as if she was joking,' Sheila replied doubtfully. 'When I said it was a bit sudden, she told me you'd made a pact long ago that if you hadn't married someone else by the time you were forty, then you'd marry each other.'

'Except you've only just turned thirty-eight, Nile – I don't call that near forty,' Teddy said.

'Gee, thanks,' said Nile.

'But Zelda *is* forty,' Bel pointed out helpfully. 'And she hasn't been in a relationship for ages, has she? Perhaps that's what made her remember it.'

'I do vaguely recall saying something like that when we were students, but only because she reminded me about it recently,' Nile said. 'I mean, we weren't serious then, *or* now.'

'Well, *you* weren't serious, but maybe she was?' Bel suggested.

He frowned. 'I don't think so, it was just one of those daft things you say. But you know what Zelda's like – always tossing squibs into the conversation to see what reaction she gets.'

'I suppose that's it,' Sheila said, looking strangely relieved seeing that she and the rest of the family seemed to like Zelda. 'I did think it was odd, after all this time.'

'Friends are all we've been for years, and that's the way it's staying,' he said firmly. 'She knows that; she was just winding you up.'

I wondered if she really did know it. I mean, perhaps she'd suddenly realized Mr Right had been under her nose all the time.

Teddy looked as if he was going to tease Nile again, but Bel gave her twin a quelling look and changed the subject quickly.

'You'll never guess who we met up on the hill near the Oldstone, yesterday morning – I completely forgot to tell you.'

'No, we *won't* guess, so you might as well say,' Geeta told her from her seat next to the highchair, wiping a speckling of food from her face. Casper made another expansive arm movement with a loaded spoon and Honey leaped up with surprising agility for his age and caught the flying blob mid-air.

There could be a good market for flying kitchen waste disposal units, if someone invented them.

Bel was fishing out a shape sorting game in bright colours from the carrier bag she'd brought in with her and handed it across the table. 'I just remembered I got this from the car boot sale.'

'Oh, is that for Casper?' Geeta said.

'Yes, and it's like new, but I know what you're like for germs, so I expect you'll want to disinfect it before he goes anywhere near it.'

'You can't be too careful,' Geeta said seriously. 'Remember that nasty bug he caught earlier in the year? I thought it was meningitis,' she explained to me, her beautiful brown eyes full of the remembered horror of that moment. 'I was beside myself.'

'I'm not surprised!' I said.

'Well, oddly enough, it was the doctor who came out to Casper that night that we met up by the Oldstone yesterday morning,' Bel revealed.

'What, Dr Collins?' said Sheila. 'What was she doing up there?'

'Walking a small white dog. And she wasn't that pleased to run into us, because she said she'd gone there for a bit of peace and solitude.'

'That was rude of her,' said Geeta. 'But Rilla, the receptionist at the surgery, goes to my yoga class and she told me that Dr Collins moved back here to look after her father when he became very frail, so she must have a kind heart, really.'

'Well, *I* was told that she moved back because she'd heard her father was getting too fond of his live-in carer and was afraid she'd lose her inheritance,' Bel countered. 'The cleaner told me.'

'That's probably all just gossip,' said Teddy mildly, but was ignored.

'Dr Collins can't be that young, so her father must be getting on a bit,' Bel suggested.

'She's only in her mid-fifties, like me,' Sheila said slightly indignantly. 'She could be very attractive, too, she just doesn't make the best of herself. And I think she's his stepdaughter – his late wife's child by her first marriage.'

'How do *you* know all that?' asked Bel.

'Your dad told me after we bumped into her at the garage in Upvale years ago. They'd met as teenagers at a local tennis club one summer when he was staying with his grandparents and though he couldn't have changed that much, she just brushed past us without a word as if she didn't recognize him and went out.'

'He did spend a lot of his school holidays here at Oldstone with his grandparents, didn't he?' Nile said. 'That's why he was so attached to the place.'

'And his university holidays too, until he dropped out and went to work for those family friends in Germany who had the swimming pond business,' Sheila agreed.

'So – was she an old flame?' asked Bel.

'I think they'd had a bit of a teenage summer fling, from what Paul said. I saw her at the surgery once, soon after she joined the local practice, and said I believed she'd known Paul when they were younger, but she was very brusque.'

'What did she say?' asked Bel, interested.

'She said, "I barely knew him, except as a decent tennis player. The locals played like rabbits."'

'I think if I saw her coming towards me holding a racquet, *I'd* run like a rabbit, too,' Geeta said.

'Or with a loaded syringe,' I agreed, resolving that if I registered with that practice, I'd make sure my appointments were with one of her colleagues.

To meet other early walkers as I was returning to the car with Hugo after one of our morning ambles up to the Oldstone was therefore an unwelcome and unusual intrusion – and doubly so once we came near enough for recognition.

The moment my eyes met those of the tall, red-haired woman with one of the Giddingses I knew my past had come back to haunt me, though I am certain I showed no betraying flicker of surprise – and certainly I could show no other emotion, for I felt none.

Presumably she was simply curious to view the place where she was found, though the news that she was to live in the area was unwelcome: I hope she won't attempt to stir up the old story again.

She doesn't look in the least like me, yet there is a familial resemblance that, fortunately, only I am likely to perceive.

28

Mr Wrong

First thing on Monday morning, Jack surveyed the teashop floor, which was now sealed to a warm, mellow, almost honey colour, and pronounced that I could walk on it.

This was just as well, since in two days' time the job lot of tables and chairs that Nile had found for me were to arrive. If there were any to spare, Teddy would collect them in his big four-wheel-drive pickup and ferry them out to Oldstone for the waffle house.

When I texted Nile to tell him about the floor I didn't get an answer, so he was probably busy. He'd taken himself off to his flat when we'd returned (in convoy) after lunch the previous day and I hadn't seen him since.

Ross was stripping the outside paintwork of the back windows with a small blowtorch, which looked rather dangerous, while Jack had resumed his tiling, and on a sudden impulse I slipped out of the front door and across the courtyard to Small and Perfect. Even if he was going to open, I was sure Nile wouldn't be in his shop that early and I wanted to look at the Spode jug again to confirm it really *was* the same shade of blue as my Minton teapot in case of any further argument.

There was no sign of it, though. Could he possibly have sold it to an online customer overnight and taken it out of the window to pack up? Its place had been taken by a brightly coloured porcelain parakeet, so it looked rather that way.

I knew it would have been out of my price range but I still felt disappointed and cross as I returned to the café and gave the wall above the panelling in my little office a second coat of cream paint.

Then I retired upstairs to write, though as usual I was called down several times, on the final occasion to admire the new loos and washbasins in the customer toilets, though one white suite looks much like any other.

Nile must have been out all day, because it was only late that evening, just as I was about to stop working, that the lights in his flat went on. The blind was already down, so I couldn't see him . . . and he couldn't see me being a Peeping Thomasina. But two minutes later my phone buzzed with the incoming reply to the message about the floor being finished ready for the furniture.

'*Good*,' it said, as tersely as if text messages were being charged by the letter.

I went to register at the nearby medical practice next day and was informed that the only doctor taking on new patients was the one I most wanted to avoid. But then the receptionist added that of course, since it was a group practice, I could make appointments with any of the others instead.

Her tone suggested that this wouldn't be at all unusual and her expression as she glanced at the name board, where a red light was flashing next to Dr Collins, was uneasy.

The forms being completed, I was just about to leave when the woman herself flung open a nearby door and called imperiously for her next patient.

'Mrs Clemency Jones?'

She scanned the waiting room, spotted a small, inoffensive woman cowering behind a potted palm and jerked her head.

Mrs Jones got up and scuttled in past her.

As she turned to follow, Dr Collins' basilisk gaze fell on me and for the briefest moment she looked quite startled. Perhaps she thought I was stalking her?

I hadn't seen Nile to speak to since Sunday lunch, but that afternoon I had another of his terse texts saying he'd collect me at seven on the way to the pub.

Honestly! No 'would you like to go' or anything of that kind: it appeared that with the Giddingses, you only had to do something with them once, like go to the pub or stay for a weekend, and it was assumed to be a regular fixture.

A reply didn't seem called for, so I didn't send one. And when he called for me and we walked round to the pub, I didn't know why he'd bothered, because he wasn't the liveliest of company. In fact, he seemed to be pondering a knotty problem. Maybe he'd lost an amazing Stanhope or an outstanding bit of netsuke to a higher bidder and didn't know how to break it to one of his cherished list of clients?

Whatever it was, he didn't share it with me and I was just starting to wish I'd brought a book with me, when the handsome blond barman gave me a cheery grin and a wink. I smiled back and Nile happened to look up just at that moment and caught this exchange.

He glowered at the poor man. 'Is he flirting with you?' he demanded, though what business it was of his, I don't know.

'In my dreams!' I told him. 'He's got to be at least ten years younger than me. And *you* can't talk, because I only left you alone for two minutes to go to the loo and when I got back you were chatting up a strange woman.'

'She was only a tourist, asking me to point Top Withens out on her map.'

'Yeah, right! But at least she got more conversation out of you than I have. I think the barman noticed you'd gone into a coma and was just trying to cheer me up.'

He frowned at me, his black brows knitted, as if he wasn't sure whether I was joking or not.

'I was just wondering how to explain to you about Zelda and why she told Sheila we were getting married,' he said. 'It's complicated.'

'Then *don't* explain it. It's really nothing to do with me whether you get married or not, or who to,' I told him, even though secretly I was dying to know. 'And anyway, didn't you tell the family it was just her idea of a joke?'

'Well, that's what I thought a couple of weeks ago, when she reminded me we'd made that pact about marrying each other. But I mean, we were students at the time and it was just a flip, throwaway remark.'

'But she wasn't joking? She thought you meant it?'

He ran a distracted hand through his black curls. 'That's what she told me when I got back to the flat on Sunday and rang her to ask what on earth she was playing at.'

'And you definitely *didn't* agree with her when she reminded you about the pact?'

'No, of course not!' he said, sounding totally exasperated. 'I think she's gone slightly mad ever since she realized she was about to hit forty. One minute she's a complete party animal with a string of unsuitable boyfriends and the next she's telling me she's desperate to settle down and have a baby before it's too late.'

'Well, I suppose it *would* make you think,' I said. 'I mean, it's a bit late for a first baby, but people do have them well into their forties these days, don't they?'

'They might do, but not with me!' he said firmly. 'We only went out with each other for a couple of weeks right at the start of my first university term, but it didn't work out. The difference in our ages seemed greater then and she found someone older. Since then, I've felt exactly the same towards her as I do towards Bel: brotherly.'

I suddenly wondered if he saw *me* in the same light, a sort of irritating new sister, and that's why he kept dishing out the bossy orders and advice. I mean, just because *I* found him irritating and devastatingly attractive in equal measures didn't mean he had to see me the same way. And probably just as well . . .

'So, did you tell her exactly how you feel?'

'After all these years, I shouldn't have needed to, but I did. She said she doesn't really want to bring a baby up on her own, but if she hasn't found Mr Right by now and I won't oblige, then she'll have to. She's had some kind of test done to see if she's still fertile and I think they told her to get a move on.'

He gloomed into his Guinness again.

'I expect that was what threw her into a panic, so she grabbed at the nearest man – you,' I said.

'Thanks: I feel so wanted.'

'I'm sorry for her, though,' I said. 'I thought I'd found my Mr Right, though actually he was never as keen on the idea of having children as I was. I'd have liked them, because then at least I'd have had real family that I was related to.'

'I know what you mean,' he agreed. 'I'd like a family too, only not with someone I've spent half my life thinking of as a friend . . . and I keep forgetting how recently you lost your fiancé,' he added thoughtfully.

'It's only about six months ago, but actually, the breakdown I had after he was killed seems somehow to have compressed the grieving process into a couple of months,' I said. 'I mean, I still miss him and think about him a lot, but I came out on this side of the depression feeling empty and looking for something to fill the space.'

'Hence the rash decision to buy the Branwell Café, sight unseen,' he said. 'It makes more sense now.'

'And to try to trace my birth mother. I know you think *that's* rash, too, but Dan was impulsive and happy-go-lucky and he'd have thought both were a great idea.'

'Would he?' Nile said, then gloomed into his Guinness a bit more. 'Zelda said I was unable to commit to any relationship and my girlfriends always got tired of waiting and found someone who would,' he said, this obviously rankling.

'They had better luck than I did then,' I commented slightly bitterly, then added curiously, without intending to, 'Did *all* your girlfriends dump you and marry someone else?'

'Some did – or *they* got serious and *I* got cold feet and dumped them,' he admitted.

It was just as I thought: he was Mr Commitment-phobe. Zelda's phone call was now starting to look to me less like a misunderstanding but more like an attempt to hogtie him! Maybe she regretted letting him go first time round and wanted another bite of the cherry?

He sighed. 'We're business partners, so we can't permanently fall out. I'd better go down and make things up with her, and persuade her to see sense. I'm busy till the end of the week, but then I have a country house sale to go to in Surrey, so I could call in on my way back.'

'Netsuke or Stanhopes? I asked brightly, though for some reason I wasn't feeling that cheerful about him visiting Zelda . . .

'Neither: a Black Forest carved wooden bear hall stand and a matching barometer.'

'They don't exactly sound small and perfect?'

'No, actually they're big and ugly, but this particular client loves Black Forest bear carvings so much, she'll buy anything.'

To my surprise, on the way home he invited me back to his flat for coffee for the first time and I accepted out of sheer nosiness. He clearly wasn't interested in pouncing on me, so it seemed safe enough.

He unlocked the door of the shop and put the light on, and as I went in I suddenly spotted the Spode jug, sitting on a shelf.

'Oh, you haven't sold it!' I said, picking it up and fondling it. 'I noticed it had gone from the window.'

'I like to change the display from time to time,' he said. 'And you can see now that it is nothing like that Minton teapot you got at the car boot sale!'

'I never said it was,' I told him indignantly, 'only that the blue of the pattern was the same – though you can't tell that in this light.'

He looked for a moment as if he might argue the point, but then thought better of it and said, 'Come on, let's have that coffee.'

Reluctantly (and carefully, because I'd just spotted the price sticker) I replaced the jug and followed him.

His flat was smaller than mine and his kitchen and bathroom downstairs, behind the shop and its small storeroom.

He made the coffee and we carried it up to his living room, which was furnished in a rather funky retro Swedish style, with bright fabrics and lots of light wood.

'This is fun,' I said, surprised.

'I'm a fun person,' he said gravely.

'You could have fooled me. I'd have milked you for design suggestions for the teashop if I'd known, though.'

'I think you've done pretty well on your own,' he said, and then we talked about my renovations and what still needed to be done until I spotted the time – which had flown by – and got up to leave.

He handed me a small but weighty box at the front door.

'What's this?' I asked, surprised.

'That paperweight you wanted for Lola, remember? It's Clichy, so you're going to be paying me back in afternoon teas for ever.'

'I might toss you the occasional crust,' I conceded magnanimously.

The van driver bringing the tables and chairs actually managed to follow directions and find the back of the café, which was unique among delivery men.

In fact, the first I knew of his arrival was a knock at the back door – and when I opened it, the first stack of chairs was already piled up outside and he'd gone to fetch the next.

Jack, who was grouting endless yards of tiling, helped him carry the rest in and through to the teashop, where I spent ages arranging and rearranging the tables and chairs, until I came up with a configuration I liked. I didn't want the customers jammed in together, but an airy, relaxing ambience.

There was a large, round table capable of seating six people, which fitted neatly into the bow window. Then I arranged half a dozen little square ones down the side of the room and dotted the smaller round tables about.

Finally satisfied, I half-closed my eyes and imagined the lights glittering on cutlery and glass tumblers, the sheen of the white tablecloths and the chink of cake fork against plate . . .

'You could squeeze a couple more in,' helpfully suggested Nile from right behind me, almost giving me a heart attack. I'd forgotten the door was open because Ross was out at the front, stripping paint from the door and window frames.

'I think you should be belled, like a cat,' I told him.

'Did I startle you? I didn't see you standing there until I was in, because you hadn't got the lights on. I think you need some replacement light fittings, by the way,' he added. 'Those rustic wood effect ones would look better in the waffle house.'

'You're right, but I thought they'd do for now and I could replace them later, when I found something more suitable. I'm not sure quite what.'

I gestured at a stack of chairs and tables at the back, near the counter. 'I don't want to squeeze any more in, so those are to go up to Oldstone.'

'I expect Sheila will store them in the attics until needed. Goodness knows, there's enough room in there to hide a battleship.'

'They are very spacious,' I agreed. 'Sheila could make lots more letting bedrooms there eventually, if she wanted to.'

'Don't encourage her, or we'll be a country house hotel,' he said.

'Oh, I don't think so – she couldn't do it all herself, and her pottery is her consuming interest, isn't it? She just slots one or two visitors in with the family and then it's not any trouble at all.'

I looked round the room with satisfaction at how it was coming together. 'You know, if Jack carries on at this rate, there won't be any major jobs left unfinished after next week! He's painting the outside woodwork tomorrow if it's dry – that's why Ross is stripping the old paint off – and the sign should be back, too.'

'Yes, is that boy safe with a blowtorch?' he asked.

'I hope so, but I've told him if he cracks any of the old glass in the bow window I'll kill him.'

I checked my watch. 'Well, if you just wandered in from curiosity and don't need me for anything, I'd better go and chase up the fitted double ovens that were promised for today and haven't appeared.'

'Actually, I came over to give you this,' he said, handing me a bubble-wrapped parcel. 'Early teashop opening gift.'

'Oh, you shouldn't have . . .' I began to protest, and then stopped once I'd revealed the lovely blue and white jug I'd adored from the moment I set eyes on it. 'Nile – *really*, you shouldn't have!'

'I didn't think you'd be able to resist picking it up and fondling it every time you came into the shop, so I thought I'd give it to you before you dropped it and wiped all the value off in one go.'

'But . . . I saw the price tag, so I know it really *is* valuable! You can't give all your stock away and I haven't even paid you for Lola's paperweight.'

'Actually, this is one of my mistakes. It's been mended, listen.' He pinged the side of the jug and it made a flat sort of note.

'It's been well done, though. I arrived late at an auction and bought a box of stuff sight unseen, because they held the jug up.'

'Well, I suppose you would have needed X-ray eyes to see the mend from where you were?'

He shrugged. 'It still has some value and also, I found one or two good things in that box when I got it back home. I was going to take the jug down to London to see if Zelda could sell it, before you took a fancy to it.'

'Thank you very much,' I said. 'I do love it, though I don't know why, unless it's because the pastoral scene is so idyllic and soothing.'

'Soothing redheads is my speciality,' he said.

'How many do you know?'

'Just the one, which is quite enough,' he said, then favoured me with the ghost of his shatteringly attractive smile and turned to leave. 'Don't forget dinner tomorrow – I'll drive.'

'What?' I said blankly.

He half-turned and raised a surprised eyebrow. 'Mr Rochester's Restaurant? You did say you wanted to go, so I've booked us in for tomorrow evening. I've got a flail to deliver while we're at it.'

'While we're at *what*?' I blurted out, so it was probably just as well he was halfway back to his shop and didn't hear me.

And did he say a *flail*?

I'd put the unwelcome incident out of my head – but then I opened my door to summon a tardy patient and there she was, looking at me with those strangely pale jade-green eyes.

I don't know why I was so taken aback to see her again so soon – and right there, in my surgery. But the surprise was transient for, since I'd been told she was to open a tearoom in the village, she would of course need to register with a nearby doctor at some point.

And she had registered with me, *as I elicited from the receptionist once I had got rid of my patient, a chronic hypochondriac.*

29

The Food of Love

I had to give myself a good talking to, while I was getting ready to go out. Despite what Lola thought, I was certain Nile didn't *really* fancy me – why should he when he could have practically any girl he wanted – and even if he did, I wasn't looking for a casual affair and a broken heart. Up the ladder and down the snake again . . .

What's more, I still didn't know exactly where he stood with his partner, Zelda.

No, it would be so easy to fall for Nile, but I wasn't going to let myself. This invitation to dinner was a casual thing and I'd treat it that way.

But since Nile was prone to look elegant and expensive even when he was wearing jeans, I decided to give my best dress an outing, although really it was more suited to a summer garden party than an autumn dinner at a remote moorland restaurant.

I got it in a sale, and mostly it lived a quiet life inside its cover on a padded hanger. It was long and swirly and made of silk in shades of green and amber. I wore a short dark green cashmere cardigan over it, but I hoped the restaurant was heated or I'd be an ice maiden in *minutes*.

When Nile picked me up the ensemble was hidden by a black maxi winter coat in a slightly military style, which I'd worn for so many years it was getting threadbare round the edges of the cuffs and on the collar.

'Very Russian Front,' he said, surveying me. 'It just needs one of those round fur hats.'

'Fake fur – I've got one,' I said. 'It was Edie's, but it never suited her and I'm not sure it's entirely me, either, so I only wear it if it's actually snowing.'

He led the way down the path to the car, looking good enough to eat in one of his beautiful silky suits and an open-necked shirt.

'You'll freeze like that,' I told him.

'My own version of the Russian Front coat is in the car. So's the flail – come on.'

On the way he reminded me that Henry had asked him to look out for any suitable old bits of agricultural equipment to decorate the barn walls with and he thought the flail, an antique wood and leather contraption, would be perfect.

When we got there the restaurant was buzzing with people, so the food must be brilliant to get them to drive out to such a remote spot. We were shown to a table for two in a secluded corner lit only by a candle lantern, which would have been rather romantic, had we been on those terms.

Again I wondered, had Nile and Zelda really been just friends all these years? And did it matter to me one way or the other? After all, even if I wanted to chance another go at love at some future point, it wouldn't be with a self-confessed commitment-phobe.

The waiter took my coat away, bearing it off as reverentially as if it had been an ermine mantle and I found, to my relief, that the room *was* warm.

'You look very dryad in that dress,' Nile said, sitting down on the other end of the curved corner seat.

'Is that good?' I asked, because they were certainly not good news in my books!

'Definitely – except you're getting lots of attention, which might turn your head.'

'Actually, I think the hen party on the far table are all trying to get *your* attention,' I pointed out.

Startled, he looked across and a pretty blonde – who presumably was

256

the future bride, since she had topped her bunny girl outfit with a veil – waved at him, which I thought was cheeky, since they must have assumed we were a couple.

He turned his back quickly. 'I think I've got enough troublesome women in my life for the moment,' he said. 'Alice?'

The dawn was breaking, lighting up Shaz's pink hair and sparkling on the sequin vest top that stopped just above her slim waist.

'Rumours of your beauty didn't lie – you were truly named,' said Prince S'Hallow. 'Kiss me again!'

'I don't mind if I do, love,' she said, with a glance at her boyfriend, now hand in hand with another woman. If Kev preferred fat girls with brassy blond hair, then it was his loss!

On the edge of the wood there was a fluttering of green draperies and a faint, faraway snarling. Unnoticed by the charm-crossed lovers, the dryads were regrouping and ready to take revenge for their poor, fallen sister.

'Alice?' repeated Nile patiently and I blinked and came back to reality again.

'Sorry, I just had another idea for the book. Did you say something?'

'Nothing important. How *is* the book coming along?'

'A bit quicker now, though of course I'm constantly having to break off mid-sentence. If Jack isn't interrupting me, then I'm chasing up equipment and fittings, not to mention sussing out my catering suppliers and . . . well, all the million and one other things on my lists.'

'Just as well Bel and Sheila have till next Easter to get their heads round it all for their waffle house,' he said. 'And at least now Sheila's realized she needs to employ someone else to run it for her.'

'If my tearoom is a success, then I'm sure Tilda can manage it, and I'll only have to do some early morning baking – I enjoy that – then go back to the flat and write unless I'm needed. But at first, of course, I'll have to be there most of the time.'

We studied our menus while we talked, and when our delicious-looking starters had been set in front of us, he said, 'I've finished the first of your novels and it was . . . a bit of an eye opener. I can see it owes a lot to old fairy tales and I know the earlier versions were quite horrific, but yours sets them in a contemporary world and gives them a lot more horror and some very unexpected twists.'

'I don't know about unexpected: half of my plots seem to end up reworking what happened to me in various ways, though I suppose most novelists do the same. The abandonment theme, and finding out you're really a princess and all that.'

He smiled and the soft light of the candle made his eyes gleam like silver against his olive skin. They held mine and I found somehow I couldn't look away.

'Tonight you're *my* princess, though I won't imprison you in my tower, Rapunzel, because after reading your novel, I'm afraid some hideous comeuppance would be on the cards,' he said softly.

I was still staring mesmerized into his eyes and I'm not sure what I would have replied, if anything, had Henry not appeared just then and said, 'I'm not interrupting anything, am I? Only Nico told me a customer had brought me something – I love the flail!'

'Great, isn't it?' agreed Nile. 'I know where I can get you a couple of really ancient scythes as well, if you don't think they'd be too Grim Reaper.'

'No – they'd literally give a bit of edge to the place!' Henry said, grinning.

Then we told him how wonderful his food was, which was the perfect truth, and asked after Eleri.

'She's blooming,' he said, and added that she hoped to see me again soon, though I expect he was simply being polite.

But he obviously thought Nile and I were a couple, because after he'd gone back to the kitchen the waiter brought over a bottle of champagne, courtesy of the house, and then, after our main course, the other waiter, Nico, suddenly appeared with a violin and gave us a table-side rendition of '*O Sole Mio*'.

Jack would have *loved* it and probably sung along . . .

I felt hideously embarrassed because everyone looked at us, but Nile seemed amused and played up to it, first holding my hand across the table and then edging around the bench seat until he was sitting close enough to put his arm around me.

'What are you doing?' I hissed.

'We can't disappoint them,' he said. 'Relax and get in the groove.' Then he poured me another glass of champagne, so I didn't so much relax as go limp. He was driving, so I'd already had more than my fair share.

When it was time to leave, Nile insisted on paying the bill, since he'd invited me. He wouldn't take no for an answer, so finally I left him to settle it while I went to the cloakroom. I wasn't entirely in command of my legs and I felt a bit weird, so it was a relief to find I looked fairly normal in the mirror, though a little flushed and glittery-eyed.

I returned to find Nile by the door, looking a bit like a stag at bay and with the bunny bride draped all over him.

'It was always you I really loved, Nile,' she sobbed into the lapels of his lovely suit.

'But we only went out for a few weeks, Chloe, and then you left me for Gareth,' he protested, looking even more hideously embarrassed when he spotted me.

I shrugged myself into my coat and walked on past and out of the door, just as two of the hen party started peeling Chloe off him.

'You know you adore Gareth and he thinks you're the best thing since sliced bread,' one of them was saying. The country must be lit-tered with Nile's exes, which reinforced my determination not to weaken and become one of them.

The moment the cold air hit me, so did the full effect of the alcohol and I reeled. Nile must have escaped right after I left, because suddenly his arm came round me just before I fell over.

'Hold up,' he said. 'You should have waited for me – you've had too much champagne.'

'There's no such thing as too much champagne,' I informed him. 'And I left because it was all a bit embarrassing in there.'

'Tell me about it!' he said ruefully. Then he began to steer me in a straighter line towards the car.

'The sky's so pretty,' I said, stopping dead suddenly and staring up into the midnight-blue darkness, scattered with sparkling points of light.

'Yes, lovely. Can you see your lucky star, Alice?' he asked, and when I looked heavenward again, quickly kissed me . . . or I think that was his intention until I kissed him back. I was not entirely in control of my lips.

By the time he released me, the stars had developed a tendency to spin round, but I was sure that was just the champagne.

'Sorry – but that was irresistible,' he said. '*You* were irresistible!'

'I – don't think that was a good idea,' I told him with as much firmness as I could muster.

'Perhaps not,' he agreed, looking down at me gravely. 'Put it down to an unwise impulse.' Then he added inconsequentially, 'There's an Arlo Guthrie song called "Alice's Restaurant". Apparently you can get anything there you want – except Alice.'

'I'm not opening a restaurant, just a tearoom,' I said, but I didn't shake off his arm when he put it round me again and walked me over to the car. I'd definitely overdone the bubbly, because the ground shifted underfoot and the stars were now not so much spinning as whirling about as if they'd escaped from a Van Gogh painting.

'A tea emporium,' he agreed, opening the car door and helping me in, where I'm afraid I fell into a light, befuddled doze, so he had to wake me when we got home.

Still, by the time I got out of the car again the cold night air woke me up a bit and as I unlocked the back door I remembered my manners – and that he had insisted on paying the rather large bill – and turned to say politely: 'I had a great evening, thank you so much.'

'You know, so did I, embarrassing interlude with Chloe excepted,' he replied, then casually flicked my cheek with one finger, turned and walked off up the passageway to his shop without another word, though he seemed to be humming something . . . maybe it was that song he'd been on about earlier.

I didn't even change when I got upstairs, just threw my coat over a chair, made a pot of strong coffee, then went to my desk and wrote and wrote into the night.

I was vaguely aware of Nile's window opposite, glowing with light and then, when I looked up later, dark again.

Towards dawn, just before I finally went to bed, I searched for that Arlo Guthrie song on YouTube . . .

Once I'd had time to reflect on things, I felt no more than mildly irritated by this young woman's appearance on the scene, for even were she to stir things up in a search for her birth mother, it would be unavailing.

Of course, I hoped she would not — this emotional and irrational urge to find and forge a connection with someone who clearly didn't want you in the first place is beyond my understanding.

Certainly, considering our relationship, I'd felt no warmer emotion than surprise at seeing her. How horrified my colleagues would be if they knew the true story — and how cold they would think my attitude!

30

Stand and Deliver

I woke up horribly early, with the scenes of the book I'd written late last night clear as crystal in my head, but the events at the restaurant after my third glass of champagne rather fuzzy.

I could remember the way Nile had looked at me across the table, while a violin played . . . and then a blonde in a bunny-girl outfit and a bridal veil making a scene. After that, it got even hazier: stars came into it . . . and a song about another Alice and a restaurant. And a kiss or two . . . unless I'd dreamed those up, which was entirely possible.

I pulled myself together with an effort: I was expecting the overdue delivery of the new double catering-sized oven, in another of those wonderful time slots, this one being between half past seven and twelve noon. So I carried my mug of coffee down with me to the kitchen, arriving just in time to spot through the window the tall and unmistakable figure of Nile, heading for his car.

Another early riser – and I was positive he hadn't mentioned that he was going anywhere – but then, why should he? My hazy recollections of last night were that we'd kissed, come home and then parted perfectly casually after a nice evening. Nothing to give me the right to bounce out of the back door and demand to know when he'd be back.

I had plenty of time to file the latest business receipts and update the accounts book before the inevitable phone call from the delivery driver. He was in some giant pantechnicon and the nearest he could get to the teashop in that was the cobbled main street at the end of the passage.

His satnav had told him to turn down Doorknocker's Row, but fortunately he'd had enough sense not to try it.

I went through and opened the front door to the café and a few moments later there was a rumbling noise and a disgruntled-looking man appeared, wheeling the oven on a trolley.

He said he couldn't leave his van where it was, so he'd have to drop the oven off at the door.

'No you won't,' I told him pleasantly. 'I've paid for delivery and connection, and that means you have to bring it right through to the kitchen: come along – you're in luck, because I've had a wheelchair ramp fitted so you don't have to get it down the step.'

I was so glad I'd laid a walkway of flattened cardboard boxes over my beautifully sanded new floor, too, to protect it from workmen's feet, because those trolley wheels wouldn't have done it any good at all.

Once he'd got it through the front door, he tried again to make his escape, but I stood my ground, blocking his exit, and told him that if he just got on with it instead of arguing, he'd be away the quicker. Eventually he gave in.

In sulky silence, but with the speed of practice, he ripped open the box and installed my beautiful double oven, which was merely a matter of connecting it to the newly wired socket and pushing it into place. Then he tossed all the packaging back into the box, put it on the trolley and went off, muttering darkly. I suspected he had misogynistic tendencies.

Tilda arrived to clean while I was still reading the instruction manual before switching it on and heating the ovens through. She went up to do the flat first, which took her no time at all, and then she did the best she could with the teashop, complaining all the while that as usual the workmen had left dust everywhere.

We shared a pot of stewed tea at eleven and she admired the new ovens. 'Space age, them are,' she said approvingly. 'I can feel the heat from here, too, though I can't see anything cooking.'

'No, you have to run them empty for at least an hour, before you bake anything.'

'Why's that, then?'

'I've no idea,' I confessed. 'Though new ovens smell better when you've done it, so maybe that's it?'

'If they're new, they should smell fine anyway.'

'It's one of life's great mysteries,' I agreed, passing her the chocolate digestive biscuits, and she looked around her.

'It's more like a hospital in here now, with all these white units and tiles.'

'Easy to clean – and easy to see when it *is* clean,' I explained. 'I'll add a bit of colour with new blinds and some tough vinyl flooring – I'm having the same one all the way through to the back door.'

'What about in the basement? They've taken up all the old stuff, what was nearly wore through.'

I got up and showed her the samples I'd chosen from. 'This dove-grey one – the same as upstairs. Now the tiling is finished in the customer toilets, the flooring can all go down as soon as it arrives – Jack's organizing that.'

'Nell and I will be glad when it's all done and the teashop opens, because we like to keep busy and that cleaning agency pays peanuts.'

'Isn't Nell . . . ?' I wondered how to put it tactfully. 'I mean, won't she be thinking of retiring soon?'

'No, why should she? She's fit as a fiddle and walks for miles every day with our Frank,' she said, looking astounded at the mere suggestion.

'Frank?'

'Our greyhound. There's a rescue place always trying to find homes for them. You should have one for a bit of company.'

'I'll certainly think about it, when I've settled down,' I agreed, then added, 'Nell must be fit if she's out with the dog every day.'

'She always says you have to use it or lose it,' Tilda said. 'You think on about getting a greyhound.'

'I will,' I promised.

Then I heard the back door open and assumed it was one of the workmen.

'Cooee!' called the unmistakable and unwelcome voice of Jim Voss, and then he strolled in as if he was sure of his welcome.

'Our Nell said she'd seen him here before,' Tilda said, eyeing him with disfavour. 'Does he haunt the place?'

'I might say the same about the Capsticks!' he snapped back, disconcerted. 'Don't let me keep you, if you're leaving.'

'I'm not – I work here,' she said.

'Did you want something?' I asked him bluntly.

He glanced at Tilda, who was clearly immovable, then said with an ingratiating smile, 'I'm here on a delicate mission – Mrs Muswell called us last night in great distress.'

'Has she found her conscience lying about somewhere?' asked Tilda.

'She should have called me,' I said. 'I'm the one she's cheated.'

'Quite unintentionally, it appears,' he said quickly. 'She didn't think you'd want any of those old things, they were only fit to be thrown out.'

'Yeah, right,' I said. 'So, can I have her phone number?'

'I don't have it,' he lied. 'But she's calling us again later today because, as I say, she's sent me on a delicate mission. She suddenly remembered that she'd left her mother's tea set in a box under the stairs to the basement – and it's of great sentimental value and she'd like it back.'

'But that's where the willow-pattern china was, and there isn't anything else in there, other than a vacuum cleaner.'

'She was positive it was there, behind the boxes of willow pattern – and since she has no objection to your having that, she thought you wouldn't have any objection to giving me the tea service to pass on to her.'

'Having stripped the place of anything of any value, it's kind of her not to demand that willow pattern back, too,' Tilda said drily. 'Eh, the cheek of the woman!'

'The value of the willow-pattern china is a drop in the ocean of the amount she owes me,' I said. 'And I'm entitled to keep anything I find on my premises.'

'But surely, her mother's tea set . . .' he blustered.

'Alice's already told you, it wasn't there,' said Tilda. 'The cupboard's empty apart from that clapped-out old vacuum cleaner – an antique like you, Jim Voss!'

He flushed an unbecoming dark red, right up to the top of his balding head. 'Perhaps I could see for myself.'

'Perhaps you could take yourself off,' she returned.

'Yes – we've already told you it isn't there and we're very busy, so we'd prefer your space to your presence,' I told him.

He glowered at us, clamped his lips together on whatever he was thinking of saying and marched out, slamming the back door behind him.

'Our Nell has the right of it: he's a little sneaking snirp,' Tilda said.

Later, just after Tilda had left, the teashop sign came back, newly lettered in white on dark teal to match the rest of the outside paintwork. 'The Fat Rascal' was in large script and underneath, in smaller lettering, it read, 'Afternoon Tea Emporium'.

When it was fixed up I stood there for ages, simply drinking in the wonderful effect of the sign, the glossy paintwork, the pretty trellis porch and the shining bull's-eye glass of the bow window. (That was Tilda's doing – she swore by vinegar and crumpled newspaper.)

Bel, who had driven in for some shopping, found me there and said admiringly, 'Oh, it looks perfect now, doesn't it?'

'Well, almost, but I think it still needs a couple of finishing touches,' I said consideringly. 'Nile gave me a big blue and white jug and I'll have that on the window ledge, filled with seasonal flowers, but don't you think there should be something else actually *outside* to brighten it up?'

'Yes, perhaps a tub of flowers or something,' Bel suggested. 'We could go to a garden centre over the weekend and see what we can find, if you like. You *are* coming out to Oldstone again, aren't you? You know Mum expects you to now, unless you tell her you can't make it?'

'It's very kind of her and I'll come tomorrow, but I want to work on my book tonight, when it's quiet.'

Mind you, if Nile wasn't back it might be *too* quiet in Doorknocker's Row . . . and feel a bit lonely. I liked it better when I could look across and see the comforting square of light that showed he was home.

'Is Nile going to be there this weekend?' I asked, despite myself.

'Oh, Nile seldom says what he's doing, he just turns up. Isn't he here?'

'No, he went off somewhere very early.'

'He told Mum he was taking you to Mr Rochester's Restaurant last night,' she said, looking at me sideways. 'Are you seeing each other?'

'It would be hard to avoid seeing each other, since we both live in Doorknocker's Row,' I said evasively. 'But we did go to the restaurant, because Nile had something to deliver to Henry Godet, the owner. He wanted to see what the food was like, too, so he asked me if I'd like to go with him.'

She looked disappointed – I'm not quite sure what she was expecting. 'Oh . . . right. And what *was* it like?'

'Delicious!'

She looked at me expectantly. 'And . . . ?'

'A violinist came and played at the table, which was embarrassing – but not as embarrassing as one of Nile's many ex-girlfriends making a drunken scene over him as we left.'

'Which one?'

'I think I heard her being called Chloe.'

'I remember Chloe. She left Nile for someone else, so I don't know why she would make a scene. And actually, he hasn't had many girlfriends since he moved up here,' she added.

'It makes no difference to me how many women he's gone out with,' I said. 'We're just friends.'

'Mmm . . .' Bel said, but seeing she wasn't going to tease any more out of me (which would have been difficult, given the muddled state both of my recollections of the evening and my emotions), she changed tack. 'Teddy and Geeta have volunteered to help Mum paint the new bedroom in the morning while Jan, their part-time nanny, looks after Casper, so I don't think we'll be needed till later. If you come for lunch then we could go to the garden centre afterwards?'

'That would be fun. I do love garden centres.'

'Me too, and there's a wonderful one the other side of Upvale. Oh, by the way,' she said as we went back indoors, 'Teddy's coming on

Monday in the pickup to collect the leftover tables and chairs, if that's all right?'

'Yes, fine – they stack up, as you see.'

'I could take some of the chairs back with me in the car now,' she suggested.

'Good idea, and I'll bring a couple more tomorrow and then he might get what's left into one load.'

The distant strains of a tenor voice singing something swoopingly operatic wafted up from the basement, along with the sound of an electric drill.

'Jack's back,' I said.

At lunch next day, Sheila told us that Nile had rung her from London, because he'd spotted a nice but pricey piece of Troika and wondered if she wanted him to buy it.

'And it's a huge lamp base, which is something I haven't already got, so I told him to try and haggle the price down and then go for it.'

So . . . Nile had gone off straight to London yesterday morning, presumably to see Zelda. And there was absolutely *no* reason why he should have told me he was going to do that, let alone say goodbye before he went . . .

It was ages since I'd been to a garden centre and I was surprised at the array of other things they seemed to stock now, and not just plant-related, either.

They also had a coffee shop, where we repaired after I'd chosen two very large teal-blue glazed pots for either side of the café door. They were already planted up with ball-shaped variegated holly trees surrounded by a circle of winter pansies.

That decided, I thought I'd get something for Nile, to liven up the dark green and gold frontage of Small and Perfect, so I picked a light green wooden tub, planted with a red rose tree on a long stem, that reminded me of the illustrations in my old copy of *Alice's Adventures in Wonderland*.

It was a bit pricey, but it would make me feel better about accepting that valuable jug and the expensive meal on Thursday night.

The garden centre promised to deliver the planters next afternoon, so I drew them a map of how to get to the back of the teashop. I was thinking of having it printed on cards to hand out: it would save a lot of time.

Bel and I painted the skirting boards in the new letting bedroom next morning, since Teddy and Geeta had already done their bit the previous day. I felt I ought to earn my lunch in more than just advice on catering rules and regulations.

Sheila was surprised when Nile didn't make it back for Sunday lunch, so it must have been a rare event. I didn't linger long afterwards either, for I needed to be back at the flat before the planters were delivered.

And it was just as well Nile's car *wasn't* parked there, because the plants arrived on the back of a small open-topped truck, which was manoeuvred into the alleyway parking space next to my car without any problem.

The pots and tub were wheeled through the passage to the courtyard and put into place and they looked perfect – the finishing touches to the outside. I thought Nile's rose tree, in its light green planter, looked especially elegant and hoped he would like it.

One of the men who delivered them lingered to look at the overgrown roses in my garden – if a square of paving with beds around it could be called that.

'Neglected,' he said, shaking his head sadly. 'But cut them back hard, feed them in spring and see what happens, before you dig any of them out,' he advised, and I thanked him. I'd do that, and now I'd been to the garden centre, I could imagine how my little courtyard garden *could* look with a bit of TLC, some more pots and planters and perhaps a fountain in the middle – one of those ones that burble gently through big pebbles.

Soothing . . .

I reminded myself of all the money I'd already spent this weekend and then went back upstairs to work on my book: cause and effect.

The dryads, having regrouped, were going to come back for vengeance and things could only get gory – just as the two couples were about to get sorted out into their right pairings, too . . . or not, as the case might be.

Beauty had grabbed Kev and planted a smacker right on his lips at the same moment as Prince S'Hallow did the same to Shaz, causing the Here-and-now to tremble in the air like a bubble about to pop.

But then suddenly they were all jerked apart by loud and bloodcurdling screams and turned to see the dryads running towards them, pointed teeth bared and long talons reaching out to tear limb from limb . . .

Kev leaped in front of Beauty and swung his scimitar. 'Don't you harpies come near my girl,' he yelled.

Beauty thought that was very sweet, but he'd really no idea what he was up against and might need a little help. She leaned around and took aim with the magic weapon.

'You can keep away from my prince too!' Shaz yelled, her own long pink talons curling into claws.

'Let me deal with this, my dear,' said Prince S'Hallow, unsheathing a gold-handled sword and swishing it about in the air, though not in a way that led her to think he knew what to do with it.

It all went to show that stupidity was the better part of valour.

I was still away with the wicked fairies when Nile's voice jerked me back to reality.

'Alice? Are you there?' he called from the bottom of the stairs.

I rose stiffly to my feet. 'Come up,' I invited, and he appeared a moment later. He looked tired – but then, I suppose he would after driving all the way up from London.

'I did knock on the café door first. You need a bell that rings up here, or one of those intercom things, for when the café is shut. I don't like just walking in.'

'It hasn't stopped you so far,' I pointed out. 'And you could have sent me a message saying you were on your way.'

'I did, several of them. Your car was at the back, so when you didn't answer, I got worried.'

'I was just working,' I explained, still so far away I was having trouble reconnecting to the here-and-now. 'Did you want me for anything?'

'Well, I assume you had something to do with the rose in a tub outside my shop, since there are also two pots either side of your door?'

'Oh, yes – I'd forgotten,' I said. 'Bel and I went to the garden centre yesterday. Do you like it? It's a present, for all you've done for me, not to mention the lovely jug.'

'Yes . . . and thank you. I think.'

'Think?' I repeated. 'You're not a plant lover?'

'Oh, I love them all right, only I'm away so much it'll probably die of thirst, or get pot-bound, or whatever.'

'I'll look after it, along with mine,' I offered. 'The garden centre man who delivered them has given me some advice about the old roses in the backyard, too.'

'I've brought you something else I picked up while I was away, but please don't pay me back in more plants,' he said ungratefully. 'I've left the boxes downstairs – come and see.'

And there, on the old table in the utility room, were a load of cardboard cartons, absolutely full of dusty willow-pattern china.

'Bel said you needed more, so I put the word out,' he explained.

And it seemed every dealer he knew was inundated with cheap modern willow-pattern china that they were dying to get rid of, because on the way down and back he'd collected all of this.

'I'd have made it back hours ago, in time for lunch, if I hadn't had to detour so often,' he complained. 'There's more to come, too, if you want it.'

'I don't think I can have too much, because of breakages, and I've got lots of room in the cupboards here to store it. Thank you so much, Nile,' I said gratefully. 'You're so thoughtful, and I'm always such a cow to you!' I added with sudden compunction: he did bring out the defensive hedgehog spikes.

He gave me one of those undermining smiles. 'Not quite always . . . and anyway, I like your acerbic edge – it keeps me on my toes.' He bent down and hauled a bigger box out from under the table. 'I brought this in first, because it's a bit delicate. I spotted it in a friend's shop and thought it would be perfect for the café.'

I unfolded the lid to reveal an old chandelier in a wide, shallow and rather art deco style, with matching wall lights.

'Oh, it's lovely!' I said, as he held it up. 'But it must have cost a *fortune*!'

'No, I did a deal with some stuff of mine he wanted. Anyway, it's another way of burdening you with gratitude and getting you in my evil power.' He stroked an imaginary handlebar moustache and leered.

'Huh!' I said, unimpressed, then added, 'Do you want to come upstairs?'

'That's not an offer I get every day,' he said, raising one eyebrow.

'For a cup of coffee,' I said pointedly, though going slightly pink, because I'd suddenly remembered our smoochy moment outside the restaurant. It only showed how far I'd vanished into the book, that I'd totally forgotten it until that moment. 'Maybe something to eat, too, because I haven't had anything for hours and I'm ravenous.'

I cooked pasta, added a jar of pesto sauce and a sprinkling of grated Parmesan (hardly up to Henry Godet's standards, but good and filling) and while we were eating it, Nile told me where he'd been.

'I had to go to Norfolk first and then across to a place near Guildford, so I thought I might as well call in on Zelda this morning before I came home, to clear the air with her.'

'And . . . did you manage to do that?' I asked.

He frowned. 'It's odd: you've known someone for years and years and think you understand what makes them tick, and then they throw you a curve ball that makes you see you really didn't at all.'

'A new curve ball, or the old one?'

'A new dimension: the reason she thought I'd be up for marrying her and starting a family is that she was under the illusion that I'd kept a torch burning for her ever since we briefly went out with each other at university.'

'And have you?' I asked bluntly, the words just marching right out there.

'No, of course I haven't!' he snapped. 'I've already told you that I only see her as a friend and that's how I thought she saw me, too. Yet all the time she really thought . . . I mean, she's very *pretty* but she doesn't ring my bells.' He looked across at me, his light grey eyes inscrutable. 'I seem to go for an entirely different kind of girl these days.'

'Presumably she usually prefers a different kind of man – so you're a desperation measure.'

'Yes – thanks for that,' he said tartly. 'But what it all boils down to is that she's obsessed with the idea of having a baby before it's too late and would rather do it with a partner than on her own. And she genuinely thought that I'd never found someone else because I was in love with her. I wondered why she was so affectionate all of a sudden, and kept ringing me about stuff she'd usually sort without my going down to London.'

'Yeah, right,' I said disbelievingly. 'I'm sure I've read that novel.' I was starting to think Zelda could have a second career as a writer. 'So, did you put her straight?'

'Yes, and she says she's going to have to go it alone, with AI.'

'Lots of women do, these days,' I said.

'I warned her to weigh it all up carefully first, but she said she hadn't got time, the clock was ticking.'

'It does sound as if she can't think of anything else, now.'

'No, she can't, because then I suggested that since she'd been left a bit of money lately, she should buy me out of the antiques stall and throw herself into expanding the business. She said she'd consider it, but she might need the money to buy a flat, because living on a house boat wouldn't be ideal with a child.'

'I suppose that's true,' I said. 'You'll just have to wait and see how things pan out.'

'That's the conclusion I came to, as well,' he said, getting up. 'And now I'd better go and unpack the rest of the car and leave you to do some more work.'

'I'd just about got to the staring-into-space phase of trying to fig-ure out how it will all end,' I said. 'I can't do any more tonight, so perhaps, before you go, you wouldn't mind helping me with some-thing in the tearoom? I need you to hand me the crockery I want to display on the shelves, so I don't have to keep going up and down the ladder. It'll only take a few minutes.'

'Opportunist!' he said, though after watching me sway about on the top of the ladder for a few moments, he told me I was unnerving him and took over.

Bossy as always.

Still, despite my colleagues evidently considering me to be completely devoid of human emotions, I wasn't entirely immune to curiosity. I therefore asked to see the files of patients who had recently registered, a perfectly reasonable request and one I'd made before. I discovered Alice Rose lived not far from the surgery and thought I might walk in that direction one day.

31

Distant Echoes

Robbie, having heard about Dan's death from mutual friends, actually rang me, all the way from Australia! This wasn't something he was prone to do. In fact, I didn't think I'd heard his voice since he emigrated, but he sounded just the same.

'Where did you get this landline number from?' I asked, astonished, once he'd trotted out his 'Sorry for your loss, mate' condolences, like a pale imitation Crocodile Dundee. I'm pretty sure the 'mate' was unintentional, it just slipped out.

'Edie gave it to me and told me where you were. She always had a soft spot for me,' he said smugly.

'She did until you vanished to Australia. After that, whenever your name came up, she said you were a great daftie.'

'It's probably a Scottish term of endearment and I think she's forgiven me. Anyway, I'll be coming over soon and I wanted to see you.'

'Why? You didn't bother last time, or the one before.'

'No, but that was because you were at the other end of the country, shacked up with Dan Carmichael.'

'I wasn't shacked up with him, we were engaged,' I said coldly, though actually, since Dan was still married at the time, I wasn't sure that was technically possible.

'My mother was asking after you the other day,' he said, changing the subject.

'Your *mother*?' I repeated incredulously, because the only time he'd taken me to visit his parents, she hadn't exactly made me welcome.

'Why? I mean, she didn't like me and thought I wasn't good enough for you.'

'You're quite wrong,' he said earnestly. 'She said you were a nice girl who kept me grounded.'

Even a sheet anchor wouldn't keep Robbie grounded when he felt the urge to jump off a cliff, holding a bit of canvas canopy, or catch the next monster wave.

'Remember that time you took me to visit them, Robbie? The moment you and your dad sloped off to the pub before lunch, she said they'd always hoped you'd marry someone with a *profession*, not a waitress. When I told her I wasn't a waitress and she needn't get her knickers in a twist, because we weren't engaged or even living together, she was delirious with happiness.'

'I think you must have misunderstood her, because she's never said a word against you,' he assured me. 'In fact, that time a couple of years ago when she and Dad came over to visit me just as things were getting serious with Lucy, they asked me why I couldn't come back home and settle down with a nice girl like you.'

'Was Lucy the one who got arrested for mooning at people on the beach?' I asked, interested.

'Yes, but she was drunk. It's the sort of thing anyone might do.'

'*I've* managed to resist the urge so far,' I said, but he wasn't listening: he never had. It had been one of his many drawbacks as a boyfriend.

'So when Mum mentioned you the other day,' he carried on, as if I'd never spoken, 'I told her you'd lost your fiancé and bought a café in Haworth and she said she'd love to see you again and I should take you down for the weekend.'

'That's very kind of her,' I said, even though I'd rather gnaw my arm off than spend a weekend in Wimbledon with the Frays. 'But I'm afraid I'm way too busy to go anywhere, because my teashop opens at the start of November.'

'I'll have to come up to see you there, then. I'm thinking of moving back to the UK and it would be nice to talk it over.'

'Are you *seriously* thinking of it?' I asked, surprised. 'I thought you were set to be an eternal beach bum?'

'I'm more into microlight aircraft and white-water rafting these days,' he said. 'My best mate had a chunk taken out of his leg by a Great White last year and it's put me off a bit.'

'That isn't something that generally happens to surfers in Cornwall, that's for sure.'

'No,' he said. 'Another reason to come back. Anyway, I thought I'd put my stuff into storage and come over for three months, while I made my mind up.'

'What about your job?'

'I gave up the dentistry and became a beach lifeguard ages ago – didn't you know?' he said, as if I could divine every aspect of his life through his Facebook posts. 'But I can always take it up again. There's a shortage of NHS dentists in the UK.'

I pitied any patients if he did, because he wasn't that brilliant a dentist in the first place, so he'd probably be even worse after a long break.

'You'd like to see me, wouldn't you, Alice?' he coaxed.

'I suppose it would be good to catch up with you,' I agreed, remembering that I had been quite fond of the large, friendly and almost entirely harmless lump. 'Give me a ring when you've landed and we'll try and arrange something, though I really *am* busy just now. I need to finish my next book before the tearoom opens, too.'

'*Book*?' He sounded baffled, which reinforced what I'd always thought: he never noticed a thing I was doing, or listened to a word I said.

'I'll explain when I see you,' I said patiently and put the phone down, thinking that I certainly didn't need anything else to distract me from my work. And that was even truer when I checked my emails, because there was one from Senga reminding me that the new novel had to be delivered by 24 October, which was now less than three weeks away! I'd been convinced it was November, but when I checked my contract, she was quite right.

I had an 'Oh my God!' moment and then, since it was a rare, workman-free day, spent all of it writing like fury and carried on well into the night.

Even when Nile texted to say did I want to go over to his place for supper (a first) I just said no, I was too busy writing, and he went quiet.

Later, something made me glance up from my desk and there was Nile in the window opposite, drawing his curtains. He stopped and looked straight across at me, gravely.

I waved, but then slid off back into my fictional world, though feeling just a *little* emotionally ruffled. I had no idea why.

Still, there's nothing like a good bloodletting to make you feel better, is there?

Beauty soon saw that if they were to survive, she must take charge of the situation herself, so when the magic stick refused to launch any more bolts from the blue upon the advancing throng of nymphs, she grabbed Kev's scimitar and laid about her with a vengeance.

The magic words 'Made in Sheffield' flashed in the sun and soon her enemies were in retreat.

Bits of dryad and pools of blood lay on the smooth turf, though since the blood was grass green, it blended in quite nicely . . . and even as Kev and Shaz stood there gazing at the scene in deep shock, moon-flowers began to unfurl wherever a drop had spattered.

Edie called next day to warn me she'd given Robbie my phone number and new address and was amazed to be told he'd already called.

'You didn't mind, did you?' she asked. 'Only he said he hoped to see you when he came over and he'd only just heard about Dan and was very sorry.'

'He's emailed me from time to time, but I hadn't mentioned Dan. And I don't really mind if he wants to see me – he's harmless. Self-absorbed, but harmless.'

'I suppose you've been too busy to get any further with trying to trace your birth mother?' she asked.

'Yes, what with the teashop and trying to finish my new novel, but I really should get on with talking to the two people who found me on the moors, though I'm sure it will be a dead end. The only way I'm going to find her is if I put something in the local paper and she comes forward.'

'I expect you're right, but you'll be the better for talking to them and hearing first-hand about it.'

'Actually, I know now where one of them lives – the farmer, Joe Godet – so I thought I might go over there on Thursday morning and see if he'll talk to me. I'm going to be too busy tomorrow.'

'I don't see why he shouldn't talk to you. Let me know how you get on.'

'OK, I'll email you all the details. And Sheila Giddings thinks the other witness, Emily Rhymer, might still live in Upvale, so I've no excuse for not getting on with it, really.'

'No, you might as well tie up the loose ends,' Edie agreed.

I'd been relying on Edie's experiences in the hotel trade to help me set up the teashop, so now I told her I'd followed her latest advice and bought simple, plain, inexpensive but classic cutlery, since she'd assured me it had a tendency to vanish into pockets and handbags.

'I've never understood why customers think it isn't theft to take the cutlery home with them,' I said.

'I've no idea either, but in my experience, people staying in hotels often leave with the soap, towels and toilet rolls, too,' she said.

I told her about the cartons of linen-look tablecloths and napkins that had arrived that morning all the way from China. 'They seemed to arrive faster than things I've ordered from this country! And I've found a local laundry already, so I can tick that off my list.'

'I can see it's all starting to take shape,' she said approvingly.

'Yes, and I'm starting on the fine details now – the fun bit.'

In fact, the only thing I *hadn't* managed to source were willow-pattern tiered cake stands, as I said to Nile later when he turned up and positively marched me to the pub, where he insisted I eat a square meal and think about something other than my novel for five minutes.

'Though I suppose the tearoom *is* another topic,' he said. 'But I can't say that the struggle to find the right cake stand is one that moves me deeply.'

'You're right, it's not that important, because I could always have plain white ones instead,' I agreed, and then fully absorbed what he'd just said and looked at him with a wry smile. 'Have I become a writing and tearoom bore?'

'Not entirely, now I've read your book and started to get the hang of what's going on in that twisty little mind of yours,' he said. 'You're a bit like a graceful swan swimming serenely along, while underneath the water, the legs are frantically paddling.'

I looked at him doubtfully. I liked the swan bit, but I wasn't too sure about the rest.

'Well, you're a complete enigma to me,' I told him frankly. 'I know you love antiques and enjoy hunting them down for clients.'

'Yes, the thrill of the chase.'

'But what do you do for fun, Nile?'

'Coerce stunning redheads to go to the pub with me, then go home alone and read gory, warped fairy stories,' he said.

When we got back I declined his offer of coffee and worked even later that night to make up for going out, and also because I wanted to take a couple of hours off the following morning to finalize my teashop menu.

Most of the recipes I intended to use were old favourites, but there were one or two new ones I needed to try out first.

So next day, while Jack and Ross were laying the vinyl flooring in the kitchen, their last big job, I was baking up a miniature storm in my flat kitchen.

Then I called them up for a taste test, along with Nile, who appeared to have let himself in again.

'I've been to get a sandwich and bought an extra one in case you were working and had forgotten to eat. But I think it was a bit redundant,' he added, eyeing the table groaning under the weight of a morning's baking, 'so I'll eat it myself: I need to build my strength up.'

He didn't say for what.

'A woman can't live by cake alone,' I told him. 'I'd love the sandwich.'

Jack and Ross took the tasting session seriously and everything passed with flying colours. I divided what was left (not a huge amount, due to Ross's having popped morsels into his mouth one after the other, in a kind of conveyer-belt action) between them to take home.

When they'd gone back to the floor-laying, Nile and I ate the sandwiches and a few of the savouries I'd kept back.

'I've got the electrician coming to put up the chandelier and the new wall lights this afternoon,' I told him. 'But then it's back to work on the book.'

'I'm out for the rest of the day, probably home very late, and I bet you're still working when I get back,' he said.

He didn't tell me where he was going and I didn't like to ask. He did go out a lot, so perhaps he was seeing someone else, and that was why he was so against Zelda's idea that they should get together? I supposed I was just someone to tease and flirt with when the fancy took him.

I'd fully intended telling him I was going in search of Joe Godet next morning, but he dashed off before I got the chance.

Still, it was something I needed to do alone anyway.

'What's happening to us, Shaz?' asked Kev. 'I thought I was having a weird dream at first but it doesn't stop and . . . it feels sort of real.'

Then he looked admiringly at the golden-haired princess beside him, the scimitar still dripping green gloop on to the grass, and added, 'Beauty, you're a real kick-ass kind of girl!'

'You're Beauty?' the prince asked, looking at her narrowly. He'd suspected it when she'd grabbed that strange sword and gone into action – which he was happy to let her do, because there was nothing like dryad blood for staining a velvet tunic – but she was a far cry from the slender sylph he'd hoped for.

'Yes,' replied Beauty. 'And I expect you're this Prince S'Hallow I was betrothed to in my cradle,' she went on, eyeing his willowy frame and butter-yellow hair with disapproval. Somehow, she'd hoped for something a little more dark and rugged.

'I was – but actually, I prefer Princess Shaz!' he declared defiantly. 'She's the fairest of them all.'

'You're not too bad-looking yourself, even if you do talk a bit daft,' Shazza said, letting him hold her hand.

'Well, I prefer Prince Kev to you,' Beauty told him.

'You tell him,' Kev said smugly, then added, 'This place yours, Princess?'

'Of course – it's my bower.'

'Right . . . and is that roof made of metal?'

'Solid gold – what else?' she said. 'We can live here happily ever after.'

'No, we can flog it and live somewhere else, instead,' he said, and gave her plump waist a squeeze. 'Better than winning the Lottery, you are.'

It was the early hours of the morning before I went to bed and I'd had the curtains in the living room open until then, waiting to see the warm, friendly square of light that meant Nile was home.

It never came.

On perusing her records, I saw that Alice Rose seemed to have been physically healthy throughout her life, apart from the usual minor childhood ailments. But I noted her more recent medication and hoped she hadn't inherited the thread of hysteria and hypochondria that ran through my mother's side of the family. She hadn't struck me as the type, but appearances can be deceptive.

It would appear that she has moved about the country a good deal, never settling in one place for more than a few years, so possibly she may before long also tire of Haworth and take herself off elsewhere.

32

Cold Comfort

I wasn't sure what was the best time to visit a sheep farmer – or even if there *was* a good time. Anyway, I picked late morning and drove out of Haworth feeling really nervous, though I'm not sure exactly why.

As I passed the turn to the Giddingses, it was almost too tempting to just go there instead, but I resolutely went on.

I'd bought a large-scale map of the area, so I knew that I needed to follow a tiny thread of a lane that turned off just before Henry's restaurant.

It ended at Withen Bottom Farm, a low stone building sitting gloomily in a hollow, with the Oldstone hidden by the crowding hillside above.

The metal gate to the cobbled yard hung open, creaking slightly in the cold breeze, and a large tractor was about to come out.

We stopped nose to nose. The driver was a small, thin, dark, grim-looking man with a long beaky nose, who first gestured to me to go away – though there was nowhere to turn other than the yard behind him – then glowered at me and switched off his engine.

'You've taken the wrong turn. Could you not see the signs for the fancy restaurant further along?' he shouted.

'I don't want the restaurant,' I called out of the side window. 'I'm looking for Joe Godet.'

He climbed down from his tractor and trudged over. 'What do you want with him?' he asked with deep suspicion. 'Are you from the income tax? You're a bit late, if so: he's been dead these last fifteen years.'

'Oh, no!' I cried, shaken, for I'd taken Henry's words to mean he was alive.

'Well, he is, then, and nowt to be done about it,' the man said dourly.

'I'm very sorry – and I'm not from the income tax.'

'Who the hell are you, then?'

Clearly he was a graduate of the same charm school as Nell and Tilda.

'I'm . . . I was an abandoned baby and Joe Godet rescued me. He found me on the moors,' I blurted out, thrown off course by the news. 'I'm Alice – Alice Oldstone.'

His expression didn't change, but after another glowering scrutiny he said grudgingly, 'Happen you'd best come into the house, then.'

I turned off my engine too and we left our vehicles standing like dogs sizing each other up. I followed him into the farmhouse, which showed signs of bachelor occupancy, though there was an elderly woman attacking the pine table with a large scrubbing brush and a lot of energy.

'This is Val, who does,' he said, by way of introduction.

'And I've done for the day,' she told him, tossing the brush back into the sink and peeling off her bright pink Marigolds.

She gave me a nod and a narrow, curious scrutiny, then said to him, 'If you want more dog hair off the carpet, you'll need to buy a better vac, because that one belongs in a museum. Like me.'

'There's nowt wrong with it.'

'There's nowt *right* with it,' she said, and then, throwing on an old plaid coat, left without a goodbye, other than the slamming of the front door.

I wondered where she was going, because there'd been no vehicle in sight, other than the tractor.

'Sit down, if you like,' invited the man.

'Are you by any chance Joe Godet's son?' I ventured.

'I'm George Godet, right enough, and the place is mine now.'

It was hard to guess his age, since his complexion was leathery and his eyes creased round the corners. 'You do *know* he found an abandoned baby up by the Oldstone?'

'Oh, aye, Dad often talked about you. Since he was the one found you, he thought he should have had the raising of you, too. But then, my ma was dead and he was no spring chicken, so it weren't ideal.'

'We could have been brother and sister, then,' I said, and he scowled even more.

'If you were hoping to get round him, so he'd leave you some brass, then you're years too late . . .' he began.

'No, of course I wasn't,' I assured him quickly. 'I just wanted to thank him for saving my life.'

'Well, it weren't like he had a choice! What was he to do, stick you back down the burrow and leave you to die?' He ruminated for a moment and I really wasn't sure which way it would have gone, had *he* been in his father's place. 'He told them social worker types to call you Alice, after Ma.'

'Oh, how lovely!' I said. 'And I'm still Alice, because my adoptive parents kept my first name, though of course I'm not Oldstone any more, I'm Rose.'

'And you're just visiting the area, like?'

'No, actually, I've bought a café in Haworth, which I'm renovating and hope to reopen soon as an afternoon tearoom.'

He seemed to brighten at this evidence that I really wasn't after his money. If he *had* any, that is, because he wasn't precisely living in the lap of luxury.

'This is all *so Cold Comfort Farm*,' I murmured, thinking aloud.

'Never heard of the place,' he said shortly. 'There's a Cold Cross Farm t' other side of Upvale, if you mean that?'

'No . . . sorry,' I said, 'my mind was wandering. What I'd *really* like to know is what your father said about finding me. Did he talk about it much?'

'Oh, aye, bent anyone's ear that would listen, till we were all sick of the tale.'

'Could you bear to tell me what he said?' I coaxed, and he sighed resignedly.

'He'd gone out before dawn searching for a ewe, an early lamber that liked to hide out near the base of the Oldstone, where the rocks gave a bit of shelter. There was a clear sky and a big full moon, so when he spotted a bit of white fleece, he thought he'd found her. Then when he got closer he could see it was sticking out of a hole in the rocks, so he thought it must be a dead lamb and maybe a fox had dragged it there.'

'And then?' I prompted as he stopped and looked into space.

'He pulled it out and it was a sheepskin all right, but one of those dressed ones they sell as a rug – and a baby were wrapped in it. He said he was so surprised, he thought he was dreaming – or maybe having a nightmare, because you looked a bit of a mess and he didn't think you were alive.'

'I had a harelip,' I said. 'I expect it added to the shock of the moment.'

'They've made a good job of patching you up,' he said, looking at my face with a curious gaze that was somehow not offensive.

I touched the thin silvery thread of scar. 'I think I must have had a very good surgeon, though my dad – my adoptive dad – said they'd told him that as harelips went, they'd seen a lot worse.'

'Yes, Dad said one of his cousins was born with a cleft lip and a palate the same, but even back then they mended it well enough so you didn't much notice it.'

'What did your dad do after he picked me up?' I prompted, keen to get George back on track.

'Once he'd got over the first shock and had a closer look, he realized you weren't dead because you made a little cry. The sheepskin must have kept you warm enough to survive, but you couldn't have been there long.'

'How amazingly lucky I was that he came along just at that moment,' I said.

'Dad said it was meant to be, and someone up there was determined you'd be found, because if he hadn't come across you, that Upvale woman probably would.'

'Oh, yes, I've read the newspaper accounts and they said this Emily Rhymer was on the scene right after he found me.'

'Gave him another shock, she did,' he said. 'He hadn't spotted any-one about, though he thought he'd seen car lights earlier on the road towards Upvale. But then his dog barked and another answered from up top – and there was one of the Upvale witches staring down at him.'

'Emily Rhymer, aged twenty-two, according to the newspaper reports,' I said. 'What made your dad think she was a witch?'

'What else would a young woman be doing up by the Oldstone on her lonesome in the dark?' he asked. 'Wouldn't she be fearful, if she hadn't got the Dark Powers to protect her?'

'I wondered about that, because it seemed very strange. And suspicious, too, though the police must have investigated and ruled her out?'

'If she wasn't a witch then, she's known for one now. It's rife down there in Upvale. But it wasn't her who'd had the baby,' he grudgingly agreed. 'She'd only just got there, wanting to see the sun rise over the Oldstone, or some daft idea like that. Her friend – an older woman that my dad said was another of the coven – drove up only a few minutes later and parked below, on the grass.'

'I know the place, but it sounds a surprisingly popular spot considering it was just before dawn on a cold early March night,' I said. 'What happened next?'

'They all got in this woman's car and came here to call the police and an ambulance. Dad had you stuffed down inside his vest, shirt and jumper by then, like he would a weakly lamb, to keep you warm with his body heat. It works a treat, that does.'

'He was very kind.'

'He said what with the girl, the woman driving, the two dogs and him with the baby, the car soon warmed up on the way back. I'd got up by then, so I saw them all come in,' he added. 'I was just a lad and we'd lost me ma a year before, so it was my job to get the fire going and the breakfast on, because though we had a woman come in – Val, the one you just saw – she had her own husband to see to first.'

I suddenly found myself feeling sorry for George, or at least the isolated, motherless boy he'd been. Mind you, he looked like someone who'd been born crabby and worked on honing it ever since, so my rush of sympathy might have been misplaced.

'So you live here alone now?' I asked.

'I had a wife, but I lost her,' he said tersely.

'I'm terribly sorry!'

'Good riddance. I lost her to the man from the agricultural insurance. Took me a while to figure out why he always seemed to turn up when I was out.'

'Oh . . . how awful!'

'I'm right enough, what with the dogs for company and the bar at the Standing Stones for a game of darts on a Friday night, for all it's turned itself into a fancy motel,' he said. 'So, where did you get to, then? You don't sound Yorkshire. You don't sound anything, come to that, except a bit posh.'

'My adoptive mother didn't have any accent – she came from the south. My father was from Yorkshire, though, and we lived over near Knaresborough for the first few years. Then we moved to a village just outside Shrewsbury.'

'That would account for it, then. And you haven't been back here since, in what – thirty-odd years?'

I shook my head. 'I was found thirty-six years ago and though I knew I was born round here somewhere, I never really wanted to see it till now. I – sort of thought I might come face to face with my birth mother, someone who looked exactly like me.'

It was my worst nightmare: that we recognized each other instantly, yet she rejected me again.

He eyed me thoughtfully. 'I don't remember that many redheads round here, especially with green eyes,' he said. 'And your hair's a real copper, too. Maybe your mother wasn't local?'

'I know. If I'd been driven to the Oldstone, I could have come from anywhere, couldn't I?'

'You could if whoever brought you knew the way round to the Oldstone by road.'

'Or someone local could have walked there, like Emily Rhymer did.'

'Not if they'd just given birth,' he said practically. 'They said you were only a few hours old, at most.'

I pressed him a little, but he couldn't add much more to the story and began asking me about the café and where I'd got the money from to buy it, so I told him.

'The official opening of the tearoom will be at the start of November and you'll always be welcome to come in for a cup of tea and some cake if you're in Haworth.'

'I'm not much of a one for poncy teashops, though I like a good slab of cake with a slice of cheese on the side,' he said.

'Then I'll make you one and drop it off next time I'm over in this direction,' I promised. 'What's your favourite?'

'Fruitcake, of course,' he said, as if I was stupid. 'Proper fruitcake, with cherries and almonds and stuff in it.'

'Right,' I said, 'fruitcake it is.'

'If there's no one here, put it in the milk churn on the slab in the wall outside,' he directed.

'What if there's milk in it?'

'There's never milk in it,' he said, and got up. 'I'd best move the tractor, so you can turn.'

Clearly, the audience was over.

I took a walk around Haworth after surgery one day and found the entrance to Doorknocker's Row, which I can't say I'd ever noticed before, since it was the merest slit of a narrow alleyway.

I stopped and then, taking out my phone and putting it to my ear, I stepped into the passageway as if I'd had a call and wanted a quiet spot to take it in. It's the sort of thing people do all the time and I was sure would look quite natural, should anyone have noticed me.

But there was no one to see me for the small courtyard beyond the entrance was entirely deserted. I could see the front of what must be the café to my left, and there seemed to be a shop window opposite, for a sign was hanging there, but I did not explore further.

Father is partial to a type of old-fashioned sweet called Uncle Joe's Mint Balls and I procured a tin of these on my return to the car, as a reason for my late arrival home.

33

Dogged Footsteps

Outside, two identical wall-eyed sheepdogs had appeared and began to herd me out of the courtyard with sharp nips at my ankles, while George reversed the tractor.

I jumped into the safety of my car with relief and the dogs gave me a look of disgust and then ran off after their master, who was already on his way back into the farmhouse. The door slammed and he was gone, much as the cleaner, Val, had taken her leave: it must be a particularly Yorkshire form of farewell.

I did a clumsy three-point turn and then headed back up the farm track, more than happy to reach the road again. As I paused to check for traffic, the sign for Mr Rochester's Restaurant and the Hikers' Café flapped in the stiff breeze to my right and, without conscious decision, I turned towards it like a homing pigeon.

Hot tea was what I urgently needed, and luckily the café was open, the windows steamed up from the warmth within. Inside I found two hardy-looking hikers and Val. She must have walked there, though perhaps there was a short cut?

She gave me a look of deep suspicion when I greeted her and encircled her tea and buttered teacake with both arms, as if I might snatch them away.

'Is he taking you on, to replace me?' she demanded belligerently.

'What?' I said, nonplussed.

'That George. Just because I'm knocking on a bit, it doesn't mean I can't clean like I always did.'

'Oh!' I said, suddenly enlightened. 'No, I didn't come about that at all. It was something totally different. In fact, I was looking for his father, but I didn't know he'd died.' Seeing she still looked unconvinced, I added, 'And I've just bought my own business in Haworth, so I'm not looking for work at all.'

She relaxed slightly. 'I thought he was going to replace me; he's threatened enough.'

'I keep telling you he won't, you daft bat,' said the woman behind the counter, whom I recognized by her long grey plait of hair as one of the helpers at Eleri's book launch. 'Who else would work for a miserable little snirp like that, so penny-pinching he only turns the heating on if there's ice on the inside of the windows?'

Val demolished the last bite of her teacake and got up. 'Well, it's what I'm used to, Martha. Now I'd best get on to my next job.'

She looked at me. 'And if you see George again, don't you go telling him you saw me here.'

'OK . . . though I don't see why you *shouldn't* be here.'

'He and his cousin Henry don't get on too well.'

'He must know you leave your car here, by now,' the woman behind the counter said. 'And you clean for Eleri one afternoon a week, too.'

'Yes, Martha, but if we don't mention it, then it doesn't matter, does it?' Val said with an air of logic and left, dragging on her plaid coat as she went.

'You were at the book launch, weren't you?' Martha said, taking my order, but seeming to lose interest in me once I'd agreed that yes, I had been there.

The tea was excellent and I studied the photos on the walls, which seemed to be of the first book launch. I knew it had been held in the café, since the restaurant hadn't been opened then.

There was a replica of the precious diary with the reference to Charlotte Brontë in it, too, with postcards and souvenirs next to it for sale, along with signed copies of some of Eleri's books, and I wandered across for a look until Martha brought my order out.

I was just eating an excellent warm cheese scone, so light it almost floated off the plate – but then, so did mine – when Eleri came in with

Henry. His harsh-featured but attractive face looked just as gloomily intense as always, and although he saw me he didn't say anything, just nodded and headed straight for the kitchen.

'The lass has just et the last cheese scone,' Martha called after him. 'Henry?'

There was the clashing of pots and pans and some muttering.

'Eh, our very own Mr Rochester,' Martha said to Eleri drily.

'I heard that,' said Henry's voice through the serving hatch.

Martha nodded in my direction: 'She was at the book launch.'

'Not only at the book launch, but she's a novelist and she's been taken on by my agent, Senga,' Eleri told her. 'Hi, Alice – this is a nice surprise. Can I join you?'

'Of course,' I said.

'What brings you all the way out here?' she asked, sitting opposite and smiling at me. Smiling *up* at me, in fact, since she is very petite. I felt a bit like a giraffe. 'Unless you're sizing up Henry's baking? We know you're going to open a tearoom in Haworth.'

'The scone was delicious, but actually I came here on impulse, after visiting George Godet,' I said, and then when Martha had, quite unbidden, put foaming mugs of hot chocolate and slices of sticky ginger cake in front of us, somehow I found myself confiding to her the whole story of my abandonment on the moors and subsequent discovery by Joe Godet.

'I was so disappointed to find he'd died years ago, though George told me everything he'd said about finding me. I've still got the other eyewitness, Emily Rhymer, though, if I can find her.'

'I'm not local, so I'd never heard the story,' Eleri said, a glint that I recognized as that of a novelist scenting an interesting plot idea in her eyes. 'No one's even mentioned it.'

Martha, who'd been hovering nearby on the pretext of wiping down a table, said, 'It were a long time ago, that's why.'

Then some hikers demanded more hot water for their teapot and a second round of cheese toasties and she had to tear herself away.

'I'm absolutely amazed,' Eleri said. 'But I do feel for you and understand why you need to try to find your birth mother.'

Then she leaned forward and added, 'But I'll tell you what: I know where Emily Rhymer lives, because her sister married a well-known actor and playwright and they often come to Henry's restaurant for dinner – sometimes they even bring the whole clan!'

By the time I left the Hikers' Café a good hour had whizzed by and since I'd already skived off work for so long, I thought I might as well compound the offence by calling in to see if any of the Giddingses were at home on the way back. I was dying to tell someone all about my visit to George.

Bel was out but Sheila, in her usual clay-spattered corduroy trousers, was in the kitchen stirring soup.

I poured the whole tale out to her, George's curmudgeonliness seeming quite funny in retrospect.

'And then I had tea afterwards with Eleri Groves at the Hikers' Café,' I continued. 'And guess what – she gave me the address of Emily Rhymer in Upvale.'

'So you're going to see her, too?'

'Yes – in fact, I think I'll go tomorrow morning because I'd sort of like to get it over with. She's now the only eyewitness left to what happened, you see.'

'I think it might be more upsetting than you realize to hear a first-hand account, so perhaps you should take Bel or Nile with you,' Sheila suggested.

'Oh, I'm OK on my own,' I said. 'I mean, I managed fine with George Godet, and he wasn't the friendliest man to talk to. I expect Emily Rhymer's much nicer and she won't mind describing what happened in the least.'

She looked doubtful. 'Well, you'll come back here right after you've seen her to tell us about it, won't you? And then do stay over on Saturday night. Bel said you were working till late on your book every day, but I'm sure a rest over the weekend would do you good.'

'That would be lovely,' I agreed, though I wasn't sure Senga would feel the same way . . .

'Nile was here earlier,' she said, with a change of subject. 'He visited that friend of his with the antiques barn and ended up staying the night. I expect you wondered where he'd got to?'

'Not really,' I said, which was a downright lie. 'He comes and goes and there's no reason at all why he would tell me.'

Sheila beamed at me and handed me a steaming mug. 'Chicken soup for the soul,' she said. 'Bread?'

I hadn't sworn Sheila to secrecy, but even so, I was amazed to discover when I got back to my flat that she'd already rung Nile and told him all about George Godet *and* my intention to track down Emily Rhymer next morning. He appeared barely five minutes after I got in and said he'd drive me over to Upvale himself on Saturday.

'No – there's no need,' I said firmly. 'I mean, it'll just be another version of what George told me, but from a different angle, as it were, and not second-hand.'

'Sheila thought you might be upset afterwards. I needn't come in with you, I can drop you there and then visit Angel Delights.'

'*Angel Delights*?'

'It's a shop in Upvale,' he explained. 'A weird mix of antiques, junk and New Age tat, but I've found the occasional interesting piece there.'

I hoped the interesting piece wasn't serving behind the counter . . . and I really didn't know why I kept having these jealous thoughts about Nile, when his discarded girlfriends littered the countryside as an awful warning of what might happen if I weakened.

Once he'd gone, I had the urge to kill something in my novel – so cathartic.

There was a sudden rattling noise behind them and a huge spider came out of the bower in a staggering, slightly dazed rush. Without a second's hesitation, Beauty swung the scimitar and the arachnid fell in a sprawling heap.

'That's the end of him, then,' said the mouse, who had followed the spider out. 'Not that I'm sorry, because he tried to eat me.'

'That mouse is talking,' Shaz whispered to Prince S'Hallow.

'I know – you just can't stop rodents nattering on, can you?' he replied, looking at her in a dazzled kind of way, while Beauty was winding her arms around Kev's neck and puckering up her lips invitingly.

The mouse contemplated the two mismatched couples and said, 'You do realize that you can't change things once you've made your decisions, don't you? Beauty will have to stay for ever in the Here-and-now with Kev, and the prince and Shazza in the Once-upon-a-time.'

Then he sighed, because none of them was listening to him.

Next morning, it being Friday, Tilda came to clean and brought Nell with her. She liked to pop in occasionally, to check how things were going, offer sometimes forthright advice to the workmen, and ply them with cups of treacly tea.

That day there was just Jack, fitting new paper towel holders in the kitchen, utility room and cloakrooms, so she plied me instead while Tilda cleaned my flat.

'Our Tilda only just told me about that Jim Voss having the cheek to come round and demand you give him that old tea set, on Molly Muswell's say-so,' she said, stirring the teapot before pouring the brew. By now, I think I'd built up an immunity to tannin.

'Yes, it was a bit much considering how she cheated me out of all the things I'd paid for. I expect Jim Voss told her about our finding the willow-pattern china in that cupboard and it jarred her memory, but of course, there isn't any tea set, so she must have sold it and forgotten or something, though she said it had been her mother's.'

'Oh, there is a tea set, but it's nothing to do with Mrs M,' Nell announced, to my surprise. 'I remember it well. It was a legacy to the Misses Spencer from their aunt Queenie, but it was so hideous they packed it up and put it away. They did get it out and use it once a year, though, in remembrance of her. I've got a couple of snaps of them having tea from it in my album at home.'

'Then where did it go? I mean, there's nothing except the vacuum cleaner in there now.'

'Miss Clara pushed it round the corner out of sight,' Nell said. 'Come on, we'll see if it's there.'

Old houses have strange quirks and the cupboard proved to run round to the right into a little alcove, with an exceedingly dusty box in it.

'Tilda can't know there's a space there, because the rest of the cupboard's clean as a whistle,' I said.

I opened the top and unwrapped a piece of the most hideously dark, gilded and overblown china I'd ever seen. 'It's vile!' I said.

'The Misses Spencer kept it for sentimental value, but even they didn't like it,' Nell said.

'Well, it certainly doesn't belong to Mrs Muswell, so let's just put it back where it was for now,' I said.

'It might be worth a few bob,' suggested Nell. 'Mrs M must think it is, if she sent that Voss round for it.'

'I'll ask Nile to take a look some time,' I said. 'But I don't think Mrs M really had much in the way of good taste, so it's probably not valuable.'

'Common as muck, she were,' agreed Nell, leading the way back upstairs.

When Tilda came down with the vacuum cleaner and I could get back to my flat again without being under her feet, I made the mistake of checking my emails before settling down to write, and there was the next lot of edits from my publisher!

Senga had warned me that there would be more, but they'd only be minor changes, and to my relief she was quite right.

I'd entirely forgotten the thread of my new book by the time I'd sorted those out, so when Bel rang and said she was in Haworth and was I too busy for a visitor, I told her to come straight round.

She was even more welcome when I discovered she'd brought fresh cream cakes and good news: she'd been out delivering some of her ceramic pieces to a small craft gallery in Oxenhope and stumbled across the workshop of an upcycler.

'Upcycler?' I had a mental image of someone riding a unicycle across a high wire.

'Yes, you know – they take bits of old bric-a-brac and furniture and make them into something else, so they have a new lease of life.'

'Oh, right, I know what you mean now.'

'I only went in out of curiosity, because I'm not that keen on coffee tables made out of old wooden pallets and bits of car engine, but his stuff was a lot nicer than that – and the great thing is that he makes tiered cake stands out of old plates, too.'

'Are they nice?' I asked, interested.

'Lovely. I bought one for Mum, but I left it in the car because I have shopping to get. I've got lots of pics on my phone, though,' she added, showing me.

'I had a long chat with Thom – that's his name, Thom Carey – and he can make the stands to order, in any quantity, if you supply the plates.'

'They'd be perfect in willow-pattern china and, goodness knows, I'm drowning in the stuff now Nile's put the word out that I want it.'

'How many stands do you think you'd need?' Bel asked, practically.

'At least twenty – I'll have to sit down and work it out. Ideally I'd like four-tier stands for the Classic Yorkshire and the Fat Rascal High Teas and three-tiered ones for the Light Afternoon.'

'I think I'm feeling hungry again,' she said, gazing regretfully at the empty cream cake box. We seemed to have scoffed two cakes each.

'I've got a large egg custard tart, if you'd like a slice?' I offered. 'Nell gave me the recipe, so I tried it out.'

'Oh, yes, I haven't had custard tart for ages!' she said, and while we were expanding our figures even more, I gave her all the details of my interview with George Godet. I'd entirely given up trying to keep *any* secrets from the Giddingses.

I called Bel's upcycler to discuss what I needed and the upshot was that I would take lots of plates to his workshop on Sunday morning, so he could start on the order.

I sorted them out and then packed them into my boot, for Nile had decreed (in a series of texts – he hadn't graced me with his physical presence all day) that I should leave my Beetle at Oldstone Farm on

Saturday morning and then he would pick me up and drive me to Upvale in his car.

I was now feeling rather nervous about meeting Emily Rhymer – if she was there; I hadn't tried ringing first to check. I'd just wing it, and see.

The solicitor was here today at Father's request (though I admit to having sown the idea in his mind) and he signed the forms giving me lasting power of attorney, so that in the event of his being incapacitated, I could make decisions for him, both financial and otherwise.

In return, I assured him that I had no intention of consigning him to a nursing home, should his physical or mental health deteriorate. Even had I not perceived it to be my duty, there was the advantage that in his own home I could ensure that at all times he received the high standard of care we were paying for.

34

Angel Delights

My drive to Oldstone Farm next morning was accompanied both by the clink of willow-pattern china and by Nile, whose car was right behind mine, until we came to the only straight bit of road, when he took the opportunity to zoom past me. I suppose I had been driving slowly, but then, *he* hadn't got a car full of breakable crockery.

When I pulled up next to him his passenger door was open and the engine was still running, so I hopped out of my car and into his, without even going indoors to beg a piece of toast and say hello.

Given that I'd been experimenting with new variations on cake and savoury recipes lately and then eating a lot of the results, this was probably a good move as far as my figure was concerned. Well-stacked was OK, but over-stacked definitely not.

The drive over the undulating moors to Upvale was scenic, especially the last bit, where the road beyond the Standing Stones Motel descended steeply and with two hairpin bends to the village below.

I wondered what kind of young woman would think hiking up there in the dark, with only her dog for company, was a fun idea. Maybe she really was a witch and unafraid of anyone, or anything, she might meet?

We passed one or two isolated houses, but most of the village lined the road that climbed up the other side of the valley, which could be reached by crossing an ancient stone bridge over a small stream.

We parked just before it, by a small pink-gravelled tennis court that made me recall what Sheila had said about her husband and Dr Collins having been tennis partners in their youth, and wonder if it was here they had played. I found it hard to imagine what my doctor had been like as a teenager!

We crossed the bridge and then walked up the hill until I spotted a big detached house, the only one in sight.

'There it is,' I told Nile.

'How do you know?'

'Because I googled it last night. Anyway, Eleri told me it was called The Parsonage and there's a sign on the gate,' I said. 'Where's your shop?'

'Angel Delights is back the way we came, further down from the bridge, but I wanted to see you in first.'

'You needn't bother, because if there's no one home, I'll come and find you. Otherwise, I'll see you back at the car.'

'OK,' he agreed, and left me to walk up the last steep bit of road to the gate alone. There was no one about, but I still felt that there were eyes watching me behind the windows of the tall stone terraced houses that crowded close to the road on either side.

The Parsonage door had been freshly painted a bright vermilion and the old stone house seemed a bit uncertain about this, as if it was trying to decide whether the colour made it look like mutton dressed as lamb.

I rang a bell and after a long delay, during which time I heard the distant bark of a large dog, the door swung open a fraction to reveal an ancient and wizened face under a lot of silver hair.

'What do thee want?' she demanded.

'I wondered if I could see Emily Rhymer, please? It's a private matter.'

She regarded me with disfavour. 'She's bekkin.'

'Bekkin?' I repeated, puzzled.

'Apple pie. In t' kitchen.'

A male head of a similar vintage, topped with a jade-green knitted bobble hat, popped up behind her. 'Hello!' he said, with a charming smile. 'I'm Walter and I've got no eyebrows.'

'I can see that,' I responded automatically.

'Go away, our Walter, you're shedding sawdust all over the runner,' the woman said, then turned to me and added reluctantly, 'And I suppose *you* can come in.' Then she slammed the door before I'd barely stepped on to the mat.

'You'd better not be one of them journalists,' she warned me.

'Why would I be?'

'Because of that lah-di-dah actor our Charlie married,' she said. 'Great streak of nowt that he is.'

'Eavesdroppers hear no good of themselves,' said an attractive male voice. 'But I take exception to being called lah-di-dah!'

An oddly familiar dark-haired man ran lightly downstairs as if his every move was being tracked by cameras, and suddenly I remembered what Eleri had said about one of the Rhymers marrying an actor/producer. He was not young – there were streaks of silver in his dark hair and laughter creases round his eyes – but he was still stunningly attractive in an unusual kind of way.

'You're Mace North!' I exclaimed.

'That's me,' he said cheerfully. 'And you?'

'Alice Rose. I'm hoping to talk to Emily Rhymer.'

'My sister-in-law – or one of them. She's in the kitchen cooking up a storm, as usual. Gloria, take her through.'

'I thought I'd stick her in the front parlour till I see if Em *wants* to talk to her,' she said stubbornly. 'Maybe the poltergeist thing will come out for a look. We haven't seen so much of her recently.'

I was just thinking that, on the whole, I'd rather *not* be shut into a room with a poltergeist thing, when he said, 'Just take her through – she looks harmless enough to me.'

'On your own head be it!'

Then she turned to me. 'But I'm warning you, flower, if you waste our Em's time she'll let you know about it.'

Mace North gave me an encouraging smile, unhooked a coat from the hallstand and went out, and Gloria led me down a dark passage and into an enormous kitchen, where a tall woman with a lot of greying hair was stirring a huge cast-iron pot with one hand, while holding a book with the other.

'Visitor for you, blossom,' announced Gloria.

She turned and for a moment I was startled by eyes as light in colour as my own, but palest blue, rather than green, and darkly ringed around the iris.

She gazed back at me without seeming surprised, or even very much interested.

'I wasn't expecting any effing visitors,' she said to Gloria accusingly.

Gloria shrugged. 'She wants to talk to you and that Mace said to bring her through.'

'She'd better not be an effing journalist then,' she said, letting the spoon sink into the pot and tossing the book aside. 'I thought they'd got over all the "famous actor's sister-in-law is a witch married to a vicar" stuff.'

'I'm not a journalist, and I had no idea . . .' I stammered, disconcerted.

'Then what *do* you want?'

'My name is Alice Rose and . . . I was the baby you found up near the Oldstone on Blackdog Moor.'

'Well, I'll go to the foot of ower stairs!' exclaimed Gloria, astonished, but Emily's expression of bored irritation didn't change.

'It was Joe Godet, a local farmer, who found you, not me,' she said.

'But you were on the scene almost immediately, weren't you?'

She looked at me narrowly. 'Yes, but don't let that give you the wrong idea. Joe Godet jumped to the conclusion you were mine and I'd just shoved you down that hole, but I soon put him right – and the police.'

'So *you* were that little sickly babby that was in all the papers?' Gloria asked, still marvelling. 'Eh, well, you've made fine strapping lass! Nearly as tall as our Em.'

'There do seem to be a lot more tall women round here. I don't stand out like a sore thumb quite as much.'

'I've never let it bother me: why should I?' Em said. 'We're all tall in my family except my sister Charlie: she's the runt. Sit down,' she added, which I did, for it was more a command than an invitation.

'I think it was the height combined with having bright red hair that made me feel so conspicuous, really,' I said. 'And actually, I was already sure you weren't my birth mother, because I've read all the newspaper reports from the time and it's clear the police ruled you out.'

'I was an effing vestal virgin at the time, wasn't I?' she said belligerently. 'Had to keep pure, for the magic.'

It was a little hard to think of a response to this, so I decided not even to try.

'I've just moved to Haworth and part of the reason I wanted to live there was to try to trace my birth mother.'

'I don't know how you're going to do that, after all this time,' Em said.

'No, nor me, unless she comes forward, but I thought even if I didn't, then talking to the two people who found me would at least give me some kind of closure.'

'Well, I've no idea who she was,' she said. 'Your colouring's distinctive with that hair.'

'My eyebrows are naturally dark too: I think that's quite an unusual combination.'

'Maybe, but I can't bring anyone to mind who looks like that . . . though those light green eyes of yours do ring a vague bell.' She frowned and shook her head.

'Could you describe what you saw, that night on the moors?' I asked. 'Joe Godet's dead, but his son's told me everything he remembered, which was quite a lot, because his father seems to have bored everyone with the story ever since.'

'I don't suppose I can add much to it, but if you really want to know, I'll tell you.'

She put the lid on the huge, bubbling pot and checked the oven, where I could see a vast pie baking – presumably the apple one. She pulled it out and put it on a trivet to cool.

'That's done and the casserole can take care of itself, but I'll make some scones while we talk. Sit down – and, Gloria, you wet a pot of tea,' she ordered the old woman.

Then, while casually tossing ingredients together to make scone dough, she told me in a series of short, laconic sentences how she'd planned to drive up to the Oldstone in the early hours of that morning with a friend, to see the sun rise over the rock. 'But there was a gathering at her house the night before and she'd overdone the sloe gin, so when she didn't pick me up, I thought she'd overslept and decided to walk up there with the dog.'

'Wasn't that quite a hike in the dark?'

'It's a climb up out of the valley, but after that it was easy enough and there was a bright, full moon. There's usually no traffic on those small roads to worry about at that time of the morning, either.'

'So you didn't see anyone at all?'

'I did, but not until I was in the last, narrow bit of lane before the turn into the parking place near the Oldstone – do you know where I mean?'

'Yes, I've been there.'

'The lane's deeply sunk between banks and walls and the road twists, so the car was on me so quickly I only just had time to drag the dog out of the way.'

'But that could have been my mother on her way back, couldn't it?' I said eagerly. 'Did you see who was driving, or what kind of car it was?'

'It was gone round the next bend in a flash and the headlights were on full, dazzling me. I had the impression it was a Mini, though I couldn't swear to it, so I didn't mention it to the police. There weren't that many Minis around here at the time.'

'But then, that might have made it an important clue!' I said eagerly.

'I don't think so: I put two and two together myself and made five, because there was a young girl in the village with a Mini, and it wasn't her, because I saw her getting petrol later that day and she looked just the way she always did.'

'I suppose you can't just shrug off having a baby and act perfectly normally a few hours later,' I agreed, disappointed.

'No, and when I thought about it, she wasn't that kind of girl, either.'

I remembered something. 'George said his father thought he'd seen car tail lights in the distance some time before he found me, but he didn't take any notice because he was searching for his lost sheep.'

'Well, then, that was probably the same car,' she said. 'Anyway, I thought maybe it had come from one of the isolated cottages off the lane and they'd been as startled at finding someone there at that time as I was, so I carried on and up to the Oldstone.'

'You didn't notice the farmer?'

'No, but he would already have been on the other side of the escarpment, where the rocks have tumbled down. The full moon was starting to sink, but it was still so bright everything cast long shadows.'

I shivered a little. 'It sounds scary!'

Those light eyes stared at me, puzzled. 'I don't know what you mean – the moor's the same moor, day or night, isn't it?'

'I . . . suppose it is,' I agreed. 'Do carry on with the story.'

'Right, well, I was just standing next to the Oldstone, looking in the direction of where the sun would rise, when my dog barked. Another one answered it from below, so I looked over the edge and there was a man holding what looked like a lamb. He called out to me to stay there while he climbed up, though I wasn't going anywhere.'

She rolled out the scone pastry vigorously and began thumping circles out of it with a metal cutter.

'Go on, then,' prompted Gloria, who was listening as avidly as I was.

Em shrugged. 'When he climbed up he accused me of abandoning a baby – he'd shoved you down the front of his shirt by then for warmth, but he showed me – and I told him he was mad and anyway, I'd only just got there. Then luckily I spotted my friend arriving in her car, so we all got into it, went to his farm and called the police and an ambulance.'

'And they took me away,' I finished for her.

'Yes, but once you'd gone, the police asked us a lot of questions before we could go home, and they snooped about afterwards until they were certain I wasn't the mother.'

She gave a sudden smile. 'Joe Godet was convinced I was part of a coven of witches and probably told the police I was going to sacrifice you on the rock, or something daft like that.'

'As if you ever would,' scoffed Gloria.

'Was I really wrapped in just a sheepskin, with no clothes or anything else?'

'A small sheepskin mat, the sort you have by the bed, that was all. You hadn't even been cleaned up.'

'I wonder if the police tried to trace the sheepskin rug?'

'I doubt it. They're ten a penny round here. No, where you came from remained a mystery, but it seemed likely to me you'd been brought there in that car that passed me. The police never traced it, so it wasn't from the cottages.'

'So it's still a dead end,' I said. 'Though it's good to hear what really happened from someone who was there. Thank you so much for telling me about it.'

'I've thought of you whenever I've been up there, which is quite often. The place has great spiritual significance,' she added, though she didn't define what kind.

I thought Joe Godet might have been right about the coven, but I was very sure Em hadn't taken me there for sacrificial, or any other, purpose.

As if she'd read my thoughts she grinned and said, 'Joe's son always seems to turn up when I'm there with my friends, so he probably hopes we do all the witchy things the Sunday papers go on about, like get naked and dance around.'

By now, Gloria had poured the tea into wide porcelain teacups and they swirled with big, tattered tea leaves. I'd rather it had been strained, but said nothing and sipped carefully. The roughage, should I inadvertently swallow any of it, would probably do me good.

Gloria took my cup when I'd drained it and I thought she was going to refill it, but instead she swirled the dregs round and peered into it.

'See anything interesting?' asked Em, seriously.

'There's what everyone expects me to find: a tall, dark, handsome man has come into her life.'

'Can you read fortunes in tea leaves?' I said, interested. 'The man's just my nearest neighbour, though – he's tall, dark and *very* handsome.'

'He's nearer than you think,' she said obscurely.

'In what way?'

'I don't know, do I?' she snapped crossly. 'The tea leaves aren't like reading a book.'

'Sorry,' I said quickly. 'Can you see anything else?'

She scrutinized the pattern of leaves again. 'You've taken a long and roundabout journey to get here, but it's not finished quite yet.'

I could have told *her* that.

Em looked up from laying discs of scone dough on a large baking tray. 'Those light green eyes . . . so unusual,' she murmured, absently.

I did try one or two other locations for my early morning walks with the dog, but constantly found myself drawn back to the area around the Oldstone. Besides, our visits had quickly become a part of my regular routine and I find change unsettling. Hugo seemed to feel the same way, for he whined if I turned the car in another direction.

Luckily I had not seen Alice Rose there again, so I hoped her curiosity was sated by her earlier visits.

35

Tiers before Bedtime

Outside I found Nile seated on the wall at the side of the road waiting for me.

'Sitting on cold stone gives you piles. My granny used to say so,' I told him.

'I'll bear it in mind,' he said in his usual grave way. 'Did she have any other bits of helpful advice?'

'Yes – eating too much sugar gives you worms.'

'I should have asked if she had any other bits of advice that weren't revolting.' He got up and stretched, so he must have been waiting for a while.

'Oh, she had lots, like eating bread crusts gives you curly hair.'

'We must both have eaten a lot of crusts, then,' he said, as we headed back down to where we'd parked the car. 'And I take it you saw Emily Rhymer. Was it illuminating?'

'It was certainly interesting,' I said, then repeated what she'd told me about a car passing her in the narrow lane just before the turn-off to the Oldstone. 'She thought it was a Mini, but didn't tell the police that bit, since she couldn't be sure.'

'But if she had, it might have helped?'

'I don't know. It might have implicated someone innocent. Emily said a young local girl had one, but she knew it wasn't her because she saw her the same day I was found, looking just the same as usual.'

'But she didn't tell you who it was?'

'No, and they don't know anyone locally with my shade of red hair, though Em said she'd seen someone with pale green eyes like mine before, she just couldn't remember who it was. Gloria agreed with her, so I left my phone number, in case it came back to them.'

'Gloria?'

'The elderly lady who let me in. I don't know if she was a relative, or the cleaner, or what. She made tea while we were talking, then read my tea leaves!'

'Betty at Angel Delights insisted on reading my Angel Cards,' he said. 'Like the tarot, but less doomy.'

'Did they say anything exciting?' I asked, interested.

'The usual: big changes were coming, I should embrace the future . . . that kind of thing. What about your tea leaves?'

I shrugged. 'A dark, handsome man was going to come into my life. I told them he already had, because he was living practically on the doorstep, but the full description should have been "dark, handsome and bossy".'

'I'm not bossy,' he stated, then blew it by adding, 'By the way, we're going out for lunch.'

'There you are: bossy,' I said. 'Case proven! And won't Sheila wonder where we've got to?'

'No, because I rang her to say I'd heard from a contact in Skipton, so we'd have lunch there and see what he's found for me. Nice place, Skipton.'

'I was going to spend my afternoon in the library, working on my book,' I objected.

'You're surely entitled to a bit of free time?'

'Not according to my agent . . . and it's now less than two weeks to the book delivery deadline. But I suppose I could take the afternoon off, because actually after this morning I don't think I could concentrate,' I admitted. 'Tomorrow morning I've got to deliver those plates to the man Bel found who can turn them into cake stands, but I'll go straight back to my flat after lunch and work all afternoon and evening to make up.'

'I'll be having an early night tomorrow, because I'm headed for bonny Scotland at the crack of dawn on Monday and I'll be away a few days,' he said. 'There's an auction I want to attend and a few contacts to go round while I'm there.'

'You could call in at my friend Edie's guesthouse if you're anywhere near,' I suggested, and when I told him where it was he said he could make a slight detour if I liked. 'I suspect you have an ulterior motive?'

'Yes, I'd like to send her one or two things, but only if it's not too much trouble for you.'

'I expect I'll survive. Is there anything I can bring you back? A haggis, perhaps?' he teased.

'Yes – a box of Edinburgh rock, I loooove it,' I told him.

'It'll rot your teeth,' he said seriously, but with a glint of laughter in his smoke-grey eyes, 'not to mention give you worms!'

By unspoken mutual consent we didn't talk about anything contentious, so that our expedition to Skipton turned into one of those magical days you look back on for ever afterwards with a warm, golden, fuzzy feeling.

First we had lunch in an ancient pub and then afterwards walked around Skipton, while Nile told me snippets about its really interesting history. There was even a canal full of narrow boats and Nile took my hand as we walked along the towpath, which was slick from earlier rain. After that it seemed the most natural thing in the world to stroll hand in hand around the remains of Skipton Castle, and I found myself telling him how, when I was a little girl and we lived near Granny Rose in Knaresborough, she would walk with me to the Dropping Well, where I was fascinated by all the strange things visitors had hung up to be petrified.

In return, he described some of the madder things the Giddings family did when he first went to live with them, like suddenly deciding to have a long weekend in France at an hour's notice and then only realizing they hadn't brought the tent poles when on the wrong side of the channel.

'And we couldn't all fit in the VW campervan, but luckily it was warm weather so some of us slept under the awning, instead.'

'It sounds like the sort of fun I had with Lola's family after we moved to Shropshire when I was eight,' I said. 'When you put the good times in the balance, they always outweigh the worst, don't they?'

'That's true,' he agreed, squeezing my hand. 'You don't forget the bad bits, but they're overlaid with the happier memories.'

Then he looked at his watch and said we'd better go and visit his contact before she shut up for the day – and by then I'd totally forgotten the reason for our trip!

Violet Grange was a small, thin, upright lady with a head of upswept white hair and a sharp pair of blue eyes. She kept a tiny but very expensive antiques shop off the main street and while Nile was looking through the things she'd put to one side for him, I drooled over a locked case of jewellery, especially a glorious ring with a single large sparkling pale yellow stone.

'Yellow diamond on a platinum band,' she said, spotting my interest with a honed hawk eye for a sale.

'Oh?' I said, disappointed that it wasn't a citrine, which I might just have been able to afford. But before I could say anything else, she'd unlocked the lid and was sliding it on to the ring finger of my left hand.

'It would be the perfect engagement ring, wouldn't it, Nile?' she asked, so I guessed she'd spotted us walking up hand in hand and leaped to the wrong conclusion.

'I suppose it would – for the right person,' he agreed. 'It certainly suits you, Alice.' He turned back to Violet wearing his by now familiar dealer's poker face. 'Might be a bit overpriced, though, Violet. Not everyone wants a yellow diamond – it's a limited market.'

'It's a very good stone . . . and, of course, for *you* I might reduce it,' she suggested.

'*I* can't afford it at any price,' I said firmly and, pulling it off, handed it back, though by then I was feeling distinctly Gollum and desperately wanted it, my Precious. But there was a thin paper band looped through it bearing the price and it really *was* precious – way outside my reach.

Nile picked it up and examined it. 'I don't deal in a lot of jewellery, but I might have a customer for this,' he said. 'At the right price, of course.'

Then he turned to me. 'This is the boring bit, Alice, where we haggle and I settle up with Violet for what I want – so why don't you go next door to the teashop and I'll join you in a few minutes?'

I ordered afternoon tea for two with a lavish disregard for the expense (and a keen interest in what their idea of a good tea would be like).

Then I slipped into a daydream in which Nile and I had just got engaged and were in Violet's shop to pick a ring . . .

But when the tall, dark and stunning real Nile walked in a few minutes later and every female head in the place turned as one to stare at him, I remembered why that daydream was never actually likely to become reality.

Really, if I went on like this I might as well start writing romantic fiction, instead of fairy-tale horror!

The waitress brought a stand of fairly run-of-the-mill-looking sandwiches, cakes and scones, then almost put the teapot down in my lap, because she couldn't seem to tear her eyes away from Nile.

He appeared quite oblivious to all of it and told me ruefully that, as always, Violet had got him to pay her more than he intended to for his purchases.

I managed not to ask him then if the beautiful ring had been one of them, or later, on the drive back to Oldstone Farm. I didn't want him to think I was angling for yet another expensive present from his stock, but it didn't stop me wanting to pick his pockets and find out.

If he had, I hoped whichever of his clients it was meant for appreciated it.

Teddy and Geeta had taken baby Casper over to his grandparents for the day, and dinner that night was an Indian takeaway, in that most of it had been cooked by Geeta's mother and brought back.

'She always makes twice as much as anyone can eat and her freezer will explode if she tries to cram anything else in there,' Geeta explained, as we stuffed ourselves.

Casper had been so tired when they got back that he'd gone straight into his cot, and the baby monitor lay to hand on the table, though he has such good lungs that if he woke up, we could have heard him crying clearly even without it.

As I'd long since given up trying to keep secrets from any of the Giddingses, I gave everyone an update on what I'd discovered from talking to George Godet and Emily Rhymer, so they were all up to speed.

'I don't know if Emily will ever remember who has light green eyes like mine, or if she'll tell me even if she does,' I finished. 'It probably wouldn't lead anywhere anyway.'

'It does look as if your only remaining hope of finding your birth mother will be through an article in the paper, if she comes forward,' Teddy said.

'Yes, but at least I'll have done my best to find her, so if she doesn't I can finally put it all behind me and move on,' I said, then since Nile was giving me one of his 'you know I don't think that's a good idea' stares I added, 'Nile's been buying dollies and teddy bears today. It's probably his second childhood.'

'Two Schuco miniature bear-shaped perfume bottles—' he began.

'Sweet, except you have to pull their heads off to get at the perfume,' I put in.

'And an early Victorian china doll's house family,' he finished.

'They had big families,' I said. 'There are about seven children, including twin babies.'

'It's a great find, especially since all the clothes are original,' he said. 'I can sell them on at a profit with just a quick email or two. The same with the bears: I have two collectors for those, so I can offer them one each.'

'What about the ring?' I asked. My tongue got loose, even though I hadn't had the least intention of asking about it. 'Did you get it?'

'Yes – you have a good eye and it's a beauty. I have someone special in mind for it.'

'Ring!' exclaimed Sheila, and we all stared at her. 'I entirely forgot – Zelda rang you *hours* ago and wanted you to call her back. Your mobile wasn't picking up.'

Nile fished it out from his pocket. 'Dead as a dodo – must have forgotten to charge it up again,' he said. 'Never mind, I'm sure it wasn't urgent and I'll see what she wants after dinner. Maybe she's thought over my suggestion about buying me out of the business with that money her uncle left her.'

'It does seem a good idea, when you're living so far away now,' Sheila said. 'I know you travel about a lot anyway, but at least you wouldn't need to go up and down to London so much.'

'What are we having for dessert?' asked Teddy, abandoning the topic for something closer to his heart.

'Norwegian waffles and home-made vanilla ice cream,' Bel said happily.

'That's not the traditional end to an Indian meal,' said Teddy.

'No, but Sheila knows it's my favourite,' Geeta said.

Floppy waffles spread with jam and eaten with ice cream were also my favourite dessert after that . . . and possibly the total downfall of my figure, should I ever weaken and buy my own waffle pan.

We stayed in the kitchen, drinking coffee and clearing up, while Nile went to ring Zelda back on the phone extension in the library. It might have been as well if he'd closed the door, because we suddenly heard his raised voice saying angrily, 'No! No, Zelda, absolutely not! No way!'

Bel and I exchanged glances. What *could* she be asking him now?

Nile came back looking like a thundercloud and poured himself a cup of coffee in silence.

'She's actually called the banns this time?' Teddy teased.

Nile gave him a look, said he had some more calls to make and emails to send, and then took his coffee off back to the library with him, this time closing the door with a decisive click.

Our sunny, happy afternoon might never have happened . . . and it was just as well I didn't want to work in the library that night!

'Oh dear,' said Sheila. 'I could have told her that the more you try to pressurize Nile into doing something, the harder he resists. But then, perhaps it's just as well I didn't, Alice, isn't it?'

She gave me one of her most sunny, innocent smiles.

*

Nile still seemed to be seething in a gently volcanic kind of way at breakfast, but he insisted on coming to Oxenhope with Bel and me, so we transferred all the willow-pattern plates to his boot and let him drive.

I didn't need him to do any haggling, because Thom Carey, the upcycling man, was offering me very reasonable terms for my bulk order – though of course I was providing the plates, he was just turning them into stands.

I think he saw making them as his bread and butter for years to come, customers tending to be clumsy with the crockery. Though on the other hand, even the most light-fingered of them would have trouble getting a tiered cake stand into a handbag.

When we'd finalized the deal he made us tea and then invited us to see his work in progress in the shed at the bottom of the garden. It turned out that the upcycling of small items like the cake stands was just to keep the wolf from the door and his real interest was in building one-off unique pieces of furniture from reclaimed wood. There was a half-completed tree-shaped wall shelf unit I coveted, the branches supporting bookshelves, but I took a firm grip on myself, because luxuries would have to wait until later.

He was a pleasant, unassuming man with a thick head of dark brown hair and eyes to match and I was starting to suspect that Bel was interested in more than his plates . . .

'What a nice man Thom is,' I said as we drove back. I was sitting next to Nile in front and he slid me one of his more unfathomable sideways looks.

'Yes, isn't he?' said Bel innocently, 'and a very talented woodworker too. It's a pity he can't make his living from the bigger pieces.'

'Not a pity for me, or I wouldn't get my cake stands,' I pointed out.

'I don't mind going there to fetch the first lot for you, when he's made them,' she offered. 'I'd like to see that tree bookshelf when it's finished – it was so realistic, as if it was growing up the wall.'

I glanced across at Nile and we exchanged smiles: I didn't think Bel's avowed intention not to get involved with another man was going to hold up for very much longer.

Quite suddenly Father's mobility seems to be dwindling at a faster rate, so that I have had to arrange for extra carers and have ordered special equipment to help them move him more easily and see to his personal care. He was never an even-tempered man, or one who suffered fools gladly, and they have learned to do what they are employed for without undue familiarity.

Father likes to hear the details of my patients and offer irrelevant and out-of-date advice — he was never in general practice and though he might still be sharp as a tack on the subject of ophthalmic surgery he has not kept up with other medical advances.

Other than this, he has the TV and his computer for entertainment, and Hugo also spends a lot of time with him. For a man who once had no use for pets, he dotes on the creature just as much as he did on his predecessor, Drogo, which I find rather strange, though I presume it is simply a sign of the slow eroding of his faculties.

36

Well Fruited

When I got back to my flat after lunch, I dashed straight out again into the village and bought a Brontë jigsaw for Edie (her secret passion – she always had a large and complicated one on the go), and a box of clotted cream fudge. Then I carried them across to Small and Perfect, which was, for once, open.

A customer was examining a selection of antique paper knives of the kind you imagine sticking out of a victim's back in old murder mysteries.

Nile looked up and raised a dark eyebrow at me.

'This box is for Edie – I'll just pop it in the back room for you,' I said quickly, and when I had, I left, because I didn't want to hang around and possibly scotch his sale . . . and that wasn't intended to be a pun, though I repeated it to Edie when I rang her later to say that Nile would be dropping in some time soon.

'Very droll – and I'll look forward to meeting your *friend*,' she added, with strange emphasis, before ringing off to attend to some hotel-keeping crisis that was going on in the background.

Friend? Was that what Nile was? I really didn't know any more.

I thought Nile might come over later, but he didn't – and I know he went to bed early, as he'd said he would, because as usual I had my living-room curtains open while I was working and I saw his light go out.

*

Despite working late, I was still up and at it again early next morning – and just in time to see Nile locking the door of Small and Perfect and then heading for his car, though he didn't look up.

Since he wasn't carrying anything, I assumed he'd already loaded his luggage in, and I hoped he'd remembered the box for Edie.

I had no idea when he was coming back, either, but goodness knows, I had enough to keep me occupied. I now had a week and a half to finish the new book, so this was the Big Push. Then as soon as I'd got that off, there would be the mad dash to get the final preparations completed in time for the grand opening of The Fat Rascal.

I wasn't at all sure Jack had grasped that writing is also work, not something I was doing for fun, preferably without interruptions. Still, he wasn't here very much by then, just popping in between jobs for other customers in order to do all the minor things, like putting up a curtain track in the bow window of the café and fitting the inside of the kitchen cupboards with sliding and swinging racks to make getting at the contents easier. There were a million and one tiny touches like this and I had given him a fairly comprehensive list already, to which I continued adding afterthoughts.

And I kept doing sums and watching the expenses eat up the dwindling pool of insurance money, wondering if it would last until we opened.

I made an appointment with Nile's accountant, which, though it took me away from the writing for a couple of hours, was helpful. I'd been unemployed since Dan's death and I hadn't earned enough from the writing alone to pay income tax, but now I needed to register as self-employed. The accountant would also help with all the staff employment and payroll issues, so he was going to make my life easier.

I'd already registered the teashop and now I heard that the premises would be inspected on a date less than three weeks away!

Apart from a slight panic when I got the notification in the post, the rest of the day was quiet – no Jack, no interruptions other than signing for a Special Delivery parcel for Nile. It was small, and probably perfect. I wondered when he was coming home and I missed him dragging me away from my book to go to the pub that evening. But I had a nice long telephone chat with Lola instead.

She and the girls had now settled into the annexe, and were luxuriating in the space.

'It's bliss!' she sighed. 'I've got my furniture and everything out of storage and it all looks lovely. And there's a galley kitchen and our own living room, too, so Mum and Dad can have their house back.'

'I should think they love having you and the children around, so they won't think of it that way,' I told her.

'I know, but I'm sure they'll enjoy a bit of peace occasionally, and then they can close the doors upstairs and down.'

'I bet the girls have fun on the smallholding, just like we did. I always loved feeding the hens and goats and helping to water the herbs in the big polytunnels for your dad.'

'Yes, the twins seem most interested in the animals, but Rosie's keener on gardening with Dad. How is that lovely Nile?' she added.

'I can't imagine what I've said to make you think he's lovely, but he's away on a trip to Scotland, though I've barely noticed his absence,' I lied, 'because I'm working so hard on the book.'

'Yeah, right,' she said disbelievingly.

That's the trouble with best friends: they can read between all the lines, even invisible ones.

Early on Wednesday morning I baked three different types of fruitcake in the interests of teashop research and then left them cooling on a rack.

Jack, having appeared with the intention of planing down the bottom of the back door, which tended to stick when the weather was damp, said the smell of them was driving him mad, so I told him to help himself to the Dundee cake with the glazed top. I had plans for the other two.

At lunchtime, when Jack and half the cake had vanished, but the door had ceased to stick, I took a break from writing and drove across the moors to keep my promise to George Godet.

His was the traditional-style cake I'd made, stuffed full of fruit, nuts and cherries. I'd put it in a plastic container, which was just as well because there was nobody home – not even the dogs, though actually, that was a relief. I left it where he'd told me to: popped in the old milk churn in the wall alcove. I put a note through the door, in case he didn't check for random cakes on a regular basis.

I stopped at Oldstone Farm briefly on the way back, but there was no one in the house. I could see a light on in the Pondlife offices and hear the rhythmic thumping of clay from Sheila's workshop but I didn't want to disturb anyone and just left the final fruitcake in the kitchen with a note inviting the whole family to come and see the almost-finished teashop on Saturday morning.

Yes, I *am* the Blackdog Moor cake fairy.

Bel's absence from home was explained when she called in later – having asked if it was OK to disturb me first – because she'd been to see Thom Carey again.

'Geeta loved Mum's cake stand so much, I thought I'd get her one too,' she said a little self-consciously.

'Any pretext to see Thom again?' I teased.

'No!' she protested, going faintly and becomingly pink. 'I mean, he's *nice* . . . but my divorce has barely come through and I'm really not looking for anyone new: once bitten, twice shy.'

'I feel the same. I seem to have a knack of choosing men who won't commit and I really don't want to do it all over again.'

'I know Nile's track record isn't *great*—' she began.

'Who mentioned Nile?' I demanded indignantly.

'Come off it, you can't fool me. The way you two look at each other is the elephant in the room that we don't talk about. He *really* likes you, Alice. This time, it could be different.'

'Or it could be even worse – and anyway, I'm sure you're wrong and he's not seriously interested in me.'

'Mum says his past has made him afraid of being hurt and yours has made it hard for you to trust another man, so you're both holding back, thinking the other one doesn't want to commit.'

'Well, it's a theory, but it's not the right one,' I told her and she laughed and said I was hopeless.

'Your young man stayed with me last night and he's a bonny laddie,' said Edie approvingly down the phone, seemingly under the same misapprehension as Sheila and Bel. 'I canna remember when I've seen a more handsome one.'

'He's not my young man! In fact, he's not even that young, because he's a couple of years older than me – and handsome is as handsome does,' I added primly.

'He's of an age to stop gallivanting around and settle down, and he spoke fondly of you, so don't go cutting off your nose to spite your face, Alice,' she advised me.

'I'm not cutting anything off!' I protested. 'He's never settled with one girl for long so he's not going to break the habit of a lifetime for me, is he? He's like a hummingbird going from flower to flower.'

She laughed and said one flower had to be sweeter than all the others, and then rang off.

I woke from a strange dream in the early hours of the morning, thinking I could hear the unmistakable roar of a tractor. Then I remembered I was living in the middle of a village, so it was highly unlikely to have been real, and fell asleep again.

However, Jack discovered a box of eggs on the doorstep later – large and obviously very free-range ones with bits of straw and muck stuck to them.

An obscure message had been pencilled on the box: 'Thank you for your kind remembrance,' it said. I'd take a guess at that being from George, but he couldn't possibly have come all the way over the moors on his tractor to deliver them, could he?

I had a big, fluffy cheese omelette for lunch and it was delicious. I'd have invited Nile, had there been any sign of him . . .

On Friday morning, although I was vaguely conscious that Jack had returned yet again and was drilling away at something, I didn't go down because I was far away in the book and heading for the end of the first draft.

But when I finally opened the flat door, there was one of those tartan cardboard sporrans full of Edinburgh rock leaning against it. The traveller had evidently returned.

I could hear Tilda talking to Jack and found them in the kitchen drinking tea and eating biscuits, while admiring the electric fly zapper on the wall that he'd just fixed up.

'That'll get any of the little buggers who make it through the fly screening,' Tilda said approvingly.

'Great,' I said. 'By the way, Jack, if a delivery of flatware and pans arrives while you're here, just get them to stack them in the back room.'

'Will do,' he said, 'though I'm off to another job in a bit.' Then he got up and went off to fix the now bright and shiny old bell back on to the door spring, so that it jangled louder than ever when the door was opened.

I'd missed it, in a strange kind of way.

Tilda offered me the last cup of treacle and the box that contained a minute sliver of the Dundee cake and a collection of crumbs, but I declined both.

'Well, back to work,' she said. 'Shall I give the flat a quick do? I didn't want to disturb you, because Jack said you were at that writing again.'

The way she said it made it sound like a really bad habit, similar to opium eating.

'That would be great: I'm just going to have a break and then I'll carry on this afternoon. The book needs to be finished by the end of next week. Just as well, because I'll need to concentrate on the teashop after that, if we're to open on 4 November.'

'I can't see any problem. It's as near as dammit finished now, isn't it? Though when I put that last lot of willow pattern what Nile brought through the dishwasher, it was making a funny noise.'

'It is very old and I suspect it's on its last legs,' I agreed. 'I only hope it lasts out until we've got the tearoom going and then I'll have to bite the bullet and buy a big new commercial one as soon as I can afford it.'

'There'll be a lot of stuff for washing by hand that *won't* go into the dishwasher,' she pointed out.

'Yes, especially cooking utensils, though I do tend to wash up as I go.'

'Our Daisy would be glad of a little evening job after college, washing up, filling and emptying the dishwasher and helping me with the cleaning,' she suggested. 'Nell will be ready to head home and get the tea on after we finish up serving of an afternoon, but me and Daisy could have the place readied up for next day in no time. Of course, I'd come once a week on a day we were closed, to give the place a good bottoming as well.'

'That would be perfect – but only if you want to take on the extra work? Otherwise I could get cleaners in . . . ?'

'No need to go paying other people when I can do it better myself and be glad of the extra money,' Tilda said firmly. 'Shall I ask our Daisy?'

'Great idea, if you think she'd like a job.'

'They all want a bit of money, don't they? And she'll finish early enough so she can still go out gallivanting. I'll get her to pop in and talk to you. She's not chatty, mind – wears a lot of black and says she's an emu.'

'Emo?' I asked after a minute. 'Like a Goth, but gloomier?'

'Sounds about right,' she agreed.

I went to thank Nile for the Edinburgh rock, but he was out again so instead I texted him and he rang me back from his mobile to ask if I'd like to go to the pub later.

'It's Friday,' I pointed out.

'That's OK, they open on Fridays.'

'I thought you were a creature of habit, so we only went on Tuesdays.'

'I'm infinitely adaptable – I can learn new ones. What about it?'

'I really can't,' I said, torn between wanting to go and a compulsion to keep working. 'I've only got one last chapter of the first draft to write, though I think it's going to take me till late.' And even then, it would only be roughly blocked out, like all of the last few chapters, because the words never seemed to take wing towards the end until I was rewriting the whole novel.

'You've still got to eat.'

'I'm going to make a plate of sandwiches to keep me going. This could be a marathon session.'

'I was going to show you my sporran,' he said enticingly.

'Which sporran?' I asked.

'A lovely old one that was at the bottom of a box of oddments I bid on in an auction. I know someone who'd buy it like a shot, but it's quite handy to put my loose change in.'

'I hope you're joking,' I said severely. 'And now, though I'm terribly tempted by the idea of escaping for a bit, my Fear of Agent means I'll have to resist.'

'OK, see you in the morning then, with the rest of the clan,' he said.

'You're coming over in the morning?'

'Of course! Sheila told me you'd invited the whole family to see the finished tea emporium and I'm looking forward to it.'

'But you know it's not totally finished. This is simply a kind of trial run and then I'll have just over two weeks to iron out any kinks before we open on 4 November – and anyway, you see it all the time!'

'Then I'll see it again with fresh eyes – and perhaps you should open on Bonfire Night, instead, so it all goes with a bang?'

'Ho, ho,' I said. 'I don't want there to be any fireworks, just a quiet, civilized opening welcome and then straight into the teas.'

'It sounds a riot of gentility,' he said drily, then added, 'I like your friend Edie and she gave me lots of good advice.'

'What about?' I asked suspiciously.

'Oh – all kinds of things,' he said vaguely, and then rang off.

The bright, friendly rectangle of Nile's window glowed warmly that evening as I worked on, laying down the bones of that last chapter and, when I'd finally finished and noticed the empty box of Edinburgh rock at my elbow, I felt quite sick, but in a *good* way.

The lasting powers of attorney were signed in the nick of time, for Father's mental faculties have definitely begun to fail, too. His memory in particular is not what it was, so that he continually repeats information he's already given me – a trait that in other people used to infuriate him.

Yesterday, I caught him engaged in a one-sided conversation with Hugo. In my opinion, this is not the action of a rational mind.

It is sad to see the decline of so sharp an intellect.

37

Ancestral Traces

Despite my late night I was still up and baking in the teashop kitchen early the following morning – cheese and tomato tartlets, mini fat rascals and iced fairy cakes.

Then I set the large round table in the bay window with a crisp, snowy cloth and napkins, plates, glasses and cutlery – a kind of trial run. I unfolded one of the highchairs recommended by Geeta, too, ready for Casper.

It all looked lovely, if I said it myself, and by the time the family arrived, closely followed by Nile (not, I was pleased to observe, wearing an antique sporran), everything was ready apart from putting out the cake stands and making tea and coffee.

The soft turquoise and dusky pale raspberry-pink glass of the art deco chandelier and wall lights were reflected in the mirror behind the counter, so that what might have looked quite a long, narrow cave appeared to go on for ever.

Bel and Nile had, of course, seen the evolution of both flat and café, but trooped upstairs with everyone else – I thought we'd start at the top and work down – and at least Sheila admired my dried flower door wreath and then stood in deep, appreciative silence in front of Dad's portrait of me for quite ten minutes.

'Wonderful!' she said, finally. Then she peered out of the front window and remarked, 'When you're sitting here at your desk, you must practically be able to have a conversation with Nile in his flat!'

'Well not really, it isn't *that* close,' I said quickly.

'I often see Alice working away when I pull down my blind,' Nile said. 'But usually she's so lost in what she's writing, she doesn't notice.'

'Perhaps you should have a rope and pulley across the gap, so you can send baskets to and fro,' Sheila suggested. 'The hooks on the wall outside were probably for laundry lines that went across like that.'

'You know, I hadn't noticed those,' I said, amazed, and then we all went back downstairs and viewed the immaculately hygienic kitchens.

There was no place for a single germ to hide and all the cleaning rotas, daily and weekly, were up on the wall already, as were charts near the fridges and freezer for marking when and where from the various food products had arrived.

'Luckily Tilda managed the Branwell Café and kept herself up to date with all the rules, regulations and paperwork, because I don't think Mrs Muswell was very interested,' I told them. 'Tilda ran a very tight ship and she's still going to do the day-to-day management once we're up and running, so I can take more of a back seat, apart from the baking.'

'It all looks perfect to me, especially now I understand more about what's involved,' Sheila said, and the others agreed.

'I think we've got our café plans right too, thanks to your advice,' Teddy said. Casper had suddenly fallen asleep against his shoulder and looked angelic, though he'd done his best to grab the dried flower garland from the flat door as we came down.

We did a final loop down to the boiler room and then through the fire door to the now rather palatial cloakrooms.

'I'm taking notes for the Oldstone Farm customer conveniences,' Teddy said. 'The sanitary ware, I mean – I'm not really into interior design.'

'You're not into interior design at all,' Geeta told him. 'Left to you, the apartment would have been all gloomy dark leather and decorated with old railway signs.'

'We'll sort the décor out anyway,' Bel assured him. 'It's the fun bit, isn't it, Alice?'

'It's probably the *only* fun bit,' I agreed.

Emerging up the short flight of stairs into the teashop, I left them to make themselves comfortable at the window table while I warmed the fat rascals and filled the cake stands. Bel helped ferry everything through, while Nile made the tea and coffee behind the counter, as if he'd been a Fat Rascal employee for years.

Casper, secured in one of the new highchairs, was drinking a cup of juice Geeta had brought for him, but it occurred to me that I ought to buy one of those little baby-bottle warming machines, even though I didn't think I'd get many small children coming in.

Everything passed the taste test with flying colours, especially the fat rascals, warm, split in half and buttered.

'Was your trip to Scotland successful?' Teddy asked his brother, beating him to the last one.

'Oh, yes, I think you could say it was,' replied Nile.

'He bought a sporran,' I told them.

'I thought it would be handy for keeping my small change in,' he said with a straight face. 'But then I mentioned it in an email to an American client who loves anything Scottish and he's snapped it up.'

'I'm afraid I snapped up all that Edinburgh rock you brought me back, too,' I said ruefully, 'but it did keep me going while I roughed out the last chapter.'

'Sugar gives you worms,' he reminded me.

'Don't be revolting, Nile!' Geeta said.

'Actually, I think that's an old wives' tale,' Bel told her brother.

'That was a lovely tea, darling,' Sheila said to me, laying her napkin on an empty plate. 'It feels delightfully decadent having such a lush tea, so I think your tearoom is *bound* to be a winner!'

'Yes, it might not be quite the mad idea I thought it was,' Nile admitted.

'There can't be much left to organize now, can there?' asked Sheila. 'Is everything finished?'

'There are bound to be several forgotten last-minute things, but no, I'm almost there. I have a list of my chosen suppliers and when I've rewritten my novel and sent it off next Friday, I'll put in the first orders and go to the cash and carry to stock up on basic ingredients.'

'And I know you're having the menus, leaflets and business cards printed,' Bel said.

'Newspaper adverts?' suggested Geeta.

'I've drafted one out, because I'm going to contact the local paper on Monday, to see if they want to run an article about how I was abandoned on the moors and my search for my mother. If the advert goes into the same issue, then even if she doesn't come forward I'll still get some good publicity out of it.'

'I think that's very sensible,' Sheila said. 'Suggest they do the interview at Oldstone Farm, if you like, so you have someone with you.'

'Thank you, that's a great idea, because I do feel nervous about it,' I replied gratefully.

'And since you finished the first draft of your novel last night, you can come back home with us now and have a little rest over the weekend, can't you?' she suggested. 'We'll have a celebratory family dinner tonight, too!'

'Anything except the sheep's head,' Teddy said, which seemed to be a running family joke.

It wasn't sheep's head, but a delicious creamy pasta dish, preceded by mackerel pâté with thin, crisp toast, and followed by a sherry trifle and thick cream. I could feel the waistband of my jeans tightening with every bite . . . or maybe that was the Edinburgh rock still expanding.

'How is Zelda?' asked Sheila, scraping the last of the trifle into Teddy's bowl, which he'd been holding out mutely for a second helping, like a well-nourished version of Oliver Twist.

'Yes, has she decided yet if she's going to buy you out of the antiques stall?' asked Bel. 'You haven't said.'

'That's because I don't know. She doesn't seem to be speaking to me at the moment,' he said tersely.

'Have you been arguing again?' asked Sheila. 'You sounded cross when she rang you last week and I thought how odd it was, because you've never disagreed all the years you've known each other and now suddenly you keep falling out.'

'She's never propositioned me with one loopy idea after another, before,' said Nile. 'That's why.'

'But I thought you said the marriage thing was a joke?' asked Teddy.

'It was to me, until she suddenly thought we should give it a go. And when I turned that one down, she came up with another bright idea . . .'

Bel said cheerily, 'Well, are you going to tell us, or shall we try to guess?'

'I don't know that it's any of our business,' Geeta said.

'Well, she was the one who announced they were getting married when they weren't,' Bel pointed out. 'He might as well tell us, before our imaginations run riot.'

I think mine already had . . .

'She wanted me to be her sperm donor and then play a part in the baby's life,' he said. 'I mean, if there was one.'

I stared at him: no wonder he'd seemed a bit distracted lately!

'I think that might be taking friendship a little *too* far,' Geeta said.

'But you can see why she'd rather have someone she knows really well, like Nile, than an anonymous donor,' Bel said. 'But it's a big commitment, because Nile isn't the kind of man to walk away and *not* get involved.'

'No, and I feel she's put me on the spot by asking me,' he said, looking right at me, though I don't know why.

Sheila frowned. 'I really don't think it's a good idea, darling. People do ask friends to be their sperm donors, or even egg donors, but there can be all kinds of drawbacks when you think it through.'

'Yes there are, and though it seemed mean to say no, there was no way I could do it.'

'I'm sure you're right,' Bel said. 'I mean, just think what would happen if Zelda got into another relationship with one of those dreadful men she favours and he moved in with her. It could all get a bit messy.'

'Or you found someone else you wanted to settle down with,' said Sheila brightly.

'I can see where she's coming from, since you're already friends and business partners, so you're up and down to London all the time,' Teddy said.

'But I'm hoping she's going to buy me out of the stall so I *don't* have to go up and down all the time!'

'Then you could do it, but make it clear she'll have to go it alone afterwards,' Teddy suggested. 'It does seem mean not to help her at all, when you're such old friends.'

'You do it, then,' snapped Nile.

'No way!' exclaimed Geeta.

'I do make very nice babies,' Teddy said, rather smugly regarding his offspring, who was messily eating a piece of banana.

'*We* make nice babies,' Geeta said emphatically.

'I think Nile's right not to do it, don't you, Alice?' asked Sheila.

'Me?' I said, turning slightly pink. 'It's nothing to do with me . . . But if she does go ahead with AI one way or the other, then one day the child will want to know who his father is, won't he or she?'

Nile gave me one of his unfathomable looks. 'I think children of registered sperm donors can find out about their fathers when they turn eighteen now.'

'Yes, I'm sure I've read that somewhere,' agreed Teddy.

'It would be lovely to trace *either* of mine,' I said ruefully, and then Teddy, who is into family history in a big way, told me about the genealogy site he used and that it was possible to take a DNA test through them.

'Oh, yes – Nile mentioned that once, but I'm not sure what it would show if I did it.'

'If people related to you have taken one and registered on the database, then you might find some relatives,' he suggested. 'But at the very least you'd learn all kinds of interesting information about where your ancestors are from, so it's worth the outlay.'

'How do they do it?' I asked.

'Oh, it's a simple saliva test. They send you a kit in the post and you complete it and send it back.'

'Paul took the test as soon as they started offering it, a few years ago,' Sheila said. 'And he did find another branch of the family.'

'It's quite expensive and I think the chances of it helping Alice are slim,' Nile said, and then there was one of those long family debates that seemed set to go on for the rest of the evening.

Partway through it I caught Teddy's eye and said, 'Let's do it!' And we went into the library, where he signed me up for the DNA testing on the spot, using his account with the website.

Trisha Ashley

'Everything will come here, but I'll let you know when it does,' he said.

I had vague ideas about swabbing the inside of my mouth and sending the cotton bud off in a test tube, or something like that. It had to be easy, if you did it yourself.

'You are kind,' I said gratefully, and then the others came in and Teddy got out the Giddings family tree to show me. Paul had started it off and now Teddy was working his way further and further back.

Later, when I was in bed and falling asleep, I decided the DNA test was probably money down the drain, but on the other hand, even tiny amounts of information about my genetic makeup would be more than I knew right now!

Today when I returned from the surgery and went to visit Father, I found him staring blankly at his computer screen, unable to remember the next move in a game of chess.

'Your memory has been deteriorating of late,' I said. 'It would be as well to have your own doctor look at you, for there are interesting advances in the early stages of Alzheimer's and dementia.'

'Don't be foolish – as if I wouldn't know if I had either of those things!' he snapped. 'No, I simply had a small memory lapse, which is quite common at my age.'

He had evidently forgotten all the other lapses, so I could tell that each new one from now on would be, to him, the first, so I said as tactfully as I knew how, 'Of course – but it wouldn't hurt to have a check-up, would it?'

'There's no point – there's nothing wrong with me,' he stated adamantly and wouldn't be budged about it.

He must realize the decline in his faculties, and is afraid to have his fears confirmed, which is entirely illogical when there might well be medication to slow the rapidity of the symptoms.

38

The Birds and the Bees

Next morning Sheila urged me to rest and get some fresh air, and some-how I found myself walking up the hill towards the Oldstone, hand in hand with a still slightly morose Nile, Honey pottering happily along behind us.

The weather had mercurially changed and there was a bright sun and only the hint of a breeze. Large clouds were slowly drifting across the light cerulean sky, stately as galleons.

There was no one else about and potentially we gave ourselves piles by sitting on one of the fallen monoliths to admire the view.

'I wasn't brought up in Yorkshire, but this area always feels like home,' Nile said.

'It did to me too, almost as soon as I'd arrived,' I agreed. 'I feel some-how rooted, even though I don't know my past, and I certainly never want to leave.'

He turned his head and looked at me. 'Edie told me how you became estranged from your adoptive mother after your father died, but never really settled anywhere.'

'I almost did once,' I said wryly. 'I thought I was going to marry Dan, but I'm not sure that would have ever come off, even if he hadn't been killed in that accident.'

'Yes, Edie said he'd never got round to divorcing his wife. And I know you had a breakdown . . .' He looked at me, his grey eyes serious. 'She said you needed time to get over him and to learn to trust another man, but that you have a very loving heart.'

'She reads too many romances,' I said, looking away. 'And I *am* over Dan – I won't forget him, but I've moved on from grieving.'

'She's very shrewd – and she told *me* a couple of home truths, too!'

'Like what?' I asked, curiously.

'I'm not saying, though she told me I was getting too old for galli-vanting around, and then there was something about hummingbirds and flowers I never quite got my head round. Perhaps you could enlighten me?'

'No idea,' I said innocently, and he gave me a look, then got up and held out his hand. 'Let's flit off back to the car then, flower,' he said in a passable local accent and called Honey away from an interesting burrow.

On the way down he said abruptly, 'You don't need to worry about Zelda. I hope we'll always be friends, but I can't do what she's asking me. And she's so strange lately that I'm starting to think I never really knew her at all!'

'Why would I worry about Zelda? I've never even met the woman!' I asked tartly, but he carried on as if I hadn't spoken.

'You may never meet her, because I definitely want out of the antiques stall now. I'm going to tell her that either we sell up, or she can buy me out, whichever she chooses.'

He sounded very determined and he still had my hand in a strong grip that now tightened. 'From now on, I'll want to spend as much time at home as I can.'

'That'll make a change.'

'Wouldn't you like to see more of me?' One dark eyebrow rose quizzically.

There wasn't really any answer to that: I'd like to see *all* of him . . . I went quite hot just thinking about it.

'You'll always have to travel quite a bit, for business, though, won't you?' I pointed out.

'Well, you keep vanishing, too – into your writing,' he said. 'I suspect you'll always do that.'

'Yes. In fact, I'll be vanishing into it the moment I get back to the flat this afternoon and I may be gone some time . . .'

*

341

Although I was so full of Sunday lunch that I wasn't sure I'd ever want to eat again, Sheila sent us back to Haworth with enough soup and sandwiches to feed a small army and Nile insisted that I go over to his flat later so we could have supper together and he could be sure I'd eaten something that evening.

What with Sheila's cooking and all that Edinburgh rock, I was hardly wasting away, but it was rather nice to have someone care enough to think about me.

First thing next morning I emailed the local newspaper, before I got cold feet about the idea, then for the next couple of days slithered off into the Once-upon-a-time, though of course there were interruptions.

On the Tuesday, Daisy, Tilda's niece, called in to see me and she was exactly how Tilda had described her: dressed head to foot in black and very gloomy, with world-weary blue eyes ringed in smudgy dark eyeliner and an uncompromisingly straight-lipped mouth enhanced by deep plum lipstick. In fact, there was more than a hint of Morticia Addams about her.

She was evidently cut from the same terse, brusque mould as Tilda and Nell, and I suspected would have the same ideas about customer service. I asked her about her college course and her ambitions and it turned out she wanted to work in hospitality . . .

But anyway, I offered her the part-time job helping Tilda to clear and clean, and she accepted it, so that was another thing sorted.

When I let her out, I found a small package in the letter box: there was a note with it from Geeta, saying Teddy had asked her to drop it off while she was in town shopping, but she hadn't wanted to disturb me.

It was the DNA test kit that we'd sent for, and when I took it up to the flat and read the instructions, I realized I was totally out of date with how these things were done.

It wasn't a matter of simply swabbing the inside of my mouth with a cotton bud, but instead involved spitting into a test tube – yes, really.

Yuck.

By now I was totally convinced I'd wasted my money on it, but I did it, then put it in the enclosed pre-paid packaging and went out to pop it in the post box.

You know you've been cooped up writing for too many hours when the weak October sun seems unbearably bright and everything sort of shimmers.

But the pull of the story drew me right back – and just as well, because when I turned on the laptop again there was a message from Senga, reminding me, as if I needed it, that the book must be emailed to her on Friday.

Just before I flitted back into Fairyland, it occurred to me that it was ages since I'd heard from Robbie. Maybe he'd found another girlfriend in Australia and changed his mind about coming over? Or was still intending to come over, but had changed his mind about wanting to see me?

The *Upvale and District Gazette* was eager to interview me for an article and fell in with my suggestion that it should take place at Oldstone Farm on Saturday. By then I'd have finished and sent off my book and be back in what passed for my right mind.

They sent a photographer round to take some pictures of the teashop first, though since I wasn't expecting him to take any of me, I probably looked like a loopy bag lady in them.

But apart from this slightly unsettling interlude, by Thursday afternoon my writing was flying along, my head full of evil fairies, stroppy princesses and the joyful exhilaration of dashing towards the finishing post.

Beauty kissed Kev again and this time he responded with such enthusiasm that buds broke out on the interlaced branches above their heads, bluebirds swooped across the sky and a unicorn appeared and began to crop the emerald-green turf . . .

They were too lost in the moment to notice the portal that had opened behind them, but Prince S'Hallow did.

'Let us go back to my own world,' he said, leading Shaz towards it. 'Your lovely hair will be crowned with gold and your white throat encircled by diamonds no less sparkling than your eyes.'

'What, real ones?' she asked, as they stepped through and vanished into the Once-upon-a-time.

The mouse hastened to follow before the portal closed, carrying a half-eaten chocolate bar, purloined from Kev's jacket pocket while he was otherwise occupied. It wasn't the heavenly single estate Criollo chocolate he'd tasted on a previous trip, but it was better than nothing . . .

'Alice, you've got a visitor,' shouted Jack up the stairs, jerking me suddenly back to the Here-and-now, and then, before I'd completely registered what he was saying, there was a loud thundering of heavy feet and the next second Robbie was in the room.

'What on earth . . . ?' I began, getting up, and then lost my breath as I was swept into a crushing bear hug.

'Alice – beautiful as ever!' he said, planting a kiss on my lips before I could take evasive action. I was a bit slow, because most of my head was still in Fairyland and I didn't feel remotely pleased to be wrenched out of it.

I pushed him away and told him so in no uncertain terms, and he looked hurt.

'But I've hired a car and driven all the way up here from London to see you – and that's all the welcome I get!'

I softened slightly; he looked so big, so boyish and so very crestfallen! 'Of course I'm pleased to see you, you daft lump, but I wish you'd warned me you were coming, because I'd no idea you were even in the country yet.'

'I thought I had,' he said, giving me that kicked-puppy look again. He didn't seem to have changed much in the seven or so years since I'd last seen him, but *I* certainly had, and although I was still fond of him, I found him slightly exasperating, too.

'Well, you didn't,' I said with some asperity, 'and I've got to finish my new book and email it off to my agent tomorrow, so I simply don't have time for a visitor right now.'

'Oh, but you don't need to worry about *me*,' he said breezily, recovering his bounce. 'I'll bring my bag up and settle in and you'll hardly know I'm here. Then we can spend the weekend together, can't we?'

'Look, Robbie, I can't do with you or anyone else around until I've finished,' I said bluntly.

'Oh, come on, Alice,' he coaxed, putting his arms around me again. 'You know you're glad to see me really, and I promise not to disturb you till tomorrow.'

He'd left the door open and Bel put her head in at this point. 'Alice, are you there? I don't want to interrupt but—'

Then she broke off, registering that I was clasped in the arms of a strange man and began to back out again, apologizing.

'Sorry – I didn't realize . . .'

'Come in, Bel, you're not interrupting anything – or not any more than Robbie has. He's just unexpectedly arrived.'

'Pleased to meet you. I'm the boyfriend,' Robbie greeted her helpfully.

'The long-ago *ex*-boyfriend,' I amended. 'I think I mentioned him to you, Bel – he's over here from Australia.'

Robbie was wearing his deeply hurt expression again. 'I dashed straight up here to see you, Alice, but you don't seem at all pleased.'

'It's just bad timing,' I explained. 'Of course I'm pleased to see you, you should just have checked this was a good time, you great daft lump.'

He brightened up a bit. 'Well. I suppose I could find somewhere to stay in Haworth till you've sent this important book off tomorrow,' he conceded magnanimously. 'It's a bit far to return to Wimbledon and come back again.'

Bel, having had time to sum up the situation and my probably far-from-welcoming expression, said, 'I've got a good idea, Robbie. My mother takes in paying guests at our house just outside the village and she'd be very happy to put you up. And Alice will be staying with us this weekend too – she needs to relax after all her hard work – so it would all fit in nicely, wouldn't it?'

'Great idea,' I said gratefully. 'Please do take him away!'

'How about you just put me up for one night and then I come back here so Alice and I can have the weekend to ourselves and . . . catch up with each other,' he suggested, a worryingly keen expression in his eyes.

'Oh, no,' I said quickly and emphatically, without thinking. Then I softened it by explaining, 'I've promised Sheila, Bel's mum, that I'd be there for dinner tomorrow and then I've got a reporter from the local newspaper coming to interview me on Saturday morning.'

'Interview you?' he echoed, looking baffled. 'I don't know what on earth's happening any more!'

'You should keep up with the plot,' I said tartly. 'I told you about my novels taking off and the teashop I'm opening.'

'You'd better come with me and I'll explain everything when we get to Oldstone Farm,' Bel promised him. 'We'll leave Alice in peace and you can see her tomorrow evening.'

'Bel, you're an angel,' I told her.

'I only popped in because I've brought you the first batch of cake stands from Thom – I happened to be over there this morning,' she said, slightly self-consciously. 'They're downstairs in the back kitchen and they look exactly what you wanted.'

Then she steered Robbie out and I could hear her asking him on the stairs whether he'd driven up and if so, where he'd parked.

Unsurprisingly, it took me a while to get back into the novel again after that, but once I *was* in, I flew on into the night, barely registering when the light across the way went out . . .

I swooped down and landed on the closing sentence in the early hours of the morning and sat there, slowly coming back to the Here-and-now.

'Where'd the other two go?' Kev asked, finally looking up and no-ticing they were alone . . . well, apart from a funny cow with one horn. He'd never been in the country but he'd seen cows on the TV and they hadn't looked quite like that.

Suddenly the animal made a neighing noise, then cantered past him at speed before leaping into a curtain of shimmering haze.

'The portal's going to close and it's pulling all the Fairyland crea-tures back to Once-upon-a-time,' Beauty said. 'See – there go our enemies,' she added, as the depleted group of dryads were sucked through the hazy patch in their turn, snarling and struggling.

'That's it, it has no power over me now,' Beauty said. 'We can get married and live happily ever after in your kingdom.'

The blue-clad man staggered out of the bower, holding his head.

'What happened?' he groaned, looking about him fuzzily.

'You fell down and knocked yourself out, Officer – don't you remember?' Kev said. 'Me and my fiancée were just wondering whether to send for an ambulance or not – weren't we, Beauty?'

The policeman narrowed his eyes. 'Beauty? But you've been going out with that Shaz for years.'

'Not any longer,' Beauty told him. 'She had too much fairy dust and she's never going to come back.'

'Like that, is it?' he said, and then, his head throbbing, wound his way down the path between some bushes and found himself in the middle of the familiar estate of shabby, run-down houses.

Would the two mismatched couples live happily ever after? I wasn't sure and I thought the story still had legs. There might be room for a sequel . . . but for the moment, I was empty as a shell scoured out by the sea and my ears were echoing with exhaustion.

When I opened the window for a moment, Haworth lay silently and deeply sleeping under a starry sky.

I flung myself into bed and followed suit.

I made an appointment for Father's doctor to come out and visit him in the end, because should he be in the early stage of Alzheimer's, then there are new drugs on the market to try.

Of course I didn't consult Father this time, because he would have vetoed any such suggestion and insisted there was nothing in the least the matter with him. But though he may be medically qualified, self-diagnosis can only go so far and when it comes to the treatment of your own family members, then an independent second opinion is called for.

39

Put Straight

Unsurprisingly, I didn't wake until very late next morning and only then because the phone was ringing.

It had stopped by the time I got to it, but immediately rang again and it was Nile, worried because he'd sent me loads of messages this morning and I hadn't answered.

'I finally finished the book just before five this morning and went to bed – and now you've woken me up,' I complained, yawning.

'Sorry, I didn't imagine you'd be working that late! But when you didn't answer and your curtains were still drawn, I got worried. If you hadn't picked up the phone this time I was going to come over and see if you were ill.'

'Never mind, it was probably just as well you *did* wake me, because I'll have to email the book off to my agent in a minute and I need a clear head for that or goodness knows where I'll send it instead. But once it's gone . . . oh, happy day!'

'And then perhaps you can concentrate on something else?' he suggested.

'True: I'll certainly have to shift up a gear or two if the teashop is going to be ready for opening day. The bills are starting to give me nightmares.'

'That wasn't quite what I had in mind,' he said, a laugh in his voice.

'What did you want me for?' I asked, starting to wake up a bit.

'Bel says your boyfriend's staying at Oldstone.' There was a question in his voice.

'I'd forgotten all about him!' I exclaimed. 'How awful of me, just landing them with him, though Bel did suggest it. And by the way, Robbie's an *ex*-boyfriend – an unexpected arrival in the lost baggage department.'

'Bel said he seemed to think you were expecting him?'

'Robbie always thinks *everyone* is expecting him, even when he hasn't told them he was coming. I knew he might be in the country before long – he's been living in Australia – but I'd no idea when, or that he was heading up here.'

'Apparently you're going to Oldstone for dinner tonight and then staying on for the weekend – unless you and this Robbie are coming back to your flat instead, of course?'

'We're certainly *not*,' I said emphatically. Being cooped up here with me might give Robbie the wrong idea. He'd certainly sounded as if he was already tending that way. 'And remember, I've got that newspaper reporter interviewing me tomorrow and Sheila says we can use the library.'

'It's going to be practically standing-room only for dinner at Oldstone tonight,' he said. 'I'll be there too – and so will Zelda, because she just rang Sheila and asked her if she'd collect her from the station.'

My heart did one of those funny thud and flip-flop things. 'Did you invite her or is she another unexpected ex in the baggage department?'

'I haven't heard from her since we had the last argument, so I don't know why she's turning up like this – unless,' he added grimly, 'she's going to try to change my mind . . . maybe even attempt to get Sheila onside. She knows how soft-hearted she is.'

'Gosh, this sounds like it's going to be a fun weekend!' I said tartly. 'And *I'm* so tired I can barely talk.'

'Then let's hope you regain the power of speech in time for your interview tomorrow,' he said, before adding that he would be heading out to Oldstone about six.

'Me too. I have a few things to sort out, and I need to find something to wear for the interview, because the reporter said he might take another picture of me. He wasn't keen on the ones the photographer took at the teashop yesterday.'

'You could wear that lovely dress you had on at the restaurant?'

'It's way too over-the-top for a Saturday morning in the country,' I protested.

'I don't think you can be too over-the-top when you're being interviewed, and anyway, the dryad look suits you.'

I shuddered slightly. 'Don't call me a dryad. They're not the sweet, gentle nymphs you might think they are.'

'Red in tooth and claw?'

'Green,' I told him.

The first thing I did after I put the phone down was wash my face in cold water to shock my brain into action, and then email off the book.

But then, the moment it vanished into the ether, I felt like a puppet with cut strings and wished I could just have a peaceful, laid-back weekend with the Giddings family to recover.

Instead, I'd have to sort Robbie out. If he imagined that I was going to fall into his arms now he was back, I'd have to put him right straight away. Already I felt guilty for landing him on the Giddingses and wondered what he'd been doing all day.

And now the almost mythically impossible-sounding Zelda would be there, too – and what with her late-onset baby fixation, being convinced Nile had been carrying a torch for her for over twenty years and expecting him to fall in with all her mad plans, I have to admit I was dying to see her . . . while stifling some lurking feelings of nervousness, jealousy and trepidation. What if she'd come to talk him round – and succeeded?

When I went downstairs to the teashop kitchen everything was quiet and empty. Jack wouldn't be coming now unless I sent for him to do odd jobs, so apart from one final bill, that was it. I'd sort of miss him singing snippets of opera around the place, and Ross looming silently about.

It was a very clean place too, for Tilda had been and gone, leaving me a note downstairs saying she'd thought I was having a lie-in so she hadn't disturbed me and she'd give the flat an extra good going over next time instead. She'd ripped out some catalogue pictures of steam mops and hand-held steam cleaners and left them under the teapot. I can recognize a hint when I see one. I just wasn't sure the finances would run to anything else.

The teashop's official inspection was on Monday, so I sorted one or two things out in the office, made a couple of calls, then noticed the time and dashed back up to the flat to pack a bag. I disregarded Nile's suggestion about what to wear for the newspaper interview and instead packed a long jersey tunic with a silk front panel in autumn shades that I knew set off my hair, and a pair of narrow black trousers. That would do it . . . and then I thought of Zelda being at dinner and that maybe she would be London-smart and I would feel a mess in my usual jeans and a T-shirt, with one of Edie's weird and wonderful knitted cardies over it.

But on the other hand, I didn't want anyone to think I was dressing up for any particular reason . . .

I had a rummage on the rail that was doing service until I found an inexpensive wardrobe.

'My new jeans, the Italian emerald-green linen top with lace inserts – and where are my malachite earrings?' I muttered to myself, quickly folding the garments away in a slightly bigger bag than the first one I'd got out.

I was later setting off than I intended, but not as late as Nile, for I was barely half a mile along the road when his dark estate zoomed up behind me and followed me the rest of the way, despite my loitering temptingly on the straight bit in the hope he'd overtake me.

We found Sheila in the kitchen, making a start on dinner.

'Hello, darlings – chicken casserole with herb dumplings and apple crumble with cream for afters,' she said.

'Straight in with the important information, as usual,' Nile said, giving her a hug, and I followed suit.

'I'm so sorry I landed Robbie on you without any notice yesterday,' I apologized.

'Oh, it's no problem,' she assured me. 'He's very nice and I got him wedging clay for me first thing, which was really useful. I've put him in the room almost opposite yours but he's using the bathroom at the end of the corridor. But now Zelda's arrived, I'm afraid she's in the room that shares your bathroom, since we haven't finished decorating the other letting bedroom.'

'That's all right,' I said.

'We really must sort out one of the bedrooms in the family side for you soon, darling,' she added, to my surprise, until I realized that in tourist season they'd need my room for paying visitors.

'There's no need, because if you ever want my room for a paying guest, I can just stay at the flat instead,' I told her.

'I expect we'd squeeze you in somewhere,' Nile said. Then he asked Sheila whether Zelda had told her why she'd turned up so suddenly.

'No, perhaps she just wants to put things right between you,' she suggested. 'I didn't really have time to chat because after I'd picked her up from the station I had work to finish off, so she and Robbie went out in his car.'

She looked at the clock. 'I expect they'll be back soon.'

'I'll take my bag up and then give you a hand with dinner,' I offered. 'Is everyone coming tonight?'

'Yes, the more the merrier, I thought, and safety in numbers,' Sheila said vaguely.

'To dilute the awkward elements?' suggested Nile.

'I hope there won't be any,' she said optimistically.

Upstairs, my bathroom smelled of unfamiliar perfume and half the shelf space was now occupied by a large sponge bag, several lush-looking bottles and jars of cream and potions.

I felt slightly resentful of this occupation, though I shouldn't have; I could have found myself sharing it with a random paying guest at any point. Anyway, when one of us was in the bathroom, the door to the other bedroom could be bolted, so it wasn't a big deal.

I washed and tidied myself, then changed into my linen top and new jeans, before attempting to coax my hair into loose curls. A little makeup . . . and I was about to go down when there was a knock at my door.

I'd managed to forget all about Robbie again, but there before me stood six foot two of handsome, well-meaning stupidity.

'Alice! Sheila said you'd arrived at last,' he said, pulling me into his arms and attempting to plant a smacker on my lips, which seemed to have become an unfortunate habit. I twisted my head away and over his shoulder spotted a small, slim dark-haired woman watching us, her hand on the bedroom door further along.

'Get off me, you idiot,' I said, fending him away.

'I thought you'd be glad to see me, now you'd got that damned book out of the way,' he said, looking hurt. 'I was telling Zelda – this is Zelda, by the way – that I didn't warn you exactly when I was coming up because I wanted to surprise you and anyway, I couldn't wait to see you.'

'Hi,' I said to Zelda, and she stared at me out of a pair of enormous pansy-brown eyes.

'Sheila was telling me about you. In fact, you seem to be flavour of the moment around here, even though no one's ever even mentioned you before,' she drawled huskily. Her eyes narrowed and looked me up and down. 'I can't imagine why.'

'I stayed here while I was getting my flat ready to move into, and since then I've been back quite a lot because I'm helping Bel and Sheila to create a café in the pottery,' I said. Then I added pointedly, 'I've heard quite a bit about *you*, too.'

'From Nile, I expect,' she said.

'Zelda's got things to discuss with Nile that are better done in person than on the phone,' Robbie broke in before I could answer. '*She* arrived without telling anyone she was coming, too. Odd we should both turn up on impulse at the same time, wasn't it?'

'Yes, weird,' I said. From the way they were looking at each other, like a pair of conspirators, I guessed they'd been exchanging confidences. In fact, they'd probably spent the entire afternoon telling each other their life histories.

'*We* need to talk, too,' Robbie said to me meaningfully.

'Do we? Then I'm afraid it will just have to wait, because I'm going down to give Sheila a hand with dinner,' I said quickly. 'Where did you both get to, today, somewhere nice?'

'Oh, we found a pub – the Standing Stones,' he said.

'I know it, it's over Blackdog Moor towards Upvale.'

'No idea where it was – we just drove and stopped at the first sign of civilization. It was cosy, with a wood fire, and since the rain was setting in we stayed put. It had good internet connection, too.'

'Your joy must have been unconfined,' I said, and he gave me an uncertain look. He'd never really understood my sense of humour.

'I'd better go and change,' Zelda said. 'I'll leave you two to have a chat.'

'Yes, come on, Alice,' Robbie said. 'I'm sure they can manage dinner without you.'

'Oh, all right,' I said, giving in and letting him into my room, though I left the door open like a Victorian miss.

He is not the sharpest knife in the box, but after five minutes I'd managed to get it into his head that although delighted to see him, and very fond of him, I hadn't the slightest intention of ever being more than good friends.

'I don't know why you thought we could just take up where we left off when you emigrated to Australia,' I said. 'I mean, a lot of water has passed under the bridge since then and we're different people from when we first met. I can't simply turn the clock back on my emotions.'

'But I was hoping to take you back to visit my parents,' he said, as if that made any difference to anything.

'Robbie, I'm opening a teashop in less than a fortnight and I'm *over-whelmed* with things to do before that. I put everything on hold while I finished the novel, but now I've got to get on with it and there's no way I'm going anywhere for weeks, if not months!'

He looked baffled. I think he'd had a scenario in his head and things were not going the way he'd expected them to.

'Think it through,' I said to him. 'I'm now permanently settled up here, while you live in Australia. That's rather a long distance away.'

'But I told you I might move back – with the right incentive.'

'If you mean me, then forget it!'

'Have you met someone else?' he asked with sudden suspicion.

'Yes, I'm secretly betrothed to Prince William,' I said rather wearily and he grinned. It was just as well I'd only switched on the shaded wall lights, because I could feel my face burning slightly.

'No, I mean really, have you?' he repeated.

'Just wait till you see the tiara I've borrowed from the Queen to wear for dinner tonight,' I said flippantly.

We went round the conversational circle for a little while longer, but after a bit he seemed to have convinced himself that he'd just been a bit quick off the mark after Dan's death and I simply needed a little more time to adjust to the idea of us getting back together again. Then he took himself off to get ready for dinner, while I went down.

Zelda had looked very small and extremely pretty in a cute kind of way and, remembering that, I suddenly felt as huge as a dinosaur.

I wondered if Sheila was right about why she'd turned up.

'Dr Tompkins is coming to see you later today, Father,' I told him.

'Why is he coming?' he snapped, frowning.

'You rang and asked him to call in,' I said. 'Don't you remember?'

He stared at me a moment longer, then his eyes slid away vaguely.

'Oh, yes – of course,' he murmured, finally.

'I'll ask Ron to remind you later and Kim will bring in tea and sultana scones when he arrives.'

Ron, who was on duty today, had been dispatched to the garden with Hugo, who was always noisily insistent when he wished to relieve himself. I could see them both through the bay window, walking across the lawn.

'I don't need reminding,' Father said crossly. 'Anyone would think I'd lost my marbles!'

40

Scenes Off

Sheila had changed her clay-stained cords for clean denim jeans and a long, loose, blue-checked shirt, in which she looked not that much older than Bel.

Dinner was almost ready and I laid the table while she put plates in to warm and sliced bread.

'I've had a sneaky gin and tonic,' she said. 'I had a feeling I might need it, because although I *hope* Zelda only wants to make up with Nile, she might have come here with the idea of changing his mind about the AI instead.'

'Surely not? I think he's already told her in no uncertain terms he's not going to do it. She's extremely pretty, though,' I added morosely. 'And probably very persuasive.'

'I was dying to ask her while I was driving back from the station after picking her up,' she confessed. 'Only I didn't think she had any idea that I knew about it, so I thought I'd better not.'

'That's true – she'd probably be mortified if she realized we *all* knew about it. And by the way, I'm sorry I dumped Robbie on you without any warning.'

'Oh, it was no trouble. He wanted to drive into Haworth and talk to you this morning, but I asked him to help me wedge absolutely *tons* of clay, which kept him occupied.'

'I have no idea what wedging clay involves,' I confessed, 'but thank you for diverting him, anyway!'

'Wedging clay is a bit like kneading dough, only on a larger and heavier scale,' she explained. 'While he was at it, he told me he hoped you two would get back together and he'd been surprised you weren't more pleased to see him when he arrived.'

'He chose the wrong moment – and he's chosen the wrong girl, too, because getting back together isn't going to happen.'

'No, I was sure it wasn't, but I was very tactful and pointed out to him that you'd need some time to get over your fiancé's death and you were fully occupied with your writing and the teashop.'

So that was what had put that idea into Robbie's thick skull!

'Well, of course I do still think about Dan a lot, but as I told Nile a while back, the nervous breakdown seemed to have somehow enabled me to move on.'

'Oh?' she brightened. 'I'm not sure Nile's entirely taken that on board, because he seems to think you still need a little space . . . though eventually I do hope you two will—'

'We're just friends,' I said quickly, guessing where she was heading. 'But not in the Zelda sense of the word,' I added, hearing her voice in the hall, calling imperatively: 'Nile – can we talk?'

'I suppose so, though it's almost dinner time – come into the library,' he replied, sounding tight-lipped but resigned.

Then there was the click of the library door shutting and we exchanged a glance.

'I think we might have a few issues to resolve before there can be happy-ever-afters all round,' Sheila said thoughtfully.

'They don't exist anyway,' I told her. 'Not even in my fairy tales.'

The rest of us had already gathered round the table and made a start on Geeta's delicious vegetable samosa starters, by the time they emerged together, though not, judging by Zelda's expression, together in any other sense than temporarily inhabiting the same space.

I got my first good look at her, for the passage light upstairs was quite dim. She was tiny, with black, glossy hair falling in two perfect wings to frame a face that could only be described as cutely pretty. She was also thin and elegant, in a garnet-coloured slinky jumpsuit that probably cost the earth.

Nile was wearing his best thundercloud expression and a black shirt, probably to reflect his mood.

'Zelda does some modelling for catalogues,' Bel whispered in my ear.

'What, for children's clothes?' I hissed back cattily, and Bel snorted.

Zelda looked at us suspiciously, then went and sat next to Robbie, while Nile took the last chair, which was opposite me. His eyes rested on me for a moment as blank and hard as grey quartz. Then the angry expression went out of them and was replaced by a wicked glint.

'You're looking very Lizzie Siddal tonight, Alice – all lace and flowing curls,' he said, with the obvious intention of winding me up, though I could never resist that smile.

'Don't tease, Nile,' said Sheila, and then, to my relief, the give and take of normal family conversation started up again and Teddy began feeding Casper spoonfuls of lumpy gloop, while Bel told her mother that she'd just remembered that she'd invited Thom Carey to Sunday lunch, and asked if that was all right.

'Of course, darling,' she said predictably.

When I turned my head I caught Zelda eyeing me closely, then she began whispering away to Robbie, which was rather rude. Whatever she said made *him* stare first at Nile, and then at me, though it didn't stop him eating. Nothing ever did get between Robbie and his dinner.

'What time is your interview tomorrow, darling?' Sheila asked me. 'Only we must leave the library free for that.'

'About ten,' I said. 'I'm quite nervous about it and I'd like to get it over with.'

'Are you going to take my advice and wear the dryad dress, for the photographs?' Nile asked.

'What interview?' asked Robbie plaintively. 'And why is someone taking your photograph, Alice?'

So then we had to give him and Zelda a potted history of my being found abandoned and my hope that my natural mother would come forward if she saw an article about it in the local paper.

'I had no idea about any of that,' Robbie said blankly.

'But I told you all about it years ago, Robbie,' I said patiently.

'Did you?' His eyes opened wide. 'I must have forgotten. I mean, I knew you were adopted, it was all the rest I didn't remember.'

'It all sounds very *Wuthering Heights*,' drawled Zelda. 'Who have you cast as Heathcliff?' She glanced at Nile. 'Or should I guess?'

'I've always thought Heathcliff was more a force of nature than a real character,' Sheila said, holding Casper who, having finished his dinner, was being passed from lap to lap around the table. I noticed Zelda hadn't shown any interest in him, which was odd considering her desire for a baby, but perhaps she was one of those women who only liked their own children?

But Casper was so adorable, I didn't know how anyone could resist him! Geeta took him off to bed eventually, when we took our coffee through into the living room. I only lingered long enough to be polite before I gave in to the enormous rolling waves of sleepiness that were finally catching up with me from last night's marathon writing session.

'I'm afraid I'll have to go to bed,' I confessed. 'I'm sorry, but I only had a couple of hours' sleep last night, before Nile woke me up.'

Zelda gave me another of those long stares, sniggered, then muttered something to Robbie, who was sitting next to her on the cushioned window seat.

I felt myself going pink and Nile looked angry.

'Yes, do go, darling,' Sheila said quickly. 'You want to be nice and fresh for the newspaper reporter in the morning.'

'I feel tired too – I think I might do the same,' announced Zelda, suddenly getting up.

I might have guessed she had an ulterior motive if I'd been less thick-headed with sleep, because she grabbed my arm as we reached the landing and said, 'I want to talk to you.'

'I don't know what about, but it will have to wait till tomorrow – I'm bushed.'

'It'll only take a minute,' she said, following me uninvited into my room and sinking on to the only chair.

'Let's stop playing games and clear the air: when Nile and I had our talk in the library, he said he'd told you I wanted him to be my sperm donor – but he doesn't want to do it because he's in a relationship with you. Not that I didn't realize that for myself at dinner,' she added.

That blew some of the clouds of sleep away and I stared blankly at her: 'What? *Nile* told you we were in a relationship?'

'I'm not a complete fool and I could see it for myself as soon as I saw the way you were looking at each other at dinner. He says this time it's serious, but then, he's been out with loads of girls and he always says that.'

'But . . .' Cogs slowly turned and I realized that Nile had only told her that to put her off. My first impulse was to deny it hotly – but it didn't sound as if she'd believe me. 'Nile and I—'

'Look,' she interrupted, 'you can tell him you don't mind him doing it. I mean, he needn't have anything to do with the baby, if he doesn't want to. There's no reason why you *should* mind, is there? So you could talk him round and—'

'No!' I exclaimed with more force than I meant to. 'Zelda, you've entirely got hold of the wrong end of the stick. It's nothing to do with me! And now I'm so tired I can't even think straight any more and I'd like you to *go away* so I can get into bed,' I finished forcefully.

'Oh, all right,' she said, getting up. 'But you can't fool me about what's going on, so you think about it and we'll talk again tomorrow.'

'There's nothing else to say. Please go away!' I snapped, and she flounced out, giving me daggers as she went.

Wait until I got my hands on Nile tomorrow, using me as a scapegoat!

I woke late next morning so it was a scramble to get ready and downstairs in time to snatch a cup of coffee and piece of toast before the reporter arrived.

Bel was on breakfast duty and told me I was still down before Robbie and Zelda, though Sheila had long since retreated to her studio.

'And Nile's in the library emailing – he's left bids for a couple of auctions today, I think,' she added. 'You'd better remind him you need the room.'

'I'll do that,' I said, heading for the door. *And* I'd ask him what on earth he'd told Zelda!

*

'But she was convinced she could talk me round if she saw me face to face and she went on, and on, and on, like water dripping on a stone,' Nile explained. 'So in the end, I thought the easiest way of getting her off my back was to tell her I couldn't do it because I was in a serious relationship with someone else. I didn't say who – she filled in the lines between the dots herself,' he added innocently.

I glared at him. 'Yes, she did – and you're lucky I didn't tell her that we're *not* in a relationship, serious or otherwise!'

'Yes, we are. *I'm* seriously attracted to you and *you* seriously doubt my intentions,' he said flippantly.

'Don't be daft!' I snapped. 'You realize she'll tell Robbie the first chance she gets? If she hasn't already!'

'Well, that's all right because you don't want him, do you? Or . . . do you?' He eyed me narrowly.

'No, of course I don't!'

'Bel said she walked into your flat just after he'd arrived and found you both in a clinch.'

'It was one-sided: Robbie had just pounced on me and was being a bit overenthusiastic,' I snapped. 'Not that I wasn't pleased to see him – I'm very fond of him – and anyway, it isn't any of your business!'

'Right: that puts me in my place, then,' he said sarcastically. 'But if you seriously don't want him back, then I don't know what you're making such a fuss about, because by telling Zelda you and I are an item, I've solved two problems in one.'

'You might at least have warned me what you'd said!'

'I didn't get a chance, or I expect I would have, but I really didn't expect her to buttonhole you so soon.'

'She didn't waste any time: when she followed me upstairs last night it was to ask me to persuade you to help her get pregnant.'

'Then I hope you told her that wasn't going to happen. You look really pretty in that top, by the way,' he added. 'Not a bit Lizzie Siddal – *or* dryad.'

'I'm glad to hear it,' I told him, slightly baffled. 'And stop trying to change the subject.'

'I wasn't – I meant it.' He raised that quizzical dark eyebrow again, looking slightly piratical. 'And here's your reporter arriving to interview you,' he said, hearing the distant ring of the doorbell and unleashing one of those sudden and demoralizing smiles on me. 'I'll bring him into the library and head everyone else off.'

The reporter was young, keen and enthusiastic and had already read all the articles printed from the time I was found. He said it would make a great human interest story and my having come back to the place where I was born to open up a teashop added a nice extra dimension.

Both the article and the advert about the opening of The Fat Rascal would be in Thursday's edition. There was no going back now.

He took a couple more photographs of me with his digital camera and said he'd hoped it would be a nice day, not a misty wet one, so we could have gone outside and got the distant Oldstone into the background.

'But we've got lots of stock pictures of it: maybe I could Photoshop something?' he said, perking up, then took himself off.

Going over the whole story again had been more draining than I'd expected and I really didn't want any more confrontations with Zelda, or an aggrieved Robbie, should she have revealed everything to him by now, so I stuck my head cautiously out of the library door and listened before emerging.

The house was eerily quiet except for a faint clattering in the kitchen. When I went in I found Sheila alone there, brewing herself a cup of coffee and popping something into the toaster.

'Teacake?' she said. 'I need a bit of soothing carbohydrate, and you look as if you do, too.'

I nodded and she sliced another in half and gave me the first one when it popped out, lightly browned and smelling fruitily delicious.

'Zelda just told me Nile wouldn't help her with the AI, because he was in a serious relationship with you,' she remarked casually.

'Last night she told *me* that too, but I've just had it out with Nile and he only said it to get her off his back,' I explained.

'Yes, I know it's early days in your relationship, and really you would both prefer not to tell everyone about it yet, but I suppose he felt he had to.'

I stared at her and she gave me one of her warm smiles, like the sun coming out.

'Unfortunately, Zelda doesn't give up easily. She asked me to try to persuade you to persuade Nile – how complicated things are getting! – and I had to be very, very firm with her about not interfering. Now I'm afraid she's rather angry and upset and, since she said all this right in front of poor Robbie, he's much the same.'

'When he arrived he seemed to be cherishing the mad idea that we could carry on from where we left off when he went to Australia. You'd think I'd been sitting in a tower like Rapunzel for the last few years, waiting for him to come back.'

'I expect by now it's starting to dawn on him that you're not the girl he left behind, but a strong, independent woman: just what Nile needs.'

'Sheila!' I exclaimed, and she opened big, innocent blue eyes wide.

I liked the strong, independent bit but I still wasn't sure I was what Nile needed – *or* vice versa. Anyway, it made me feel a bit like medicine, to be taken until the symptoms cleared and then the bottle could be thrown away.

'Zelda had already started confiding in Robbie when they went to the pub yesterday, so I think he's now chief confidant,' I said. 'Where is everyone now? The house is very quiet.'

'I made Bel and Nile take them for a walk on the moors. It's stopped raining and I expect it will clear the air.'

I thought that was optimistic: it was probably sulphurous with banked-down emotions.

Unkindly, I suddenly thought how nice it would be if Bel and Nile simply abandoned Zelda and Robbie somewhere in the middle of the moors without a map.

Father seemed to have thought Dr Tompkins' visit a social one, since they were old golfing acquaintances, but that he had insisted on checking him over while he was there.

'Load of nonsense!' he snorted. 'But he said now he was semi-retired he needed to keep his hand in, the old fool!'

However, when I had a little chat with my colleague my fears were confirmed, though I saw no point in telling Father.

I knew he'd never notice the additional pills I slipped in among the others he had to take.

41

Strong Reservations

I spotted the walking party returning from the kitchen window. Bel and Nile were in front, with Robbie and Zelda lagging way behind, their heads together like a pair of conspirators.

They passed out of sight round the side of the house and a few moments later the front door slammed and we heard voices in the hall.

Bel followed Nile into the kitchen and rolled her eyes.

'Phew! I feel as if I've been sucked through a vortex of emotion and spat out on the other side.'

'It was OK for you – *you* weren't directly involved,' Nile said morosely, sitting down at the kitchen table and stretching out his long, jeans-clad legs. They looked like designer jeans – but then, everything he wore looked expensive, even when I knew it wasn't.

'I got to hear every last detail anyway, since we were changing partners more often than during a country dance,' Bel pointed out. 'First, Robbie spent ages telling me he felt Alice had got him all the way up to Yorkshire under false pretences, while Zelda was buttonholing Nile—'

'That was her great renunciation scene,' he put in.

'I know: she gave it to me, word for word, right after she'd finished winding Robbie up to the point where he went to have things out with you. I feel quite exhausted!'

'I'm not surprised,' I said. 'It sounds like the walk from hell – but I'm glad no one seems to have actually come to blows!'

Nile glanced up. 'Robbie accused me of being a quick worker and toying with Alice's heart when she was at her most vulnerable.'

367

'I think some of Zelda's theatrical flourishes must have rubbed off on him, don't you?' Bel said. 'He doesn't usually seem to talk like a Victorian papa.'

'Did he *really* say that?' I asked Nile. 'It does sound most unlike him!'

'Yes, but I managed to persuade him my intentions were *strictly* honourable,' he said gravely.

'Of course they are, darling,' agreed Sheila, who was starting to prepare lunch.

'*Which* intentions?' I demanded.

'All of them,' he said, and his grey eyes met mine, full of limpid and, I was sure, entirely spurious innocence.

'Zelda and Robbie got their heads together on the way back and I don't know what the upshot of that was, except Robbie would like a word with you, Alice: he's in the library.'

'Oh God, is he?' I exclaimed, aghast.

'I suspect it's going to be *his* great renunciation scene,' Nile said drily. 'You'd better go and get it over with.'

He was quite right, too: it was just unfortunate that I found Robbie in resigned, forgiving and noble mode so funny that I had trouble keeping my face straight. Luckily, he seemed to assume my quivering lip was a different kind of emotion.

'I wish you'd told me you were involved with someone else before I dashed up here to see you,' he said reproachfully.

'Since you didn't even let me know you were in the country first, that would have been a little difficult,' I pointed out.

He ignored that. 'It didn't cross my mind that you'd have found someone else so soon after Dan was killed. At first I thought Nile must have taken advantage of you when you were at a low ebb, until he explained everything.'

'Oh?' I prompted, deeply interested. 'Like what?'

'Well . . . that you were taking your relationship slowly, because he didn't want to rush you into anything you might regret later.'

'Oh, right . . .' I said. 'Yes, of course: silly me!'

'Anyway, now I understand where you're coming from. But I'll always be there for you if things go wrong and you need me,' he assured me nobly.

'That's so sweet of you, Robbie,' I said, though of course his support wouldn't be a lot of use if he went off back to the Antipodes.

'I hope you'll both be very happy.'

'I expect we will,' I said, but didn't add that that might not necessarily be together . . .

He sighed heavily. 'I've decided to drive back to London after lunch.'

'But I thought you were staying till tomorrow,' I said, and added, even though the news was a relief, 'I mean, I've hardly seen you yet.'

'Well, that wasn't my fault, was it?' he said, the nobility slipping and an aggrieved note shoving its way in. 'Anyway, since I can see there's no point in my hanging about now, I thought I might as well get back to Wimbledon.'

I didn't try to dissuade him and we ended our tête-à-tête with a hug.

It was just unfortunate that Nile chose that moment to put his head into the library to tell us that lunch was ready.

Nile's brooding thundercloud look lasted until Robbie told everyone that he was leaving after lunch, after which the sun came out.

Evidently it wasn't news to Zelda, because she said, 'Yes, and I'm going with him: he's going to drop me off in Camden, which will be easier than my staying tonight and struggling with the Sunday trains. This whole journey's been a pointless waste of time.'

'Oh, I hope not, because we love seeing you, darling,' Sheila told her kindly, even though I was sure she was as relieved as the rest of us to hear she was going. 'And Robbie's always welcome to visit us again, too.'

I think she meant it; but I'm certain the rest of us were hoping they never darkened the doors of Oldstone again.

'Back to normal once more,' Sheila said with a sigh of satisfaction as we finally waved Robbie's hired car off.

We all agreed . . . though, actually, normal at the Giddingses' isn't the same as normal anywhere else, and Sheila had me, Bel and Nile sanding down the banisters on the small back staircase practically before the dust of the car had vanished down the drive.

Teddy, Geeta and the baby were out for the day, so there were only the four of us at dinner that night.

I think we were limp with relief after breasting all the crosscurrents, for we slipped back into discussing the waffle house plans and what I still needed to do during my mad dash to get the teashop ready to open on 4 November, as if the last couple of days and all the emotional upsets hadn't happened. And The Fat Rascal opening was now not much more than a week away!

'I'm going to invite some special guests for the opening tea, so leave the date free,' I told Sheila. 'I'm reserving the big table in the window for you and the family, because I really want you all to be there.'

'Of course we'll be there, darling,' she said, 'but I intended booking us in for it anyway. We'll be your first paying customers.'

It took me a while to persuade her out of this resolution and then Nile asked me who the other special guests would be.

'Well . . . Thom Carey, for one.'

'Then I'd better sit with him, because there won't be room at the big table for another person,' Bel said quickly.

'I'll make a note of that when I do the seating plan . . . which reminds me that I've ordered some small reserved signs for the tables and they haven't arrived yet, so I must chase them up.'

I got a sheet off Sheila's shopping list pad and made a couple of notes.

'I'll invite Jack and his wife, and Ross too, if he'd like to come. And then I did wonder about asking Eleri and Henry Godet . . . but then, Henry might criticize my food, so perhaps not! I'm definitely inviting Henry's cousin George, though he did say teashops weren't his thing. And Emily Rhymer and her husband.'

'What about the reporter who interviewed you this morning?' Bel suggested.

So much had happened that it seemed like days since this morning!

'Oh, yes – good idea! He might even write it up again, if he comes.'

'I thought the teashop was nearly ready and just needed a few tweaks, but it sounds as if you're going to be frantically busy right up until you open,' Bel said.

'I will,' I said, 'but at least now I don't have to juggle it with trying to finish writing a book!'

Sheila spent next morning in her studio, while Bel and I cooked lunch for a change, with Nile as skivvy. I think we'd all had more than enough of emotional scenes and explanations for the moment, so it was nice to do something so ordinary.

When Thom arrived he brought yet more cake stands and we loaded them straight into Nile's car, which was roomier than mine, so he could drop them off for me later. I now had almost enough . . . and Thom said he was getting to the point where he was having willow-pattern nightmares.

He was really nice and he and Bel seemed to hit it off so well. By the time I left, she was showing him the plans for the waffle house and then she was going to take him round the studios.

I knew they would like to convert a couple more of the stables into workshops, so perhaps Thom would be their first resident craftsman, making those lovely upcycled tree bookshelves.

I invited him to The Fat Rascal opening tea then and there, and he said he'd love to come, so that was one tick on the guest list.

I'd dashed off after lunch, saying I had something I needed to do – I just didn't say that the urgent thing was to go up to the Oldstone and think about things, Nile being the main one of them.

I don't know why I thought I could do it there better than anywhere else, but so it was.

The weather had brightened, but it was still a very cold, late October day, the kind with a hint of wood smoke hanging in the chill air. It wasn't surprising I had the place to myself. From the top, by the standing stone, I could see for miles . . . which was a lot further than I could envision where I was going with my personal life.

It had been a very confusing couple of days, but one thing had become crystal clear: Nile *was* attracted to me and *I* could so very easily let myself fall hard for him. And that would be such a mistake, because when he inevitably moved on, it would make it difficult for me to continue seeing the Giddingses and I'd lose the closest thing to being part of a real family I'd ever known.

I found I was droning out the song about someone taking another little piece of my heart and a sheep had bobbed up from behind a clump of heather and was giving me a deeply disapproving glare.

Nile had beaten me back to Doorknocker's Row: his car was parked behind the teashop and the boxes of cake stands were stacked on the table in the utility room.

He'd left me a note, too, saying he'd brought back some of Sheila's broccoli and Stilton soup and crusty rolls, so he'd bring them across later for supper. Then he'd added a postscript that he wouldn't be hanging about afterwards, because he was off on his travels again early tomorrow morning.

'Who wanted you to hang about anyway?' I told the note crossly. 'In fact, who invited you to come over at all, with or without supper?'

Feeling ruffled, I unpacked the cake stands, washed and dried them, then stood them in rows in the big cupboards in the utility room.

When Nile arrived, I found I didn't need my freshly hardened heart to discourage any advances, because we seemed to be back on our usual friendly – if slightly spiky on my side and reserved on his – terms.

He did end up staying later than he intended, but it was his own fault: when I told him that after he'd gone I was going to tweak the café website I'd made, he couldn't resist helping me, which was just as well, since he knew much more about it from designing his own than I did.

When the advert was published on Thursday it would include the website address, so I needed to put the menus up.

'We'll take bookings through the internet or by phone,' I told him. 'They'll all be written in a book kept behind the counter, for Tilda and Nell to consult . . . and I really must buy another laptop for the office. Tilda says she can take email bookings if I do, because Daisy's taught her how to use a computer, but Nell thinks the internet is the Devil's work and won't have anything to do with it.'

'Well, I suppose she might have a point,' he said, grinning. Then he got up and said he'd have to go. 'As I said, I've got an early start in the morning.'

I resisted the urge to ask him where he was going, but it was a close-run thing.

And *I* needed to be up early tomorrow too, because the teashop was having its official inspection and I wanted to make sure it was *perfect*.

And it must have been, because it passed everything with flying colours and the only recommendations were that I give my staff special training on aspects of health, hygiene and safety before I opened for business.

I thought that would go down well with Tilda and Nell, but I rang and invited them to come and be trained on Wednesday. Or at any rate, to come and have tea and discuss it.

Then I set up Facebook and Twitter pages for The Fat Rascal, linked them to the website and uploaded a really good photograph of the round table set for afternoon tea that I'd taken on the day all the Giddingses were there. I felt like a complete technobabe after that.

On impulse I looked at Robbie's Facebook page while I was on there and it still didn't mention that he wasn't currently in Australia. But then, mentally he always did seem to be on another continent – a drifting one.

On Tuesday I woke up with a hollow feeling in my stomach and the realization that in exactly a week The Fat Rascal would be open – and immediately had a major meltdown, even though I was sure, or *almost* sure, that everything was ready.

It was as if I'd had a premonition, because the moment I got downstairs the boiler switched itself on – and then made a horrible noise like a prolonged death rattle and expired.

When I got the man who'd serviced the one in the flat out to look, he confirmed my worst fears: it was dead as a dodo. I'd need a new one – and I'd *have* to have it, even if it would totally wipe out the contingency fund meant to keep the teashop afloat for the first vital weeks.

I thought Nile was still away, but he must have returned some time last night, for he appeared minutes after a flurry of panicked messages hit his inbox.

And what's more, after soothing me down to a gentle simmer, he patiently stayed and helped me work through all my lists, check the books, the stock, that I'd ordered the fresh bread and milk . . . *everything.*

'It's all going to be *fine*,' he assured me patiently. 'And since they're starting to put the new boiler in tomorrow, that will be ready in plenty of time, too. Stop worrying.'

'But it's costing so much! If the one in the flat goes as well, then I'll just have to live in an icebox. I'll be chilled but perfectly preserved by spring,' I said gloomily.

'That's right, look on the bright side,' he urged me, with a grin.

'If the customers don't flood in and keep coming, I won't be able to pay the suppliers, or the staff or—'

'Stop right there,' he ordered. 'I've already told you: the customers will pour in, it will all be a success, and Princess Alice will live happily ever after in her fairy teashop castle.'

'Yeah, right,' I said.

'And if the finances get really desperate, I'll bail you out.'

'Oh, that's kind!' I said, totally taken aback by his generous offer. 'But—'

'I won't need to, you'll see. Come on, what else is on that never-ending list of things to be done?'

'Lola's making a flying visit up on Friday, just for one night, to deliver the jams, pickles and sauces, but other than that, I think we're done.'

'Then all you need to do now is relax – and then cook up a storm.'

'I'm not sure I know how to relax any more,' I said ruefully, 'but thank you for going through it all with me, Nile. I really appreciate it.'

'You could demonstrate your appreciation by taking me out to lunch,' he suggested. 'And we'll kill two birds with one stone, because afterwards we'll spread some of that glossy pile of Fat Rascal leaflets all over the village.'

And we did, too – and some of the outlying hotels and guesthouses, all of which had information racks ready and waiting. We gave the Gondal Guesthouse a wide berth, though.

Nile went back to Small and Perfect when we returned. He still hadn't said where he'd been all of the previous day, which, of course, was none of my business.

Then Sheila rang with the glad tidings that she'd just had an indication that planning permission was likely to be granted for the development of the café in the stables.

'That means it's pretty likely to go through, doesn't it?' I said.

'I think it will, so I've asked Michelle, the sister of Casper's nanny, if she'd like to run the café for me. She said she'd love to, so I'm going to teach her to make waffles. She's a very nice girl.'

'Great, because I'm sure during tourist season you'll have more than enough to do looking after the paying guests.'

'I don't actually do very much really, except cook dinner if they want it,' she said. 'Bel does the breakfasts and the cleaner changes the beds and towels. Oh, and Alice, Thom might become our first resident craftsman next year, if we convert another stable!' she added brightly. 'If he charged more for those lovely big pieces of reclaimed wooden furniture Bel showed me pictures of, he wouldn't have to bother so much with upcycling smaller items.'

'That's true,' I agreed. 'I did love the tree bookshelf he was making and I'm certain people would pay a fortune for those.'

'His neighbours have been complaining about the noise when he's sawing and sanding wood. Some people have no soul. But it doesn't matter to us and it will be rather nice to have another craftsman working here – perhaps nice in more ways than one, because I can tell Bel's very taken with him.'

'I'd noticed, but I'm sure she's not in any hurry to start a new relationship – and neither am I, come to that,' I added pointedly, since I was now certain from her hints that she was cherishing hopes.

'You know, that's exactly what I told Nile when he called in on his way up to that country house sale in Northumberland. Take things slowly, I said.' She smiled at me, undeterred.

'Oh, so *that's* where he was?' I said involuntarily.

'Yes, did he forget to tell you? I'm sure he thought he had – and he says you're both going to the pub tonight, with Bel and Thom.'

'That's the first I've heard of it!'

After I'd put the phone down, I thought that Nile made too many assumptions about me and I really ought to tell him I had something else to do tonight, except it would probably be fun for us all to go out together.

And we did have a nice, relaxing evening and then went back to Nile's for coffee, which he brewed up in a big snazzy machine. Then Thom drove Bel home, meaning he'd be spending half the night crisscrossing the moors, and I pleaded exhaustion and went home too.

Nile didn't try to persuade me to stay with him a little longer, but then, that was what I wanted, wasn't it? So there was no reason for me to feel disappointed . . .

On Tilda and Nell's training day I sat them down and explained about the new boiler.

'So you see, since I've spent all my money on replacing it, there won't be any left to pay your salaries, or anything else, if the teashop isn't an immediate success.'

'It will be, and anyway, we'll wait for our wages, if necessary,' Tilda said.

'Why not sell that old tea set Jim Voss came round after?' Nell suggested. 'There was one just like it on the *Antiques Roadshow* on Sunday and it fetched about five thousand pounds. I were struck dumb.'

'I don't think it can be the same as that one downstairs – it's so ugly!'

'Oh, yes, it were just as hideous,' she assured me. 'It were French,' she added, as if that explained it. 'I've brought that snap out of the album that shows the ladies having their tea from it, like I said they did once a year.'

The black-and-white photo was small, but the details surprisingly clear: two rather Edwardian-looking ladies were sitting behind a small bamboo table on which, unmistakably, was the tea service. There was a younger version of Nell standing next to them, her white cap pulled down low over her brow.

'Well . . . I did mean to get Nile to take a look at it,' I said doubtfully.

'Maybe do it sooner than later, then, flower,' suggested Tilda. 'If it's valuable, no wonder Molly Muswell was so keen to get it back!'

I wasn't convinced, but I agreed I'd definitely ask Nile's opinion, and we got on with the training, which was a hoot.

I solemnly read through all the rules for ensuring safety in the work-place, food preparation, and general good hygiene and how to wash your hands.

'I haven't killed any bugger yet,' Nell said.

'Paper towels are the most hygienic option for drying hands and you can use a clean one to turn off the tap,' I continued, sticking to the script. 'The dirty laundry – that's the tablecloths and napkins – should be bagged and put in the rear hall ready for collection each evening, and the clean laundry put away in the designated cupboard until needed.'

'Well, I'll go t' foot of ower stairs,' said Nell sarkily.

'All tea towels, handtowels and dishcloths will be run through the washing machine on a hot cycle every single day . . .'

I turned a page and said with relief: 'Lastly, be careful to tick off the boxes on the whiteboard when daily and weekly cleaning tasks are com-pleted, and the stock charts logging in the dates of perishable items.'

I sat back. 'There, that's about it.'

'Go teach your grandmother to suck eggs,' Tilda said, having sat with folded arms and an impassive face as she listened to the whole thing.

'Well, *I* know that *you* know, but I had to do it anyway.'

'Never mind, it was right entertaining, like a play,' said Nell. 'Did you say our aprons have come?'

They were Victorian-style with a bib top, frilled edges and a generous wrap-around, and when they tried them on I think Nell's would have gone around her twice, except she threaded the strings through holes in the waistband and tied them in a large bow in front.

'That's how we did it when I worked at the Copper Kettle,' she said.

They had decided between them to wear black tops and trousers underneath, and Nell had requested the sort of headband with a white frill attached that I'd only previously seen in ancient films.

It's surprising what you can get on the internet.

'Not long now till opening day, and I'll come along early with our Tilda,' Nell said. 'We'll be all revved up and ready to go, when the doors open.'

She made it sound like the opening day of a sale, when we might be trampled by a crush of customers.

'Eh, it'll be grand to be back in harness again and somewhere proper, too,' Nell said happily.

'Before you go,' I said, 'there's something I need to tell you about myself, before you read it in the local paper tomorrow.'

'Go on then,' urged Tilda. 'You've got my interest right piqued now!'

When they'd gone I rang Nile and said, 'Can you come over? I've got something I want to show you.'

'Promises, promises,' he said. 'I'll be right there.'

'Don't get your hopes up – it's only your *professional* expertise I want,' I told him, and he laughed.

When he arrived I'd already brought the tea set upstairs to the back room and was unwrapping and laying it out, piece by piece, on the old table.

'Where did that come from?' he asked, picking a cup up and turning it over to examine the base.

'You know I told you Mrs Muswell had sent Jim Voss to ask me for her mother's tea set, because she'd left it behind, only it wasn't in the cupboard where she said it was?'

He nodded.

'Well, it *was* there after all, just tucked out of sight. Nell knew where it was and she said it dated back to the Misses Spencer, who had the Copper Kettle, so Mrs Muswell had lied about it being her mother's. Nell even has a little black-and-white photograph showing herself serving the Misses Spencer tea with it – she brought it to show me earlier.'

'So Mrs M had only just remembered it and was trying to get it back?'

'Yes, I expect Jim Voss told her about our finding the willow-pattern china in the cupboard under the basement stairs, and that jogged her memory.'

'Well, I'm not surprised – it's quite valuable.'

'Really?' I stared at him. 'Nell and I think it's hideously ugly, but recently she saw something similar on the *Antiques Roadshow*.'

'I think it's ugly too,' he agreed, 'but it's Sèvres, and there are lots of collectors out there who don't share our opinion.'

He scrutinized each piece carefully, then said finally, 'It's all genuine – there are a lot of fakes about – and complete with the original tray. In perfect condition, too.'

'So how much do you think it's worth?' I asked eagerly.

'I'll have to check some auction estimates, but I think it's good for *at least* four thousand, and possibly quite a bit more.'

'Wow!' I said. 'I think the Misses Spencer just gave me back a bit of financial wiggle room!'

I expect if they knew, they'd be pleased to be helping restore their beloved teashop to its former glory, and I was happy I could even the score with Mrs Muswell at the same time!

I don't usually read the local paper, but there was a pile of the latest edition on the counter when I was paying for my petrol in the village. A photograph of the Oldstone and the headline on the front page leaped out at me: 'Woman abandoned as Baby returns to seek Birth Mother,' it said sensationally.

Of course, I didn't buy a copy there, but instead stopped at a newsagent where they wouldn't recognize me, when I was on my way to the surgery. When I had read the article I thought how tiresome of Alice Rose to want the schmaltzy happy-ever-after meeting with her birth mother that so seldom ever worked out that way. It certainly wouldn't in this case.

I blame all these TV shows for encouraging misguided people to search out lost relatives who, I am quite sure, would in nine cases out of ten have preferred to stay that way.

42

Perfectly Poised

The day the newspaper article came out, I went out early to buy a copy – and narrowly missed bumping into Dr Collins, who came out of the shop and got into her car as I walked along the street. She drove off the other way, though, so I don't think she saw me.

On the way back to the teashop I felt exactly like a snail without its shell, though I don't suppose many people had read the paper yet, or if they had, were interested.

Would my birth mother see it? And if she did, how would she feel? I hoped she'd be happy that I was searching for her and eager to meet me, but there was a current of pessimism running through me (probably caught from Nile) that suggested an alternative scenario.

I was so engrossed in these thoughts that I only came back to reality when I caught the sound of a loud altercation as I turned into Doorknocker's Row – a shrill female voice and the more familiar deep tones of Nile's.

I stopped dead at the sight of Nile and an enormously fat woman engaged in what looked like a heated argument outside The Fat Rascal.

It was unmistakably Mrs Muswell, but either she'd used an old photograph on the internet, or she'd put on a lot of weight recently, because her beady dark eyes were sunk deep into her doughy face.

'I'm not listening to any more of your cheek!' she told Nile.

'You're not going anywhere before you've paid me for those antiques of mine you sold.'

Mrs M opened her eyes as wide as they would go – not far – and said innocently, 'I told you, I just I forgot to put that cheque through your door before I left.'

'Yes, just like you forgot to answer the letter I sent you through your solicitor.'

'I've been moving around,' she said evasively. 'I haven't caught up with my mail yet.'

'I reported what happened to the police,' he told her grimly.

'There wasn't any call to do that – it was just an oversight!' she said indignantly. 'And what's more, I didn't sell everything and I can't be held responsible for any that were left.'

'Alice – the woman you sold the café to – found them and has given them back to me. And here she is,' he added pleasantly.

Mrs M whirled around as fast as her bulk would let her and stared at me.

'I sent you a letter through your solicitor, too,' I said. 'It concerned the small matter of every item of any value that was listed on the sales agreement when I bought the café having been removed before my arrival.'

I think she'd have tried to flee at that moment, if I hadn't been standing in front of the only exit, but instead she rallied and brazened it out.

'Now, that's exactly what I'd come to see you about, only you were out,' she said.

'I caught her peering through the café window,' Nile explained.

'I came over from Spain yesterday and I'm staying with friends – the Vosses at the guesthouse – and Jim told me you'd got hold of the wrong end of the stick about the things I'd got rid of, so I thought I'd just pop round and explain.'

'Right, explain away,' I told her. 'And we'd better go inside while you do it,' I added, unlocking the door and ushering her in.

Nile brought up the rear – he obviously wasn't letting her go any-where until he'd got his money.

She came in reluctantly and then stood looking round in surprise. 'You wouldn't think it was the same place! The Vosses told me about your grand plans and that you stand to make a mint out of this up-market teashop of yours, so you don't seem to have done too badly out of our bargain. Had the place at a snip, you did.'

'I haven't opened yet, so who is to say how it will go?' I said. 'And when I arrived, it looked like an entirely different place from the one in the photographs you showed me before I bought it, too.'

'They were the only ones I had and I didn't *tell* you it still looked like that.'

'Perhaps not, but you did sign an agreement stating what equipment, furniture and fittings were included in the sale, and practically none of them were there.'

'Ah, that's where the misunderstanding came in,' she said menda-ciously. 'I thought that was just a list of what was there at the time, but of course I threw out the old things when I started renovating. If you remember, I explained I'd only put the café on the market to see if anyone wanted to buy it and do it up themselves, before I spent any money on it.'

She *had* said something like that, but still, she knew she'd cheated me.

'I left you all that lovely willow-pattern china too,' she said, man-aging to sound aggrieved.

'You can't give that modern stuff away, these days,' Nile put in. 'It's worthless.'

'So you say,' Mrs M told him rudely, then swung round to face me again. 'I don't think you've got a leg to stand on, dearie. And while I'm here, I'll take away that old tea set of my mother's that was in the cup-board with the willow pattern. I can't think how I came to forget it.'

'Nice try, but no deal,' I said. 'I've already told Jim Voss that I'm keeping it – and I know it wasn't your mother's, because Nell told me it was left in a will to the people who owned the Copper Kettle café, and she has photographs to prove it.'

Mrs M's doughy face was suffused with a flush of fury. 'You're a liar, just making that up because you know it's valuable!'

'You know very well that you're the liar, and I'm going to sell the tea set to make up for some of the equipment you cheated me out of.'

'And if you pay me now for those antiques you sold, I won't have you arrested for theft,' Nile put in, and Mrs M made a gobbling noise.

'Like you could, when it was all a little misunderstanding!'

'Want to try me?' he offered.

'There's no call to be like that about it. I'll write you a cheque when I get back to the guesthouse.'

'You'll give it to me in cash before I let you out of my sight,' he insisted, and told her how much she owed him.

The flush faded into a shocked pallor. 'It can't be that much!'

'It certainly is – and think yourself lucky I deducted your commission.'

Since he was still standing in front of the door, after a moment she gave in, pulled a fat wallet out of her handbag and peeled off some high-denomination notes from a fat wad. 'I've only got euros,' she said sulkily.

'I'll take anything except Monopoly money,' he said, and counted it when she thrust it at him.

'That looks about right,' he said at last.

'Then perhaps you'd like to move over and let me out?' she suggested. 'I've never heard so many accusations – and me only coming here out of the kindness of my heart to explain things to Alice when she got hold of the wrong end of the stick.'

'It was the right end,' I said. 'Goodbye, Mrs Muswell. I hope we don't meet again.'

She made a noise curiously like a kettle coming to the boil and flounced out. From the teashop window we watched her blunder off in a blind fury down the alleyway and, we hoped, out of our lives.

Nile turned to me. 'Funnily enough, when I caught her looking in your window I was on my way to tell you that the Sèvres set was a *very* rare design and the last one to go up for auction fetched nearly eight thousand pounds.'

Then we looked at each other and burst out laughing.

The newspaper *did* circulate, for I had my first telephone booking after lunch – Eleri, who, like Sheila, insisted on paying rather than coming as my guest.

'I only hope Henry approves of my baking,' I said nervously, and she laughed and said she'd forbid him to say anything that wasn't totally complimentary about it.

George left a message turning down the invitation I'd sent him, but adding that any time I was passing and wanted to drop off a cake, I'd be welcome. I think he really meant the *cake* would be welcome, not me.

And I must get into the habit of saying 'Fat Rascal Teashop' when answering the downstairs phone and not just announcing 'Fat Rascal!' which was open to misinterpretation.

The moment all my cupboards, fridges and freezers were full right up, I felt as happy as an autumn squirrel with an overflowing nut hoard.

I'd spent an entire afternoon making fruitcakes, too, which were wrapped in greaseproof and stored in tins, because they keep so well.

Then later that same day, when I checked for telephone bookings again, I found a second message from George Godet, who had completely changed his mind and was coming to the opening tea after all! I decided I'd put him at the same table as the newspaper reporter, so he could give him the uncut version of how his father had found me.

On the Friday, Lola drove herself up in a new, smart little van with 'Dolly and Lola's Perfectly Pickled and Preserved Company' emblazoned up the side.

She'd brought the first consignment of preserves, as well as a modest stock to be displayed for sale in the glass cabinet on the counter. Tilda had now polished it to an eye-dazzling sparkle, along with the mirror behind.

Since she'd got the whole place so clean that you could eat off any surface, there wasn't much to challenge her until we opened, but if she steam-cleaned the loos any more with that hand-held device she'd persuaded me we needed, I was convinced they'd shrink.

Nile suggested that we meet up with Bel and Thom at the nearby pub that evening for dinner, which was enjoyable, though Lola said afterwards, when we got back to the flat, 'I like your Nile, but what with Thom and Bel obviously pairing off too, I felt a bit of a gooseberry!'

'What do you mean, *too*? He's not *my* Nile, so you needn't feel like a gooseberry on *my* account.'

'Oh, come off it,' she said. 'It's time you both stopped pussyfooting around and got together. He's in love with you and you're in love with him – what's preventing you getting together?'

'Do you really think he's in love with me?' I asked. 'I think he's attracted to me, so perhaps he thinks he is . . . but it wouldn't last. I told you, he's a commitment-phobe.'

'And you're only going to commit if you get the gold-plated guaranteed happy-ever-after,' she said with a grin. 'It's a stand-off!'

'It's got even more complicated lately,' I said, then gave her the full, unabridged version of the Zelda and Robbie weekend, including what Nile had said about our 'serious relationship'.

'I don't know where I am with him,' I finished. 'Or even where I want to be.'

'He's probably as confused as you are; but it does show him in a nice light, that although he's attracted to you, he's been taking things slowly because he thinks you need time to get over Dan.'

'Or so he says. And anyway, I explained ages ago that although I still thought about Dan a lot, I was ready to move on.'

'Men can never take a hint,' she said.

'Lola!' I exclaimed, and she grinned.

Then she insisted on going across to Small and Perfect to say goodbye to Nile next morning, before setting off home.

'He says he'll be glad when your head isn't exclusively occupied by bad fairies and teashops,' she reported, when she returned. 'So now we know what he's waiting for.'

'If he's waiting for anything . . . and I suppose I *have* become a bit of a bore on both counts lately,' I said, 'though once the tearoom has opened Tilda will run it and I can take a back seat.'

'That's what I told him, but I warned him you'd always been away with the fairies and he'd just have to get used to it.'

'I do keep wondering how the characters from the book I've just finished are getting on now,' I admitted. 'I'm sure there's a sequel gathering itself together somewhere in my head.'

'Let's hope this one has a bit more happy-ever-after,' she said, but I told her not to get her hopes up.

When I'd waved her off, I went back indoors. Although I was going out to Oldstone for Sunday lunch next day, I had too much to do this weekend to stay over. There was now less than four days to go till we opened!

But after I'd marzipaned one of the fruitcakes, so I could ice it later, I made the mistake of having a scroll down through my email inbox to see if anything needed answering urgently – and there was one from my editor saying Senga had forwarded the manuscript of my new book and she loved it!

The next bit wasn't quite so good: the edits for it would be with me in a couple of weeks.

I could see the pace was going to be relentless . . . and shortly, the telephone messages booking tables began to be relentless, too. I don't know if it was the draw of my having been the abandoned baby of the moors, or the lure of a teashop promising to feature the rudest waitresses in Yorkshire, but by afternoon, the phone was ringing off the hook with bookings, and there were more by email, too.

I'd begun to check for email hourly anyway, just in case my birth mother chose to communicate that way, but there was nothing from her then or later.

I knew it was still early days, yet with every hour that passed, the faint hope of her contacting me died a little.

Finally, it was the evening before The Fat Rascal opened and we were as ready as we'd ever be.

Tilda, Nell and Daisy had come in that afternoon and laid the tables ready with snowy white cloths and napkins and gleaming cutlery. The float was in the till, the reserved signs put out on every table, and a healthy number of bookings for the rest of the week written into the ledger behind the counter, next to the phone extension.

The beautiful blue and white jug in the bow window was now full of flowers presented to me earlier by Nile, along with a bottle of champagne, and when the others had finally gone home, we retired to my flat with fish and chips and swilled them down with glasses of bubbly . . . as you do.

'Have you heard anything from Robbie?' Nile asked afterwards as he bagged up the greasy wrappers, ready to put in the bin.

'No – but then, I haven't really had time to think about him since he went back to London with Zelda. I've been way too busy. Have *you* heard from Zelda?'

'Well, that's just the thing,' he said, a glint of something that looked very like amusement in his grey eyes. 'She'd gone quiet again and wasn't picking up her phone, so I checked her Facebook status earlier and . . . she says she's in a relationship.'

I stared at him. 'You can't *possibly* mean . . . ?'

He nodded. 'Yes – it's now the Robbie and Zelda Show. I finally got her on the phone and she said Robbie was everything she'd ever looked for in a man.'

'If she was looking for someone big, good-natured and stupid, then she's certainly found her match – but I have to say I didn't see that one coming.'

'Nor me: it seems a very unlikely pairing.' He looked at me more seriously. 'Do you mind?'

'What, about Robbie? No, of course not!' I said. 'I hope it works out well for both of them.'

'That's how I feel. And now she wants us to sell the antiques stall and she's putting her houseboat on the market, because they're going back to Australia. They're talking about setting up some kind of white-water rafting adventure centre, or something like that. It's so un-Zelda, I think she must have had a personality transplant.'

'Well, I hope she's soon got a little Joey in her pouch, too,' I said generously, then suddenly yawned.

'I feel boneless with exhaustion – but excited at the same time!' I said.

'I think you need an early night, ready for your big day,' Nile agreed, 'so I'd better leave you to it – but just tell me if you need my help with anything in the morning and I'll be right across.'

Then he smiled, cupped my face in his hands and kissed me lingeringly on the lips, before going off downstairs to let himself out. Despite my best intentions, there may have been a bit of reciprocal lip action going on there. I was starting to think my attempts at resistance were futile.

Despite my exhaustion, I didn't get to bed immediately because both Lola and Edie rang to wish me every success the next day.

I wished they'd been able to come for the opening, but at least I'd have Nile and the rest of the Giddingses to support me. And even if my natural mother never came forward to claim me, I had a new family, for the Giddingses seemed to have absorbed me into the clan by some kind of osmosis.

As I finally drifted off to sleep, I felt as if I was at the top of a helter-skelter, about to get on my mat and slide off into an unknown future.

I put the newspaper in my bag and read the article again while I was having an extended coffee break, my patients appearing a little thin on the ground that day.

I found it extremely galling that my perfectly logical actions of that night had been ascribed to some kind of mental instability caused by the shock of unwanted childbirth. However, there was no way I could correct this inaccuracy and defend myself without risking the disclosure of my identity.

I disposed of the newspaper in a rubbish bin on my way out of Haworth.

43

Fat rascals

I'd dreamed of this moment for so long that when it finally came, I had to keep pinching myself to make sure I was awake.

The first service was in full swing and I peeped through the kitchen door into the tearoom. Every single table was occupied, and a constant buzz of conversation filled the air like the sound of a happy hive. Nell and Tilda, in their all-enveloping white frilled aprons, bustled busily about.

There had been a round of applause when I'd opened the door to welcome everyone to the opening of The Fat Rascal, and the reporter had insisted on taking my photograph, flanked by Nell and Tilda, before I beat a hasty retreat to the back premises.

Luckily he now appeared too busy stuffing his face with sandwiches and cake to think about taking any more. George Godet was sitting opposite him and, with his beaky nose and grey-streaked black hair sticking up in an angry crest, looked like a slightly demonic cockatoo. He'd shaved and spruced himself up for the occasion, though, in a tweed jacket with leather patches on the elbows and a finely checked shirt.

'It's going well, isn't it?' I whispered to Tilda as she paused briefly next to me, holding a fully loaded tea-tray. 'I think I'd better do a little circuit round the tables and talk to some of the customers.'

'It's like Blackpool on a bank holiday in here!' Tilda said, which from her expression I took to be a good thing, then with a nod at George's table added, 'Them two seem to be having some kind of eating competition. Eh, you'd think it was an all-you-can-eat buffet!'

'I suppose it is, in a way,' I said. 'An all-you-can-eat tea.'

'Tables three, six and nine are the competition,' she hissed, though they were well out of earshot. 'Come to see how much threat you are to their business.'

'The competition? You mean from other local cafés?'

'That's right, and the expressions on their faces could curdle milk,' she said with satisfaction, then headed off back into the fray, while I worked my way round the room, having a brief word with everyone.

Most were friends: the Giddingses, of course, were seated in the bow window, though Nile had been in and out of the kitchen helping me, and Bel was with Thom at one of the smaller tables down the side of the room. Ross had brought his mum and they were sharing a round table with Jack and his wife, Viviane.

When I got to Henry and Eleri, she said the Bump had made her ravenous and she was eating for six.

'Why not?' I encouraged her, thinking how glowingly pretty pregnancy had made her. 'I'm glad you're enjoying your tea. Just ask Nell or Tilda if you'd like some more of anything.'

'Those scones weren't *too* bad, but—' began Henry critically, and then I think Eleri must have kicked him under the table because he suddenly shut up and glowered at her. She didn't look noticeably impressed by this, so I expect it's simply his default expression.

'It's all delicious,' she assured me.

'That's right, flower, and you need to keep your strength up, when you're expecting,' chimed in Tilda, neatly decanting lemon and orange curd tartlets on to the depleted top tier of the cake stand. 'Don't let yon great streak of nowt snaffle all the tarts, this time.'

Henry seemed pleased with this rudeness and grinned at her. 'Couldn't I entice you into coming to work for me, instead? Seeing such a vision of loveliness and hearing your dulcet voice every day would be worth paying good money for.'

'Give over, you daft bugger,' she said amiably, and I left them to their verbal sparring and moved on to greet Emily Rhymer and her husband. I was sure she'd said he was a vicar, but if so, he wasn't in the traditional style, since he had long grey hair tied back in a ponytail and wore gold crosses in his ears. They'd both arrived in black motorbike leathers, though after a while they'd hung their jackets over the backs of their chairs, probably because it had got hot in the teashop.

I promised to give Em my fat rascal recipe and was about to stop by George's table when I heard Nell tell him roundly, 'If you ask me for any more of them cheese scones, greedy guts, *you'll* be the fat rascal and we'll be able to hire you for a mascot!'

'If I'd wanted to be insulted by a skinny old bat, I could have stayed at home,' he rejoined dourly.

'Think thisen lucky any decent body talks to thee, tha miserable little snirp,' she told him. Going by his dropped jaw and mottling red face, I think he must have missed the advertising about the rudest waitresses in Yorkshire, so I beat a strategic retreat to the kitchen.

I have to admit that I'd wondered if perhaps my natural mother might have booked a table today, so that she could see me without making herself known, but none of the women present struck me as an obvious candidate.

But then, maybe we humans don't possess an innate ability to tell our parents from the rest of the herd?

I had to bake more cheese scones for the second sitting, mainly due to George taking such a liking to them, and while I was mixing the dough Sheila came in with Nile to say goodbye.

'Congratulations, darling. It's a huge success!' she said, kissing me.

'Yes, and I apologize for ever doubting it would be,' Nile agreed.

'It *will* be a success if business carries on being so brisk – but will it last?' I said anxiously. 'How many of them only came today out of curiosity?'

'Some of them *may* have come out of curiosity, but they'll return for the food,' Sheila assured me.

After she'd gone, Nile stayed for a while longer, plying me with coffee and stacking the dishwasher whenever Nell or Tilda cleared a table. Then he had a call and had to go over to his shop.

'One of my clients is coming to collect a Clarice Cliff milk jug – an unusual design and the last piece she needs to complete a whole tea service,' he said. 'I won't be long.'

He wasn't, either, for he returned just as the scones were cooling on the rack.

'What perfect timing,' he said, taking one and looking for butter. 'You bake like an angel.'

'Do angels bake?' I asked.

'Pre-Raphaelite angels do.'

'Put that scone down, tha' great lummock, and fill some of them little pots with jam,' ordered Nell, who had reversed through the swinging door carrying a full tray of dirty dishes with the ease of long practice. She looked amazingly perky, considering she was no spring chicken and had been trotting to and fro ever since we opened.

'All right,' he agreed. 'Cream, too?'

'Yes, a dozen of both, before the next lot come in – I'm putting the reserved signs back on t' tables as fast as this lot go, though some of them are hanging about so long you'd think their bottoms had been glued to t' chairs.'

She went out again.

'Was it my imagination, or was Nell jingling?' I asked.

'Her pockets are weighed down with tips. I noticed the same with Tilda,' he said. 'The ruder they are, the more money people seem to give them. That was a promotional brainwave!'

The second sitting mainly consisted of strangers, though I did recognize one or two, like the receptionist from my doctor's surgery, who was one of Geeta's friends, and Geeta and Teddy's nanny, Jan, but it seemed to go with as much of a swing as the first sitting.

When the bell had finally jangled behind the very last departing happy customers, clutching card carriers filled with leftover cake and little pots of Lola's preserves, the tearoom suddenly looked strangely empty.

Tilda was in the little office, cashing up, while I was stashing left-over cheese straws into a tin.

'Only one person wanted a totally savoury afternoon tea, so I overestimated the number of savouries I'd need,' I said to Nile.

'I'll eat anything that won't keep,' he offered helpfully.

'I seem to remember promising you a takeaway of savouries for ever, in return for Lola's paperweight,' I reminded him. 'And you've been so brilliant today, helping out whenever we needed it, that you deserve it!'

'Just feed me the leftovers and I'll be happy,' he said.

'Here's our Daisy, come to help clear the last tables and then give Tilda a hand with the cleaning up,' Nell said, sticking her head through the hatch, like a puppet in a Punch and Judy show.

At last the teashop was clean, tidy and quiet, except for the chugging of the dishwasher, and Nile and I were alone.

I felt tired but also still somewhat wired from the adrenalin rush, so when he suggested we go over to his place so he could cook me his supper speciality, I agreed.

His signature dish turned out to be Welsh Rarebit, and delicious it was, too. But right after that I suddenly went so spaced-out with sleepiness that even a cup of his very good coffee couldn't keep my eyes from closing, so he walked me back over to my door, kissed me quickly and then pushed me through it. Maybe he thought if he kissed me fast enough, I wouldn't notice. It's a theory, anyway . . .

I noted on the way through the teashop that there were twelve messages on the answer phone, but the only one I answered that night was a brief text on my mobile from Edie.

Count your cutlery, it said.

But of course Tilda, who was even less trusting than Edie, already had.

*I assumed that when Alice Rose heard nothing from her appeal, she
would think her birth mother dead, or moved away from the district —
or even that she had seen the article in the paper but did not wish to
reveal herself. Perhaps then she would finally cease to rake the whole
thing up.*

*I half-hoped her teashop venture would be a flop, which might have
been an extra incentive to move her unwelcome presence elsewhere, but
it seemed quite likely the opposite would happen: everyone, it seemed,
was talking about it.*

*The great draw (apart from the quality of the teas, which apparently
is high) is that the waitresses are plain-speaking Yorkshirewomen. I can't
see what there is amusing in that, but there is, as they say around here,
no accounting for folk.*

44

Tried and Tested

I was up again at dawn, baking dozens more miniature fat rascals and a large marmalade cake, which I meant to finish off with a tangy orange icing later, when it had cooled. I suspected I'd soon be able to make fat rascals in my sleep . . .

The laundry collected yesterday's table linen and then the artisan bread maker dropped off my order, which had to be checked and put away . . . and suddenly the morning had slipped away and it was time for Tilda to come in and start cutting the finger sandwiches.

Then we were off again with a repeat performance of the previous day, though with a whole new set of customers and no Nile to help, since he was out all day and wasn't due back until late. I missed him . . .

That evening, when I'd closed the teashop door after Tilda and Daisy, and switched off the lights, I went up to the flat and rang Lola to tell her how popular her preserves had been.

'You'll have to bring a lot more. I made small open tarts with the lemon and orange curds and people were buying jars of it to take home.'

Then I told her all the amusing bits about the opening day, like George eating so many cheese scones he should be in *The Guinness Book of Records* and what Nell had said to him.

She couldn't chat for long, because she was going to a firework display with the girls – what with everything going on, I'd entirely forgotten it was Bonfire Night! – but I made an omelette and then went to bed, since I was so tired I was seeing Catherine wheels anyway.

*

It's surprising how quickly you slip into a new routine, though of course Nell and Tilda were already an experienced double act and I expect they could have managed without me. But then, the teas wouldn't have been so good. I mean, call me immodest, but nobody's scones and fairy cakes float off the plate quite like mine do, even though I suspect Henry Godet might beg to differ with me on that one.

Thursday's edition of the local paper carried a further article about the teashop, with the Rudest Waitresses in Yorkshire coming in for special mention, along with photographs featuring Nell, with her headband pulled low down over her forehead as she glowered at a rather startled-looking customer.

Tilda said she was going to order copies of all the photos of her and Nell, and I asked her to order me a complete set while she was at it – they would be a nice memento of the day, framed and hanging on the walls.

Nile had taken some photographs for my website the day we opened, too, which he helped me to put up.

And on the Friday came the first internet reviews on the Travel-Oracle site, with the benison of a scattering of stars, and I heaved a huge sigh of relief and began to truly believe it was going to work!

Food and insults for tea! The prices may be steep, but the new Fat Rascal teashop delivered on the quality of both the food and the backchat from the waitresses – and you could have as much of both as you wanted . . .

Bel rang on Saturday morning with a message from Teddy to say my DNA results had arrived.

'Or the link has – you follow it to the page with your results,' she explained.

'I've been so preoccupied I'd forgotten all about it,' I exclaimed. 'Still, it's long odds I'll find even a distant relative, and the rest of the results probably won't mean anything to me. I think I'll need Teddy to interpret them.'

'Shall I ask him to do that, then?' asked Bel.

'Yes, if he has time, because then he could explain the findings when I come over tonight, couldn't he?'

'OK, I'll do that. *I* think it's quite exciting, even if you don't!'

'To be honest, I'm looking forward much more to spending a restful night at Oldstone,' I said frankly, because I'd be heading over there the moment we closed up the teashop that afternoon.

Still, I was sure that soon Tilda would be able to manage the day-to-day running of the teashop herself, as she had before, and I'd have time to write again, which was just as well, because Beauty and the rest of them had started clamouring to tell me what was happening to them now so I really was going to have to write that sequel.

'Them birds have got very long beaks . . . and arms as well as wings,' Shazza said, frowning at the creatures flitting about in the trees. She was short-sighted, but she'd rather die than wear glasses.

'Long noses, beloved,' corrected Prince S'Hallow. 'Do you not have fairies in the Here-and-now?'

Most of the family were already gathered in the big, warm farmhouse kitchen when I arrived, though Teddy was apparently still in the library, going through my DNA results.

'He's been ages, so perhaps it's something exciting, like you're the last of the Romanovs,' Geeta said.

'More likely a direct descendant of Lizzie Siddal,' suggested Nile with a glint in his eye, and I gave him a look.

'I'm just going to go and tidy up and dump my bag,' I said. 'I'll be right down.'

I was only about ten minutes, mostly spent untangling my hair, which the wind had blown into a demented cloud in the few short steps from the car to the house, but when I went back downstairs and opened the kitchen door on a babble of conversation, there was a sudden silence and everyone turned and stared at me, as if they'd never seen me before in their lives.

'What is it?' I stammered, totally disconcerted. 'What's happened? Is there something wrong?'

'No, not wrong. Come and sit down, darling,' Sheila said. 'Teddy's got something to say to you – some exciting news.'

'Yes . . .' Teddy said, running a distracted hand through his fair hair and opening his blue eyes wide. 'It's the DNA result, Alice. I'm still finding it hard to believe, but I've checked carefully and—'

'We've got the same father!' Bel broke in impatiently. 'Alice, isn't that *amazing*?'

She sprang up and gave me an impulsive hug, but when she let me go the room spun so dizzyingly that I sank down on to the empty chair next to Nile. He took my hand and held it in a warm, strong clasp.

'You mean . . . Paul Giddings was my father?' I asked blankly.

'It's true, Alice,' Nile assured me.

'But how can that possibly *be*? And how do you *know*?' I appealed to Teddy.

'Oh, I realized as soon as I started to look through your results,' he said. 'Dad was right at the top of the list of your closest relatives, linked to his entry in the database with our family tree, and of course I know the user name for that.'

'You're Bel and Teddy's half-sister, darling,' Sheila said, looking surprisingly joyful about it. 'There, I just knew you were part of the family the moment I met you!'

'Another sister for me and Nile,' Geeta said.

'Leave me out of it: I don't feel remotely brotherly towards Alice,' Nile said. 'In fact, for the first time, I'm glad I've no blood relationship with the Giddingses at all!'

'It rubs off, though: you're a Giddings in all other ways,' Teddy told him.

I barely took in what they were saying, for I was still struggling to take in the whole overwhelming revelation. 'But it's bizarre!' I said at last. 'I mean, how *can* it be true? There must be a mistake!'

'No, there isn't,' Bel assured me. 'Teddy's the expert and he says so.'

Then Nile asked the million-dollar question. 'What we haven't discussed yet is: if Paul is Alice's father, then can we trace who her mother was?'

'Not through the DNA test results, because all the rest of the relations listed are ones I recognize, so not her mother's side,' Teddy said.

'You know, in all the excitement, I hadn't thought of that!' Sheila said. 'Let's count back to how old Paul would have been at the time you were conceived. You're thirty-six, aren't you, Alice?'

I nodded mutely, my hand still comfortingly held by Nile. One freshly discovered parent seemed enough to get used to at the moment. 'And my birthday is the second of March, though they thought I was slightly premature.'

'So . . . we're looking at early in the summer before Paul started his first year of university – is that right, Teddy?'

Teddy, who had been scribbling numbers on a bit of paper, nodded. 'I think so. He told me he used to spend the long holidays visiting Old-stone, until he dropped out after the first year of his degree course and went to Germany.'

'We met in Germany,' Sheila said reminiscently. 'Love at first sight . . .'

'So he must have had a girlfriend up here the year before he met you,' Geeta said rather tactlessly, though it didn't seem to throw Sheila.

'Well, when we visited Oldstone soon after we got engaged, we *did* run into someone he'd once dated,' Sheila said. 'I'm sure I've told you that.'

'You can't mean Dr Collins?' Bel exclaimed incredulously. 'I don't think she was born with human emotions. In fact, she's probably an android.'

'But she would only have been a teenager at the time and was prob-ably an extremely *pretty* android,' pointed out Sheila. 'She still would be attractive, if her expression and manner weren't so off-putting.'

'It can't be Dr Collins,' I said with certainty. 'I've met her and . . . there was *nothing*, no spark of recognition or anything. It must be some-one else!'

'I don't know, darling. It seems improbable that he would have had another mystery local girlfriend at the same time,' she said. 'The other thing is that when Paul and I ran into her at the Upvale garage, she cut him dead, and that was when he told me they'd had a brief teenage fling, but they'd broken up and it was his fault.'

She looked up, her expression troubled all at once. 'Oh dear! I think now he must have dumped her and gone off to university, mustn't he?'

'It sounds like it, but Paul can't have had any idea she was pregnant, if so – I mean, if she really was Alice's mother,' Nile said.

'That's true!' Sheila looked relieved. 'He wasn't the sort of man to walk away from someone in trouble.'

'Why wouldn't she tell him?' I found myself asking.

'I don't know. Perhaps she didn't realize she was pregnant until long after he'd gone and she couldn't get in touch with him, except through his grandparents. She wouldn't want to do that.'

'She might have been afraid to tell her parents, too. Or even didn't know she was having a baby until it arrived. That's more common than you'd think,' Bel suggested.

'I'm already having trouble accepting who my father is, even though Teddy seems sure about it, but there isn't any proof that Dr Collins is my mother. It's all speculation . . .' I said, feeling dazed.

'I know, it's been a shock, albeit a good one. Let's not worry about it at the moment, but celebrate your being part of the Giddings family, Alice,' Sheila said, as if finding your late husband had fathered a child with a previous partner was something joyous and welcome.

'Nile, there's a bottle of champagne in the fridge – go and open it at once!' she commanded. 'And, Geeta, find the best glasses – this calls for a toast!'

I went into the village shop to buy stamps and when I emerged, I saw Emily Rhymer on the other side of the road, with one of those over-large rough-haired dogs she favours. She stopped and gave me a very strange stare, then nodded as if she'd just confirmed something she'd only previously suspected, before walking off.

Of course the Rhymers, a local clan, were all a little odd, but Emily more so than the rest. Still, I felt somewhat unsettled by this, since she was the woman I'd passed in the lane leading to the Oldstone that night so many years ago . . .

But then, even if she had her suspicions, without proof she could hardly come out and accuse me after such a length of time, and I suspect that gossiping is a pastime just as alien and incomprehensible to her as it is to me.

45

Mixed Messages

'I'm still overwhelmed that suddenly I've got a family of my own – and Sheila was so very generous about it,' I said to Nile next morning.

I'd been so overcome by emotion and champagne that I'd hardly slept and we were the first down to breakfast other than Sheila; there were signs that she'd already eaten and gone to her studio.

'She's honestly delighted. It wouldn't be in her nature not to be,' he assured me. 'The only thing that upset her was that Paul didn't know about your mother being pregnant, so she had to cope alone. Or *not* cope, considering what happened.'

'That doesn't sound like Dr Collins, does it? I mean, the whole scenario doesn't seem to chime with anything I know about her character.'

'But she was a teenager at the time, not the woman you've met now,' he pointed out. 'We all do silly things when we're young.'

'I still find it hard to accept that she's my mother – but then, I have to agree with Sheila that she's really the only candidate. I don't see how I can find out, though, without asking her straight out, and she's scary.'

'If it is her, she's obviously not going to come forward and contact you, or she'd have done it by now,' he said, putting a freshly brewed cup of coffee down in front of me and pushing the toast and butter nearer.

I was thinking. 'I wonder . . . remember I told you that Emily Rhymer originally suspected a girl from Upvale of being the driver of the Mini that passed her in the early hours of the morning, after I was abandoned?'

'Yes, but didn't she see her later the same day, going about things perfectly normally?'

'She did . . . but if the girl was Dr Collins, then she was probably as cold and self-contained then as she is now, and wouldn't show any emotion, would she?'

'I suppose it's possible,' he conceded.

'So if I ring Emily up and tell her who I suspect is my mother, maybe she'll confirm or deny that that's the person *she* was thinking of?'

'Perhaps she will – but isn't the entire Giddings clan enough family for you?' he asked, raising one eyebrow.

'Oh, more than enough!' I exclaimed. 'But still, I just want to know the whole of it, having got this far.'

And when I got Em on the phone later and told her what we'd found out, then asked her point-blank if Dr Collins was the girl she'd suspected of being my mother, she confirmed it.

'I thought it was her straight away, because she was seventeen and her father had just bought her a new Mini after she passed her driving test. And there was something else that made me think: when the police had finally finished with us and we were going home, I noticed the iron gates in front of the Collinses' house were closed, but they'd been open when I'd walked past them earlier.'

'But then you saw her later that day and thought it couldn't have been her after all?' I prompted.

'That's right. She was getting petrol and she looked pale and serious – but then, she always did. There was nothing to show . . . So anyway, I thought I must have been mistaken.'

She paused and then said slowly, 'Gloria remembered where she'd seen light green eyes like yours – Liz Collins' mother had them. Liz didn't inherit them, hers are blue, but they're obviously in the family.'

'Really? That sounds a bit of a clincher,' I said. 'I don't know where the red hair came from, but I got my height from the Giddings side . . . and frankly, I'm finding all of this a bit much to take in!'

'I'm not surprised, but I'm glad the Giddingses welcomed you into the family. We Rhymers are an oddly linked bunch ourselves,' she said, but didn't explain in what way.

'Yes, but we'll have to keep the relationship as a family secret, because Sheila pointed out that if we went public with it, other people who were around at the time I was conceived might put two and two together and guess who my mother was, too.'

'*My* lips are sealed,' she said. 'Are you going to ask Liz Collins outright if she's your mother?'

I shuddered. 'I can't imagine doing that – and she'd probably deny it, or threaten me with legal action for defamation of character, or something. No,' I finished. 'I don't really see how I can, without actual proof, and there isn't any.'

'There's an awful lot of circumstantial evidence, though,' Em said. '*I'd* ask her.'

'I'll think about it,' I said.

I gave the family the gist of all this over Sunday lunch. Nile, of course, thought I ought to let the matter lie now, but the rest of the family were in two minds.

'If she's your mother, I'd like to tell her that I'm so sorry Paul didn't know she was pregnant, because I'm positive that if he had, he wouldn't have just abandoned her and walked away,' said Sheila, soft-hearted as ever.

'I don't think she's been brooding about it for the last thirty-six years: in fact, I'd say she put it right out of her head and got on with her life,' Bel said. 'She has to know about you being back and opening the tea-shop, Alice, so she's *chosen* not to contact you.'

'It would be good to tie up the last loose ends, even if she doesn't want to acknowledge you in public,' suggested Teddy. 'I'm going to add you to the family tree this afternoon, but I'll have to leave your maternal side out of things until we do know for certain. There's a chance some of your maternal relatives might sign up to the DNA database later too, so we can trace her that way.'

'I think I need time to get used to being part of the Giddings family before I ask her,' I said.

'I'd like to tell *everyone* that you're really Alice Giddings!' said Sheila.

'Yes, me too,' Nile agreed, and then favoured me with one of his more enigmatic and unnerving smiles.

After lunch, Nile went over to World's End Antiques, where his friend Rick had a couple of items for him to look at, while I stayed at Oldstone and went through the family photograph albums with Sheila.

It was amazing to think that this was now *my* family too – something I'd never had!

Now we knew about the relationship, my resemblance to some of the ancestors was very obvious and made me feel very strange, but also connected in a way I'd never been before.

Later, as I drove home over the moors to Haworth, despite what I'd said earlier to Teddy, the feeling slowly grew inside me that I *couldn't* just leave it at that. It didn't matter if my mother publicly acknowledged me or not: I just wanted to *know*.

So the moment I got back to the flat I sat down at my desk to write a letter.

It took several attempts and over an hour before I was satisfied that I'd got the tone right.

Dear Dr Collins,

Having discovered through DNA testing that my father was Paul Giddings of Oldstone Farm, strong circumstantial evidence points to your being my natural mother. Since you didn't come forward to contact me after the newspaper article, I assume you don't wish to acknowledge me, but truly I don't want anything from you, except just the certainty of having this confirmed. Then the matter will be closed and the information will go no further.

I hoped that sounded unthreatening and reasonable.

Then I added my contact details, sealed the letter in an envelope marked 'Strictly Personal' and enclosed it inside another addressed to her at the surgery.

It was dark when I let myself out of the teashop door, the letter in my hand . . . at exactly the wrong moment, because Nile was just emerging from the passage, heading for Small and Perfect.

'Hello,' he said, surprised. 'Where are you off to?'

I might have asked what business it was of his, but instead I replied feebly, 'I'm going for a walk.'

'Isn't it a bit . . . dark? And cold? It's trying to sleet.' Then he came up closer and eyed me suspiciously in the light from the lamp over the door. 'What are you up to?'

'Nothing, I just wanted some fresh air,' I said. 'And I've got something to post, so I thought I'd do it now.'

'Give me a minute to drop my bag off in the shop and I'll come with you.'

'Oh, don't bother, I won't be long and—'

But he wasn't listening and having pushed his bag through the door of Small and Perfect and locked up again, led the way out of Doorknocker's Row.

'So . . . you're going to post a letter, but it doesn't seem to have a stamp on it,' he observed, as we walked down the street. 'By which I deduce that you're going to stick it through a letter box – just call me Sherlock. And let me take another inspired guess: it's for Dr Collins?'

'All right, it is,' I admitted. 'But I've only asked her to say yes or no to whether she's my mother, nothing else.'

'You realize if it isn't true and you persist in trying to contact her, she could very well report you to the police for stalking, or something?'

'This will be my only attempt because the evidence all points to her, doesn't it? What Em Rhymer said clinches it.'

'Yes, so why not let it lie there?' he asked, then tried to persuade me out of posting my note, though that had the unfortunate effect of making me turn stubborn.

Mind you, the moment I'd popped it through the letter box of the surgery, I wished I could snatch it back again, but it was too late.

We set off back by a roundabout route that brought us to the top of the village and the quiet churchyard. I was so preoccupied with my thoughts that at some point, without my noticing, Nile had put his arm around me.

'Infuriating woman,' he said, stopping suddenly and looking down at me. 'You know there's a good chance she won't respond to that letter at all?'

'It's still worth a go, but even if she won't talk to me, at least I now know I'm a Giddings.'

'Yes, and it's just as well I'm only one by name, because I've never felt less brotherly in my life,' he said with some force.

'Yes, so you said before,' I told him and he made an exasperated noise before pulling me close and kissing me senseless.

My response was instinctive and his grip tightened crushingly.

Time stood still and probably several planets collided and stars moved out of their orbits.

Finally, he was the one to break contact and stared down at me sombrely. 'Edie told me to give you time . . . and Lola warned me that unless I was serious about you, I should leave you alone.'

'That was good advice,' I murmured, still half-dazed. My arms seemed to be around his neck, even though I had no recollection of putting them there, and my knees had totally dissolved. It was just as well he was still holding me.

'Which bit?' he asked.

'The "leaving me alone unless you're serious" part.'

'But I am – I think I love you!'

'*Think* isn't good enough,' I snapped, coming back to life and belatedly trying to push him away.

'All right: if you really want me to wear my heart on my sleeve, I admit I fell in love with you the first time I set eyes on you, standing on a chair in the café and wearing that hideous mobcap. It just took me time to realize it, because I'd never felt that way before.'

I stared up at what I could see of him. He sounded serious.

'I think we could really make a go of it, Alice,' he added softly. 'Let's give it a try?'

He didn't define what he wanted us to try . . . but it sounded like I'd be on a kind of trial, to be returned in my original packaging if unsuitable for his purpose.

'I don't think so,' I said. 'You have a name for backing off at the moment your girlfriends expect a bit of commitment, remember? And anyway, do I really want a man I can't leave alone for five minutes, without coming back to find him draped in strange women?'

And twisting suddenly out of his grip, I set off for home at such a pace that we were almost back before he caught up with me.

'Alice . . . ?' he said and his voice sounded as if he was laughing. I went straight in and closed the door with a slam.

Then I leaned against it and cried and cried, though I'm not sure why. So much had happened in so short a time, so many life-changing things: I expect it was all just too much for me.

Surprisingly once I got to bed I slept well and then, since next morning was a Monday when we were closed, Tilda appeared and threw herself into a deep cleaning session as if it was a high treat. Not that she and Daisy hadn't left it clean as a new pin on Saturday evening, but she wasn't satisfied and scoured the place, then began giving the fridge, oven and microwave an extra good going-over.

I could have done with having her scour Nile out of my heart, too, because he seemed to have established himself there without my wanting him to in the least. While I was running through the checklist of tasks I'd need to do so we were ready to open the teashop next day, my mind kept going back to what he'd said last night.

Thinking he loved me just wasn't good enough . . . and suggesting we give our relationship a go was hardly the romantic proposal of a girl's dreams. But if he'd asked *me* whether I loved him, what would I have said? Would my subconscious have popped up like a jack-in-the-box and yelled, 'Yes, yes! I'll settle for whatever you give me – take me, I'm yours'?

It took my mind off worrying about how Dr Collins was going to react – or *if* she would react. She'd probably read the letter by now, and if we'd got it all totally wrong and she *wasn't* my mother, maybe she was even at this moment ringing her solicitor to sue me for defamation of character, or something like that.

I checked for messages and emails about every ten minutes, not *really* expecting anything – but then suddenly, late in the afternoon, up popped a text.

At the Oldstone, dawn tomorrow. Don't tell anyone and come alone – I will not talk to you before witnesses.

I am horrified that Alice has somehow discovered her true father and my long-ago connection with him. I must move quickly to scotch this story before rumours spread like a new creature springing from that original monstrous birth. Alice must be made to understand my position and tell anyone she has confided in that she was mistaken.

Father, despite all my efforts, is fast deteriorating, both mentally and physically. I think once he acknowledged to himself that he was losing his faculties, he metaphorically turned his face to the wall.

Though continuing to ensure he has the best care money can buy, I now long for the day I inherit and can leave this place and the memory of what happened for ever. I will leave Hugo here for ever too – after my father, the person he is most attached to is the housekeeper, Kim, so I will make her a leaving present of him.

I have informed the letting agency that they must now take my villa in Portugal off their books, for I wish to have it entirely refurbished with a view to moving there permanently at some not-too-distant date.

46

On the Rocks

The message was terse, but it at least confirmed we'd been right, for she wouldn't have suggested a meeting if she wasn't my natural mother. And tomorrow she would reveal how she came to abandon me at that godforsaken spot.

I shivered. I was sure this would be a one-off meeting, because I'd reluctantly forced her hand by my persistence, and I was certain she wasn't going to fall on my neck like a character in a Victorian novel, crying, 'At last, dear child, I can hold you in my arms!'

I set the alarm for a ridiculous hour of the morning and intended going to bed early, though I wasn't sure just how much sleep I would get that night.

But what I didn't bargain for was Nile texting me to say we needed to talk and he'd collect me on the way to the pub in ten minutes. It never seemed to enter his head that I might be doing something else.

I replied that there was nothing left to say and reminded him I had to be up early to bake fresh scones and cakes, but he just said we needn't stay long, and stopped answering my messages.

It was easier to go than argue the toss on the doorstep, but I might have known he'd guess I had something on my mind other than the events of last night, not to mention the sudden revelation that I had a family of my own . . .

I avoided the dangerous ground of the first and focused on the latter. 'Sheila's taken to ringing and asking me how her new daughter is today!' I told him brightly. 'She's so kind – I mean, lots of women wouldn't be very happy to discover their husband had an illegitimate child.'

'You've already said that twice tonight, by which I deduce you've got something else on your mind,' he said shrewdly. 'Let me take a stab in the dark: has Dr Collins got in touch with you?'

He knew me too well . . .

I didn't reply, but my face must have given me away, because he said, 'I see she has – so you'd better tell me about it!'

'Oh, all right, but it's a secret because she warned me not to tell any-one else.'

I got out my phone and showed him the message.

'Why *there* and at such a godforsaken time of the morning?' he demanded.

'I suppose because it's where it all began for me – and at dawn it will be totally deserted. I'm sure this will be the only time she ever talks to me about it and she doesn't want anyone to witness the meeting.'

'I don't like the idea of you going alone. I'd better come with you.'

'You can't! She won't talk to me if you do, she says so.'

'Then I'll drive you there, but stay in the car,' he suggested.

'There's only the one place to park nearby and she might spot you – and then it would scupper what's probably my only opportunity to find out her side of the story.'

'We could go early and I'd duck down when she arrives, so she won't know I'm there,' he persisted stubbornly.

'No, I want to go alone, and anyway, I don't know what you're wor-ried about. She's hardly going to push me over the edge in case anyone finds out her guilty secret, is she? I mean, we're not in the Victorian era now; she isn't going to be ostracized by everyone for being a scarlet woman.'

'People might not be that understanding about the way she aban-doned you, though. And I suspect her privacy and professional status are important to her.'

'You've been reading too many old murder mysteries: don't think I haven't noticed that the bookshelves in your flat are filled with them.'

'So is my Kindle,' he admitted. 'My guilty secret is out.'

'At least that one is fairly harmless. Have you got any worse ones you want to confess?'

'No, that's as bad as it gets – and you're trying to change the subject again. I still don't think you should meet her entirely alone, because she won't be pleasant to deal with. I don't suppose she wants her stepfather to hear of it even now, either – Bel's been talking to the surgery receptionist again and she says he's very frail.'

'I hadn't thought of that aspect. She must have hidden the pregnancy from her parents, so it would be a shock to him. Not that I intend spreading the information about, and I'm sure Emily Rhymer won't,' I added. 'That just leaves the family and we know they won't talk, either.'

'But Liz Collins doesn't know that.'

'I'll make it clear to her that her secret's safe.'

He still didn't like my going alone, but he finally capitulated, though with conditions.

'I'm going home for the night, so you can ring me as soon as you've had the meeting tomorrow morning and I'll practically be on the spot,' he said. 'I can be there in minutes, if you need me.'

'That's the first I've heard of you going out to Oldstone tonight, and it's going to be a bit late when you get there, isn't it?' I said suspiciously.

'It's never too late to play trains with Teddy,' he said innocently. 'It's my turn to be the Fat Controller.'

I tossed and turned all night and then got up in the dark, shivering with cold and nerves, and set off over the moors for the rendezvous.

I only hoped Nile hadn't gone home to Oldstone last night because he intended setting out even earlier and lurking around the meeting place, but I relaxed when I arrived and there was no sign of him.

Dawn had only just started to seep upwards on the horizon when I parked on the short, sheep-nibbled turf near the weathered picnic tables, but Dr Collins' familiar hatchback was already there. It was empty and there was no sign of her, so she must have walked up the hill in the dark.

I zipped up my coat and set off after her and I don't think I've ever felt more alone.

I found her by the upright stone, standing a little back from the edge and looking out at the rapidly greying moors. She turned when a pebble rattled under my feet.

'You've come,' she stated in a flat voice and there was no softening of her usual cold and severe expression. 'So, what's all this circumstantial evidence?' she demanded, straight to the point. 'And who have you told your story to?'

'I haven't told it to anyone,' I said. 'Sheila Giddings knew you'd gone out with Paul and we worked out the dates – it all seemed to fit. Besides, you were seen as you drove home after leaving me here.'

I shivered again – not from the icy blast of the November breeze, but from an internal chill sparked by that remote, passionless voice.

'I knew that Rhymer woman was suspicious, but I didn't think she'd broadcast it about.'

'She didn't – she won't,' I assured her. 'But I'd already talked to her and knew she was holding something back – so when I asked her directly if she suspected you, she said she did. And it's true, isn't it? I only want to know,' I pleaded.

'My affair with Paul Giddings – if you could call it that – was nothing but a brief folly. I learned my lesson,' she said harshly. 'So, the Giddings woman knows about it and Emily Rhymer; who else?'

'Look, apart from Emily Rhymer, who won't tell anyone, we're keeping it all in the family. I've no interest in exposing you – that's not what this is about. I'd just like to understand how and why you came to leave me here and then that's it.'

'I was sure Emily Rhymer had recognized my car, but I put some doubts in her mind later,' she said, then turned to look over the moors again. 'It was a colder night than this when I brought you out here. It was early March and there was a stiff frost on the grass.'

'I don't know how you managed it. Weren't you only about seventeen or eighteen?'

'Seventeen. I'd just passed my driving test and Father had bought me a car. I knew these roads well and it was a bright night,' she explained, as though it was all very logical and *I* was very stupid.

'But . . . I meant that you couldn't have been in a fit state for driving?'

'I'd had a great shock, but my faculties were working perfectly well, though I fear my overwhelming feelings of horror and revulsion at your arrival prevented me from checking that you really *were* dead, instead of presuming it.'

'*Horror and revulsion?*' I repeated, feeling sick.

'I believe those to have been my predominant emotions,' she told me precisely. 'And an urgent desire to expunge the evidence of what had happened, so that Father never found out. Being only my stepfather, I felt sure he would have immediately disowned me.'

'But did your mother know—' I began.

'My mother was a weak, hysterical, stupid woman, only concerned with concealing what had happened,' she said, and I thought I caught the slightest trace of a dark bitterness there, the first hint of emotion she'd shown. 'Once she'd died, I thought no one else would ever find out the truth.'

Somewhere below the Oldstone, there was a sudden rattle of pebbles.

'Who's there?' she asked sharply. 'Did you bring someone with you, after all?'

'No,' I assured her, going right to the edge of the lip of rock and leaning over to peer down, one hand on the Oldstone to steady myself. 'It's just a sheep, and I don't think it's likely to gossip.'

She came up behind me and her hand suddenly closed on my shoulder in a strong, bony grip. For a moment I was frozen to the spot, with the mad idea that she might be about to give me a push and so get rid of the evidence once and for all . . .

Then she said prosaically, 'Come away from the edge. I have an irrational fear of heights and you are too close.'

By the time I'd turned she was already putting some distance between us and wiping her hand on her coat, as if contact with another human being, even one so closely related to her, was contaminating.

'It's very odd to have found my mother, yet for there to be no emotional connection between us at all,' I said.

'Oh – emotional connection!' she snapped, as if they were dirty words, then added harshly, 'I was such a little fool back then. I thought Paul and I were so in love . . . until one day I went home earlier than I was expected and found him in bed with my mother.'

'Y-your mother? Oh, how horrible for you – I'm so sorry!' I stammered, stunned. 'I can see that—'

'You see *nothing*!' she said savagely. 'Afterwards he wrote a letter saying it had all been a bit Mrs Robinson, but he shouldn't have let my mother seduce him and he was ashamed of what he'd done. I burned it . . . and after that, I only spoke to my mother when it was absolutely necessary – till the night she gave birth to you.'

My knees gave and I sat down suddenly on one of the fallen stones. 'Your *mother* gave birth to me? You mean . . . I'm your *half-sister*?'

'I suppose so,' she said indifferently. 'But you can imagine my feelings when I heard a noise in the middle of the night and walked into her room – and there you were on the bed, a horrible sight. I knew immediately you had to be Paul's, because my stepfather couldn't have children.'

My mind, at first struggling to accept all this, began to work again: it made sense. 'Hence the shock and revulsion,' I said slowly.

'My mother had originally trained as a nurse, so she should have realized she was pregnant and done something about it,' she said callously. 'So there you were, puny and a mess. I didn't look too closely and only found out later you had a harelip. You gave one cry and that was it, so we assumed you were dead.'

'And decided to get rid of me?'

'Of course. My mother was terrified that Father would find out and so was I. It was sheer luck he happened to be away on a three-month trip. She threatened to tell him it was mine, if I didn't get rid of it – you – but I could see it had to be done in any case. And then the Oldstone just popped into my head.'

'Because it was so remote, so there was little chance of anyone finding me?'

'Of course: there you were, dead, as we both thought, so we needed to get rid of the evidence,' she said logically. 'I didn't think there'd be anything to find by spring when the hikers were about again. The bed-side rug was messed anyway, so I rolled you in that and drove out here with you.'

'Then pushed me into the nearest hole and left me?'

Like a bit of rubbish after a picnic, I thought.

She frowned. 'I must have left a piece of the rug sticking out.'

'Yes, that's what the farmer who discovered me said,' I agreed.

'Well, that's that,' she said more briskly, as if she'd just broken some bad news to one of her patients. 'Perhaps you understand now why I wanted you to drop the whole business and of course I still prefer that Father never finds out.'

'But – did my mother never mention me again?'

'Not really. When it turned out that you were alive, we were glad you'd been found, but we never spoke of it after that.'

Seeing this might be my only opportunity, and she was preparing to leave, I asked quickly: 'What was she like?'

'Like? Oh, a very stupid, neurotic woman,' she said dispassionately, 'though crafty enough to get Father to marry her. You have her green eyes and red hair, though she always bleached hers, because she hated it.'

That seemed to be it.

'Thank you for telling me the truth – and I understand now why you don't want anything further to do with me. I'll respect that and it won't get out, I'm sure of it.'

'If we meet again, it will be as strangers: this conversation never hap-pened,' she warned me.

I nodded numbly and she turned and strode off down the hill towards her car.

I waited until she was a good distance away, then went back to the edge of the overhanging rock and called down: 'You can come up now, Mr Sheep!' Then I sat down on the stone again and waited, staring out across the beautiful, cruel moors.

A few moments later I heard the scrunch of Nile's feet on the stony path and then his arms closed around me. I turned thankfully into his warm embrace, my emotions chilled to the bone.

'Where did you hide the car?' I asked.

'In Henry's car park. Then I hiked over before you got here. I was sitting down there so long I'd become part of the landscape.'

'You heard everything?'

'Every word.' He pulled me to my feet and held me close.

'Now you've got to the end of that particular rocky road, can you be happy with the family who *do* want you?' he asked.

I nodded mutely.

'And can you concentrate on something else for a while? Because I really want you to be Alice Giddings and I've been trying to find a way of telling you.'

'But I already am . . . sort of,' I said, staring up at him.

'But you'd be one by name, if you married me. And I've wanted to ask you for ages, only I thought I should give you more time . . . and I wasn't sure how you felt about me.'

'Are you serious? I thought you were just asking me to have an affair with you the other night, a sort of trial run.'

He held me away slightly and looked down at me. 'I don't know why you always seem to think the worst of me. I was trying to propose!'

'It didn't sound like that,' I said defensively.

'I haven't had any practice,' he said drily. 'All my life I've been waiting for you: the one woman I know will never let me down, just as I will never fail you. I really do love you, Alice, and everyone can see it except you!'

'You'd better mean that, because I'm not settling for anything else,' I warned him, though my heart was doing that thump and flutter thing again.

'I've something here that might help persuade you,' he said, reaching into his pocket and then sliding a familiar big yellow diamond on to my finger.

I stared down at it: even in the half-light of dawn it sparkled with a fire of its own. '*I* was the special client you thought would like it?' I said. 'All that time ago, you knew you wanted to marry me?'

'You're a very *special client*, but a bit of a tricky customer – and yes, as soon as Violet said it would make a perfect engagement ring, bells, whistles and sirens went off in my head and I realized you were the one I'd been waiting for all my life,' he said.

I sighed happily. 'It was such a perfect afternoon I wanted it to go on for ever – and I realized how easy it would be to fall in love with you.'

'And did you?'

For answer, I wound my arms around his neck and kissed him, and by the time our lips reluctantly parted, the sky had gone a Technicolor pink, as if a rosy lightbulb had been switched on by a romantic lighting technician.

'Pink sky in morning, shepherd's warning,' I murmured dreamily.

'I'll take that kiss as a "yes, I love you madly, Nile". Let's do it again – we need more practice,' he suggested, but just then the harsh cry of some bird broke the moment.

'Oh, God – the time!' I exclaimed. 'I have to get back and bake fat rascals before the teashop opens.'

'Speaking of fat rascals, look who's here,' Nile said drily, looking over my shoulder, and I turned to see George Godet trudging up towards us, his two dogs slinking at his heels.

'What is it about the Godets and Blackdog Moor? Do you haunt it like Heathcliff looking for Cathy?' I demanded, when he was within earshot.

'Cathy who?' asked George.

I felt reasonably sure that Alice now understood my position and that there never had been, nor ever would be, any emotional connection between us. We would meet, if at all, as the strangers to each other we truly were.

Since all my actions had been to preserve my professional integrity and reputation and to conceal what had happened from Father, it was both shocking and ironic that tonight he suddenly asked me what had become of my baby, the one Mum had told him about just before she died.

'She was delirious,' I said. 'I never had a baby.'

'Who mentioned babies?' he demanded querulously, for already his mind had wandered off elsewhere again.

I sincerely hoped it would stay there.

47

Some Enchanted Evening

It had been a hot August day, only the thick walls of Oldstone providing any respite from the sun until we all went down to the swimming pond in the late afternoon with a picnic tea.

I was floating there on my back in the pleasantly cool water, dreamily looking up at the sky and thinking how all the various knots and dropped stitches in the fabric of my life had now been reworked into a whole exciting new tapestry.

I'd found Nile and a family that were my own by birth as well as marriage, and if I'd also found a dark secret and a half-sister who didn't want to know me, I'd accepted that as the price I had to pay.

I realized I cared enough about Dr Collins to hope she had found her own kind of happy ending, for we'd heard on the grapevine that her stepfather had died and she'd gone to live permanently in her villa in Portugal, leaving her little dog behind with the cleaner, to whom he was apparently attached.

The tearoom had become a resounding success and Nell and Tilda were famous – or infamous – worldwide. The attention might have turned the heads of lesser mortals, but Tilda and Nell didn't even turn a single hair.

And Daisy had just completed her hospitality course and was going to be trained up to help run the teashop – she'd proved to have a surprisingly light hand with baking.

Just as well, because I'd need to rest and take a little time off, soon . . .

Nile's dark head suddenly popped up next to me like a seal's.

'You look just like Millais' *Ophelia*, except for the lack of flowers and half-witted expression,' he said.

'You know how to turn a pretty compliment,' I said, splashing water at him, and he grabbed me and gave me a kiss.

'Oooh, Mr Giddings, this is so sudden!' I said.

'You asked for it, Mrs Giddings . . . but aren't you getting chilled?' he added anxiously. 'Come on out and have something to eat.'

I laughed. 'I'm not at all cold, the water's delicious – and the baby won't come to any harm, because right now it's only about the size of a grapefruit. You didn't hear Teddy fussing round Geeta, did you?'

'No, but it's not her first baby,' he said, still looking worried.

'I'm fine, but I'm also hungry,' I said, giving in and making for the little jetty. It was lovely that Geeta and I had discovered we were expecting only a week apart – which could mean the babies arrived at the same time, if one was early or the other late.

'I was thinking that everything has worked out just like a fairy tale,' I said to Nile, as I reached the wooden ladder and he caught up with me.

'Not one of yours, I hope!'

'No, this time *I'm* the heroine and you're the right prince, so for once there will definitely be a happy-ever-after!

Recipes

You'll be everyone's favourite if you copy Alice's example and whip these up for afternoon tea . . .

Little fat rascals

Fat rascals are a Yorkshire delicacy, somewhere between a rock cake and a scone, and no one can come close to those baked to a secret recipe by Betty's Café in Harrogate. However, this recipe was devised by a friend, the late author Angela Dracup, and is quick, easy and delicious.

I have added a couple of tweaks – instead of currants, I have used raisins, added a little more spice and then divided up the mixture into afternoon-tea sized morsels: Little rascals, in fact!

I love these split while warm and buttered, but they are also good spread with jam and cream, as you would a scone.

Ingredients
3oz/75g butter or margarine
8oz/200g self-raising flour
A quarter tsp each of ground cinnamon, grated nutmeg and mixed spice
Pinch of salt
3oz/75g mixed dried fruit with peel
2oz/50g raisins
3oz/75g caster sugar
One large egg, lightly beaten with two tbsp milk

Method

1) Preheat the oven to gas mark 6/200°C/400°F and line an oven tray with baking paper.
2) Put the butter into a large mixing bowl and sift in the flour and spices. Add the pinch of salt.
3) Mix together using the rubbing-in method until it looks like very fine breadcrumbs.
4) Add the dried fruit and sugar and mix well.
5) Stir in the egg and milk mixture one spoonful at a time, until you have a stiff dough.
6) Divide the mixture up into twelve small rounds on the baking tray.
7) Bake for about 15 minutes, or until pale golden brown, then remove from the oven and put on a cooling rack.
8) They are irresistible warm from the oven, but they can be stored in a cake tin once cooled.

Welsh rarebit

A true Welsh rarebit is a tasty and luxurious version of cheese on toast and there are many opinions on the best way of making it: some like to use bread toasted on one side only, while others prefer it made with English mustard, rather than dry mustard. But this is how I make mine – and luckily, living in Wales, I can even use lovely Welsh cheese for greater authenticity!

Ingredients
4 slices wholegrain bread (I prefer it quite thickly sliced)
1 level tsp dry mustard
2 heaped tsp plain flour
1 tbsp butter
4 tbsp any dark beer (though milk can be substituted)
8oz/200g strong cheese, such as mature Cheddar, grated
A pinch of black pepper
2 generous tsp Worcestershire sauce

Method
1) Toast the bread and butter it.
2) Mix the mustard powder and flour together.
3) Melt the butter in a saucepan over a very low heat and stir in the flour and mustard mixture to form a roux.
4) Now, slowly stir in the beer.
5) Add the cheese and stir till it is melted.
6) By this point it should be a nice, thick paste, so add the pinch of pepper and mix in the Worcestershire sauce.
7) Divide the mixture between the slices of bread and spread it out. Then toast under the grill until it goes brown and bubbly.
8) Serve immediately!

Sticky ginger cake loaf

A delicious sticky, dark and spicy ginger cake. Fragrant and warming for even the rainiest of Yorkshire days, this classic northern recipe is perfect with a nice cup of tea!

Ingredients
1 tsp ground mixed spice
1½ tsp ground cinnamon
½ tsp ground nutmeg
4oz/125g plain flour
1 tsp bicarbonate of soda
3oz/75g butter (cut into cubes and a little extra for greasing)
3oz/75g light brown sugar
3oz/75g treacle
3oz/75g golden syrup
2 tbsp milk
3oz/80g drained stem ginger, finely grated
1 egg (beaten)

Method

1) Preheat the oven to gas mark 4/160°C/320°F and line and grease a cake loaf tin.
2) Mix the spices together with the flour and bicarbonate of soda in a bowl.
3) Add the cubes of butter and rub together between fingertips until the mixture resembles fine breadcrumbs.
4) Put the sugar, treacle, syrup and milk in a medium saucepan and heat gently, stirring until all the sugar has dissolved.
5) Turn the heat up but do not allow mixture to boil.
6) Add the stem ginger to the flour mixture and mix in to distribute evenly.
7) Slowly pour the syrupy mixture into the flour mixture, stirring as you go with a wooden spoon until all the ingredients are combined and of a smooth texture.
8) Add the beaten egg to this slowly, and beat vigorously until combined and mixture now resembles a thick pancake batter.
9) Pour mixture into cake tin, filling to just below the rim, and bake in the centre of the oven for 50 minutes to an hour until it is well risen and firm to the touch. You can additionally check if it is cooked in the centre by inserting and removing a skewer which once pulled out should be fairly clean.
10) Once cooked, remove the cake from the oven, allowing it to cool in the tin for 5 minutes before turning it out.
11) If possible, store it in a cake tin, still in its lining, for 24 hours before eating to allow the flavours and stickiness to really set in!

Very cheesy cheese straws

If Welsh rarebits aren't enough to satisfy your cheese cravings (and to be perfectly honest, can you ever have too much cheese?), try this recipe for incredibly moreish cheese straws. If you prefer them without heat, then simply leave out the paprika and cayenne pepper.

Ingredients
3oz/75g Parmesan cheese, finely grated
3oz/75g Cheddar, finely grated
7oz/200g plain flour, plus more for dusting
½ tsp smoked paprika
¼ tsp cayenne pepper
Pinch of freshly ground black pepper
3½ oz/100g butter, chilled, plus more for greasing
1 free-range egg (white and yolk separated)

Method
1) Preheat the oven to gas mark 7/220°C/425°F. Lightly grease a large baking tray.
2) Put the cheese into a mixing bowl. Sift in the flour and then add the paprika, cayenne and black pepper, and mix.
3) Cut the butter into little cubes and rub them into the flour mix with your fingertips, until the butter has disappeared into the flour and you have a crumbly mixture, then stir in the egg yolk to reach a dough-like consistency.
4) Next, still in the bowl, knead into a ball.
5) Dust your work top with plenty of flour to avoid any sticking, then carefully roll out the dough with a rolling pin into a roughly square shape about ¼ inch thick. You can square up the edges gently by patting with your hands.
6) Taking a sharp knife, cut the dough square into vertical strips about 1 inch thick, then cut sideways to halve the length. Twist each straw into a spiral pattern.
7) Gently place straws on to the baking tray, leaving a little space between each one as they will expand whilst cooking.
8) Whisk your egg white, then taking a pastry brush, coat the straws with this mixture.
9) Place the baking tray in the oven and bake for about 8-10 minutes. The cheese straws should be a very pale golden brown when cooked.
10) The straws may be fragile once removed from the oven, so leave them to sit for about 5 minutes before you remove them.

About the Author

Trisha Ashley was born in St Helens, west Lancashire, and believes that her typically dark Lancashire sense of humour in adversity, crossed with a good dose of Celtic creativity from her Welsh grandmother, have made her what she is today . . . whatever that is. Nowadays she lives in North Wales, together with the neurotic Border Collie foisted on to her by her son, and a very chancy Muse.

A Christmas Cracker was her eighth consecutive *Sunday Times* Top Ten bestseller. Her novels have twice been short-listed for the Melissa Nathan Award for Romantic Comedy and *Every Woman for Herself* was nominated by readers as one of the top three romantic novels of the last fifty years.

For more information about Trisha please visit her Facebook fan page (Trisha Ashley books) or follow her on Twitter @trishaashley.

A Leap Of Faith

Trisha Ashley

Sappho Jones stopped counting birthdays when she reached thirty but, even with her hazy grip on mathematics, she realizes that she's on the slippery slope to the big four-oh! With the thought suddenly lodged in her mind that she's a mere cat's whisker away from becoming a single eccentric female living in a country cottage in Wales, she has the urge to do something dramatic before it's too late.

The trouble is, as an adventurous woman of a certain age, Sappho's pretty much been there, done that, got the T-shirt. In fact, the only thing she hasn't tried is motherhood. And with sexy potter Nye on hand as a potential daddy – or at least donor – is it time for her to consider the biggest leap of all? It's either that or buy a cat . . .

'One of the best writers around!'
Katie Fforde